NO PHULE LIKE AN OLD PHULE

IT'S A PHULE TIME JOB!

PHULE'S COMPANY BOOK #5

NO PHULE LIKE AN OLD PHULE

IT'S A PHULE TIME JOB!

PHULE'S COMPANY BOOK #5

NEW YORK TIMES BESTSELLING AUTHOR

ROBERT ASPRIN
AND PETER J. HECK

WordFire Press
Colorado Springs, Colorado

NO PHULE LIKE AN OLD PHULE
Copyright © 2004 Robert Asprin
Originally published by Ace, 2004

ISBN: 978-1-61475-460-2

Cover design by Janet McDonald

Cover Image by Jeff Herndon

Art Director, Kevin J. Anderson

Book Design by RuneWright, LLC
www.RuneWright.com

Published by
WordFire Press, LLC
PO Box 1840
Monument, CO 80132

Kevin J. Anderson & Rebecca Moesta Publishers

WordFire Press Trade Paperback Edition August 2017
Printed in the USA
wordfirepress.com

PROLOGUE

General Blitzkrieg was just lining up a tricky four-meter putt when a buzzer sounded on his desk. He flinched at the noise, and the ball jerked to the right, missing the target by a good half meter. "Damn it all to hell, what is it now?" he snarled, stomping over to the desk and pressing a button.

"Colonel Battleax to see you, sir," came the voice of Major Sparrowhawk, his adjutant. "Shall I send her in?"

Blitzkrieg stifled another curse, and nodded. Then, realizing that Sparrowhawk couldn't hear him, he said, "Sure, sure, send her in." He quickly stashed his custom-made ultracarbon putter behind the desk and turned to stare out the window behind him. The view of the North Rahnsome Mountains behind the old city wasn't anything to get ecstatic over, but he was pleased at the thought of having his back turned to Battleax when she entered the office—a subtle slight, but nothing she could take overt offense at. If he'd been able to contrive a way to make her cool her heels in the outer office for fifteen or twenty minutes, he'd have enjoyed it even more—but that would have required some advance planning. Might as well just get the unpleasant confrontation over with. He didn't know what the colonel was here for, but it was bound to be unpleasant.

He heard the door slide open, but he resisted the impulse to turn; let the old harpy wait until he was good and ready. He let a thin smile cross his face as he heard the colonel come into the office. "I think you've forgotten something, General," came a voice from behind him.

Blitzkrieg turned, just in time to see Colonel Battleax toss him the golf ball he'd left sitting in the middle of his office floor. Caught off guard, he snatched at it clumsily, and stifled another curse as it bounced off his chest, then ricocheted off his toe to roll under the desk. He determinedly ignored it. "What brings you here today, Colonel?" he asked, doing his best not to show his annoyance at her.

"I've got the latest intelligence reports on the Zenobian situation," she said. "You'll be glad to know ..."

"I won't be glad unless you're going to tell me those blasted overgrown lizards have eaten Captain Jester," said the general, losing his composure after all. "That's the planet he's on, and the less I hear about it, the less I'll have to ruin my appetite."

"I doubt there's much that could do that," said Battleax, eyeing his ample midsection. "Anyhow, you need to know this, whether you like it or not. The second race that Jester found on Zenobia—the Nanoids—claim to be indigenous to the planet."

"Very interesting, I'm sure," said Blitzkrieg. He poked his toe under the desk, experimentally, hoping he could kick out the golf ball without bending over to look for it. No such luck.

"More interesting than you may realize, General," said Battleax, smugly, "We have two technologically advanced races inhabiting one planet—and both are apparently legitimately native to that world. Now, as you may recall, Captain Jester's company was called there because the Zenobians had detected the Nanoids conducting surveillance of their major cities. This suggests that the Nanoids may be looking to expand their territory—and you can surely guess what that would lead to."

"Civil war," said Blitzkrieg, waving a hand dismissively. "Not our problem, as long as the conflict doesn't break out into Alliance space. We keep a strict hands-off policy, and provide sophontitarian aid where appropriate. They covered that in second year MilSci at the academy—or did you miss that lecture?"

"No, General," said Battleax, smiling. "Did you miss the fact that the Zenobians signed a mutual defense treaty with the Alliance just over a year ago, and that we're now making diplomatic overtures to the Nanoids, to get a treaty with *them?* That planet already *is* Alliance space, and if we're not careful, we're going to be deeply entangled with both sides in the conflict. And the only combat-ready Alliance military unit in the entire system is one Legion company."

Blitzkrieg's eyes lit up. "Yessss!" he hissed.

"No," said Battleax, shaking her head. "We can't just leave them in the line of fire."

"Of course we can. It's the Legion way," said Blitzkrieg, a feral grin on his face.

"Maybe I did miss a lecture at the academy, after all," said Battleax, coldly. "Or is that one of the lessons reserved for the old boy network?"

"Nothing more than learning to look at the big picture," said Blitzkrieg. A superior smirk came to his face. "If you're ever going to get stars on your shoulders, that's the kind of choice you have to be ready to make, *Colonel.* They don't play this game in short pants, you know."

"I'll take your word for that," said Battleax. She leaned forward and picked up the golf ball, which had rolled out of the far side of the desk and come to rest at her feet. She handed it to the general, and said, "But if Phule's company is going to be in the middle of a civil war, I'm going to make sure they know in advance just what kind of game they're in—and what kind of pants their superior officers are wearing. In your case ..." She paused and looked Blitzkrieg up and down. "No, it's too easy. I won't say it." She saluted, then turned and walked out of the office with a mischievous grin.

Blitzkrieg spent the rest of the day trying to figure out just what she'd meant by it.

Chapter One

After his success in the Zenobian affair, my employer had naturally assumed that his Legion career was back on track. He had scored not only a diplomatic, but a scientific, coup in discovering a new alien race, the Nanoids. He had managed to discredit the new commander sent by headquarters to take over his unit. And he had successfully cemented trade relations with our hosts, the Zenobians.

Little did he realize that there were machinations under way in several distant worlds, all of which were destined to intrude on his peace of mind.

O   O   O

The yellowing poster in the dirty store window hung crookedly between two nondescript advertising signs, and its once-bright colors had long since faded into shades of off-white. But Zigger found it beautiful, nonetheless. He had been admiring its picture of a heroic figure in a black jumpsuit ever since his father had brought him down this street and he had seen the store. To a small Lepoid from a second-rate factory town on the planet Teloon, it was the stuff of his dreams. He hadn't been able to read the words the first time he saw it, but he'd gotten his father to read them to him: "Join the Space Legion and See the Galaxy!"

Zigger hadn't known what a galaxy was back then. But he knew magic when he saw it. It made his nose twitch and his ears snap to attention, and as far as he was concerned, whatever the poster was selling had to be the real thing. And every time he came down that street—even when he was running errands for his mom, or late for school—he'd stop for a brief moment in front of the store and gaze upon the poster with loving eyes.

It was something of a letdown when Zigger realized what kind of merchandise the store sold. The store (its name was Spotty's) sold nothing at all heroic or magical—just stupid ordinary things like fur restorer, groot repellant, stupid entertainment capsules, and a selection of print-zines. The Space Legion recruiter had come by one day and put the poster in the window, one of many crowded into the space. Several years later, it was still there. But not even that could detract from the allure. Zigger had already made up his mind that he was going to join the Space Legion—and everything else was second to that.

His parents didn't necessarily approve, but they were smart enough to use it to motivate him to do well in school. "You'll never get into the Space Legion if you don't do your math problems," his father would say, and that was all Zigger needed to dig in for another round of attrition and subduction. Or, if he didn't like something his mother had made for supper, she would say, "Eat up, little one—you have to be a big, strong, healthy Lepoid to join the Space Legion!" And Zigger would gobble down the last few pieces of brittleroot on his plate. It worked every time, and even after Zigger figured out what his mom was doing, he didn't stop listening. After all, it stood to reason that she was probably right. And so young Zigger grew up strong and smart, and all his teachers said he could be anything he wanted to when he grew up.

That pleased Zigger. But all he really cared about in life was joining the Space Legion when he grew up. So when he hopped onto the stage to receive his school diploma (with honors in three subjects, though not the highest honors—those went to Snickly, who was a grind and a suck-up anyway), and citations as an All-Teloon athlete in three different sports, and a plaque for Good Citizenship, everyone expected great things of him. The commencement speaker had told the young Lepoids that the universe was their tuber, and even though the graduates knew it was a cliché, most of them were willing to believe it for a moment, at least.

So it came as a considerable shock to Zigger when his parents put their feet firmly down in opposition to his announcement that he was going to join the Space Legion instead of going on to Harevard University, where his grades (not to mention his prowess at running and jumping) were certain to earn him a scholarship. "You can't just throw away an opportunity like this," said his father, glowering at him from the head of the breakfast table. "With a Harevard education, you can do anything you want to."

"But I can do what I want to without it," said Zigger, with a forkful of synveggies halfway to his mouth. "Besides, if I'm good enough to get in now, I'll still be good enough after I've served a term in the Legion. And they let you save up your pay to cover college expenses. It's a really smelliferous deal, Dad!"

"It smells pretty bad to me," muttered Zigger's dad.

"Now, Oswald, you know that's just the slang these youngsters use nowadays," said Zigger's mother, in a conciliatory tone. "When he says smelliferous, he just means it's very shuropteous."

"Well, why doesn't he say so, then?" said Oswald. "Have to get a dictionary to figure out what kids mean these days."

"What I mean is that I'm not going to Harevard," said Zigger. "Not until I find out if I can make it in the Legion. It's the only thing I've always wanted. You know that, Dad."

Oswald shook his head, started to say something, then took a deep breath. "You know what? I think I'm going to let you do it ..."

"Yaay!" cheered Zigger, hopping out of his seat and prancing around the table.

"... With a couple of conditions," his father continued. "First, if you get accepted to Harevard—and if they agree to hold a place for you while you complete one tour of duty in the Legion. If you still want to stay in the Legion after that, I guess there's not much I can do for you."

"I'll accept those conditions, Dad," said Zigger, pausing in his celebratory dance. "They don't matter, anyhow. All I've ever wanted is to join the Legion."

7

"There's an old saying," said Zigger's mother. "'Be careful what you wish for—you just might get it.' I hope the Legion is everything you want it to be. And if not, there's always Harevard."

But Zigger wasn't listening anymore.

O O O

"Sergeant Brandy, may I ask a question?"

It took all of Brandy's self-control not to permit herself a deep sigh. "What is it, Mahatma?" she asked. She knew even before she heard the question that it was going to take all her resources to come up with an answer. Mahatma could twist almost anything she said into a refutation of all the discipline and authority the Legion depended on. But that was just part of a day's work for the Top Sergeant of Omega Company.

"We have been on Zenobia nearly six months," said the young legionnaire, smiling beatifically—it was his invariable expression. If she hadn't known better, Brandy would have assumed Mahatma was on some kind of meds, legal or otherwise. (In this outfit, it was most likely otherwise.)

Brandy waited for Mahatma; he hadn't asked any question yet, so she knew he wasn't done. The silence lingered. Finally, as the rest of the training squad fidgeted, she said, as calmly as she could manage, "That's right, Mahatma. We've been here six months." Sometimes she thought half that time had been spent with her answering Mahatma's questions, but she carried on with only a hint of impatience. "Now, what was your question?"

Mahatma's smile never wavered. "When we had finished our job on Landoor, we were sent to this planet. You told us it was because we had done a good job there." He paused again.

"That's right," said Brandy, not letting the pause stretch out this time. "What did you ..."

"Have we not done a good job here?" Mahatma broke in. "Or have we not finished the job we came to do?"

"Neither one," said Brandy. "We came as military advisers to the Zenobians, and we've been able to solve their problems without any fighting at all. That's doing a damned good job, if you want my opinion."

"But we have not been sent to another posting," argued Mahatma. "That must mean the brass don't think we've finished the job."

"Dude's makin' sense," came a voice from the back of the squad, before Brandy could answer. She was pretty sure she knew who it was, but she thought she'd be better off dealing directly with Mahatma instead of being drawn off into side issues. At least, unless she needed to divert everyone's attention from whatever point Mahatma was leading up to. The little legionnaire always had a point—usually one that undermined some basic tenet of military doctrine. She still hadn't figured out what he was doing in the military. Luckily for Brandy, most of his points were too subtle for anyone but her and Mahatma to understand. And she wasn't sure *she* always understood them ...

"The job *isn't* over," Brandy conceded. "But that doesn't mean we haven't done well. In fact, if we'd messed up the job, we'd damn well know it by now."

"Uh, Sarge ..." Another of the training squad had a hand up.

Brandy frowned. She'd hoped the answer she'd given would end the digression and let her get back to the training session. "Yeah, Slayer, what is it?"

"Uh, if we were doin' so well, why did headquarters send that Major Botchup to take over the company?"

"Headquarters usually doesn't know squat about conditions in the field," said Brandy. "You all saw how out of touch the major was when he finally got here. Things didn't get straightened out until the captain came back from his trip to the Zenobian capital. And you notice they haven't tried replacing the major. In fact, rumor has it, the captain's in for a promotion. If that doesn't mean we're doing things right, I don't know what does."

"Hey, yeah, that makes sense," said Slayer. The rest of the squad murmured its agreement, and Brandy relaxed. Now she had a chance to regain control of the exercise. If only Mahatma didn't start up again ...

"All right, people," she said. "Today we're going to talk about desert survival techniques. What's the first thing you need if you get stranded away from the camp?"

"Weapons," said one voice.

"Nah, you need shelter," said another.

"A map," said a third.

"That's all good stuff to have," said Brandy. "But none of it's going to do you much good without a supply of safe drinking water. I'm going to show you some ways to find water out in the desert …"

From that point, the exercise went ahead as planned. By the end of the morning session, Brandy was actually pleased with the legionnaires' progress. Even Mahatma managed to keep from asking any more irrelevant questions. Not that she expected that to last long …

O O O

If there is any port in the Alliance where private space yachts might dock without undue flurry, it is undoubtedly Lorelei, a space station that spends its every waking hour as a playground for the wealthy. So while the unannounced appearance of a Logan 350—one of the sleekest and most distinguished vessels available to a private citizen—caused the traffic control officers on duty at Lorelei to give their undivided attention to getting docked smoothly and without delay, it caused no comment. Its electronic signature, revealing a high level of quasi-military hardware on board, might have raised a few eyebrows on other worlds and stations, but Lorelei took it in without a blink.

Nor were many eyebrows raised when the yacht unloaded a vintage hoverlimo. Rich people often brought their own transport vehicles to Lorelei. Those paying attention might have recognized this one as an exception—a top-of-the-line Fleutz-Royale, which to the trained eye revealed subtle security modifications worthy of a planetary chief executive's state limo. Despite its arrogantly plain exterior, this was a vehicle many billionaires might consider a bit pricey. Its performance and safety more than justified the price, but even so, few of them would have been willing to pay it.

As soon as the hoverlimo was unloaded, a compactly built woman and a well-muscled man emerged from the Logan, escorting a lean, energetic, middle-aged man into the passenger seat. Racing fans might have recognized the woman as Maria Delia Fanatico, a Formula-Ultra race driver who had mysteriously retired about fifteen years ago, after an impressive string of victories. The man was Eddie Grossman, whose face was familiar to veterans of the elite Red Eagles army unit if not to the general public. As the unit's small-arms instructor, he had built an almost uncanny reputation for never missing a shot he had called.

There weren't any immediate alarm bells at the Fat Chance Casino's communications center a few moments later, when the passenger appeared on their screens, calling from the comm unit in his vehicle. He asked (in a tone that made it clear he was issuing an order, not making a request) to be connected with Willard Phule.

"One moment, sir, I'll have him paged," said the junior clerk who took the call. It says a certain amount for the clerk's training that he not only recognized Captain Jester's civilian name, but knew that anyone asking for the casino's majority stockholder under that name ought to be put through without delay. "Whom should I say is calling, sir?"

"Victor Phule," said the caller. And that, at last, set off the alarms.

"Y-yes, s-ss-sir," said the junior clerk, and it was something of a miracle that he managed to put the caller on hold without disconnecting him. This was *not* one of the contingencies that the clerk's training had anticipated.

The clerk's face disappeared, to be replaced by an ad for the Fat Chance Casino's supper club and floor show, featuring several shots of Dee Dee Watkins in revealing costumes. A few moments later, a different young man's face appeared on Victor Phule's view screen. He peered at the view screen mounted below the on-line camera, and said, enthusiastically, "Captain Jester here. What can I do for you?"

Victor Phule peered suspiciously at the view screen for perhaps three whole seconds. "I asked for Willard, not for his screening service," he growled. "Get him on. If he's in a meeting, get him out of it. And if I have to wait much longer, there'll be a bunch of people looking for new jobs. Now, let me talk to my son, you miserable impostor, or you'll be the first one on the list!"

The young actor somehow managed to keep his composure. "Please hold, sir," he said. Before Victor Phule could get in another word, the screen returned to shots of Dee Dee's dance routine interspersed with happy diners enjoying the four-star cuisine. (Not visible to the unsuspecting eye were various subliminals touting the casino's primary business.)

By this time, Phule's hoverlimo had floated to within eyeball range of the Fat Chance. Impatiently, the weapons magnate reached out and broke the connection. "Incompetent idiots," he muttered. "Willard will have some explaining to do when I get him in my sights. I thought the boy had better sense." In the front seat, the driver and bodyguard said nothing.

In a few moments more, the limo had pulled in front of the casino's marquee front. Eddie Grossman hopped out almost before the vehicle had stopped moving. He scanned the various gawking onlookers and uniformed hotel flunkies with professional thoroughness before opening the door to allow Victor Phule to storm out, making a beeline for the hotel entrance. Not missing a beat, Grossman followed a half pace behind him.

At the wheel of the hoverlimo, Maria Delia Fanatico watched them go, with a sigh. Phule rarely got this angry. She was almost sorry not to get a chance to see the inevitable explosion. She wasn't at all sorry that she was not the one her boss was mad at. She'd risked her life plenty of times on the race track, but there were some things far more dangerous than that. Getting one of the richest men in the galaxy mad at you was one of them.

O O O

The Reverend Jordan Ayres ("Rev" to his friends and followers) wore a pensive look, somewhere between a sulk and a pout. A casual observer might have taken this to mean that something was bothering the chaplain of Omega Company. But no—the pout was merely his normal expression when he was calm or thoughtful. It was a direct and intentional result of the extensive facial remodeling that all devout members of the Church of the King underwent in order to more perfectly resemble their prophet. In any case, to someone meeting Rev for the first time, the pout was probably less off-putting than the sneer that his face assumed when he was actually in a cheerful frame of mind.

Rev's initial success in converting the members of Omega Company to the Church of the New Revelation—or, as it was often known, the Church of the King—had been nothing short of phenomenal. But, as even he had to admit, recently the stream of converts had slowed to a trickle. For various doctrinal reasons, particularly the strong pressure for church members to have their face remodeled in the image of their prophet, Rev's denomination was somewhat lacking in appeal to the nonhuman sophonts among his larger flock. And even among the humans, a fair number were attached to some other denomination, while others were frankly uninterested in any religion per se.

While the company had been stationed on Lorelei, or on Landoor, this had not been of particular concern to Rev. In both localities, he had found plenty of potential converts in the indigenous human populations. But here on Zenobia, populated by a race of sentient saurians, the King's message appeared to be falling on barren ground.

Rev had turned to some of his favorite texts for inspiration. Elder Aaron's personal memoir, *Anyplace Is Paradise,* had reinforced Rev's belief that the King was present everywhere, and Bishop Scott E. Moore's *Gonna Be Cool* affirmed that true believers would survive even the heat death of the universe. But, as always, the deepest meanings came from the King's own words—above all, the soulful admonition, "Don't be cruel." Rev's heart went flippity-flop every time he heard the King pronounce that sentiment. The words had lost absolutely none of their power as they'd come down the centuries. And yet, to his puzzlement, the Zenobians seemed deaf to all that. In fact, they seemed completely uninterested in anything the King had said or done.

He drummed his fingers, staring out the window of the small office he occupied in the administrative wing of Omega Company's Zenobia headquarters module. Out on the parade ground, Flight

Leftenant Qual and two of his fellow Zenobians were making adjustments to some piece of equipment they'd brought along when they'd come to the Legion camp. The lizardlike sophonts who had invited the Legion to this planet were every bit as intelligent as humans, or any of the other races that had become part of the Alliance. They showed as much imagination, as much curiosity about the universe they inhabited, as other species. Why, then, weren't they interested in the King's message?

There was only one way to find out, Rev realized. He rose to his feet, with a sigh at the stiffness in his legs. Not for the first time, he reminded himself that he'd been neglecting his exercise program. There wasn't any excuse for that—not with a fully equipped gym right around the corner from his office, and the best instructors available, completely paid for by the Space Legion—or, more precisely, by Captain Jester. The King wouldn't have wanted one of his followers to let himself go ... not when it was so easy to stay in shape.

But at the moment, Rev was on a mission. He strode down the corridor to a convenient exit and came out onto the parade ground a short distance from where the Zenobians were working. He walked over to them, humming a favorite melodic pattern. *Dum, dumba dumba dum, dumba dumba dum ...*

Qual looked up at the chaplain's approach. "Greetings, Crank!" said the Zenobian officer, flashing his array of sharp reptilian teeth.

"Crank?" said Rev, momentarily confused. Then he realized it must be another of the apparently random mistranslations the Zenobian's autotranslator spit out from time to time. Try as they might, the Legion's techs had never been able to adjust Qual's translator to render the name of Omega Company's commanding officer as anything but "Captain Clown." A few members of the company privately suspected that Qual's mangling of human language was not entirely an artifact of his equipment ... but they had never been able to prove anything, and since the little Zenobian was popular with the troops, nobody saw much point in making an issue of it.

Remembering his purpose, Rev said, "Good afternoon, Flight Leftenant Qual. Do you have a moment to talk?"

"It is a long time since we converse," said Qual. "It would be my gratification."

Rev relaxed—he'd been worried that the Zenobian officer might be too involved in his work to answer his questions. "You know, I have a kinda special job here," he began. "Sort of a mission, you might say."

"Yes, I have seen that," said Qual. His two coworkers stood listening—evidently their officer's translator gave them the gist of what Rev was saying. (Rev worried that what they heard might be a very distorted version of his actual words, but again, there was very little he could do about it.) "You are an officer, but one who gives advice, not orders," added the Zenobian.

"Yeah, that's the idea," said Rev. "Now, you must've heard me talk about the King ..."

"Many times, Crank," said Qual, still smiling. "You hardly speak of anything else."

"That's right," said Rev. "Now, what I want to know is, what do you all think about that? I mean, you people don't seem really interested in Him."

"Oh, this King of yours is very interesting," said Qual, and the other two Zenobians nodded eagerly.

Rev smiled. "Well, I didn't expect you to say that ..."

"But of course you cannot expect us to take him seriously," Qual added. "Humans ought to create their own myths instead of borrowing from more ancient species."

Rev scratched his head, puzzled. "Borrowing? I don't understand."

The two Zenobian crew members opened their mouths in the posture Rev had come to recognize as laughter, but Qual kept a serious expression. "Possibly you tell the truth, friend Crank," the Zenobian officer said. "I have noticed that you do not much understand the humor. But I have perhaps already said more than I should. We Zenobians do not lightly speak of our deepest racial beliefs, and I do not wish to expose our doctrines to you. I will tell you only that you need to convince one of our High Shamans to tell you the tale of 'L'Viz. It will be highly instructive, I can assure you. Now, if you will pardon me, I and my crew must complete our calibration of the *sklern*. Good diurnal period, Crank."

Rev stood there with his mouth open as Qual and his crew resumed their work. But after a moment, he retreated, shaking his head. He hadn't learned everything he'd hoped he might, but what he had learned left him plenty of food for thought. *'L'Viz*—he'd remember that name, and when occasion arose, he'd follow up Qual's suggestion. There was a mystery here, and he meant to get to the bottom of it.

Evening rush hour in Bu-Tse, the capital city of Kerr's Trio, was as hectic as rush hour in any other major city in human space. Try as they might, city planners had never figured out a way to eliminate the mass exodus of office workers into the transit system at the beginning and end of the business day. At some point or another, urban planners had tried any number of strategies to decentralize the business district, to stagger work hours, to facilitate telecommuting—none to any lasting effect. Centuries of complaints to the contrary, neither the employers nor the work force really wanted to change what had apparently become as fixed a pattern as the alternation of day and night.

But while the dark-haired woman getting off the Bu-Tse slideway with two huge grocery bags at the Dedisco loop was almost certainly unaware of the history behind her crowded ride home, she was by no means reconciled to it. She stalked up to the nondescript apartment building at the corner, elbowed her way into the gravshaft, and glared at her fellow denizens of the Dedisco Towers as they rose through the shaft together. There was an audible sigh of relief as she swung off on the fifth level and stomped down the hallway to her apartment door.

She palmed the lock, bustled through the door, and headed for the kitchen. From the living room came the sound of a tri-vee set turned to a gravball game. She ignored it and noisily dumped the bags on the kitchen table. From the other room came a male voice: "Lola?" She ignored that, too, muttering angrily as she began to unload the bags.

"Lola, you better come in here," said the voice, louder this time.

"Wait a minute," she barked. *Schmuck can't even come out and talk to me, let alone help,* she thought darkly. *I ought to make him get his own meals …*

"Lola, we got trouble," said the voice again.

"You're the one that's got trouble," she snapped, turning to face the entrance to the living room. That's when she saw the stranger with a beamer pointed at her. "Uh—who are you?" she finished, lamely. Unfortunately, she already had a very good idea what the answer had to be.

"I'm askin' the questions, sister," said the man, gesturing with the weapon. "You get in there with yer buddy and don't try nothin' fancy."

The way he handled the beamer was all the proof she needed that he knew what to do with it in the event something fancy did occur. She went into the living room. There sat Ernie, in a straight-backed chair facing the tri-vee set. His arms were bound to his sides, and a wide band of elasteel around his torso bound him to the chair. On the couch next to him sat a small man in an expensive suit.

"Good, everybody's here," said the small man. "Why don't you have a seat, Lola? We have business to discuss."

"Who are you?" said Lola. "We haven't done anything."

"That's exactly the problem," said the little man. "Sit down, please—it makes me uncomfortable to see you standing up." He gestured toward the other chair in the room.

Lola was not by nature docile. But something in the man's manner told her this would be a very bad time to make herself disagreeable. She sat.

"Good, that's very good," said the small man. "It makes things so unpleasant when people aren't in a cooperative mood. I really hate it when we have to persuade people to go along with us."

"What do you want?" said Lola. "Who are you, anyway?"

The little man inspected his fingernails, then said, "My name doesn't matter, but if you wish, you can call me Mr. V. My partner and I represent certain parties from whom you accepted an employment contract some time back. Perhaps you're familiar with the agreement I'm referring to?"

Lola did her best to appear calm. "This wouldn't have anything to do with Lorelei Station, would it?" she asked.

"*Very* good," said Mr. V, nodding enthusiastically. "It's always good to start from a position of mutual understanding. I was afraid that little matter might have slipped your mind. May I inquire when we can expect you to fulfill your contractual obligations?"

"In fact, we made every effort to do exactly that," said Lola, twisting her neck to peer up at him. "There was an unexpected development …"

"An unexpected development," the little man repeated her words, sympathetically. "That's the way things sometimes go in our business, isn't it? They never quite go the way you plan." Lola nodded, smiling.

Then Mr. V clapped his hands together loudly. "But a professional doesn't let those little setbacks get in the way of completing the job. A professional knows how to overcome obstacles. You and your colleague *are* professionals, aren't you?"

"Of course we are," said Lola. "But …"

"But me no buts, young lady," said the little man, leaning forward to look her in the eyes. "You were engaged to deliver a certain package to a certain location. Now, it's been quite a long time, and the delivery has not taken place."

"I can explain that," said Lola. Her mouth was suddenly dry.

"I'm sure you can," said Mr. V. "But I'm going to save you the trouble, young lady. My principals aren't really interested in explanations, and neither am I. If we want explanations, there are any number of professional explainers whose services we can engage. At the moment, we would much rather see results. Do you grasp my meaning, young lady?"

"I think so," said Lola, in a very quiet voice.

"Very good again," said the little man, turning away from her and pacing. He stopped and turned, and said, "Now, to the point. Your contract calls for the delivery of certain goods. We are going to insist that you fulfill that contract. And we are furthermore going to insist that it be done without any further unnecessary delay. Do you understand me?"

Lola nodded. "There may be additional expenses involved in retrieving the goods ..." she began.

Mr. V held up a finger, like a scolding schoolteacher. "Young lady, I wouldn't be eager to ask for more money when I hadn't finished the job I'd contracted to do," he said. "Not if I were in your shoes. Certain people might get very impatient with you."

"I was merely pointing out the possibility," said Lola, with a gulp. "It might not be a problem, in any case. We can discuss that when everything's wrapped up."

"Good," said Mr. V, smiling again. "And I notice that you say *when* everything's wrapped up—can I take that as meaning you intend to go ahead with your operation?"

"Yes, of course," said Lola. She smiled. "We never intended anything else."

"Good, it's a pleasure doing business," said Mr. V, rubbing his hands together. "I'll tell my principals that everything is in order, then. And when can they expect delivery?"

Lola began calculating in her head. The big variable would be travel time; hyperspace had unpredictable twists and wrinkles, and a ship might well arrive some time before it had set out—or months later. Still, the expected travel time back to Lorelei ought to be something like three weeks. "You want the package delivered to the same place as before?" she asked.

"Precisely," said the little man, with a nod.

"Sixty days from now," said Lola. "That's cutting it close, but I think we can do that."

"We'll hold you to it," said Mr. V. "And just in case you're tempted to think about slipping out of your obligations again, I think we'll give you something else to think about." He snapped his fingers, and the man with the beamer stepped into the room. Ernie's eyes grew wide ...

CHAPTER TWO

Journal #649

T|he excesses of youth, as amusing as they may seem to those of riper experience, are nonetheless productive of worthwhile results. Youthful exuberance, wedded to the seemingly inexhaustible energies of the young, can achieve things that sober maturity would never attempt. It is undoubtedly for this reason that armies are made up of the young.

The negative corollary of this verity is that, despite almost comically elaborate efforts to arrive at correct intelligence, armies are more easily duped than almost any other institution of similar size and complexity. And the same can be said of their individual members—only more so ...

O   O   O

"Here's a package for you from Legion Headquarters, Captain," said Lieutenant Rembrandt, bustling into her commander's office.

"Oh, good—maybe it's the promotion Ambassador Gottesman said I'm supposed to be getting," said Phule. He took the package from her hands and eagerly began to tear it open. "I never thought I'd make it to major," he said. "I mean, I suppose I always hoped I'd do well in the Legion—maybe even make it to general. It's every officer's dream, I guess. But realistically, if you keep butting heads with the top brass—and I've pretty much made a full-time career of that ..." He stopped suddenly, his face a snapshot of disappointment.

"What is it, sir?" said Rembrandt.

"This isn't my promotion," said Phule. "It's a set of environmental impact forms from the Alliance Ecological Interplanetary Observation Union. The AEIOU."

"That's interesting," said Rembrandt. "Have we had any previous dealings with the AEIOU?"

"Sometimes. Why?" Phule asked his lieutenant.

"I just wondered what they wanted," said Rembrandt.

Phule looked at the cover letter. "They want us to document our compliance with ecological preservation directives for undeveloped planets, and to submit our updated environmental preservation plan. There's a list of regulations..."

"Undeveloped?" Rembrandt frowned. "Where do they get that? This is an inhabited world, last I looked. The desert out here may be fairly empty, but that Zenobian capital city you were in is about as developed as it gets."

"That was pretty much my impression," said Phule, scratching his head. "Somebody's gotten the wrong information."

"That could be a first-class pain," said Rembrandt. "You know these bureaucrats. Once they get the wrong idea, it's as good as gospel. I remember when the newstapers mixed up my uncle Daryll with another guy who was killed in a skimmer accident. It took him nearly sixteen years to convince the Planetary Employment Bureau he was still alive—and poor Uncle Daryll *worked* for them ..."

"Well, this is obviously irrelevant to a Legion mission," said Phule. "We've never had to file environmental impact forms before..."

"Don't bet anything on it," said Tusk-anini, who'd been sitting in one corner of the office, reading. "Environment all around us, so we having impact every day. Bureaucats right to worry. I think is smart to fill out forms."

"How about you do it, then," said Phule, handing the pile of papers to the huge Volton legionnaire. "You fill out the paperwork, I'll sign it, and we'll send it back to the AEIOU. That'll get 'em off our back."

"I do it," said Tusk-anini. "When you want back?"

"I don't know—a week or so ought to be enough time," said Phule. "It's your baby, now—you can use the spare desk in the comm center to work on it. Let me know if you run into any problems."

"Will take good care of baby," said Tusk-anini. He tucked the papers under his arm and headed for the comm center.

Rembrandt watched him go, a trace of worry on her face. "Are you sure it's a good idea to give that job to him, Captain?" she said. "He's likely to come up with very strange answers to some of those questions—you know how his mind works. Sometimes I think he's too smart for his own good."

"Oh, I'm not worried about the AEIOU," said Phule. "You know what happens to paperwork—it just sits on some secretary's desk until they file it and forget it. Odds are nobody will even glance at those forms, except to make sure we've filled them out and that I've signed them."

"I hope you're right," said Rembrandt. "There are enough people looking for ways to make trouble for you—and for this company—that I'd hate to see somebody else have an excuse to get on your case. It worries me that this came from Legion Headquarters instead of directly from the AEIOU."

"You don't need to worry," said Phule, waving his hand. "Remember, I'm the guy who handles problems from upstairs. And as long as Colonel Battleax and Ambassador Gottesman are on our side, we've got two people who can keep the trouble from ever getting as far as me. And I've got a pretty good idea how to keep them happy."

"I sure hope so, Captain," said Rembrandt. She let her frown relax. Phule was probably right. Ever since he'd been on board, life with Omega Company had been steadily improving. Who was to say it wouldn't keep getting better and better?

O   O   O

Three men met Victor Phule as he entered the casino offices. Two were dressed in well-tailored civilian garb, the third in a black

Space Legion officer's uniform. Only someone familiar with the minutiae of Legion uniforms would have noticed that the various patches and insignia he wore were completely bogus.

"All right, where's my son?" barked Victor Phule, ignoring the proffered handshake. "I've been trying to catch up with him for weeks, and every time I call I either get some actor or a bunch of excuses. I want to see Willard—or talk directly to him, if he's not on the station."

The elder of the two men in business suits answered him, in a quiet but urgent voice. "Mr. Phule, I'm Tullie Bascomb, head of gambling operations at the Fat Chance. I understand your concern. But I think this is a discussion that ought to take place in private," he said.

Phule glared at him, but after seeing the man's expression, he nodded. "All right, then," he said. "This had better be good." The man who'd spoken to him indicated a doorway to one side, through which a comfortably appointed small conference room was visible.

At a nod from his boss, Phule's bodyguard stepped inside, quickly scanned the room, then nodded. "Nothing obvious," he said.

"It's clean," said one of the men who'd greeted Phule. "Your son made sure of that. Come on in, Mr. Phule. Would you like coffee, tea, something else?"

"I'd like to talk to Willard," said Victor Phule. "And I've had about enough of your stalling. Where is he?"

"Off-station," said Bascomb. "And at last word, he was doing just fine. Come sit down, Mr. Phule. I'll give you the full story. And, if you insist, we can connect you to him—he's close enough so we can use regular intrasystem comm."

Phule grumbled, but took a seat. Bascomb introduced the others in the room: Gunther Rafael Jr., former owner of the casino, and Doc—a veteran character actor Phule had hired to impersonate a legionnaire in order to keep the crooked operators who ran Lorelei Station from learning that Omega Company had been transferred to another post, leaving the casino unguarded.

"This isn't for general publication, you understand," said Bascomb. "The captain is off-station because he's decided that his military command takes priority over his other businesses. For the interim, he's left the place in our hands. And I don't mind telling you, Mr. Phule, if the captain walked in here unannounced five minutes from now, I don't think he'd find one thing that isn't being done exactly the way he'd do it himself."

"I'll be the judge of that, thank you," said Victor Phule, displaying no emotion. "From what I've seen so far, the boy hasn't entirely lost his head for business. But the devil is in the details, as you gentlemen know. And I'm going to withhold judgment until I've had a look at your books and your operations."

"Can he do that?" asked Gunther Rafael, turning to Bascomb. He had a perpetually nervous look, as if he expected to be called on the carpet.

"Technically, probably not," said Bascomb. He held up a hand to forestall Phule's protest. "But I'd be a damned fool if I didn't let him satisfy himself that the place is on a sound footing. Unless the captain explicitly forbids it, that is. Mr. Phule carries a lot of weight around here, but as far as I'm concerned, the captain carries more. No offense, Mr. Phule—but he's the man who put me in this job."

"I appreciate your loyalty to my son," said Victor Phule. "But loyalty only goes so far, Bascomb. I've done business with the military long enough to know how much it values loyalty. That's all well and good—but where I disagree with it is when it elevates loyalty over competence. If a man can't do the job, I want another man in that job—before the first one costs me more money than his loyalty is worth. Do you understand me?"

"I understand you, Mr. Phule," said Bascomb, with a shrug. "Maybe I wouldn't be so quick to put a price on loyalty, but I agree with you on competence—I don't think I'm flattering myself to say that your son hired me because I've shown a fair bit of competence in the casino business. Now, would it be convenient for you to look over those books after lunch? While you're eating—on the house, of course—we can set up one of the executive offices for you to use."

"Bring me the books now," said Phule, brusquely. "I want to see both sets—the real ones, and the phony ones you use for the tax auditors. And I'll work at the desk my son uses when he's here. I don't expect there's anybody else who needs that particular space."

"I'll need you to excuse me a minute for that," said Bascomb, standing up. "I'll send in a waiter to take your drink order."

"Forget the waiter," snapped Phule. "Just bring me the books. And it better not be too long."

"It'll take as long as it takes," growled Bascomb. He turned on his heel and marched out of the room.

Twenty minutes later Bascomb returned, with a determined expression on his face. Without saying a word, he unlocked a file drawer, removed a pair of memory modules, and handed them to Victor Phule. "These have both sets of books on them," he said. "I guess you'll want to use your own computer, but we can give you one to use if you'd like."

"I'll let you know," said the elder Phule, brusquely. "Now, have that impostor clear off the desk and get out of my way. I want to get to work."

O O O

"Aw right, smarty, so what's the plan now?" Ernie grumbled. Their unwanted visitors had left, but he'd had to wait until Lola managed to find a tool strong enough to cut the plasteel tape Mr. V's muscle man had used to confine him before he could get out of the chair they'd put him in. He still had sticky patches on his arms from where the tape had held them. Touching them made him shudder. He didn't even want to *think* about what might have happened ...

She shrugged. "We go back to Lorelei, of course," she said. "That's our only choice."

"And when we get there?"

She shrugged again. "I'll figure something out."

"*You'll* figure something out?" Ernie's voice rose an octave. "You bet you will! You're the one who got us in this whole farkin' mess to begin with!"

"I seem to remember you agreeing to taking the job way back when it was first offered," said Lola. "In fact, you were pretty gung ho about it."

Ernie scoffed. "Yeah, that's before we tried snatching that damn robot, which had us both fooled into thinking it was Phule. Then, when we try to smuggle it off-planet, it manages to steal a lifeboat off a space liner and bail out right in the middle of hyperspace. I don't think I'll ever figure that one out. We might as well forget about snatching that punk."

"Great idea," said Lola. "Except that Mr. V and his clients aren't going to let us forget it. At least, not until we show them enough of an effort to convince them we're playing the game their way. If there's some way for us to bail out when things get sticky, I'll find it. Don't you worry."

Ernie's eyes bulged out. "Don't *me* worry?" he growled. "Next time, see how *you* like sitting there with ten yards of plasteel tape holding you to the chair, and an ugly guy with a beamer aimed up your nostrils. I've been there, and I don't like it worth an unplugged virt."

"Oh, come on," said Lola, grinning mischievously. "You look really cute when you're helpless, you know?"

"Gee, thanks," said Ernie. He thought a moment, frowning, before he continued. "Does this mean …"

"Forget about it," said Lola, in a tone that left no room for doubt. "Right now, my main priority is keeping my skin intact. Which means getting a ticket on the next space liner headed back to Lorelei."

"That's going to cost us an arm and a leg," grumbled Ernie.

Lola fixed him with an exasperated stare. "And what do you think it'll cost us *not* to go back?"

"I know, I know," said Ernie. "We've gotta look as if we're gonna try to finish the job. But what if we can't, anyway? We'll be out all that money, and running for our lives, to boot. If we're gonna spend the rest of our lives running, what's the point of blowing all our money right from the git-go? Worse, what's the point of spending it to get someplace where the guys who're trying to do us in are running the show?"

"If they were really running the show on Lorelei, they wouldn't have to bring us in to snatch Phule," said Lola. "Hey, they might even have figured out that Phule's got a robot there to impersonate him. That little fact could be worth a nice bundle, all by itself."

Ernie frowned again. "Why didn't you think of that when those bastards were getting ready to work me over?"

"It wasn't the right time to play that card," said Lola, calmly. "Those guys didn't come here looking for information, so why should we give it to them? We have to hang on to it until we can trade it for something we want."

"Yeah, huh?" said Ernie. "Next time the big guys have *you* tied up with plasteel, ready to slice and dice and barbecue, I can guarantee you—you'll have a damn good idea what you want."

"Ernie, Ernie," said Lola, shaking her head. "I got us out of that little fix, didn't I? If we keep obsessing about every little setback, we'll never make any progress toward our long-range goals. You understand that, don't you?"

"My longest-range goal is to keep on breathing," said Ernie. "It ain't such a bad idea to avoid unnecessary pain, either. Come to think of it, there's no such thing as necessary pain, in my book."

"Well, we'll do what we can to avoid pain," said Lola. "But the best way to ensure that, right about now, is to get ourselves on a starship headed for Lorelei. So give me your credit chip, and I'll get busy on that—and once we're on the way, we'll have plenty of time to work out the next steps."

"All right," said Ernie, reaching for his wallet. "But this better be good."

"Don't worry," said Lola, brightly. "I expect everything to work out perfectly this time." Her smile as she took his credit chip was almost sincere enough to convince him.

O O O

Sergeant Mayhem's eyes bulged out in disbelief. He'd been assigned as the Space Legion recruiting officer on Teloon for close to fifteen years—ever since he'd managed to pyramid a minor injury sustained during the Stoddard's World police action into a cushy desk job far from any chance of action. Little had he realized just how far he was going to be from the action. In his entire time on

Teloon, he'd averaged less than one recruit a year—on a planet with a population pushing the three billion mark!

He still didn't understand how the Legion could afford to keep him here. Probably some clerk had figured out that letting him retire, paying his pension (a hefty sum, considering his years in service), giving him passage to a world of his choice, and shipping a replacement out to Teloon would cost the Legion more than keeping him on the rolls. Assuming they were ever going to replace him—given his results over the years, it hardly seemed worth the Legion's while.

But sure enough, here sat one of the planet's natives on the other side of his desk, practically begging to enlist! It took all his will power to keep from drooling at the prospect. "Well, sonny, do you think you have what it takes to be a legionnaire?" he asked. The question blithely skimmed over the fact that all it really took to be a legionnaire was the ability to walk, stumble, or crawl into a recruiting station and do something—almost anything—that could reasonably be interpreted as an effort to enlist. The Legion was far from picky.

"I honestly don't know, sir," said the native. "All I can say is that I've been doing everything I possibly can to prepare myself. I've got excellent grades in school …"

"Good, very good," said Sergeant Mayhem, nodding enthusiastically. He himself had left school as early as the law on his home planet allowed—at roughly age fourteen, if he remembered correctly. It had been a good while back. His lack of education hadn't hampered his Legion career, as far as he could tell. How smart did a guy have to be to carry a gun and dig ditches?

"And I think I'm in excellent physical condition," the native continued. "I've played three varsity sports, and I've got belts in two different martial arts …"

"Great," said Mayhem. That made it slightly more likely that the recruit would complete basic Legion training—which he needed to do if the recruiting officer was going to get his bonus for bringing in a live one. Mayhem had lost the bonus on about a third of his recruits. He always hated it when that happened. But this one sounded as if he might actually make it through the not-too-rigorous Legion boot camp ... as long as he didn't mind being treated like dirt.

"You have any idea what you're getting yourself in for?" he asked, somewhat reluctantly. He certainly didn't want to scare the kid off, but the regulations required him to make it more or less clear that this wasn't going to be any kind of picnic. "The Legion's not for softies, you know," he continued. "If the Alliance winds up in a war, it's the Legion that's going to get sent to fight it. You understand what that means, don't you?"

"I understand, sir, and I'm ready," said the native. "What do I have to do to join?"

"Read this paper and sign it," said Mayhem. "You'll take a copy home, and think about it for twenty-four hours. If you haven't changed your mind by tomorrow, you're in."

"Yes, *sir!*" said the native. He practically bounced over the desk to grab the stylus out of Mayhem's hands and quickly put his signature on the enlistment form, then handed the top copy back to the sergeant.

"Zigger," said Mayhem, looking at the form. "Well, you'll want to choose a Legion name before you report for training. You might start thinking about what name you want."

"Oh, I've thought about it a long time," said Zigger. "I've already made up my mind ..."

"Don't tell me," said Mayhem. "Once you join, nobody should know your civilian name. The pay computer will keep your records so everything is in order, but I can tell you for a fact that nobody in the Legion will look into it during your actual term of service. That way, you'll be judged by what you do in the Legion uniform: not what you've done before or who your parents were."

The latter was a polite fiction. In fact, a lot of Legion officers were where they were because of who their parents were—and how much they'd been willing to spend to put them in an officer's uniform. But there was no point in telling this kid the hard facts of life. He'd figure them out soon enough, probably at the hand of a snotty junior officer who'd spent most of his life ordering servants around and considered enlisted legionnaires one more variety of servant.

Mayhem didn't particularly care, as long as he'd cashed the recruitment bonus well before the kid learned what a rotten deal he'd signed up for. Whatever happened to the kid after that was the kid's own lookout. Mayhem grinned, just thinking about the bonus, and the kid grinned back. *Sucker,* thought Mayhem. *I wish I had a million more like you. But you'll do. You'll do just fine, for now.*

O O O

"Hello, sweetie," came Mother's insinuating voice over the intercom in Phule's office. "That cute Ambassador Gottesman is on the line, asking for you."

"Great, put him through," said Phule. He wondered what the Alliance's ambassador was calling about this time. By now, Phule and his Legion company had established themselves as firm favorites with the diplomatic branch. Their successful peacekeeping mission on Landoor, then their performance in the delicate position of establishing the first Alliance presence on Zenobia, had given State two comparatively easy victories in situations where a good deal had been at stake. But it was too soon for the authorities to be considering a new mission for the Omega Mob. And it was as sure a bet as anything in the galaxy that Gottesman was not spending State's money on an interstellar voice call just to chat up his old friend. Something interesting was undoubtedly on deck.

The light on Phule's desk came on, then the ambassador's voice came through. "Hello, Captain Jester—I hope all's well out your way," said the ambassador.

"Coming along very smoothly, sir," said Phule. "The Zenobians have pretty much accepted us as the logical go-betweens in their attempts to establish relations with the Nanoids. And our talks with the Nanoids have progressed to the point where we can begin to address substantive issues."

"Good, good," said the ambassador. "State's hoping to get a xenological team there to handle these negotiations on a more professional basis, but until one of the two native parties makes a formal request we can't very well stick our nose in. Have you seen any sign that either side is likely to make such a request?"

"Nothing so far, sir," said Phule. "But the Zenobians are still not convinced that the Nanoids aren't off-planet intruders, and to be honest with you we can't prove that, either. We're moving along as best we can, but I can't say there's any sign of a major breakthrough yet."

"Well, if you're doing your best, that's likely to be as good a job as anyone can do," said Gottesman. "We'll just have to bide our time. Ghu knows, we're used to that in the diplomatic branch. But here's something you can do for us in the meantime, Captain. I understand Zenobia is pretty much an untamed world, out beyond the natives' urban centers."

"I suppose so," said Phule. "Out where we are is certainly wild enough. What do you have in mind, sir?"

The ambassador cleared his throat, and said, "Well, as it happens, we've got a number of civilians who've done the government a few favors over the years, if you know what I mean. And it so happens that some of them have gotten the idea that there might be some fairly large game running loose on Zenobia—something on the order of the larger dinosaurs. Am I right about that, Captain?"

"Well, there are some fairly large specimens here, if what I saw in the zoo back in the capital city is any indication," said Phule. "I can't say I've seen any such in the wild, though—we're out here in the desert, you know, and most of the animals I've seen out here are fairly small—although a few of them are pretty nasty. But most of the larger creatures on this world seem to be swamp-dwellers. Anyway, the natives don't really seem to want us trampling through their swamps—I get the idea those are prime recreation areas, from their point of view."

"I see," said the ambassador. "Well, I may ask you to talk to some of their people to see if we can get some exceptions made. There are a couple of VIPs who've taken a fancy to do some serious big-game hunting, and they've gotten the notion that some of the beasties there on Zenobia are about as big as they come. Have you heard anything about an animal the natives call a *gryff?*"

"Not much more than the name," admitted Phule. "From what the natives say, I'd guess it's a big, slow-moving, and rather stupid herbivore. Not very exciting to hunt, I'd imagine."

"Nothing's very exciting to hunt, as far as I'm concerned," said the ambassador. "Much more civilized to play TetraGo in a comfortable chair with a cold drink close to hand. But there's no accounting for tastes. I get the impression that if it's big enough, that's all the justification some of these fellows need. How much trouble do you think it'd be to get the Zenobians' permission for a party of off-worlders to come in and bag a few trophies?"

"All I can promise is to give it a try," said Phule, dubiously. "Give me a couple of days, and I'll get back to you if I can convince them …"

"Great, I knew I could count on you," said Ambassador Gottesman. "And remember, you can always call on me if you need anything that State can help with. Gotta run …" And he closed the connection.

"Well, the Zenobians aren't going to like this one bit," said Phule, looking across the office at Beeker, who'd sat there silently during the call. "I can imagine Chief Potentary Korg's face when I run this idea past him."

"Something like this was inevitable, sir," said the butler. "The State Department didn't support you for this assignment out of altruism, you know. It was just a matter of time before the quid pro quo became obvious."

"Well, Gottesman has taken our side against the general more than once," said Phule. "I can't refuse him something in return. It's only fair."

Beeker sniffed. "There's nothing fair about it," he said. "In fact, it has a distinct odor …"

"So we'll hold our noses and do what we can," said Phule, with a resigned tone. "If the Zenobians say no, that'll be an end to it."

"I doubt it, sir," said Beeker, but Phule wasn't listening.

CHAPTER THREE

Journal #653

The job description of a junior Legion officer—and make no mistake about it, my employer was extremely junior—does not in the normal course of affairs include diplomatic negotiations with the supreme rulers of alien planets. For the most part, a Legion captain is expected to avoid attracting the notice of anyone other than his immediate superiors. As far as any actual decision-making, that is best left to those qualified, which in practice usually means the sergeants nominally under his command.

In this matter as in many others, my employer had made himself the exception, as much by sheer luck as by any great personal initiative. Having been the first human to make contact with the Zenobians, he found himself invited to lead the first military expedition to the home world of that unusual race. And, more or less by default, once on Zenobia, he became the senior representative of the Alliance government. As a result, he was responsible for the negotiation of all kinds of business between off-worlders and the natives.

As the astute reader will already have grasped, this had both its advantages—notably the possibility of putting himself in the position of prime beneficiary of any unusually lucrative business—and its disadvantages. After a number of months on the planet, my employer had just begun to realize just what some of the latter might be.

O O O

"That is impossible, Captain," said Chief Potentary Korg. Phule couldn't read the Zenobian leader's face, but there wasn't much doubt about what his words meant. The translator's confidence-level readout was sitting on 93% +/-5%. Between the languages of two races of sophonts that had evolved on separate planets with no interspecies contact until the last couple of years, electronic translation didn't get any more confident than that. At least, the machine seemed to think so ...

"The Legion doesn't like to use that word," said Phule, with a smile he hoped the Zenobian would read the same way a human would. A display of teeth wasn't necessarily a friendly gesture, especially when dealing with a race of carnivorous dinosaur-like aliens, but so far he hadn't had any adverse reactions to the expression.

"The Legion's lexical preferences are not my affair," said Korg. He showed his own teeth—which Phule knew was probably equivalent to a human smile. At least, when Flight Leftenant Qual showed his teeth, it was a smile. So at least the Zenobian didn't seem to be personally offended by the request. It looked more as if his refusal was a policy matter that Phule could turn around by offering a few incentives.

Phule had dealt with that kind of problem before. "Of course, we wouldn't expect to bring a party of off-world hunters onto your planet without some compensation ..." he began.

"Compensation?" Korg blinked. "It is not a matter that can be orthagonalized by compensation, Captain. This is the sacred ancestral swampland of the Zenobian race that you propose I allow your off-world hunters to invade."

Phule held up his hands. "Chief Korg, I hope you don't think I'd come to you with such an unseemly proposal. In fact, we off-worlders are only here at your invitation. It would be very bad form for us to try to tell you to open up any particular areas of your beautiful planet for off-world visitors. But you were willing to open an area that your people weren't using for our Legion camp. Why not another area for off-world people to hunt in—for appropriate compensation, of course?"

Korg stood up and went to the window, staring out at the huge asparagus-like trees that lined the street outside. After a moment he turned to face the video pickup, and said, "I will take this under consideration. There may be areas we can allow your hunters to visit—as long as they remain within the bounds specified, and destroy only those species we permit. And at the same time I shall determine what compensation ought to be appropriate—if your hunters are prosperous enough to come visit Zenobia simply to hunt, I would expect that they can sustain a significant disbursement for the privilege."

"That sounds like something we can agree on," said Phule. "Could you have some of your people give me a list of areas that might become available for hunting? And, if possible, some indication of what kind of game would be available in those areas? Once I have that in hand, we can begin to find out how much our bigwigs might be willing to pay for the privilege of coming here to hunt."

"So let it be encoded," said Chief Potentary Korg. "So let it be done." He closed the videophone connection.

Phule turned to Beeker, who had sat just out of the video pickup's field of view, monitoring the exchange. "Well, Beeks, I think we've got what we're after—assuming the old lizard doesn't set too high a price for shooting his dinos."

"Since State will be footing the bill, I suspect the price will be no object, sir," said Beeker. "They can simply have the IRS pass the cost along to the taxpayers—business as usual, in other words."

"IRS?" said Phule. "Ugh—don't remind me. If you hadn't found me a galaxy-sized loophole, those bloodsuckers would have drained me dry. I'm amazed they gave up so easily."

"Don't be so sure that they have, sir," said Beeker. "Or alternatively, that they haven't persuaded their friends in other government agencies to single you out for their attentions. It may be no coincidence that the Alliance Ecological Interplanetary Observation Union has chosen to request an environmental impact statement from you, not exactly the thing one would expect them to require of a military unit, if you follow me."

"Oh, I doubt that's anything to worry about," said Phule. He leaned back in his chair and propped his feet up on the desk. "Odds are, it's just some bureaucrat looking for a way to pressure us into tossing him a bribe. I don't mind that—as long as the rascal stays properly bribed, once I've paid him."

"There's never any real guarantee of that, sir," said Beeker. "The best one can hope for is that not too many other bureaucrats learn where the pot of gold is located. But sooner or later, they're certain to sniff it out."

"We'll worry about that if it happens," said Phule. "And unless I get old and fat before my time, I'll have moved on to something else by the time they realize they might be able to get a few credits out of me. It's hard to pick a man's pockets when he won't stand still and wait for you."

"I hope you're right, sir," said Beeker. "One never ought to underestimate one's enemies—especially when they wield the power to tax and to imprison."

"Oh, I won't underestimate them, old bean," said Phule. "But I'm not about to let them scare me, either."

"Very well, sir," said Beeker, but his expression made it clear that he had ample reservations.

O O O

"Well, if you're trying to hide anything from me, you're doing a damned good job of it," said Victor Phule, grudgingly.

"The captain brought in some pretty slick accountants," said Tullie Bascomb, with a shrug. "In this business, your bookkeeper can make you almost as much money as your bookmaker."

"Understood," said Victor Phule. "That's precisely why I asked to examine both sets of books—more to the point, it's why I'm still not entirely convinced they're accurate. Are you certain you don't have a third set you're hiding from me?"

"If there's a third set, the captain hasn't told me anything about it," said Bascomb. The casino manager stood comfortably at the foot of the desk where Phule was working, showing no signs of anxiety. "Not that it's any of my business, you understand," he continued. "I make sure the floor's running smoothly, and leave the rest up to the people the captain's put in charge. He wants my opinion, all he has to do is ask. But I'm not going to stick my nose into their business."

Victor Phule shuffled the hard copy pages, thinking. He knew better than to comment on Bascomb's unstated corollary: that a certain nose was being stuck into the captain's business and that it didn't belong there. Still, he made a mental note of the crack. Bascomb was, as far as he could tell, a thoroughly competent manager, but it was worth remembering that his loyalty lay with the younger Phule. That was all right with Victor Phule, as long as Bascomb was willing to do as good a job for the father as he'd done for the son—assuming, of course, that Bascomb *had* been doing a good job for the son. As long as he was sticking his nose into his son's business, Victor Phule intended to find that out as well. If he was going to stir up resentment, he might as well do a thorough job of it.

He stood up from the desk and said to Bascomb, "I can see already that the gambling operations are driving the entire business—it looks as if everything else you're doing is designed to attract customers to the casino floor to bet. So I want you to show me through the casino, give me a satellite view of all that's involved in that end of the business."

"OK," said Bascomb, without any great show of enthusiasm. "You want the tour right now?"

"Right now," said Victor Phule, his voice absolutely level. It was time to show Bascomb who was boss. Phule hadn't built a galaxy-wide munitions business by being soft on his people. That appeared to be a lesson his son had failed to learn. Well, if the boy couldn't do a man's job, there was a man here ready to do it. He smiled coldly. "Lead the way," he said, and fell in behind Bascomb as the casino boss led him out of the office. Behind Phule came his bodyguard, quiet and unobtrusive.

Their first stop was a large room filled with video screens showing the casino from the viewpoint of the myriad cameras mounted above the floors. For every two or three screens, there was a casino employee intently peering at the scenes on display. "This is the nerve center of the whole operation," said Bascomb. "Everything that goes on is recorded, so any funny business that goes on can be nipped in the bud. There's always somebody who thinks he can beat us at our own game. We don't mind the system players—in the long run no system can change the fact that the odds are rigged in the house's favor. If a few people win in the short run, that just encourages more people to try to beat us. And the bigger the handle, the bigger our profit."

"So what are you looking for?" asked Victor Phule. "You've got a lot of expensive equipment here, and a lot of people sitting here watching it. What are they doing to earn their pay?"

"We're looking for two things," said Bascomb. "Professional cheaters can cost us, at least if they can get in and out before we catch them. We've got a database of known cheaters that we share with the other major betting houses, and we can spot most of the grifters before they even get to the betting tables—sometimes even before they set foot in the casinos. Watch this."

He touched a remote control and a nearby monitor changed its display. Now it showed an elderly Asian woman pumping chips into a bank of quantum slots, with the zombielike effect of so many bored retired people. "Can you see what made us pick her out?" asked Bascomb.

Victor Phule squinted at the display. "No," he said, then, "Wait a minute. She's not using the same tokens as everybody else, is she? They're counterfeits!"

"Pretty good," said Bascomb, grudgingly. "Maybe we could get you a job as a spotter. But here's the real catch—she's not just putting in counterfeit tokens, they're specially improved. Every one of them has a chip designed to increase her odds of winning one of the big jackpots. We might not have spotted it except she got caught five years ago doing the same thing at the Horny Toad Casino. She changed her disguise, but we still got her once the computer matched up her appearance with her MO. And a good thing—if we'd let her play a couple of hours, she was likely to walk out with ten or twenty thousand. Now look at this one."

The grandmotherly type disappeared and was replaced by a middle-aged businessman in ostentatiously casual garb at the craps table. At the end of a play, the man scooped a pile of chips off the table and walked casually toward the cashier's booth. "Do you see the hustle?" asked Bascomb.

Victor Phule scratched his head. "Run it again," he said, annoyed that he hadn't noticed anything out of the ordinary.

"OK, keep your eyes open," said Bascomb, with a smirk. Again the scene played out—perhaps ten seconds long.

"I've got it!" said Phule. "Right where he turns, and his hand goes in his pocket—I don't know what he's doing, but that's got to be when he does it."

Bascomb laughed. "Nah, he's just putting his hand in his pocket, maybe to check his hotel key. As far as we can tell, he wasn't doing anything this time."

Victor Phule glowered. "So what's the point, then?"

Bascomb toggled the remote, and the display changed to show the businessman and the Asian woman side by side. "The point is, this is the same hustler you saw before. Different day, different disguise."

"That's hard to believe," said Phule, peering intently at the two faces. "They're so different ..."

"Right, and so are these," said Bascomb, toggling the remote to show a series of other faces: a flashily dressed young male, a weary-looking little fellow who might have been a file clerk, a statuesque black woman ..." And the damnedest part is, the hustler isn't even human," he added. "You see what we have to deal with?"

"I guess I do," said Victor Phule, shaking his head. "What do you do when you catch ... *it?*"

"Put them on the first ship leaving the station and send the pic to the guards at the port of entry," said Bascomb, with a smile. Now he'd shown the elder Phule that he was in charge, and that he belonged in charge. "With any luck, you'll catch the hustlers before they even get to the casinos. That's one of the advantages of operating on a self-governing space station—you have a chance keep the troublemakers out altogether, instead of having to catch them in the act."

"A good policy," said Phule, nodding. "The same idea works in the weapons business. You might be able to dodge missiles once they're launched, but it's a lot more effective to keep the other side from launching them to begin with."

"Makes sense to me," said Bascomb. "The same idea is behind our employee screening program. We do an intensive background check on anybody applying for a job where they'll handle money. That prevents most of the potential problems. These monitors here are our best shot at catching the ones we can't interdict at the hiring stage. Every employee comes through this room as part of the orientation process, so they know their every move is being watched. That keeps most of 'em honest."

"And the rest?"

"The rest we catch in the act," said Bascomb. "And when we do, it's a one-way ticket off Lorelei—forever."

"When?" Victor Phule's voice had a skeptical edge to it. "I think you mean *if*. You don't mean to say you catch all of them, do you?"

"You better believe we catch all of them," said Bascomb, stubbornly. "Nobody gets away with ripping off the Fat Chance."

"Overconfidence is your worst enemy," said Victor Phule. "If you think you're catching everything, you're bound to be overlooking something. Come on, admit it—you can't stop it all."

"We can, and we do," said Bascomb, his jaw set even harder.

"You can't," said Victor Phule. "And I'm going to prove it!"

"That I want to see," growled Bascomb. "Exactly how are you going to prove it?"

"If I tell you, you'll be looking for it," said Phule. "Now, excuse me—I think I'll go take a look at things from ground level. I have an idea exactly where you're going wrong, and I'm going to rub your nose in it. And when I do, I think my son will want to know just what kind of man he's put in charge of this casino." He turned and stalked away, his bodyguard a pace behind him.

"He already knows what kind of man I am, Mr. Phule," muttered Bascomb. "Too bad you don't know him well enough to trust his judgment." He smiled, then turned to the casino employees watching the monitors. "Did you see that man who just left? I want you to watch him like a hawk every second he's on camera. Here's what I think he's going to try ..."

O   O   O

The Reverend Jordan Ayres was frustrated. For the first time in his career as a minister of the Church of the New Revelation, popularly known as the Church of the King, Rev had run into a problem he couldn't solve by consulting the sacred texts and commentaries. Not even applying his good common sense—a commodity he believed himself to possess in ample measure—had he been able to get to the bottom of it. He tapped his fingers on his desk, staring at the useless computer readout, trying to decide what avenue to follow next.

The problem was, there just wasn't enough known about the Zenobians. It had been only a few short years since the human race had encountered the reptilian sophonts, who in their appearance and habits resembled nothing so much as miniature allosaurs. That had been back on Haskin's Planet, where Captain Jester's troops had intercepted one of their spaceships—an exploring party commanded by none other than Flight Leftenant Qual. And to the best of Rev's knowledge, other than the members of Omega Company, no human being had set foot on the Zenobians' home world. Of course, the Alliance had done a fair amount of crash research into this new race when the Zenobians had requested formal membership—but much of that research remained unpublished, or at least inaccessible to someone with Rev's resources, which were far more comprehensive than those available to most civilians.

In particular, nothing of the Zenobians' religious beliefs had been recorded by the diplomatic, military, and commercial interview teams that did the groundwork for the Alliance treaty. It wasn't even known for certain that they had any such beliefs. Except for the intriguing morsel that Flight Leftenant Qual had offered in response to Rev's questions about the King ...

'L'Viz. Qual had claimed that Zenobian myth spoke of a figure with that name, a name that resonated curiously with that by which the King had gone in his Earthly days. Even more intriguingly, Qual had remarked that, when Zenobians had first learned of the King, they had taken Him as a human borrowing from their own mythology. Could the King have manifested Himself on Zenobia, bringing his message to the reptilian sophonts of a world far distant from his own home? Rev knew he had to penetrate to the bottom of this mystery, one of the deepest he had found in all his years of reading the sacred texts. Its implications for the Church were staggering—and its solution could catapult him to the first rank of its spokesmen.

But where to begin? Qual had implied that Zenobians were not comfortable speaking of such things to outsiders. That meant that Rev would need to take some sort of indirect approach. Did the little reptiles have sacred texts he might access somehow? Their libraries must have the information he wanted—but so far they had not linked their data to the Alliance's interplanetary UniNet. Doubtless there were technicians who could make the connection unilaterally and find what Rev wanted. But where was he going to get a tech wizard with that level of expertise, and how was he going to pay him?

Rev stood up from his desk. He paced over to his office window and stared out onto the Legion camp's parade ground, thinking. The King had always said that no problem was too difficult to tackle—if the highest mountain stood between him and his goal, he would just climb it. All Rev needed to do was put his mind to it. There had to be a way. There *had* to be a way …

O   O   O

Zigger had never been aboard a space liner before. In fact, as far as he knew, nobody in his whole family had ever left their home world—not before he had decided to realize his ambition to join the Space Legion. The experience was considerably less dramatic than he had expected.

For one thing, the spaceport had apparently been designed with the idea of giving travelers as forgettable an experience as possible. The furniture, the decor, the sights and sounds and smells—

everything might as well have been designed to linger just below the threshold of annoyance, without ever breaking out into anything that evoked a specific response.

And the ship itself—it might as well have been a crosstown hoverbus, for all the passengers' awareness of being in deep space. Zigger found himself in one of a row of identical seats in the main cabin, unless he preferred to stay in his spartan bunk in the dormitory-like sleeping area. The Space Legion, for all its attempt to woo its new recruits, had made it perfectly clear that it was not going to pay for anything more than the basic intersystem fare from the Lepoid's home world to the nearest Legion training camp. That meant a steerage-class ticket, with a very strict weight allowance for personal belongings. "Don't you worry about extra clothes," the recruiting sergeant had told him when he handed him the ticket. "You'll be wearing Legion black before long."

Zigger would have liked to have at least a view screen in the cabin so he could watch the stars outside, even though he knew that hyperspace travel wildly distorted the appearance of everything outside the ship. Supposedly there *was* a view screen in the first-class lounge. Zigger was tempted to sneak up and take a look for himself, but he couldn't figure out how to get past the heavy plasteel doors firmly protecting the People Who Mattered from curious Legion recruits and other such rabble. The population in steerage did seem to have a particularly high proportion of nonhuman sophonts, Zigger thought. Well, where he was going, that would be different.

Meanwhile, there was nothing else to do but sit in the main cabin and view his Poot-Poot Brothers tri-vees. They were almost the only reminders of his youth that he hadn't been prepared to leave behind as he embarked on his new life. His broad-jump medals, his talking ukulele, the lucky eighter he'd found on the street the day he'd won the math contest—even the favorite winter hat he'd worn until his mother had to mend the earholes three times: All were left behind. Even if he'd been sentimental about those artifacts, the exorbitant charges for overweight luggage would have changed his mind quickly enough.

But the spaceline provided cheap tri-vee viewers for its passengers, and a reasonable library of current hits and all-time favorites, knowing full well that it offered little enough else to keep them from going slowly nuts in the long stretches between stars. And tri-vees took up almost no weight or space. So Zigger's old friends, the Poot-Poot brothers, came along—and so did Oncle Poot-Poot and Mam'selle Toni and all the other series regulars.

Zigger was scrolling through one of the early episodes, "Oncle Poot-Poot Meets Barky," when he became aware of someone looking over his shoulder. He turned around to see a human—a young one, he thought, although he wasn't familiar enough with the species to be entirely sure of his judgment. "Hey, I hope I'm not bothering you," said the human. "It's just been a long while since I saw a Poot-Poot tri-vee—that stuff's really sly. I loved it when I was a kid. Especially that one with Barky, the Environmental Dog."

"I still like it," said Zigger. "Are you from Teloon?"

"No, I got on back at Fiano," said the human. "I'm on my way to Mussina's World to join the Space Legion."

"No goofing!" said Zigger. "That's where I'm bound, as well. I guess we're going to be comrades in arms. What's your name?"

"Well, they say that legionnaires don't tell anybody their real names," said the human. "They only go by their Legion names. The only problem is, I haven't decided on mine yet. Have you got one picked out?"

"Sure," said Zigger. He'd been thinking about his Legion name ever since his first decision to enlist. He'd looked into several books about Old Earth, hunting for something with just the right feeling. The answer, when he'd found it, seemed just right. "You can call me 'Thumper,'" he said.

"*Thumper.* That's pretty sly," said the human. He wrinkled his brow, then confided. "I've been thinking about calling myself 'Sharky'—you think that fits?"

Zigger looked the human up and down, then nodded. "It's *you,*" he said, not quite sure what made him say so.

But it was obviously the right thing to say. "All right!" said Sharky. "Thumper, you and me gotta stick together. They say the Legion drill sergeants eat recruits for breakfast. Between the two of us, I bet we can keep each other one step ahead of the game. Is it a deal?"

"Sure," said Zigger—no, his name was *Thumper* now. Thumper grinned, and said, "I've got a whole bunch of Poot-Poot tri-vees. Come sit next to me and we can watch 'em while we figure out what we want to do now that we're Legion buddies."

"All right," said Sharky again. "Look out, sergeants—here we come!"

O O O

"Yo, Soosh, c'mere," said Do-Wop, grinning evilly. "I got a swindle that can't lose."

"Right," said Sushi, raising an eyebrow. He'd been listening to Do-Wop's harebrained schemes ever since Captain Jester had made the two of them partners. Almost without exception, he'd ended up having to talk Do-Wop out of his grandiose plans—most of which had some loophole big enough to drive a space liner through. "What's the plan this time?"

"This one's as solid as neutronium," confided Do-Wop. "You know how Chocolate Harry runs a big-ass poker game every time he wants some spare cash, which is like every couple-three days?"

"Sure," said Sushi, leaning back on the fender of a cargo carrier. He folded his arms over his chest and looked Do-Wop in the eye. "Don't tell me you're going to try to cheat the sarge at his own game. It'll never work."

"Nah, this is even sleener," said Do-Wop. "I'm gonna get up my own game and swindle everybody else."

"Not very likely," said Sushi. "I know you. You lose every time you play poker with C. H., and every other time I've ever seen you play. What makes you think it'll be any different just because you're the one running the game?"

"Because I've been watching the sarge, and I finally figured out how he cheats," said Do-Wop. "It's so evil, I don't know why I didn't think of it myself."

"Really?" Sushi was impressed in spite of himself. If Do-Wop had actually caught the Supply sergeant cheating, he'd done something that had defied the best efforts of the entire company for as long as anyone remembered. "How does he do it?"

"Scope this out," said Do-Wop. He glanced around to make sure there were no eavesdroppers, and lowered his voice. In a dramatic whisper, he said, "The fat old snarkler *drops out of a hand when he ain't got good cards.*"

"*What?*" Sushi's voice rose nearly an octave, and his mouth fell open in surprise.

"Shh, you want everybody to hear what it is?" said Do-Wop, peering around worriedly. "I tell ya, it's a pure stroke of genius. Why, a dude could get rich overnight doin' that.

"Do-Wop, that's not cheating," said Sushi. "It's the way you're *supposed* to play poker."

"Oh, su-u-ure," said Do-Wop, scornfully. "Go try that one out on Tusk-anini—it ain't gonna fly with me. If what you said was true, why don't everybody play that way?"

"Now there's a question well worth asking," said Sushi, grinning. "In fact, I think I'm going listen to myself and ask it. Why don't *you* play that way?"

Do-Wop's jaw dropped. "What, and miss the chance of winning a really big one? Believe me, Soosh—there ain't no bigger rush than when everybody looks at your hand and thinks it's total crunk, and tries to boost the betting so's to clean you out, and then your last hole card gives you that sure winner."

"Right," said Sushi, with a sigh. "So how often does that happen?"

"All the time, man," said Do-Wop, excitedly. "I had a hand like that just a couple weeks ago. Had to draw a six to make my straight on the last card. I hung in there and got the sucker, on the last card. Woulda cleaned house, too—but all the dudes except Double-X had folded before then, and I only won seven-eight bucks on it."

"Uh-huh," said Sushi, unimpressed. "And how many times do you play for that kind of hand and wind up with crunk anyhow?"

"Sometimes it happens," Do-Wop admitted. "But hey, like C. H. says—you never go for it, you never get it!"

"Yeah, he *would* say that," said Sushi. "You know, I'd be tempted to give you a lesson about poker odds, except I seem to remember that you got one of those from Tullie Bascomb back on Lorelei, and it obviously didn't take. Maybe he was right—it's a waste of time to wise up a sucker."

"Hey, who you callin' sucker?" said Do-Wop. "If you wasn't my buddy ..."

Whatever he was about to say, it was cut off by a fresh voice. "Good mornin', boys. Would y'all be interested in a little special project I just cooked up?"

The two legionnaires turned to see Rev standing just behind them, with the half sneer that was the closest he came to a smile.

"Yo, Rev, what's up?" said Do-Wop.

"A li'l ol' electronic reconnaissance project, I think would be the best thing to call it," said Rev. "When I ran into this here problem, I couldn't help but think of you boys, rememberin' how you were the ones that cracked the Nanoids' transmissions. How'd you like to do somethin' along that line for me?"

Sushi shrugged. "Depends on what you've got in mind," he said. "Why don't you start talking, and we'll let you know whether it interests us."

"Sure, sure," said Rev, glancing around the parade ground. "But I'll tell you what—why don't y'all come into my office, where maybe it's a little more private? Then I can tell you the whole thing."

"Lead the way," said Sushi. "Come on, Do-Wop, this might be fun."

"What the hell, it's a slow day," said Do-Wop. The two legionnaires fell into line behind Rev and followed him to his office. At first, Sushi didn't know whether or not to make anything of the fact that Rev led them on a roundabout route instead of using the entrance nearest to his office, where Flight Leftenant Qual and two of his fellow Zenobians were working on some of their electronic equipment.

But when Rev began to describe his plan, Sushi understood.

O O O

"All right, tell me about these games," said Victor Phule, standing in the middle of the Fat Chance Casino's main gambling floor. "How do they work, and what does the house get from them?"

"Yes, sir," chirped the young resort PR person Tullie Bascomb had assigned to show him around. Marti Mallard was blond and perky, dressed in a short, tight skirt—the very image of a cheery bubblehead. Phule knew better than to take her at face value. He'd already had a look at the casino's personnel files, and noticed that Ms. Mallard had graduated *magna cum laude* in Interspecies Studies from Libra Arts University, followed by a business degree from Taurus Tech. Underneath that perky exterior was a steel trap of a mind, and her presence on the Fat Chance Casino's staff showed that his son's personnel department hadn't been completely asleep when it put her on the job.

"The most popular attraction in almost all casinos is the slot machines," said Marti, leading Victor Phule into a large bay filled with customers happily pumping tokens into an array of quantum slots. "One of the leading points of our ad campaign has been Captain Jester's decision to make the Fat Chance Casino's slot machine payouts the highest on Landoor ..."

"I wish you wouldn't call my son by that stupid Legion name," growled Victor Phule. "What exactly is the payout percentage on these machines, and why did my idiot son have to go raise it? That sounds like it'd cut into profits."

Marti moved closer to Victor Phule, and said in a low voice, "You probably don't want to talk about that in front of all these players, Mr. Phule. The fact is, even after your son shaved off one percent of the casino's percentage on the slots, it's still by far the most profitable of all the games we offer. No matter how big the jackpots are, on the whole, we're taking in a steady twenty percent of every dollar played."

Just then a bell began ringing, accompanied by bright flashing lights and a honking Klaxon. "*Yes-s-s-s!*" shouted an enthusiastic voice, and along the ranks of avid quantum slots players, many (but far from all) heads turned to see what had set off the noise, which now included an electronically amplified victory march. "There's one now," said Marti. "The bells and lights mean it's at least a thousand dollars. We want to make sure everybody knows when there's a big winner."

Victor Phule was incredulous. "You're giving away a thousand dollars?"

"Of course," said Marti. She managed somehow to whisper out of the corner of her mouth without losing her bright smile. "The players have to believe that they have a chance to win—and win big—if they're going to come here instead of one of the other casinos. On any given play, a player has a chance to win a jackpot of a hundred, a thousand, even ten thousand dollars—and when one of them does hit a jackpot, we give them the bells and lights so nobody can forget they have that chance."

Victor Phule's expression was skeptical. "To tell you the truth, I've never understood why anybody would bet on anything but a sure winner," he said. "And when you're giving somebody a chance to take away a thousand dollars—or more, if what you say is right—then the casino is betting on a losing proposition. On top of that, we give them free drinks and free food—and entertainment at a bargain price, as well. Why aren't we charging a competitive price for that, when we're giving away money hand over fist in the casinos?"

Marti's voice dropped even lower. "Because for every big jackpot, there are hundreds of losing bets, and that's the foundation of the business. Every single day of the year, as inevitably as taxes, the casino takes in many times what even the luckiest player can expect to win. Over the long run, the casino comes out solidly in the black."

"Solidly in the black is all right," said Victor Phule. "But I got my MBA at Rakeitin School of Business, and they taught us that any businessman worth his salt aims to maximize profits. I've built my arms business into the biggest in the galaxy by following that principle, and I can't see why it doesn't apply to this so-called business, as well."

"You saw the books, Mr. Phule," said Marti, shrugging. Even now, the smile never left her face. "If you don't want to believe what you saw, there's not much I can do to change your mind. The odds are stacked in the house's favor, and always will be."

Phule frowned. "There's a loophole somewhere," he said. "If the odds are so heavily stacked, none of these people would keep coming back to play. Yet I've already heard several of them say they're back for a fourth or fifth visit. There are obviously some consistent winners. That's what worries me. If one person can keep winning, then others can—and if enough learn how, they can put this place out of business."

Marti shook her head. "It doesn't work that way, Mr. Phule," she said patiently. "There's no way around the odds. In the long run …"

"Long run? Pfui!" said Victor Phule. "Your whole business principle is wrong, and I'm going to prove it. Where do I get tokens to play these machines?"

"Right over there, Mr. Phule," said Marti, pointing. She smiled quietly. It wasn't the first time somebody had refused to believe the simple facts. Nor would it be the last. Every casino in the galaxy made its money because of people who didn't believe in the odds. It looked as if Victor Phule was about to find that out—the hard way.

CHAPTER FOUR

Excessive displays of zeal, should always be grounds for suspicion. The religious bigot, the superpatriot, and the zealous company man have in common an emotion—loyalty to something larger than their individual interest. Loyalty to the greater cause is an emotion that everyone shares to some degree, and that in due proportion ought to be considered a good thing. But the zealots carry it to such an extreme that any reasonable person would feel a degree of embarrassment. Even more than the fanatical fixity of their loyalties, it is the lack of a sense of proportion that makes them suspect. Anyone with a balanced view of the world around him inevitably becomes to some degree a cynic.

I consider myself to have an exceptionally well-balanced view of the world around me. In consequence, I am frequently annoyed by the impositions of those less-balanced persons I find myself surrounded by . . .

O   O   O

The shuttle settled down roughly a kilometer south of the Legion camp. Phule and Beeker watched the landing from within the camp perimeter, then—as the cloud of dust began to settle—Phule gave a signal to his driver, Gears. The hoverjeep moved forward toward the landing site.

Ahead of them, the shuttle door was already open, and two men—presumably the hunters—were standing idly by, watching the crew piling luggage and equipment on a crawler. They'd evidently brought enough to last them twice as long as their little expedition was scheduled for—either that, or they'd assumed there wouldn't be laundry facilities at a Legion camp. Actually, thought Phule, fastidious visitors might have been advised not to trust their clothing to the mercies of a Legion field laundry—as much to avoid the likelihood of rough handling as on account of pilferage. With its own state-of-the-art automatic laundry facility built into the encampment module, Omega Company was miles ahead of the normal Legion standard. But the visitors could be excused for not having known that in advance.

Gears brought the hoverjeep to a halt next to the equipment crawler, and Phule leapt lightly to the ground. "Good afternoon, gentlemen," he said, holding out his hand. "I'm your host, Captain Jester. Welcome to Zenobia."

The men had been staring at Jester during the hoverjeep's approach. Now one of them took the captain's offered hand and shook it. "Our host, eh?" he said. "Not quite the way most people describe a visit from us. But I'm glad you're taking it in good spirits, Captain. It'll make our work here a lot easier."

Phule chuckled. "Work isn't exactly how I'd describe your visit, either," he said, heartily. "We've convinced the Zenobians to open up an area where no off-worlder has ever been—I'd call it virgin territory, gentlemen. It won't be exactly a weekend in the Waldorf, but I think you'll find it worth the effort. They tell me there are some spectacular beasts in there."

"Opened up virgin territory?" It was a woman's voice that replied, and Phule turned automatically to face the speaker. She was tall, with sharp features under a bowl haircut, and was dressed in the same dull-colored jumpsuit as the men (Phule now realized). The name tag on her breast read *C. I. Snieff.* "I certainly hope that's an exaggeration, Captain," she added, pursing her lips. "We want to keep this planet's indigenous territory unspoiled, wherever possible. Your company's presence is enough of a problem."

Phule wrinkled his brow, slowly beginning to realize that there was something going on he didn't quite follow. "Excuse me," he began. Before he could finish the thought, a new creature emerged from the shuttle hatchway and made a beeline for the Legion hoverjeep, uttering a steady stream of angry barks.

"What the hell?" said Gears, jumping back into the jeep to escape the agitated animal.

"Hey there, big fellow," said Phule, going down on one knee and stretching out a hand to the dog. "What's your name, huh?" The dog, ignoring him, circled the hoverjeep, staring balefully at Gears and snarling.

"Surely you recognize Barky, the famous Environmental Dog," said Snieff, "He's been on tri-vee all over the galaxy. Every schoolchild loves to watch him sniff out pollution and other dangers to the natural balance. Your hoverjeep's emissions must not be properly controlled."

"I beg your pardon, ma'am," said Gears, who had climbed up on the seat to avoid the attentions of Barky. "I set this vehicle up myself, and if it ain't totally up to spec, I'll eat it one piece at a time, without no ketchup, neither. Hey, can you call your dog off?" he added, with a note of concern.

"Barky is *never* wrong about pollution," said Snieff. She turned to one of her companions, and said, "Inspector Slurry, please impound that vehicle until we can have it properly tested."

"Woof!" said Barky, the Environmental Dog, his front paws up on the running board of the hoverjeep. It was not a friendly "woof." Gears cringed.

"Wait a minute," said Phule, interposing himself between Snieff's two assistants and the hoverjeep. "That's a Legion vehicle. You can't impound that ..."

"We certainly can," said Snieff, haughtily. "Inspector Gardner, show him the subpoena."

The third member of the team, a tall thin man with long reddish blond hair and a goatee, grinned and handed Phule a folded envelope. On one side it was marked, "Recycled Paper." Phule turned it over to read the other side: "Alliance Ecological Interplanetary Observation Union: Inspection Order and Subpoena."

"Subpoena?" asked Phule, blinking. "Inspection?"

"Sir, I believe I understand the situation," said Beeker. "This is obviously not the party of, ah, visitors we were expecting. This is an Environmental Inspection team from the Alliance Ecological Interplanetary Observation Union. And I'm afraid, sir, that they are perfectly within their rights to impound any vehicle suspected of improper emissions. The laws are quite explicit on that subject, sir."

"Alliance Ecological Interplanetary Observation Union?" Phule stared at the three inspectors, a puzzled look on his face. "But we shouldn't be under their jurisdiction. This planet has its own sovereign government ..."

"That may be so, Captain," said Snieff. "But we certainly aren't about to take your word for it. All the preliminary reports indicate that we might just be in time to prevent an environmental disaster. And nothing I've seen so far suggests anything to the contrary. Beginning with your driving a vehicle out to our landing site. Are you Legionnaires so lazy you can't use your own feet? Have you forgotten how to march?"

"Wh-what?" sputtered Phule. "I don't understand ..."

"Sir, I think we'd best get out of the inspectors' way and let them do their work," said Beeker. "And next time you receive an environmental impact questionnaire, I suggest you give it to someone other than Tusk-anini to fill out."

Phule nodded, understanding at last. "In that case, I think we'd best head back to camp. Inspector Snieff ..."

"*Chief* Inspector Snieff, thank you," said the woman.

"Yes, of course, Chief Inspector," said Phule. "If there's anything you need from my people, please let me know. We'll be happy to cooperate."

"I certainly hope so," said Chief Inspector Snieff. "The law provides very hefty penalties for obstruction of an environmental inspection."

"We don't have anything to hide," said Phule. "You'll see when you arrive at our guest quarters ..."

"Oh, no," said Snieff. "Regulations prohibit us from accepting accommodations with a suspected violator. We'll be setting up our own camp, Captain. I think you'll find it an instructive example of a minimal-impact inhabitation. Now, if you'll excuse us, we have to finish unloading."

"Of course," said Phule.

"Excuse me, ma'am," came Gears's voice. "If you'll just call off your dog ..." Snieff ignored him as she plastered a bright orange sticker to the door of the hoverjeep. It said in block letters, "IMPOUNDED FOR POLLUTION."

"Woof!" said Barky, the Environmental Dog. "Woof woof, woof woof woof!"

O O O

Legion boot camp was like nothing Thumper (as Zigger now called himself) had ever seen before. For one thing, the population was predominantly made up of humans—although there were enough members of other species to keep him from feeling completely outnumbered. He was the only Lepoid on the base, though—at least, the only one he'd seen in his bewilderingly rapid trip through the initial processing area.

That had been an experience he'd just as soon forget. Luckily, it had gone quickly enough that it seemed to be over almost before it started. But not before he'd been poked and prodded by doctors, and the autodoc had jabbed his arm with at least a dozen inoculations for diseases the Legion thought his race might be susceptible to on distant planets. (The doctors had spent a good half hour looking him up on the base's medical expert system before deciding which inoculations he was likely to need and which were likely to be more danger than help. He'd still been woozy most of the next day—maybe a reaction to the shots, maybe something else.)

All the humans were given ultrashort regulation haircuts. Being of a short-furred species, Thumper was spared that indignity, at least. But he was issued a black Legion jumpsuit at least three sizes too large, and combat boots that no imaginable breaking-in would ever make comfortable for his elongated feet. He was all ready to protest this treatment, but he realized that none of the other new recruits' uniforms were the right size, either. Half an hour of searching and trading found him a jumpsuit that fit him better, and his was the almost right size for another recruit—a lanky, bespectacled human who had adopted the Legion name "Spider." Nobody in the outfit had a pair of boots that fit Thumper. Since appearing without boots was defined as being out of uniform, a serious offense against Legion discipline, that was going to be a problem.

But Thumper had plenty of other problems to distract him from the boots. Prime among these was his drill instructor, Sergeant Pitbull, who seemed to be of primarily human origin, although there were whispers that he was at least part something else. Exactly what that something else might be, none of the recruits was willing to say—at least not where the sergeant might hear it, which was apparently everywhere in the barracks. At least, the sergeant had an uncanny ability to storm into a room immediately after one of the recruits had said something mildly critical of Legion discipline and to chew out the offender in terms none of them had dreamed of before they had joined the Legion.

It was on their third night of training that Thumper and his new comrades simultaneously realized that the Legion recruiters had actually told them the truth about one thing: Legion boot camp wasn't going to be easy. "By St. Elrod and all powers, I never knew there were so many places I could hurt," said Sharky, lying flat on his bunk, just after lights out.

"That ain't nothing," said Spider. "I never knew there were so many different wrong ways to wear a uniform. Seems like I jes' can't do it right, nohow."

Thumper nodded. Even having found a uniform that fit properly, he was still having trouble getting it to look right—or so the sergeants seemed to think. "I guess they want us to pay attention to all the details," he said; "When you're in a hostile environment, one little detail could make the difference ..."

"Oh, bull," said Spider. "Tell me what difference it gonna make how I fasten my sleeve button!"

"That's not what I mean," said Thumper. "The point is, they want to train us so we don't overlook anything. Then, when you're in a combat situation, you're less likely to overlook something that could kill you ..."

"Ain't nobody ever been killed by a sleeve button that I heard of," insisted Spider.

Thumper was about to try his explanation again when somebody hissed *"Pitbull!"* and the entire bunkroom fell silent in fear of the sergeant's wrath. For once the sergeant didn't materialize; but by the time the recruits realized it was a false alarm, half of them were asleep, and nobody else seemed inclined to take up the thread.

The one part of Legion life that Thumper found congenial was the healthy dose of physical activity: drill, exercise, hard labor, and more drill. Perhaps this was because he had come to the Legion not as a last chance to escape from an intolerable existence back home, but as an actual lifelong goal. Running, marching, and doing endless calisthenics shouldn't bother someone who had kept himself in good physical condition, he kept telling his buddies. Most of the time, they were too exhausted to answer him. But the looks they shot in his direction were eloquent, had he only been able to read them.

At last, even his friend Sharky, whom he'd met on the space liner that brought them to Legion boot camp, warned him that he was getting "too gung ho." They'd ended up in the same recruit platoon by the simple expedient of showing up at the processing center at the same time.

"What's wrong with being gung ho?" asked Thumper.

"You're making the other guys look bad," said Sharky. "We're all in this together, you know. It ain't good if you show up your buddies."

"I'm not trying to show anybody up," Thumper protested. "I've always wanted to be a legionnaire. Now that I am one, why shouldn't I try to be a good one?"

"'Cause you make things harder for the rest of us," Sharky explained. "If most of us want to punk out after a hundred push-ups and you keep on going, the sarge is going to get on our asses to keep up with you."

"Gee, I never thought of that," said Thumper. "But don't you want to be all that you can be? If you do more pushups, you'll get stronger. That could be important when the crunch comes ..."

"Crunch? What crunch?" Sharky scoffed. "The Alliance hasn't been in a real war since my grandpa was a kid."

"No, but that doesn't mean it won't happen ..."

"Against who?" Sharky demanded. "Every time we meet a new race, they want to join up with us on account of the trade advantages. Like those lizards out on Zenobia."

Thumper shook his head. "There was a civil war on Landoor ..."

"Sure, and that wasn't much more than a food fight, from what I hear tell," said Sharky. "Nobody except the locals got hurt. All the Legion did was go in to mop up, and they spent more time lying on the beach than anything else. So why make things any tougher than you have to?"

"You can't assume just because things have been easy lately that it's always going to be like that," insisted Thumper.

"Hey, I'm just trying to give you a clue," said Sharky. "If you play along with the other guys, everybody's happy. Make too many waves, nobody's gonna be happy—and they're gonna know whose fault it is."

"All right, I understand you," said Thumper, with a nod and a smile. He didn't say what he was thinking. He didn't have to. His actions would do the talking for him, when the time came.

O O O

"The slots, huh?" Tullie Bascomb shook his head in disbelief at what the security monitors were showing. "Most of the guys who think they can beat the house by playing some kind of homemade system go for blackjack," he said. "Or poker, if they think they can win steady enough to cover the house percentage."

Doc grinned. "That's for sure. Only suckers play the quantum slots—they're the worst bet in the joint. You showed us that, back when the captain first brought us to Lorelei."

"Yeah," said Bascomb. "I guess the captain didn't tell his old man that, though. Look at him pumping the tokens into those machines!"

"Yeah, I saw him pretty near knock down two white-haired little old ladies who tried to horn in on a machine he'd been priming," said Doc. "He's got the fever, all right."

"Well, he's a grown man," said Bascomb. "And I guess he can afford to lose a few bucks. Hell, I doubt we could put a serious dent in his bankroll if we set up a row of thousand-dollar-a-pull machines. That doesn't mean I'm not tempted, though ..."

"Nah, what's the point? At that price, nobody but Victor Phule could ever afford to play 'em," said Doc. "And what would the payouts have to be ...?"

"High enough to make a billionaire's palms sweaty," said Bascomb. "Right now, I think he's just playing on principle—he thinks the payouts are too generous, and he's trying to prove the point. To really get him hooked, we'd need to offer something big—even a million bucks is probably small potatoes, when you're talking about someone who's used to supplying armaments to entire planets."

Doc rubbed his chin and leaned forward to point at Victor Phule's image on the security monitor. "What if we did set up a bank of machines for nobody but Pop Phule to play? Offer him a jackpot that'll make even *his* mouth water—title to the whole darn casino, for example—but at impossibly long odds. Once he's thrown enough tokens down the slot, then he'll have to admit that we aren't giving away money."

"You've got an evil mind," said Bascomb, chuckling. "Only one problem I can see with it. We don't own the casino—Omega Company does, and we can't offer a prize we aren't able to deliver if somebody does win it. Not even on Lorelei, where the house rules and the laws of the land are pretty damn close to one and the same."

"So we make the odds so impossible that he can't possibly win, is all," Doc insisted. "Let's say he's got to get five simultaneous jackpots on five different machines ... or some other combination that only comes up once in a trillion times."

Bascomb shook his head. "It's tempting, you know, Doc? But we can't do anything as screwy as that without getting the captain to sign off on it. I don't care if we *would* be setting those crooked slots to teach his father a lesson—bad business is bad business, even when you keep it in the family."

"I guess you're right," said Doc. "In fact, has anybody gotten in touch with Captain Jester? He'd want us to tell him that his father's here, I'm pretty sure of that."

"I got his OK before showing the old man the books," said Bascomb, snapping his fingers. "But this is a new wrinkle, and I'm not sure whether he'd go along with it. Guess the only thing to do is get him on the horn and ask."

"Right," said Doc. He pressed one of the studs on his wrist chronometer and nodded. "It's midafternoon at Zenobia Base, so he's likely to be in reach of a vidphone. Do you want to call him, or shall I? Or shall we just send a priority message and let him get back to us?"

"Seeing that it's during his business hours, I think we better tell him this in person," said Bascomb. "And since I'm in charge of the gambling end of the business, I guess I ought to be the one to make the call. You want to talk to him, too? He might have a few questions you can answer as well as I can."

"Sure, why not?" said Doc. He waved a hand in the direction of the monitor. "One good thing—our main problem's not going anywhere. Except maybe to the cashier's window for another batch of tokens."

"Let's hope he makes that particular trip a lot of times," said Bascomb, with a thin smile. He gestured toward a door, and the two men went to the office to place a call to Captain Jester.

O O O

"YOU FARKING SLUGS *DISGUST* ME!" roared a voice that seemed far too loud for an ordinary human's vocal apparatus. Thumper jerked his eyes open, awaking from the utterly exhausted sleep he'd been in a fraction of a second before. He automatically checked the time: Five in the morning. The drill instructor, Sergeant Pitbull, was right on time, fully dressed and ready to eat raw recruits for breakfast. Thumper had last seen him only six hours before, when he'd put the squad of new legionnaires to bed with threats and curses.

Thumper still hadn't figured out how the drill instructor managed to stay alert and fit on what must be even less rest than the recruits were getting, but he'd come to take it for granted. Every task he demanded of the recruits—including some that at first had seemed impossible—Sergeant Pitbull could perform better than any of them, despite being at least ten years older. Even Thumper, who had already learned that he was in better physical condition than almost all his fellow recruits, couldn't beat the sergeant in any direct competition—especially in hand-to-hand combat, where the sergeant seemed to have a bottomless repertory of dirty tricks. Even in an outright sprint, where Thumper was sure he had the advantage, Sergeant Pitbull had somehow managed to make him trip and fall before he got three steps from the start.

Worst of all, it seemed as if the sergeant was always angry. One night, after lights out, the whispered conversation in the bunkhouse got to the subject of whether anyone could remember hearing a friendly remark pass Pitbull's lips. The closest anyone could come was, "THAT'S RIGHT, WAY TO STOMP HIS WORTHLESS CIVVY ASS!" when a hulking recruit named Crunch put Spider in the infirmary with a dislocated shoulder during judo practice. And while Crunch was probably right that the sergeant meant it as a compliment on his judo technique, most of the other recruits agreed with Spider's heated protestation that congratulating one of the recruits for injuring another wasn't *his* idea of a "friendly word."

Then Sergeant Pitbull slammed the door open and bellowed, "SHUT UP, YOU STINKING BUGS!" (He seemed never to have learned to speak softly.) In the utter silence that followed this remark, he continued, "WHEN I TURN THE LIGHTS OUT, YOU'RE SUPPOSED TO FARKING SLEEP, NOT YAMMER LIKE A BUNCH OF SCHOOLGIRLS! THERE'LL BE PUNISHMENT DETAIL FOR THE WHOLE FARKING SQUAD!" After that, even Crunch conceded the point. Pitbull had been as good as his word—next morning, there were a hundred extra push-ups for everyone.

But this was another morning, which meant another chance for Pitbull to deal out arbitrary punishment. Thumper and all his buddies scrambled out of their bunks and came to attention. There was just a glimmer of a chance that today they might manage to avoid extra pushups or some other equally unpleasant task. Not much of a chance, but Thumper had gotten in the habit of grasping at even minuscule chances. Along the way, he'd gotten much better at push-ups than he'd ever imagined being. It wasn't what he'd seen himself doing when he'd dreamed of joining the Legion, but if his experience so far was any indication, push-ups were a significant component of Legion life.

"LISTEN UP, YOU FILTHY SKIME-EATERS," roared Sergeant Pitbull. Thumper wasn't sure what a skime was, but after hearing the sergeant, he knew he didn't want to eat one. Or maybe it was a *filthy* one he didn't want to eat … He had only a brief moment to meditate on that question, as the sergeant continued with his high-volume harangue. "TODAY WE'RE GOING OUT TO THE OBSTACLE COURSE," the sergeant boomed. "THAT'S WHERE WE SEPARATE THE REAL LEGIONNAIRES FROM THE FARKING WEAK-SIBLING CIVVIES. *DO YOU BUGS WANT TO BE REAL LEGIONNAIRES?*"

"YES, SERGEANT PITBULL!" the squad shouted in chorus. They'd long since learned that any less enthusiastic response would be greeted with scorn. Privately, Thumper wondered whether Sergeant Pitbull might have stood too close to an explosion at some point in his earlier career, damaging his ears in the process. If he were partly deaf, that would explain a lot … but no, the autodocs could fix that …

"FOLLOW ME, YOU BUGS!" said the sergeant, and he set off at a flat-out run—the only speed at which a Legion recruit was allowed to move. Luckily for Thumper, he could outrun everyone in the squad without particularly trying. It was one of the minor advantages of being a Lepoid. He hadn't found very many of them here in the Legion, so he had acquired a finer appreciation for the ones he'd found. Running easily, he stayed just behind the sergeant until the squad arrived—many of them huffing and puffing despite several weeks of rigorous exercise—at the obstacle course.

In front of him, Thumper saw a tract of land that would probably feel flattered to be described as "ruined." Or even "devastated." It was a mud-filled morass with craters and chunks of broken stone wall or the jagged stumps of trees at seemingly random intervals. The few open stretches were strewn with skeins of ugly-looking barbed wire laid parallel to the ground. Here and there were wide water-filled ditches and eight-foot wooden walls. At the far side Thumper could make out sandbagged bunkers, from which the muzzles of machine guns protruded. "LISTEN UP, YOU BUGS," explained Sergeant Pitbull. "THIS HERE IS WHAT WE CALL A STIMULATED BATTLEFIELD, WHICH IF YOU'RE EVER IN A FARKING SHOOTING WAR YOU'RE GONNA SEE A SHIT-LOAD OF 'EM. THE DRILL IS, WHEN I BLOW MY WHISTLE, YOU GET TO THE OTHER SIDE AS FAST AS YOU FARKIN' CAN. BUT CHECK THIS OUT—THEM SKIME-EATERS WITH THE MACHINE GUNS GONNA SHOOT LIVE FARKIN' AMMO OVER YOUR HEADS, SO YOU BETTER KEEP 'EM THE HELL DOWN. WE LOSE A COUPLE-THREE STUPID-ASS RECRUITS EVERY MONTH ON ACCOUNT OF THEY JUMPED UP AND TRIED TO RUN AWAY"

Thumper nodded as the sergeant explained the drill. Looking at the course, he could see that the machine guns were limited to a narrow field of fire. Outside that area, the main problem was dodging around the craters and rubble, but if one didn't mind a bit of mud, there was no reason to go at less than full speed. After all, the sergeant *had* said that the point of the exercise was to get to the other side as quickly as possible.

So when the sergeant blew his whistle, Thumper was off and running ...

O   O   O

Phule stared blankly at the sheaf of papers that had just landed on his desk. "What's all this?" he asked in an annoyed voice. It was obviously not the promotion papers he'd been expecting from Legion Headquarters.

"Environmental impact forms from those AEIOU guys," said Roadkill, one of the two legionnaires who'd carried in the mountain of paperwork. "That Chief Inspector Snieff brought it over in some kind of wheelbarrow. Street and I just happened to be the first legionnaires she saw, and she took that as a license to order us around."

65

"Order you around?" Lieutenant Armstrong looked up from the adjacent desk, where he was filling out work assignment forms. "I think I'm going to have to talk to her myself. I've been trying to get some of you rascals to follow orders ever since I became an officer in this outfit, with little or no sign that I'm getting anywhere."

"Jeez, some thanks we get for being good legionnaires," grumbled Street. "I'd have given her a piece of my mind, if she hadn't had that stupid dog with her. That ugly mutt looked at me as if it was gonna take a bite out of my tail end."

"Barky, the Environmental Dog?" asked Phule. "He seemed pretty harmless to me."

"I think he thought Street was a polluter," said Roadkill, deadpan. "Or maybe a litterer—it's hard to tell what that dog thinks when all he'll say is 'woof!'"

"Stupid mutt can't prove nothing on me," said Street, scowling.

"Are you saying that because you haven't done anything, or because you think you've covered up your tracks?" said Armstrong, raising one eyebrow just a fraction. He pointed at the two legionnaires, and added, "Don't be too sure Barky can't sniff you out, if you've been polluting."

"I already told ya, I ain't done nothin'," said Street. He stared at the floor, squirming as if one of his schoolteachers had called on him to recite a lesson he hadn't studied.

"It's all right, Street, nobody suspects you of anything," said Phule. Then, remembering to whom he was speaking, he hastily added, "Not this time, anyway."

"Yeah, I was just joking," said Roadkill, punching his buddy on the biceps. "But we'd better get back to that job we were doing, before somebody notices we're gone—then we might really get in trouble."

"Just tell them you were bringing me something," said Phule. "And thanks—I think." He looked at the pile of papers, and his expression was anything but thankful. But Roadkill and Street were already out the door.

Phule picked up the top sheet of one of the piles of papers and began to read it, but before he'd gotten more than a couple of lines, his wrist communicator buzzed. "Yes, what is it, Mother?" he said, holding the device closer to his mouth and ear.

"Priority call from Lorelei, you silly thing," said Mother's teasing voice. "You must be an even bigger man than you look."

"Lorelei? Put them right through," said Phule. He wondered what was urgent enough for the team he'd left to run the place to call him about. Among them, there weren't many things he didn't think they could handle. He wouldn't have left the place in their hands if he'd believed otherwise.

"Tullie Bascomb here, Captain," came the familiar voice. "We've got—well, not really a problem, but a situation Doc and I think you need to know about."

"Go ahead, Tullie," said Phule. "Is it my father again?"

"Yeah, he's still being a pain in the butt," said Bascomb. "It was bad enough that he wanted to go over the casino's books …"

"You showed them to him, didn't you?" asked Phule.

"Sure, after you told me it was all right," said Bascomb. "For a while I was worried he might really find something to raise a stink about, but I guess he didn't. But then he decided to stick his nose into the gambling operation."

"That's hardly in character," said Phule, rubbing his chin speculatively. "I never knew him to have any interest in gambling. Where is he now?"

"Playing quantum slots," said Bascomb. "Somehow, he got the idea our jackpots were too big. We tried to tell him about the odds, but he didn't want to listen. So now he's trying to win a big one to prove we're wrong."

Phule chuckled. "Tullie, if my father's determined to throw away his ill-gotten fortune one token at a time, I'm not about to do anything to stop him. It's just that much more for the Company's retirement fund."

"Well, I'm glad you feel that way about it, Captain," said Tullie. There was a definite note of relief in his voice. "In that case, would you have any problem if we cooked up a way to get even more of his money out of his pockets?"

"Not in principle, I guess," said Phule. "What exactly did you have in mind?"

"Doc came up with the idea of adjusting some of the slots to take really big bets—up to a thousand bucks a pull," said Bascomb. "We'd advertise a monster jackpot, but set the odds so long nobody'd have the ghost of a chance to collect on it. What do you think?"

"I don't see why not," said Phule. He chuckled, then continued, "At a thousand dollars a pull, I doubt anyone but Papa will ever be able to afford to play. And I have no compunction whatsoever about taking his money for my troops. Go ahead, and let me know how much he loses before he gives up."

"You got it, Captain," said Bascomb, and closed the connection.

Phule stared for a moment at the wall across from his desk. His father's antics shouldn't really have surprised him, he supposed—it was typical of the old fellow to show up unannounced and try to take charge. But, as usual, he seemed to have come up with a new twist. He shook his head. There weren't many people in the galaxy who seemed more out of place in a casino than the old man—not that his father would ever let something like that stop him. Well, it was about time somebody taught Victor Phule a lesson. And he couldn't think of anyone who could better afford to pay the tuition. He sighed, then picked up the top sheet on the pile the two legionnaires had brought in, and began reading.

CHAPTER FIVE

Journal #669

When a system is set up to deal with misfits and incompetents, the addition to the mix of someone actually capable may cause a greater disturbance than the addition of a weak cog to a functioning organization. This is certainly the case in most formations of the Space Legion, where incompetence and malfeasance have become a way of life.

Thus, the arrival at the Legion's central training base on Mussina's World of a new recruit who actually had a few qualifications for a military career was almost inevitably a recipe for disaster.

o o o

"I don't understand what I did wrong," said Thumper, sullenly. He sat on the edge of his bunk, illuminated by a single handlight in Sharky's hand. The light was shining directly in his face, which made it hard to see the others standing all around him. It wasn't hard to guess who was there, though—everybody else in Recruit Squad Gamma.

"You're acting like an eager beaver, is what you did wrong," said Sharky, exasperated. "It's what you *keep* doing wrong. Why you got to set a record for the fastest run of the obstacle course?" The other squad members stood in a circle around Thumper, adding their sullen voices to his argument.

"What's wrong with doing the best you can?" Thumper asked. "That's all I did. I like running and climbing over things. Why can't I do that when I have the chance?"

Sharky groaned. "Because now the sergeants are tryin' to make everybody else run the course faster," he explained. "*IF THAT LITTLE TWERP CAN DO IT WHAT THE FARM'S WRONG WITH YOUR LAZY STINKIN' ASS?*" he said, pretending to shout without raising his voice to a level that might be heard outside the bunkhouse. There were a couple of chuckles in appreciation of the accuracy of Sharky's imitation of Sergeant Pitbull's habitual bellow, but nobody sounded in particularly good humor.

"Well, it seems to me the question is, can you guys run the course better than you've been doing it, or not?" asked Thumper. He turned his head from side to side, not so much looking at his audience as trying to get away from the persistent glare of the handlight.

"Wrong damn question," rumbled a deep voice. Thumper recognized the speaker as Pingpong, the biggest and slowest recruit in the platoon. "What you oughta ask is, should we stomp the shit out of this so-called sophont for making everybody else look bad to the sarge?"

"Hey, easy there, Pingpong," said Sharky, patting the big recruit on the shoulder. "It ain't come to stompin', yet. We're just havin' a friendly talk with good ol' Thumper here, lettin' him know how all his buddies in the squad feel about stuff."

"Oh, yeah," said Pingpong, scratching the thick fur atop his head. "Well, let me know when it's time for stompin, OK?"

"Sure," said Sharky, with a nod.

"I can't believe you guys are threatening me," said Thumper, indignation all over his face. "Just because I want to do my best ..."

"Yeah, yeah, doin' your best is triff," said Sharky. "But do you hafta do it when it makes all your buddies look bad? If you'd just save it for when there's a real enemy ..."

"We got a real enemy," said another recruit—Spider, this time. "It's all the farkin' sergeants ..."

"Damn straight!" said several of the recruits in chorus.

"No, no, no," said Thumper, holding up his forepaws. "Sure, the sergeants are tough on us, but that's because *we* have to be tough when the death rays start flashing. Really, guys, it's all for our own good ..."

"Ain't no damn death rays flashin'," said Pingpong. "There ain't been a farkin' war since my granddaddy was in the Regular farkin' Army, forty years ago. Who we gonna fight, anyhow?"

"There was a civil war someplace out in the New Baltimore sector, wasn't there?" said Spider. "The Legion was sent in to settle that one ..."

"That was on Landoor," said Sharky, dripping scorn. "And that wasn't any real war—just a bunch of backward colonials gettin' excited. Only real action was when some Legion officer shot up the peace conference. Hope he got him a couple sergeants ..."

"*Shhh—Pitbull!*" came a hoarse whisper, but it was too late.

"YOU GOT YOU A SERGEANT NOW, YOU STUPID FARKIN' CLOWNS!" roared the drill sergeant, throwing open the door to the recruits' bunkroom. The overhead light came on abruptly, catching the circle of recruits standing around Thumper's bunk like greeblers around a sweetbush. They all snapped to attention as the sergeant stomped over to the group. "WHAT THE FARK'S GOIN' ON HERE, AS IF I DIDN'T KNOW?" he bellowed.

"We was just telling old Legion stories, is all, sarge," said Sharky, stepping to the front of the group. "Tryin' to build up the squad's morale, y'know?"

"YEAH, HUH? LIKE YOUR MOTHER BUILDS UP THE ARMY'S MORALE," said Sergeant Pitbull. "YOU BARKERS SHOULDA GOT YOURSELF SOME SLEEP BEFORE NOW, BECAUSE I WAS GONNA COME GIVE YOU A FRIENDLY WARNING, LIKE. JUST A LITTLE BIT OF ADVANCE NOTICE OF THE SURPRISE INSPECTION BY THE BIG BRASS."

"Surprise inspection?" said several of the recruits in near unison.

"THAT'S RIGHT, YOU GOT WAX IN YOUR EARS?" explained Pitbull. "GENERAL BLITZKRIEG SET DOWN ON

BASE JUST AFTER DARK, AND HE'S GONNA COME INSPECT BARRACKS AT OH-EIGHT-HUNDRED HOURS TOMORROW FARKIN' MORNING. MAKE THAT *THIS* MORNING."

"Oh-eight-hundred?" groaned the recruits. The clock on the wall showed just a bit shy of oh-four-hundred.

"YOU GOT IT RIGHT THE FIRST TIME," said Pitbull. "NOW, YOU'RE JUST LUCKY YOU GOT A SERGEANT THAT REALLY CARES FOR YOUR SORRY ASSES, SO I GIVE YOU SOME ADVANCE WARNING SO YOU DON'T ALL GET REAMED OUT BY THE GENERAL. YOU THINK I'M A HARD-ASS, YOU AIN'T SEEN NOTHIN'. BLITZKRIEG EATS RECRUITS FOR TAPAS WITH HIS AFTERNOON SHERRY. YOU GOT FOUR HOURS TO MAKE THIS FARKIN' PIGHOLE LOOK LIKE A LEGION BASE. BLITZKRIEG GIVES ANY ONE OF YOU PSEUDO-SOPHONTS EVEN ONE DEMERIT, YOU'LL GET IT FROM ME TEN TIMES—EXCEPT I DON'T GIVE DEMERITS, I GIVE PUNISHMENT. YOU GOT THAT, YOU CLOWNS?"

"Got it, Sarge," said the recruits.

"THEN GET YOUR ASSES BUSY," Pitbull shouted. "AND BE QUIET ABOUT IT. I'M GONNA GET SOME FARKIN' SLEEP!"

O O O

"I dunno, man, this is some weird-ass job Rev wants us to do," said Do-Wop. As usual, he was leaning on the back of Sushi's chair, looking over his partner's shoulder at the computer screen. "How does he expect us to find out about this Zenobian guy, Leavis?"

"L'Viz." Sushi corrected him. "And how we find out about it is our business—we're the recon experts, and he isn't. It's an interesting challenge, don't you think? Find some way to access the Zenobians' archives and see if we can pull out info on this ancient legend of theirs."

"Sure, and how we gonna know it when we do find it?" said Do-Wop. "Even with a translator, that Flight Leftenant Qual don't make sense half the time. I dunno how you think we're gonna find one particular story out of all the stuff they must have written down. It's like findin' one special bush in the whole forest."

"Yeah, I know it looks that way," said Sushi. "But we do have a few clues that'll make it easier. Like the name of the main character, for example. And if the story's that well-known, we may find it in more than one place. It'd be like searching human archives for Odysseus …"

"O'Dizzy-us? Never heard of him."

Sushi sighed. "Sometimes I wonder about you," he said, looking up at his partner. "Should I send you out to find a bottle of quarks, so I can get some work done?"

"Better you should send me for a couple quarts of beer," said Do-Wop. "I know where to find that, anyhow."

"Believe me, I'm tempted," said Sushi. "But I've got some tricky work to do before I can kick back, and every now and then I'll need a fresh pair of eyes to look over my shoulder so I can tell whether I'm making any real progress. So you can't have any beer, either. What you *can* do is run over to Chocolate Harry's and see if you can get us a translator. We'll need it once I find the Zenobians' archives—and we might as well have it before we need it. If he hassles you any, go get Rev to write out a requisition for it."

Do-Wop smirked. "If he hassles me any, I'll just figure out some way to skank it. Harry thinks he's bad, but his security really stinks. I could slide into his supply depot and walk off with everything in sight, and he'd never look up from his biker magazines."

"Maybe so, but don't try it just yet," said Sushi. "That's the kind of thing we have to save for when we really need it. In fact, go to Rev first—he'll write an order for a translator and sign it over to us, and that's that. We don't have to explain where it came from if somebody sees us using it, and people aren't shooting us the evil eyeball when we really need to do something without being noticed."

"Ah, you take the fun out of everything, Soosh," said Do-Wop. "You wanna sneak into the Zenobians' archives because it's a challenge, and that's supposed to be triff. But when I want to skank a translator from Supply, that *ain't* triff, on account of I might get caught. I don't see no difference."

"You don't?" Sushi turned around in his chair and looked his partner straight in the eye. "The difference is, there's no problem getting a translator the legit way, and no awkward consequences if somebody sees us using it. But getting into the Zenobian archives is something Rev's asked us to do—and he's a Legion officer, so he's the one who takes the heat if we get caught. We're just doing a job for a superior officer, get it?"

"Maybe," said Do-Wop. "But remember back when that Major Botchup was CO when the captain was gone? There was a whole big mess about whether or not we should follow illegal orders, and who was authorized to give legal orders, and what happened if you weren't sure. I never did find out just what was OK and what wasn't, except I figured I don't follow orders enough to get in trouble, anyway."

"Well, that's one way to look at it," said Sushi. "But I think I know what you're getting at. We don't know for sure that Rev has any business spying on the Zenobians—after all, they are supposed to be our allies. But how much do you want to bet that Alliance headquarters isn't already spying on them, on a much wider level than we're planning to do?"

Do-Wop's eyebrows rose the better part of an inch. "Whoa, man, that's right! I never thought about that—but it makes sense. Maybe there's even somebody in our outfit doin' it, if we knew everything that was goin' on!"

Now it was Sushi's turn to raise his eyebrows. "You know, Do-wop, if I ever act as if I think you're stupid, remind me of this. Of course there's somebody in our company gathering intelligence on the Zenobians—there's got to be! We're the only Alliance military outfit on Zenobia. I mean, why would the government pass up a chance like this? The question is, who is it? It must be somebody who's been with us a while—we haven't had anybody new join the company since before we got the Zenobia assignment."

Do-Wop shrugged. "Well, it ain't us—unless this job for Rev is part of it. Hey, you don't think …"

"Nothing would surprise me," said Sushi. "But we're not going to figure it out just standing around jawing. Why don't you go over and get Rev to sign a chit for that translator—and see if you spot anything to make you think *he's* the spy. I suppose it's none of our business, but I must admit you've piqued my curiosity."

"I'll keep my eyes open," said Do-Wop, showing what for him was an unusual degree of enthusiasm. He winked, and slipped out the door, and Sushi returned to his attempts to penetrate the Zenobians' computer network. Maybe that weird oscillation in the 1000 kHz range was a carrier wave of some kind ...

O O O

"Hey, we just got here," protested Ernie, sprawling full length on the bed. There was no other place in the room to sit, unless he wanted to perch on a windowsill—which was currently occupied by Lola. "What's the point of turning around and going right back out again?"

Lola shrugged. "Phule's most likely to be at the Fat Chance, so that's where we go."

"Oh, sure," groaned Ernie. "That's halfway around the wheel. On a stinkin' bus, no less."

"If you have a problem with a bus, think about what happens if we don't get the job done this time," said Lola. "Or did you enjoy our last meeting with Mr. V?"

"Screw Mr. V," said Ernie, but he looked nervously over his shoulder as he said it. Here on Lorelei, the mob was as likely as not to have ears even in the shabby rented room where he and Lola had landed after their unenthusiastic return to the space station where their previous attempt to kidnap Willard Phule had gone spectacularly awry.

Despite taking the cheapest liner they could find passage on, the two freelance kidnappers had arrived at Lorelei low on funds— low enough to make finding someplace to stay a real chore. After several hours of working the spaceport's bank of pay phones, Lola had managed to find them a room in a small apartment building that normally catered not to off-station tourists but to the lowest-paid casino workers—a major comedown from the suite they'd occupied in the Fat Chance on their previous trip. The only workers who lived this far from the casinos were the least skilled and most easily replaced. The powers that ran Lorelei Station saw no reason to waste much effort making their living quarters attractive or convenient.

"There's a bus stop about half a kilometer away," said Lola, looking over the battered Public Transit handout their landlord had condescended to lend them. "Come on, get your tourist duds on. Now's as good a time as any to scope the place out and make some plans. Besides, if we look and act like players, there's free food in the casinos. Unless you've been holding out on me, we sure can't afford to eat in any of the restaurants here."

"Holding out?" Ernie protested. "After the way you searched my baggage on the ship, you think I'm holding out on you? What, do you think I keep my fortune in antique microchips built into my back teeth?"

"I wouldn't put it past you to try," said Lola. "Only reason you wouldn't do it is you're too impatient to keep your money where you couldn't get right at it if you got the itch for something expensive. And too lazy to go to the dentist, come to think of it. Which is why I want to get started *now*. Come on, Ernie, let's go see if we can finish this job before the big guys get upset at us again."

Muttering darkly, Ernie pulled himself upright. At Lola's insistence, he changed into a sportier-looking shirt and ran a comb through his thinning locks. A pair of out-sized sunglasses completed the costume. Then, with Lola similarly disguised as a tourist, together they made their way to the nearby bus stop, hopped the Clockwise Local, and soon found themselves at the entrance of the Fat Chance Hotel and Casino.

"All right, put on a big smile," whispered Lola, as they got off the bus. "And remember, we only have fifty bucks apiece to gamble with. Better try to win—it's the only way we're going to eat anything better than the free lunch."

"I always win," said Ernie.

"Sure," said Lola, straightening her hat. "So tell me again—why are you taking contract jobs from the likes of Mr. V?" Fixed smiles in place, they strolled arm in arm through the main entrance of the Fat

Chance. The black-uniformed guards, actually actors impersonating legionnaires, didn't give them even a first glance.

Inside, they swept through the entrance lobby, ignoring the hotel registration desk, and headed straight for the gambling floors. During the working day, Phule was most likely to be within easy view of the floor, watching his investment growing before his eyes. Assuming, of course, that Phule was in the casino at all. Lola and Ernie had found out on their previous trip just how risky that supposition was …

"Do you see him anywhere?" asked Lola, as they sauntered through the bar area.

Ernie peered around the glaringly lit bar area. "Not a sign of the guy … Hey! Check it out! I always wondered where she'd gone—didn't know she was into gambling!"

"Who?" said Lola, looking at the woman Ernie had indicated, a small woman leafing through a racing magazine and sipping on some tall clear drink. "I see who you mean, but I don't recognize the face. Is she a vid star or something?"

"Nah," said Ernie, scoffing. "That's Maria Delia Fanatico—hottest race driver on the Formula-Ultra circuit, in her time. Broke all the course records for the Tour di Zappi when she first came up. Shocked the hell out of everybody when she retired all of a sudden, maybe fifteen years ago. People figured she got a rich boyfriend who didn't want her to keep racing, or something like that. I thought she was the hottest thing in the world, when I was a kid. Never expected to see her someplace like here, though."

"Well, if she's got a rich boyfriend, that explains how she can afford Lorelei," said Lola. "Which we *can't* unless we hit a jackpot or two. Come on, let's check out the free lunch in the game rooms. Maybe our boy will be there, and we can finish what we came here to do."

"Sure, sure," muttered Ernie. "More likely it'll be that damn robot again." He glanced again at Delia Fanatico, then followed Lola into the next room.

O   O   O

"All right, Tusk-anini, it's time for your break," said Lieutenant Armstrong, who was OD tonight. "Get up and get out of here—I don't want to see you for half an hour."

Tusk-anini put down his book—*Black's Dictionary of Interspecies Law, Twenty-first Edition*—and looked at the clock. Oh-three-hundred hours, the middle of the night, and of his shift in the comm center. He stood and placed the book on the seat of the chair he'd been occupying. "I be back," he said gruffly, and headed out the door, ducking his head on the way through. He didn't understand why the Legion insisted on having him get up and leave the comm center, when he could relax even more effectively just by continuing to read. But Armstrong, in particular, was a stickler for regulations, and Tusk-anini had learned that arguing with the lieutenant was a waste of time. It was easier to get up, take a little while to enjoy the clear night air of the desert, and come back when it was time to resume his shift.

Being of a nocturnal species had in fact worked to his advantage in the Legion, once he got a commanding officer who didn't try to make pegs of different shapes fit into identical holes. Humans seemed to think it was a hardship to stay up all night. Sergeants in particular were in awe of any sophont who actually enjoyed being awake during the wee hours of the morning, at least unless there was a party going on. Captain Jester had almost immediately rearranged Tusk-anini's schedule so that he could work during his preferred hours. And, since most humans were sound asleep during the night, there was little reason for the Volton to waste his duty hours doing anything more strenuous than catching up with his wide-ranging reading of human literature. As long as he was there, and awake, in case something did happen, that was enough for them. It was just one of the curious facts he had gathered about this strange race.

The comm center was a short distance from an exit onto the parade ground. Phule had required that the modular unit he had purchased for Omega Company's base on Zenobia should have easy access to the outside from every point, in case of an attack or other emergency. That was smart planning, Tusk-anini thought. In a real emergency it could save not only time but lives.

He came out into the base's central area and looked up at the Zenobian sky. Out here in the desert it was clear at night, with a panoply of unfamiliar constellations visible above the campsite. Tusk-anini's home star was below the horizon at this time of night, but he knew that it was located in a small constellation the Zenobians called the Gryff's Tail. Tusk-anini could see no resemblance between the group of stars and any kind of tail, but never having seen a *gryff*, he was willing to reserve judgment for the time being.

As he stood looking at the stars, a voice nearby whispered, "Tusk-anini! Come here quickly."

He looked to see Rube, one of the three Gambolts assigned to Omega Company. Catlike aliens with excellent night vision, the Gambolts were also valuable for nocturnal work. Captain Jester liked to have at least one of them on guard duty during the dark hours. Of course, with no hostile forces on this planet, the value of the Gambolts was mostly in helping to train legionnaires of other species to move and work in conditions of low visibility. Still, conditions could change, and the captain liked to be prepared for all possibilities.

"What going on?" said Tusk-anini, keeping his voice low as he moved next to Rube, who crouched along the side of a heavy personnel carrier.

"We don't know, Tusk," said another voice—the human legionnaire Slayer. "Weird stuff out in the desert ..."

"Why you not reporting it?" asked Tusk-anini. Having just come from Comm Central, he knew that no reports of suspicious activity had come in. Nor had the base's sophisticated detection systems detected anything suspicious while he had been on duty. He knew that for a fact, because Lieutenant Armstrong was especially meticulous about recording even the faintest blip on his screens.

"We aren't sure it's dangerous," said Rube, whose auto-translator made his speech seem much more idiomatic than the Volton's. But Tusk-anini had made it a point to learn English directly so as to improve his understanding of humans—which had been his main reason for joining the Legion to begin with.

79

"Perimeter electronics no detect nothing yet," said Tusk-anini, peering out in the direction Slayer had gestured in. "What kind of weird stuff you mean? Lights, noises, smells?"

"Faint lights, moving," said Rube. "Slayer can't even see them, most of the time."

"I seen some of 'em," said Slayer, who was wearing Legion-issue night-vision goggles. "They're sorta yellow-green, and they move real slow."

"Any chance Nanoids doing this?" said Tusk-anini, thinking of the microscopic silicon-based beings the captain and Beeker had discovered out in the Zenobian desert.

"It could be," said Rube. "But don't the Nanoids show up on the electronics? That's how they were detected in the first place, I think."

"Usually they do," admitted Tusk-anini. "Don't know much about them, though. Maybe some new form of them. Or maybe some Zenobian life we don't know yet—flying bugs with taillights, maybe, like the books say on Old Earth."

"Ah, that's just a story for kids," said Slayer. "The guys that write those stupid books must take a lot of drugs to think up all that weird stuff. I bet most of 'em never been anywhere near Old Earth."

"There's another one," said Rube, pointing toward the desert. Sure enough, there was a faint but plainly visible light there—plain to Tusk-anini's night-adapted eyes, in any case. It moved slowly left to right, staying a more or less constant distance above the desert floor, then suddenly winked out.

"Well, Tusk, now you seen it. You think we ought to go out and look where it was?" asked Slayer, deferring to Tusk-anini as the most experienced legionnaire present.

"I don't know," said Tusk-anini. "Looks undangerous, but who knowing? I go back to Comm Central soon and see if sensors pick up anything. Armstrong is OD tonight—is the one who ought to decide whether to look closer or not."

"Yeah, I guess so," said Slayer, clearly relieved that he wasn't going to be sent out in the desert to investigate—at least not yet.

Tusk-anini thought a moment more, then said, "Whatever Armstrong say, tomorrow I ask Qual if any animal on Zenobia acts like that. He going to know, if anybody do."

"Good idea," said Rube, nodding. "You want me to come along when you tell Armstrong?"

"Sure, nobody attacking camp," said Tusk-anini. "I go back on duty—you come now."

But when the two legionnaires described what they had seen to Lieutenant Armstrong, he emphatically denied that the Comm Center's instruments had detected any activity in the desert. "I'm glad you spotted this," the lieutenant said. "I'm not sure what to make of it. I'll twiddle with the instruments and see if there's any signal on some energy band I haven't been monitoring. You keep an eye on those lights, Rube, and if you see anything that looks like a threat to the camp, sound the alarm right away. But for now, my gut instinct is to watch it and wait. If anything changes, let me know right away, and I'll decide whether or not to wake up the captain. Until then, keep a sharp lookout and be ready to respond."

"Yes, sir," said Rube, and he returned to guard duty. But whatever the lights were, they turned out to be undetectable on the base's electronic sensors—and after an hour or so, even the Gambolt reported that they had gone away.

O   O   O

Several parsecs distant, at the Legion's Hickman Training Center on Mussina's World, four dozen raw recruits waited anxiously in their bunkhouse. Just as some of them had begun to gripe that the threatened inspection was another ploy to cheat them out of a night's sleep, the barracks room door burst open.

"TENN-*HUT!*" bellowed Sergeant Pitbull. "GENERAL BLITZKRIEG WILL NOW INSPECT THE BARRACKS!" he added, unnecessarily, as General Blitzkrieg blustered into the bunkroom. He was followed by a female human major bearing a clipboard and a bored expression. The recruits, forewarned, were all lined up at the foot of their bunks, wearing their best uniforms and trying (for the most part without success) to conceal their nervousness. Nothing resembling a senior officer had ever deigned to appear on the post during their brief time as legionnaires. Even the colonel who nominally commanded Hickman Training Center might as well have been on another planet entirely—the recruits weren't even sure whether their post commandant was male, female, or even human.

On the other hand, there was no doubt at all that General Blitzkrieg was human. Thumper had sniffed him out even before he'd entered the barracks. Thumper had grown up on a planet with a high enough human population that he knew the race well, and was even fond of a fair number of the sophonts from Earth. But he also came from a race with a highly developed sense of smell, and he knew the odor of humans well. Especially human males who ate red meat, smoked tobacco, drank distilled alcohol, and sloshed their faces and armpits with aromatic concoctions as part of their morning ablutions. No question at all, General Blitzkrieg was one of those humans. He entered with a scowl that had been known to make strong legionnaires quake in their boots. That, in fact, was its main purpose, and on most of the recruits it worked quite well.

But as much as Thumper thought he knew about humans, he had learned very little about human psychology, and so the little Lepoid had no clue that the general might *want* to scare him. *I've done my job right, so he can't find fault with me,* thought Thumper. He stood at perfect attention, his uniform immaculate, his bunk made with exacting care to every detail. In fact, Thumper's bunk was even more perfectly made than the sample illustration of a correctly made bunk in the *Legion Drill Instructor's Manual* His trunk was equally a paragon of exactness. Whatever else the general might find wrong with this recruit company—and Sergeant Pitbull had made it clear that he didn't expect much to be *right*—there wasn't going to be anything for him to criticize about Thumper.

Sergeant Pitbull had his mouth open, ready to issue another order, when someone hissed, "Now!" and all hell broke loose. As Thumper tried to turn his head to see who had spoken, the lights went out, and he heard the sound of several pairs of running feet. There was an incoherent roar from the front of the room, about where General Blitzkrieg stood, then someone rushed up to Thumper and put something into his hand. "Hold this!" they whispered, and before he could say a word, he found himself holding something. Even as he realized it was some kind of bucket, and that the outside of the bucket was dripping something wet on his uniform pants, the lights came back on.

Even then Thumper didn't quite realize what kind of trouble he was in. Granted, the sight of General Blitzkrieg splattered head to toe with some sort of brownish sludge—*foul-smelling* brownish sludge, Thumper immediately realized—was the first thing that drew his attention. The next thing was the row of wet footprints and drips leading away from the general—toward where Thumper stood.

Only then did he recognize that the same foul smell that emanated from the general was also coming from the bucket he was holding. And, most curious of all, the sludge-covered footprints stopped right at his feet.

"WHAT THE FARKING HELL IS GOING ON HERE?" roared Sergeant Pitbull, instead of whatever else he had been about to roar when the lights went out. Then he saw the general, and his eyes grew to the size of dinner plates. "Oh, golly," he said, in a voice the recruits had to strain to hear—the first time in Thumper's memory that one of Pitbull's statements hadn't threatened to shatter his highly sensitive eardrums.

By now, every sophont in the room had managed to grasp that something dreadfully wrong had happened—that fact was probably within the intellectual grasp of the pea-sized AI that regulated the water level in the toilets. Likewise, even the dullest-witted recruit's eyes had managed to trace the damning chain of evidence that led from the general's ruined dress uniform to the odoriferous bucket in Thumper's hands. In fact, it slowly dawned on Thumper that every eye in the barracks was staring directly at him.

"I didn't do it," he managed to sputter as Sergeant Pitbull advanced toward him, mayhem in his eyes. But by then it was way too late.

CHAPTER SIX

Journal #675

Who among us does not take pleasure in the discomfort of our enemies? Such is common wisdom, noted by many observers.

It is less frequently observed that, by choosing one's enemies with a degree of care, one can significantly increase the number of occasions on which to enjoy the pleasure of seeing them discommoded. In fact, it is likely that infelicitous choice of rivals is the cause of more frustration than almost any other miscalculation. This is as true in business as in those more personal areas of human enterprise.

The subtleties of the matter are clearly illustrated by the fact that my employer, despite his lack of any salient qualities that might warn off a calculating opponent, had over and over turned unpromising situations to his own advantage and frustrated the hopes of those arrayed against him. In fact, so improbable were his victories, that the defeated party was often inclined to step right up to make another attempt at besting him. But almost inevitably, the outcome of the first encounter was only repeated in the return engagement.

That didn't stop his would-be enemies from coming back for more ...

O O O

It was 5:00 PM Galactic Standard Time on Lorelei. But it might as well have been 5:00 AM—or high noon, for all the difference it made in the casinos that were the economic lifeblood of the resort satellite. The casinos were open twenty-four hours, and there was no time of day or night when the brightly lit gaming tables or banks of quantum slot machines were without a full quorum of bettors. Even the exotic potted plants lining the hallways of the Fat Chance Casino got twenty-four-hour attention from the throng of gardeners and housekeepers who filed unobtrusively but efficiently through every public space of the hotel and casino—watering, trimming, cleaning up.

"What games are you going to play?" Lola stared suspiciously at Ernie. She'd intercepted him on the way to the Fat Chance Casino cashier's window to purchase gambling chips.

"Poker's got the best odds, the way I see it," said Ernie, shrugging. "The house just takes a percentage of every pot, and the winner keeps everything else. I figure I can swindle most of the bozos that end up at the poker table here—and beat 'em at cards, too."

"Don't get too creative—if they catch you cheating, you're on the next shuttle off the station," Lola reminded him. She took him by the arm and led him along one of the central aisles through one of the casino's middle-priced gaming rooms. Working their way through the overflowing crowds were cocktail waitresses, dispensing free drinks to the gamblers—a time-honored strategy for increasing the amount wagered. A significant majority of the gamblers were taking the bait, guzzling down the drinks (and free eats) as if they were at a permanent party. Some were undoubtedly shills, encouraging the real customers to act as if the party would never end. And here and there, casino guards in the black uniform of the Space Legion served as silent reminders who owned this casino—and what would happen to anyone caught cheating.

Lola stopped and turned to face Ernie. "Remember, you're playing it straight today. If casino security comes down on you, it's your butt that's on the grill—I don't know you, and I'm not helping you. Got it? So don't go screwing up this job just as it's getting started. Especially considering what's likely to happen to us if we mess up this time …"

"Don't worry, kid, I'll play it close to the vest," said Ernie, grumpily. He waved vaguely toward the nearby blackjack tables. "We gotta have enough spare bucks to keep ourselves flush ..."

"And we have to keep from losing what little we have," said Lola, stopping and turning to face him. She grasped him by the lapels, and said firmly, "Your budget for today is fifty dollars ..."

"Fifty lousy bucks!" Ernie grumbled. "That's barely enough to get into a decent game!"

"Build it up enough, and you'll have more tomorrow," said Lola. "No sucker bets, nothing that'll get you busted by Casino security. We've got to keep ourselves afloat long enough to get the job done—because if we don't get it done, we're really sunk. You remember Mr. V, don't you?"

"All right, I get you," said Ernie. "Fifty bucks it is. By the time I'm done, it oughta be three-four hundred."

Lola smiled, and said, "Good, and if it is, you get to keep half your winnings to play with tomorrow. Now, excuse me—I'm going to go snooping." She gave him a punch on the biceps and turned toward the high-rollers' section of the casino. Odds were, if their quarry was anywhere on the casino floor, it would be there, where the action was fastest and most furious. Lola's step quickened—even she could feel the excitement.

There were a pair of guards in Legion uniform flanking the doorway to the elite playing area, but Lola whisked right past them. The casino didn't discourage gawkers in this section, as long as they didn't interfere with the play and didn't linger an unseemly long time. The way Lola was dressed, they weren't likely to single her out—not that they seemed to be enforcing any dress code at all in this section. It wasn't unknown for someone dressed like a day laborer to enter one of the Lorelei casinos and plop down a grease-stained paper sack that turned out to be filled with thousand-dollar bills.

There was an even more private area for those upper-class gamblers who insisted on playing their games out of the sight of the common rabble—but she wasn't interested in them. She was after Willard Phule—and *he* wasn't going to hide from the paying customers. As she knew from her previous visit to the casino, he spent as much of his time as possible accessible to the patrons. She'd even seen him with his Port-a-Brain set up on a bar table, working where he'd be visible to the players, rather than anonymously in some back office.

But it didn't take more than a glance to eliminate the possibility that he was in this area. The only Legion uniforms in sight were the pair of guards at each end of the room, visible but unobtrusive. Everyone else in the room was in the casual garb of rich people on holiday—a range that ran from the garish display of the self-made to the tastefully drab leisurewear affected by Old Money.

Then Lola did a double take. To one side was a lean man pumping tokens into a bank of quantum slot machines. That was completely off the expected pattern. The high rollers had their own preferred games—obsolete games like roulette and baccarat were their style, rather than the faster-moving, high-tech games that predominated in the outer rooms. Never mind that the odds on the elite games were heavily stacked in the house's favor. The very rich enjoyed the risk, and they were willing to pay to be seen playing the more prestigious games. But slots were utterly déclassé—there was almost no pretense of skill to them, and even less of elegance. So why, suddenly, were there slots here in the high-priced area of the casino?

Then Lola peered more closely at the man playing the slots. There was something familiar about that face … She was ready to move in for a closer look when she noticed the compactly built man always hovering close by the slot player, never so close as to be obvious or obtrusive, but to her experienced eye, unmistakably a bodyguard—and he was looking at Lola. She favored the guard with an embarrassed smile, then glanced away, pretending to misunderstand the reason for his interest. It was a ploy that worked with most men; she hoped this guard wasn't *too* professional. But her curiosity was definitely piqued; who was the man he was guarding? She shuffled through her mental database of faces, trying to place him without another glance that might alert the guard to the real reason for her interest.

For the moment, she couldn't quite place him. But she was sure there was something important going on. Sooner or later she'd figure it out. And then she'd figure out how she could turn it to her profit. In the meantime, she might as well continue her search for Phule at the twenty-four-hour free lunch spread …

O   O   O

"Here are your overnight messages, sir," said Moustache, bringing a small handful of printouts to Phule's desk.

"Great," said Phule, his face lighting up. "Anything from Legion headquarters?"

"I don't believe there's anything out of the usual, sir," said Moustache, crisply. By now he knew—everyone on the base knew—that the captain was expecting a promotion. He also knew that the promotion had yet to materialize, despite several months having elapsed since the first rumors of it had reached Omega Company at its Zenobia Base. He wondered whether it might not be time for someone to tell the captain not to pin his hopes on something that evidently was stalled deep in the bowels of the Legion bureaucracy—most likely on General Blitzkrieg's desk. Perhaps it was; but Moustache couldn't find it in his heart to break the news.

Phule's face fell momentarily, but he quickly regained his composure and returned to business. "Any report from the team investigating last night's incident?"

"None yet, sir," said Moustache, standing at attention. He could have been modeling for a Legion recruiting poster, so perfect was the stance. "They've got a fair bit of territory to cover, though. Most likely it'll turn out to be some local wildlife we haven't seen before."

Phule tapped his fingers on the desktop. "Likely enough," he conceded. "Funny we haven't seen it before, though, if that's what it is. We have guards out every night, and nobody's reported moving lights before."

"That could be readily explained if the phenomenon were seasonal, sir," Beeker pointed out. "We've not been here an entire local year yet, so we've hardly had sufficient opportunity to observe all the phases of the indigenous fauna."

"True enough," said Phule. "But Flight Leftenant Qual didn't seem to know of any animal that might be causing it, either."

"Duly noted, sir," said Beeker. "However, Mr. Qual is a military person by profession, not a naturalist. Nor is he native to this region of his planet. He may be no more familiar with its denizens than we are."

"I guess that makes sense," said Phule. "Still, I'd be happier if we got some kind of definitive result from our search. If we don't, I may have to station a team out in the desert after dark, to see what they can find out. And I don't like doing that when I don't know whether I'm putting them in danger."

Moustache said, "Sir, if I may comment." He paused briefly, and at Phule's nod continued. "If whatever made those lights is dangerous, there is no reason to think it's any less so in broad daylight. If our search team finds nothing today, I myself would not hesitate to send them out again at night. The camp's safety is an overriding issue, sir."

"Thank you, Moustache, the point's well-taken," said Phule. He stood up and paced, thinking, then turned, and said, "In fact, I think we ought to plan for that. First ..."

He was interrupted by the buzz of his wrist communicator. "Yes, Mother, what is it?"

"Code Red, sweetie," came the familiar voice, with an edge of urgency Phule hadn't heard before.

"Code Red?" he asked, feeling stupid. "But that means ..."

Mother's answer removed any doubt. "The desert search team is under attack!"

O O O

"ALL RIGHT, YOU SLOBS, COME GET YER ASSIGNMENTS TO YER NEW UNITS," bellowed Sergeant Pitbull. He waved a thick sheaf of regulation Legion envelopes in his hand, presumably one for each of the recruits in his platoon.

The recruits came to their feet in an excited babble of voices. This was the moment they'd all been waiting for—the next step in their Legion careers. It meant, for one thing, that the recruits would now go on to the specialized training they'd requested when they'd joined the Legion, rather than an endless round of body building exercises and mindless drills under Pitbull's relentless eye. In fact, for most of them, just getting away from Pitbull was sufficient cause for celebration. Whatever else Legion life held for them, it was likely to be an improvement over basic training.

Thumper rose to his feet without particular enthusiasm. Whatever camaraderie he'd felt for his fellow recruits had vanished when he'd realized what had happened to him during General Blitzkrieg's inspection visit. Somebody had deliberately set him up to take the blame for the insult to the general—possibly more than one somebody had set him up, in fact. He'd spent a long time trying to plead his innocence, and a longer time in a punishment detail. He suspected that only his perfect record in all the exercises leading up to the incident with the general had kept him from being drummed out of the Legion then and there. But Sergeant Pitbull had made it amply clear that the consequences were far from over. And one of those consequences was almost certainly going to be reflected in his first assignment. Now, it looked as if there was no chance for him to end up in the elite unit he'd requested upon enlistment

Pitbull read each recruit's name and their assignments as he handed them their letters. "POPPER—FORT KABOOM," he barked. Popper, a dumpy, shortsighted humanoid from Tau Ceti IV, beamed—ever since he'd arrived in camp, he'd been talking about how much he enjoyed blowing things up. Now, at the Legion's demolitions training school, he'd get a chance to do it on a grand scale.

"SPIDER—YOU'RE ON TEAM REGULUS," said Pitbull. That was a good assignment, too, and fit Spider's personality. Team Regulus was the Legion's Home Guard unit, sharing ceremonial duties at Alliance Headquarters with elite groups from the Regular Army and Starfleet. The assignment had more to do with spit and polish than with fighting ability, but that made it all the more a plum for many legionnaires.

Several of the recruits were sent to advanced training in various behind-the-lines specialties, but at least half of them went to advanced combat training with frontline units. This was the core of the Legion's mission, of course, and Thumper had nurtured hopes, even after the disaster with General Blitzkrieg, of getting into an outfit where he could prove his worth again from the ground up—despite the fact that, as far as he knew, there were no ongoing wars anywhere in Alliance territory in which to display his martial prowess.

After most of the names had been read, Thumper began to suspect that Pitbull was saving his name for last—he'd seen him shuffle through the envelopes, obviously picking the order in which he wanted to announce assignments. This was annoying, but there was nothing Thumper could really do about it. Until the recruits were placed on a transport ship to their new units, Pitbull was still their immediate superior and could order them around as he saw fit. Being a drill instructor, he usually saw fit to do so in the most sadistic way possible. This batch of recruits would soon be gone from Mussina's World and Legion boot camp forever—or so they devoutly hoped. But Pitbull wasn't about to pass up his final opportunity to torture and humiliate them.

Finally, the last envelope was in the sergeant's hand. He grinned crookedly and held it up to the light. By now, all the recruits were aware whose envelope it was, and curiosity was even stronger than their excitement over their own assignments. Pitbull waited for silence, then announced with a flourish: "THUMPER—OMEGA COMPANY!"

"Omega Company?" Thumper was stunned. As short a time as they'd been in the Legion, all the recruits had heard rumors about Omega Company. Once the dumping ground for all the misfits and malcontents of the Legion, it had been taken over by a new commander, who reportedly had turned it around. Omega Company was in the news; in this boring interval between real fighting action, it was getting sent to interesting places. It was exactly the sort of assignment Thumper had hoped for. "Excuse me, Sergeant, is that correct?"

"YER *%!!@#-A IT'S CORRECT, RECRUIT!" Pitbull roared. "THE GENERAL INSISTED ON IT, AND THAT'S RIGHT WHERE YOUR SORRY ASS IS GOIN'! THAT CONCLUDES THE ASSIGNMENTS! AS YOU WERE, YOU SLOBS! DON'T LET ME CATCH ANYBODY GOOFING

OFF—I CAN STILL HAND OUT PUNISHMENT DETAIL!" And Pitbull turned on his heel and stalked away.

O   O   O

"Under attack?" Suddenly Phule's adrenaline began to surge, and the focus of his attention narrowed to a pinpoint. "Attack by whom? Can you patch them through to me?"

"I couldn't hear who the attackers were," said Mother. "All I got was a message from the team saying that somebody—or something—was attacking them. There was a lot of noise, but I couldn't tell exactly what was happening. The signal keeps breaking up, and I don't think they have a whole lot of time to chat with us, anyway. But hold on. I'll see if I can raise them again and put you through."

"I'll be ready," said Phule. He became aware that he was on his feet, although he had no memory of rising from his desk chair. In the corridor outside his office, he could hear the sound of running feet. "Meanwhile, sound General Quarters," he ordered. "I want every available member of the company ready to go bail them out." He turned to Moustache and Beeker, who had both heard the entire conversation. "Sergeant, get a relief party together without delay. I'll give you your orders as soon as I know what needs to be done. Beeker, grab me those stereoculars—we're going out to see if we can spot anything."

"Yes, sir!" said the two men, practically in unison, but Phule was already out the doorway, running at top speed. Turning to a shelf just behind the captain's desk, Beeker picked the stereoculars in their case and followed him out the door, a step behind Moustache. Somewhere down the corridor an alarm was sounding.

Outside, Beeker could see that word of the attack had already gotten out. A small pack of legionnaires was milling about on the south edge of the base, many of them carrying weapons and wearing helmets, others looking as if they'd been dragged out of the showers by the alert. Spotting them, Moustache nodded and strode off purposefully in their direction. For his part, Phule was sprinting toward a short observation tower at the center of the base. Again,

Beeker followed, attempting to make as much speed as he could without abandoning the last vestiges of dignity.

By the time the butler reached the base of the tower, Phule was already at its top, shading his eyes with one hand and staring out into the desert. Resignedly, Beeker put the strap of the stereoculars case over his shoulder and began climbing the ladder. Below, he could hear voices shouting, and a vibration in the ladder indicated that someone else was climbing up behind him. Gritting his teeth, he finished the climb and put the case in Phule's outstretched hand. Looking to the south, just over a kilometer away, he saw a small cloud of dust—or was it smoke?—along a line of native "trees," but nothing else he could clearly identify.

"What can you make out, Captain?" said Lieutenant Armstrong, who was the one who'd followed Beeker up the ladder.

"Not much, yet," said Phule, peering through the stereoculars. "Hard to see through the heat haze and dust ..." He was interrupted by his communicator's buzz. "Jester here, go ahead," he said, lowering the stereoculars and boosting the volume so the others on the tower could hear clearly.

"I'm getting a signal from the desert search team, Captain," said Mother's voice, now more urgent than sultry. "Stand by ..."

"Captain, do you read me?" a voice crackled through the speaker. It had the kind of mechanical inflection characteristic of an autotranslator, and Beeker thought he recognized it as Spartacus, one of the two Synthians with the company. Sluglike aliens, they were dependent on mechanical transportation to keep up with their fellow legionnaires of other species. Phule had discovered that glide-boards, a common children's antigrav toy, gave them maximum mobility at a bargain price.

"Loud and clear, Spartacus," said Phule. "What's your situation there? Anybody hurt?"

There was a blare of noise that Phule couldn't quite identify, then Spartacus's voice came through again. "...has us treed. Don't ... hostile sophont or ..." More noise drowned out whatever Spartacus said.

"There shouldn't be this much interference over such a short distance," muttered Armstrong. "If it weren't for that damned stand of trees, and all the dust, I think we could see them directly from here."

"Spartacus, I can barely follow you," said Phule, raising the communicator to his mouth again. "If you can hear this, just hold tight. Don't fire unless fired upon. I'm sending out a rescue party. Do you read?"

"... Captain ..." came the Synthian's voice, in a cloud of static.

"All right, Mr. Armstrong, I'm going to lead the relief party," said Phule, thumbing the communicator's "off" button. "With comm on the fritz, we'll have to rely on visual signals. If I fire a green flare, everything's under control. If I fire a white one, send the autodoc. A red one ..." He paused.

"Yes, sir?" said Armstrong. "A red one means?"

"I'm hoping I won't need a red one," said Phule. "But if you see it, come after us as fast as possible with everything you've got." He tucked the stereoculars under his arm and began climbing down the ladder, two rungs at a stride.

O O O

"Victor Phule!" said Lola, staring at the readout of the hotel room's Netlink. "That's the fellow playing the high-priced slots!" She'd run a routine ImageBase search on the stealthcam image she'd acquired of the man she'd met in the casino, but she knew better than to expect any clear result. To her surprise, it had given her an 83% positive ID almost at once—Victor Phule, munitions tycoon.

"Stuck-up-looking old bugger," muttered Ernie, lying back on the hotel bed and peering around Lola's shoulder at the computer screen.

"More to the point, he's the father of the man we're looking to grab," said Lola, pointing at the text underneath the picture. "Not to overlook the fact that he's one of the wealthiest men in the galaxy. You can think what you want about him, but he can afford to be stuck-up. And we can't afford to ignore what it must mean for him to be here."

"OK, I'll bite," said Ernie, managing to look somewhat more interested. "What do you think it means that he's here on Lorelei?

Rich guys like to gamble, too—like I been telling you, Lola. If you'd give me enough money to get into a few of the big-money games ..."

"Oh, encapsulate it," said Lola. "The point is, there can only be a few possible reasons why he'd be at the casino. And the most likely is that young Phule himself is out of commission somehow—in fact, that would explain why the casino had set up that robot to impersonate him."

"Maybe," said Ernie, sitting up on the edge of the bed. "But what about all those newstapes we keep seeing, of Captain Jester at the Landoor amusement park, and Captain Jester greeting those mechanical beings on some three-for-a-buck planet way the hell off the main space-lanes? Those can't all be fakes, can they?"

Lola frowned. "Well, maybe not all of them. But one thing I've learned, over the years—when you want to find out what's really going on in some racket, always look at where the money comes from and who it goes to. We all know the Fat Chance is the place where one enormous pile of money comes from. And if the people it goes to aren't right here to make sure they get what's coming to them, they're too stupid to deserve any of it. That means Willard Phule has got to be here somewhere. All we have to do is figure out where, and then make our snatch."

"Yeah, like it's that easy," said Ernie. "Why don't we snatch the old man, instead? Hell, he's got more bucks than the kid—and he ain't got the whole army guarding him, either." He began picking at an annoying nose hair, squinting at himself in the bedside mirror.

"Stop that," said Lola, swatting at his hand. Then, recalling her encounter with Victor Phule, she added, "And don't be sure the old man'd be so easy to snatch. When I spotted him, he had at least one obvious bodyguard with him—and I don't know how many more that I didn't spot. The man can afford the best, and he's in a business where he probably has plenty of job applicants with relevant experience. And I wouldn't bet a nickel that the Legion guards don't have special instructions about keeping an eye on their boss's father, either."

"No bet," conceded Ernie. Then, turning his hands palm up and spreading them apart, he said, "But if the job's that tough, what the hell are we even doin' here? We oughta just head for the most back-ass planet on the map, or maybe even off the map, and go to cover. I don't see no percentage in sticking around here if we can't do the job—especially with the enforcers looking to wale on us if we can't deliver."

"Oh, I'm not giving up on the job," said Lola, placing a forefinger against her cheek. "In fact, I think it looks better than ever for us, with the father here as well as the son. That gives us two likely targets, instead of just one. And it boosts our chances another way, too—because there are twice as many of them to guard, there's more chance for their security to slip up. We've got to study the situation just a little more, and then I'll come up with a plan ..."

"You'll come up with a plan?" said Ernie. "It was your brilliant plan that backfired the first time and got us in this mess to begin with. Why don't I ever get to make the farkin' plans?"

"Because you'd fark 'em up," said Lola, bluntly. "I mean, I won't claim everything's been a screaming success, or any other kind, so far. But if you'd been in charge, we'd both be behind bars somewhere—assuming Mr. V and his goons didn't catch with us first."

Ernie scowled. "That reminds me. I never did figure out why, if Mr. V and whoever he works for—"

"Which, believe me, you *don't* want to know," interjected Lola.

"OK, OK," said Ernie. "But tell me this: if those wise guys can run us down anyplace we escape to, why the hell do they need us to snatch Willard Phule? Why don't they just go snatch him themselves?"

Lola shook her head. "You really don't understand that? Just think about it. What goes wrong if we get caught?"

"If we're lucky, we get a vacation on some prison colony, making rocks into sand," said Ernie. "If we're unlucky, we get made into sand."

"That's about right," said Lola. "But the people who are springing for us to kidnap Phule have got a lot to lose. So they're deflecting the risk by hiring us, and making sure there's no paper trail back to them. And that's why we can't afford to know who they are—because if we do, we're too dangerous."

"Hey, dangerous—that's me, all right," said Ernie, puffing up his chest and striking a muscle-man pose.

"Yeah, well just be careful you don't get yourself in more trouble than you can get out of," said Lola, exasperated. "These people play rough, or have you forgotten that?"

"All right, you win," said Ernie. "But this time, if I don't think the plan's gonna work, I'm gonna let you know up front. I'm not as stupid as you think."

"Oh, you couldn't be," said Lola, smiling broadly. Before Ernie could figure that out, she added, "But for now, I need you to stay out of sight and relax—I've got to run out and do some spying."

"Spying? Who on?"

"Why, the big bird and the little bird," said Lola, opening the door and turning back to face Ernie. "And with a little bit of luck, we may even catch them both." Before Ernie could come up with an answer to that, she was out the door and gone.

O O O

Phule was pleased to see that Moustache had the rescue party lined up in good order near the camp perimeter. He was even more pleased to see how many of the company had turned out on such short notice, fully equipped and ready for action. But that posed a problem in its own right. Taking the bulk of his available force into an unknown situation was risking disaster.

"All right, people, listen up," he said. "We're going to break into two parties. One will go with me to see what's happening out there in the desert. The other's going to guard the camp in case this is some kind of diversion; Lieutenant Armstrong will command that party."

Phule quickly chose a dozen legionnaires to join him in the rescue party. There were plenty of volunteers to choose from— every single legionnaire present wanted to go to the aid of their comrades. Phule made it a point to include the three Gambolts, whose speed and fighting ability would be a particular asset against an unknown threat. But he was careful to leave a core of proven legionnaires with Armstrong—not only to protect against a surprise attack, but to act as a reserve rescue party in case his group couldn't finish the job. He didn't think that was going to be necessary. On the other hand, he didn't think a red flare was going to be necessary, either—but he had one in his belt.

"All right, people," he said. "The plan is to get out there as quickly as we can, so we'll take the personnel carrier. When we're about a hundred meters short, I want you three Gambolts to get off and scout ahead on foot. We'll come in at walking speed behind you. If any of you signals, or if there's any sign of danger, we'll pick up speed again and do whatever we need to. Since we don't know what we're getting into, be alert for my orders. Any questions?"

"I have a question, sir," said Mahatma, raising his hand. The little recruit's round face had its usual mellow expression, which, in combination with a raised hand, almost always spelled trouble.

Phule mentally chastised himself—he should have remembered Mahatma's tendency to question everything a superior said to him. But he'd already opened that door by choosing the little recruit for the rescue team, so he had no choice but to deal with what came through it. "Yes, Mahatma, what is it?" he asked, as patiently as he could manage.

"I notice that we are heading in the direction of the AEIOU inspectors' camp," said Mahatma. "Should we not warn them that we are about to mount an operation in their vicinity?"

"Actually, that makes sense," said Phule, nodding. He lifted his wrist communicator to his mouth, buzzed Mother, and quickly relayed Mahatma's suggestion to her. "Tell them to keep their heads down," he added. "If we have to engage in combat, there could be danger to civilians in the neighborhood."

"Sure, sweetie cakes," said Mother. "But wouldn't it be so much better just to order them off-planet while you've got a good excuse? I wouldn't mind seeing the last of that Chief Inspector Snieff."

"That's not a bad idea," said Phule. "I don't think we're in quite that much trouble, though. But I'll keep it in mind in case things get dangerous."

"All righty, you're a big boy—but don't ever say I never gave you a chance to get rid of that pest," said Mother. She cut the connection, and Phule turned to his crew. In moments, the rescue party was loaded on the personnel carrier. At Phule's command, Slayer took the controls, lifted it off, and started moving forward at top speed.

Phule stood on the forward bench, looking through his stereoculars in an attempt to see what was going on up ahead. He could hear what sounded like distant shouting, though not in any language he recognized. Had the Synthian lost his translator, or was there some other species there? He realized he didn't know who else was on the original search team—he'd left it to Brandy to choose its members, and hadn't thought to ask once the crisis had arisen. In a sense, it didn't really matter who was out there. They were all valued members of Omega Company. Their comrades in arms would do whatever it took to bring them back safe. Omega Company took care of its own. And anyone who stood in the way ... well, *too bad for them,* Phule thought.

The personnel carrier had quickly covered the ground between the camp and the trees, and was coming up on the position where Phule had decided to drop off the Gambolts. "Slayer, bring the vehicle to a halt," he ordered. "Dukes, Rube, Garbo—make ready to dismount."

Slayer expertly cut the vehicle's speed and dropped it to within a hand's breadth of the ground. The Gambolts quickly slipped off the tail end—protected from any possibility of hostile fire, although there had so far been no overt hostilities—and began working their way through the underbrush, quickly fading out of clear visibility. Phule waited until they were well clear, then signaled for the personnel carrier to move forward again. There was still no clear indication what sort of enemy had attacked the original search party. Evidently their comm units were still not working correctly—there'd been no further transmissions since the truncated conversation Phule had had with Spartacus.

It was quiet, Phule realized. *Too* quiet. The faintly purring engine of the personnel carrier was the only sound; even the shouting that Phule had heard previously had now faded into silence, leaving only an uncomfortable anticipation. Somewhere ahead of him, the Gambolts were noiselessly working their way toward the site of the disturbance ...

Suddenly, a loud sound erupted from the underbrush perhaps fifty meters off the left front of the vehicle. As Phule stood up to stare—realizing even as he did so that he was exposing himself to possible enemy fire—a Gambolt jumped seemingly two meters straight up, yowling. It was Dukes, the largest of the three catlike aliens in Omega Company. As soon as the Gambolt landed on his feet, he let out another yowl and began sprinting for the nearest tree.

"What the hell?" said a voice somewhere behind Phule. Dukes reached the tree and, without losing any of his speed, made a right-angle turn and went at least halfway up the trunk before reaching a convenient branch and stopping, with a harassed air about him. The seat of his black Legion jumpsuit was torn, Phule noticed.

At the foot of the tree, now, Phule made out a squat creature, quivering with rage. When it spoke, everything became clear. He didn't even need the stereoculars to recognize it, or to make out what it said.

"Woof!" said Barky, the Environmental Dog, taking off at top speed to find another Gambolt to chase up a tree. "Woof! Woof!"

CHAPTER SEVEN

Journal #681

There are few things more aggravating than a person whose opinions on some important subject are essentially correct, but who insists on subordinating all other matters to that one area of discourse. One might even say that, the more correct the opinion, the more annoying it becomes to see it drive out all other topics of conversation. The only remedy for such people is to avoid their company entirely. Unfortunately, they are often in a position such that avoiding them becomes difficult ...

O   O   O

"I've never met such unreasonable people in my life," said Phule, pacing around his desk. The meeting with Chief Inspector Snieff had *not* been productive.

"That's a rather frightening assessment, sir. Especially considering that you've spent the last five years in the Space Legion ..." Beeker left the thought unfinished.

Phule ignored him. "All I ask them to do is to keep their dog away from my people. You wouldn't think that would be so hard, would you?"

"The dog cannot be blamed for its response, sir," Beeker noted. "To put it frankly, sir, even a relatively sophisticated person such as

I might find the, uh, characteristic odors of some races of nonhuman sophonts rather peculiar, if not downright unpleasant. You notice that it paid particular attention to poor Spartacus, and to the Gambolts. The poor animal, which has a far more sensitive nose than you or I, simply reacts to them as it has been trained."

"It must have been raised in a humans-only environment," said Phule. "But still—my legionnaires aren't polluting the planet. I took special pains to get the most up-to-date ecological protection features built into the base. We recycle *everything*, Beeker. Nothing goes to waste in Zenobia Base. Our environmental policies are far greener than the Legion's regulations for units in the field, and we stick to them, too."

"I believe you, sir," said Beeker. "But I should remind you that I am not the one you need to persuade in this instance. The relevant parties are Ms. Snieff—and her dog."

"I don't know which is worse," said Phule, plopping himself down on the edge of his desk. "At least she didn't try to bite anybody … though maybe that'd be better than having her spout slogans at me all afternoon. If she bit me, all I'd need to do is make sure my shots were up-to-date."

"It is unfortunate that there are no inoculations against fanaticism," said Beeker. "The woman's employer is in my opinion one of the very few governmental organizations actually capable of making the world better than it finds it, and yet she seems to have the gift, so to speak, of alienating everyone around her. I suppose it is another example of the tendency of bureaucracies to promote those who most excel at bureaucratic infighting, rather than at the actual business of the organization."

Phule had picked up the remote for the office's video display wall and fiddled with it as he listened to Beeker. Now he looked at it, realized he wasn't about to use it for anything, and put it back down on his desk. "The bottom line is, we need to be able to work here," he said. "I can't just tell my people not to go near their camp, Beeker. They were out in the desert to investigate a possible threat to our security. And we never did find out what all those lights were about."

"Sir, now may be the time to prevail upon Flight Leftenant Qual to interest his government in the matter," said Beeker. "Point out to them that your mission is being jeopardized by this AEIOU team's officious meddling. Perhaps you might even persuade one or two Zenobians to stray out into the desert where they would encounter the dog. That might persuade them quickly."

"And if Barky went after them, what would stop them from shooting him?" said Phule. "Or maybe eating him for lunch. The Zenobians don't seem to eat mammals—they don't seem to have very many, in fact—but they might make an exception in this case. Getting an animal killed by the locals—not just any animal, but a beloved environmental dog with his own weekly tri-vee show, and fan clubs of adoring kids on every human-occupied planet—no, Beeks. No thank you. I've already survived more than my share of interplanetary incidents. But I don't think even Ambassador Gottesman could bail me out of that one."

"It would have a very unfortunate effect on your public image, I am sure, sir," agreed Beeker. "However, I fear that something of the sort is inevitable unless you take steps to prevent it. I am more than ever convinced that General Blitzkrieg has engineered this AEIOU visit in hopes of discrediting you."

"Old Blitzkrieg again, eh?" said Phule. "Well, by now, he's tried everything short of sending assassins. And the Mob has tried *that*. I'm still here, in case you haven't noticed, Beeks. Don't worry. It may take a little while, but I'll figure out some way to get rid that AEIOU team—and their little dog, too."

Beeker shook his head mournfully. "Sir, I really wish you had pursued a classical education," he said. "It would help you avoid many infelicitous remarks."

But Phule wasn't listening. Instead, his gaze had gone to the open window facing out onto the parade ground and beyond that, to the open land south of Zenobia Base. "Look, Beeker," he said. "There are lights moving out in the desert."

O   O   O

"YO, RABBITEARS! GET YER MOTHERLESS ASS IN HERE!" bellowed Sergeant Pitbull, glowering out of his office door.

Instinctively, Thumper jumped. "Yes, Sergeant!" he said, scurrying for the office. The half dozen other recruits remaining in the barracks room looked at him with a mixture of mild curiosity and relief that they weren't the ones Pitbull had decided to harass during their final hours on Mussina's World. Then they went back to their reading, their card games, or whatever they had chosen to pass their remaining time before leaving Legion boot camp forever.

Even though Thumper had already gotten his assignment for Omega Company, the sound of the drill sergeant's voice was equivalent to a jolt of high-voltage electricity. Most of the other recruits had already been loaded onto ships headed for their new assignments. But Omega Company was on some isolated planet, a place without regular traffic. As anxious as Thumper was to join his new outfit, he would have to wait for transport to be arranged. And as Pitbull had already made clear, nobody was going to go out of his way to get a single bad-news rookie to a company full of rejects and troublemakers.

"Recruit Thumper reporting, Sergeant!" said Thumper, coming to attention just inside the office door.

"Close the door and sit down, Legionnaire," said the sergeant. He spoke in a voice Thumper had *never* heard him use. For one thing, it would barely have been audible beyond the confines of the office. For another, it didn't carry any of the menacing inflections he was used to hearing from Pitbull—in fact, he'd called him "Legionnaire" instead of some insulting nickname. And to top it all off, Thumper had never been invited to sit in the sergeant's presence before now. Wondering just what might be wrong, Thumper took the offered seat.

"I wanted to talk to you, so's you don't get the wrong idea," said Sergeant Pitbull. He had a strange expression on his face that Thumper couldn't quite recognize. "You know, and I know, that somebody set you up to take a big fall when General Blitzkrieg came to inspect the company. And if you think about it, you probably know why it happened."

"Some of the other recruits were mad at me for running the obstacle course too fast," said Thumper, nodding. "And for trying my best at other things, when they were happy just getting by."

"That's right," said Pitbull, nodding. "I knew you were smarter than the average sophont. You were showin' 'em up, so they decided they had to make you look so bad you couldn't ever recover from it. Except they forgot one thing. Or maybe they never even knew it."

"Forgot something?" Thumper was confused, now. "What was it you think they forgot?"

"General Blitzkrieg has a ripner up his ass about Omega Company," said the sergeant. "He thinks they're total screwups. What's more, he thinks their CO, Captain Jester, is the biggest screwup of all. So when he thinks he's got another troublemaker on his hands, where does he send him? Straight to Omega, natch."

"Yes, Sergeant, I gathered as much," said Thumper. "I don't know if there's anything I can do to wipe this incident off my record …"

"Wipe it off your record?" Pitbull guffawed. "Why'd you want to do that?" He leaned forward and lowered his voice even more. "You want to know the dead-cert truth? General Blitzkrieg has been the biggest dorknose in the Legion since before I was a recruit, and that's damn near thirty years, now. I damn near hurt myself beyond repair trying to keep from laughing when he got that bucket of slop poured all over him."

"Excuse me?" said Thumper.

"You heard me right," said Pitbull. "The funniest thing is, whoever set you up there was doing you the biggest favor he could have done. I know people in Omega, and from all they tell me, it's the best damn outfit in the Legion for a heads-up guy to be in right now. You play your cards right, and Omega just might be the best thing that ever happened to you."

"Excuse me?" Thumper said again, still not quite convinced that what he was hearing made sense.

"GREAT GHU, YOU GOT THOSE BIG-ASS EARS AND YOU STILL CAN'T HEAR DIDDLYSHIT WITH 'EM?" roared Pitbull. Thumper almost reflexively flinched at the volume. Pitbull smiled and lowered his voice again. "You know those clowns outside are tryin' to listen in on us," he said, with an actual grin. "Gotta give 'em somethin' to think about."

"Er—yes, Sergeant," said Thumper, still confused.

Pitbull leaned forward, and said, in an even lower voice, "The thing I wanted to tell you is, you're damn near the best recruit I've had in ten years. You need to loosen up some, but I figure Omega will do that for you. And you need to pay more attention to getting along with your buddies—no matter how good you are as an individual, it's how you play with the team that's gonna make or break you in the Legion. You hear me?"

"Yes, Sergeant," Thumper said again, wondering if he sounded as dull to the sergeant as he did to himself.

"Good," said Pitbull, pushing his chair back from the desk. "The other thing you need to know is that we found you transport to Zenobia, which is where Omega Company is based. There's a bunch of rich civilians taking some kind of damn junket to Zenobia, and somebody convinced 'em to take on a passenger, which turns out to be you. So you'll be traveling in style, which ain't so bad after all. Don't let nobody know it—it's supposed to be punishment."

"Yes, Sergeant!" said Thumper, considerably more enthusiastically now. "When do I have to be ready to depart?"

"You have to get on the shuttle to Wayne's World, oh-six-hundred tomorrow morning." Pitbull stood up, took a deep breath, and suddenly his voice took on its normal bellow. "YOU MISS IT, I'LL KICK YOUR STINKING ASS FIVE DIFFERENT WAYS, AND THEN I'LL REALLY GO TO WORK. NOW GET THE HELL OUT OF MY SIGHT, RABBITEARS!"

"Yes, Sergeant," said Thumper, one last time, and he scuttled out the door. It was a real job to keep from grinning as he came into view of his fellow recruits, but somehow he managed it.

O O O

"If that goddamn dog wasn't an interplanetary mascot for a clean green 'vironment, knowed and beloved throughout the galaxy, I'd've shot his raggedy ass four, maybe five times, right then and there," said Double-X. He was sitting in the Desert Lounge, Zenobia Base's bar for legionnaires, with a group of his buddies, sharing a cold beer and the story of his encounters in the wilds outside the camp that day.

"Su-u-ure, I can just see the story on the tri-vee news, *Space Legionnaire Kills Beloved Environmental Mascot*," said Street, scoffing. "With your picture—nah, they wouldn't put somethin' that ugly on. They'd put on Barky, the Environmental Dog instead. Even shot full of holes, he be a little bit cute."

"Cute?" Double-X slapped his hand against his forehead. "He gets his choppers in your leg, you tell me about cute *then*. That's the bitin'est dog you ever seen—you or anybody else."

"Well, I thought I'd seen everything in the Legion," said Slayer. "But when I drove up and saw Spartacus halfway up a tree, I about busted open laughing. If the captain hadn't been there, I bet I would have. I didn't know Sythians could climb trees."

"More like, he flew up there on his glide-board," said Street. "You're right, though—if I'd seen that, I'd have bust open laughing, too."

"I don't think is funny," said Tusk-anini. "Barky try to hurt legionnaires. Captain must stop Barky."

"You Voltons must not have any pets," said Super-Gnat, sitting on a bench next to her huge partner. She grinned, then went on, "The thing is, Barky *is* kind o' cute. I mean, kids all over the Galaxy have his holo in their rooms, and they send money to save the trees because of Barky. When I was a kid, I used to think it was really blurgin' how he could sniff out pollutants ..."

"When you was a kid?" said Do-Wop. "Man, that's one long-lived dog ... OW!" he yelled, as Super-Gnat punched him.

"Barky's genetically engineered," said Sushi, laughing at his partner. "They didn't want to have to replace him every few years, so while they were giving him the genes to let him sniff out methane and fluorocarbons and so on, they made him long-lived, too. If I remember right, he'd be going on eighty years old even if he'd never started space-traveling."

"Eighty or eight, don't give him no right to bite folks," said Double-X, slapping a fist into his open hand. "I was the captain, I'd be tellin' those AEIOU suckers to lift their ship before the sun sets on 'em."

"I bet he would like to do that," said Sushi, swirling the ice cubes in his rum and Neocoke. "Problem is, the captain can't just order another government agency off the planet except under martial law, which doesn't apply here. If he could get the Zenobians to ask them to leave, that'd be another story. But so far, the Zenobians don't seem interested in them one way or another."

"Hey, maybe I can get Barky to chase Leftenant Qual up a tree," suggested Do-Wop, pointing toward the ceiling to illustrate the idea. "That'd get 'em interested, all right."

"You ever get a good look at Qual's teeth?" asked Super-Gnat. "He's got about twice as many as any dog you ever saw, and mostly twice as big—plus, he runs even faster than a Gambolt. If Barky has enough sense to find the meat in a hamburger—and at least, his bio says he does—he'll steer clear of *that* fight for all he's worth."

"Bio? The farkin' dog's got a *bio*?" said Double-X.

"Hey, watch your mouth," said Super-Gnat. "Barky, the Environmental Dog, was my favorite icon when I was a kid. I cried for a week when we moved to a new town and my mom forgot to bring along my Barky doll. You talk bad about Barky, I'll whap you." She flexed her right arm to show him she meant business.

"All right, all right," said Double-X, trying to smooth things over. He probably outweighed Super-Gnat by fifty kilos, but everybody in the company knew that what the little legionnaire started, she finished—with Tusk-anini ready to step in if he thought she wasn't getting a fair shake. He rubbed his chin, and mused, "I guess all those big media stars got bios, so why not Barky?"

"Barky's bio says he's the most intelligent dog ever, too," said Super-Gnat, somewhat placated. "I read the whole thing when I was a kid. And watched his show every week. It was really triff, watching him chase the polluters."

"Yeah, except now he seems to think that we're polluters," said Sushi. "I don't know how he got that idea—the camp's about as green as you can get—I think we recycle everything we can, certainly anything likely to be useful if we ever had to fight somebody. Of course, the AEIOU probably doesn't take that point into consideration."

"War not healthy for ecologies," said Tusk-anini. "Best reason to prevent war, I thinking."

"Maybe that dog *do* be smarter than he looks," said Street, nodding. "Course, I knowed he was right smart all along when he went bitin' on Double-X."

That set off another round of good-natured insults and arguments that went on until closing time. The legionnaires went to bed without figuring out what to do about Barky, or how to deal with the AEIOU mission to Zenobia, although they talked enough about those problems to solve them half a dozen times.

It probably would not have made them any happier to know that their superior officers were having no better luck.

O   O   O

Victor Phule popped a token into the slot of the machine facing him and pulled the lever. There was something gratifying about the activity; just enough mechanical resistance, a sound of gears engaging and wheels spinning—even though he'd been told that the sounds were actually synthesized effects, and the gears and wheels were simulations that had nothing to do with the choice of which symbols the machine would display. Instead, an elaborately sealed Heisenberg circuit determined the winning (or more often, losing) combination. Whoever had designed the machines had done her job well, Phule grudgingly admitted. It felt as if you could actually use the handle to control which symbols appeared, even when your brain knew the facts to be otherwise.

The "wheels" spun to a halt, and Victor Phule inspected the three symbols in front of him: a bell, a cherry, and a lemon. No payout, this time. Phule picked up his Slate-o-mat and entered the result. On the whole, he was forty-seven thousand dollars in the red at this point. Considering that the bank of machines he was playing took nothing less than five-thousand-dollar tokens, that was a pittance. One decent payout, and he'd be ahead of the game. One significant jackpot, and he'd rake in more for one play than any but the top casino executives made in a year. And if he hit the *big* one ...

He chuckled. It was only a matter of time.

He was mildly surprised that nobody else seemed interested in these particular machines. Yes, the price of a play was high, but the payouts were proportionately richer than anything else in the Fat Chance Casino. Even thirty-five to one, the odds for playing a single number at the roulette table, was a paltry reward compared to the million-to-one superjackpot the casino had posted for these machines. Well, if no one else played, no one else had a chance to win, did they? Determinedly, Victor Phule fished in his pocket and took out another token.

He was about to feed it into the machine when someone close behind him said, "Having any luck today?"

He turned to see a woman's face—youngish, dark-haired, and rather pretty, though not on the vidstar level. Almost inevitably, she knew who he was and how much money he had; Victor Phule was not without ego, but he had no reason to believe he was the type of man who would appeal to many women if his wealth were suddenly to disappear. On the other hand, he had an excellent notion of just how attractive that wealth was to almost everyone else he met. After all, the galaxy has room for only a limited number of multi-billionaires—which meant that the vast majority of those around him at any given time had far less money than he, and had at least some interest in altering what they perceived as an unnatural imbalance. From Victor Phule's point of view, of course, that imbalance was very much the natural state of affairs, and he saw no reason to give anyone a chance to change it to his disadvantage.

So his first response to the question was to verify, out of the corner of his eye, that his bodyguard was nearby, paying due attention to the situation. Sure enough, Eddie Grossman was only a step or two away, pretending to play the slots while looking in his direction. The guard lifted a forefinger to his left ear, signaling that he had already scanned the woman for weapons and found nothing to set off his alarms. Good—that eliminated one source of worry, although there were of course plenty of ways to damage or kill someone without carrying a detectable weapon.

That verified, Victor Phule decided to indulge himself with a few moments' conversation. "Luck doesn't enter into it," he said. "Beating these machines is easy, if you have a good system and stick to it."

"You must have a lot of faith in your system," said the woman, eyeing the machine that Phule had just been playing. "Could you teach me how you play?"

Victor Phule looked at her again, sizing her up. "You don't look as if you have enough money to play on these machines," he said. "They're five thousand dollars minimum ..."

"Yes, that's what convinced me you must have a good system," said the woman. She paused, then said, "My name's Lola, by the way."

Phule ignored her attempt to get his name. "You need to get a set of five machines and protect them from anyone else playing them until you've won your quota. So if you were thinking about putting a token in one of these, forget about it."

Lola smiled. "I'm afraid that even if I had your confidence, I don't have your bankroll. If I like your system enough to try it, it'll be on the five-dollar machines. But go ahead, Mr. ...?"

"Next thing is, you have to set yourself an amount you're going to win, and once you win it, you stop for the day. Slot machines are calibrated to take a certain percentage of the bets made on them, so you have to resist the belief that you can hit the jackpot twice in a row."

"I see," said Lola. "So you're feeding your own bank of machines until they pay off, then quitting while you're ahead."

"Yes, essentially that's it," said Victor Phule. "I'm betting that most of the players are too undisciplined to follow a system like mine. So their losses build the jackpot even bigger for me, you see."

"I guess so," said Lola, nodding dubiously. "But what happens if ..."

But by then Victor Phule had decided that the young woman was interesting, but not enough so to distract him from his mission of breaking the bank at the Fat Chance Casino. He rubbed his palms together, a signal to the bodyguard, and said, "Well, Miss, it's been a pleasure talking to you. But I really have to get back to work here." And no sooner were the words out of his mouth than Eddie Grossman was there, gently taking the woman by the elbow and steering her toward the exit, talking quietly to her. Eddie was good at what he did—most likely, the young woman would never be aware that she'd been given the brush-off. If he wanted to renew the conversation, it would be as if nothing had ever broken it off.

He put a token in the slot and pulled the lever ...

O   O   O

Lola walked out of the High Rollers' Lounge in the Fat Chance Casino burning with curiosity. Her first encounter with Victor Phule had been much stranger than she had expected. About the only thing that fit any predictable pattern was the bodyguard's moving in gently to encourage her to end the conversation with his client. Phule must have flashed him some signal she'd missed. But that was all right—she'd actually gotten to talk to him much longer than she'd hoped to.

Unfortunately, she hadn't learned very much of use. Victor Phule's explanations of why he was playing the casino's quantum slots didn't make any sense—and that set off all her alarms. She didn't see any reason to point out that nobody else but the armaments tycoon was playing the five-thousand-dollar machines. Without the undisciplined players he depended on to build up the losses, his supposed "system" was nonsense. Besides, everybody but the most unthinking fish knew that the slots gave the worst odds in the whole casino. Obviously, nobody who could build a financial empire like Phule-Proof Industries could be so cavalier about throwing away his money. So there must be something else going on here.

What was Victor Phule's real game? Was his conspicuous high rolling nothing more than shilling, meant to encourage others to play recklessly? Was his so-called system just a way to convince players that the slots might not be the bad investment that every sensible gambler claimed they were? Or was something even deeper going on here? Lola did her best to keep her face cheerful, to keep Victor Phule talking. Whatever his game was, she intended to find out—and to be there to scam him out of a share of the proceeds, whenever it did pay off.

It wasn't going to be an easy job, Lola told herself. But it had a lot better chance of paying off than Victor Phule's system for playing the slots. And whether or not he realized it, she had a lot more at stake than he did. She smiled again. *Always bet on the hungry fighter,* said the old gambler's cliché. One thing for sure: she was a lot hungrier than Victor Phule. And she was going to get her bite out of him, one way or another.

O O O

Back at Zenobia Base, Willard Phule's wrist intercom buzzed, then Mother's voice came through the speaker.

"Hate to wake you up, cutie pie, but we've detected an incoming ship. You might want to tidy up before they get here."

Phule, who had been wide-awake (it was midafternoon, after all) and working at his desk, grinned. "Thanks, Mother," he said. "That must be the party of bigwigs we've got to entertain for Ambassador Gottesman. Try to hail them, and patch me in when they answer."

"Will do, sweetums," purred Mother, and she broke the connection.

"Do you plan to meet these, uh, *bigwigs* in person?" asked Beeker, looking up from the financial program he'd been running.

"Sure, if it really is them," said Phule. "I'm not going to go charging out to meet just anybody again. I learned my lesson with those AEIOU inspectors. I all but rolled out the red carpet for them, and they've been nothing but trouble ever since."

"That's an understatement, sir," said Beeker, sniffing faintly. "I found them an unpleasant company from the beginning. I am more and more convinced that they were dispatched here by one of your enemies and now need to find sufficient violations to justify the expense of shipping them to this planet."

"It does seem like the kind of thing General Blitzkrieg would try," Phule said, musing. "Although it might even be a bit too subtle for him. He's more the kind to try something direct, like sending Major Botchup to replace me in command. That's the old Legion way, which is all Blitzkrieg seems to understand."

"I don't think I'd use the term *understand* to describe the general's mental processes," said Beeker. "Still, I wouldn't be so quick to overlook the possibility that he might from time to time come into the possession of competent advice and actually follow it. Even as you do on occasion, sir."

Phule stared at Beeker, trying to figure out whether or not the butler expected him to take offense at the comment. After a long moment, he shrugged, and said, "Well, I can't deny the possibility. But now that they're here, figuring out who sicced them on us is secondary to figuring out how to get them off the company's back. I think we're about as environment-friendly …"

"A barbarous locution," muttered Beeker.

Phule hesitated one beat, then continued, "About as environmental-friendly as we can be and still carry out our mission," he said. He was used by now to the butler's correcting his grammar and diction on the fly, although he couldn't always figure out exactly what Beeker was objecting to. Judging from Beeker's sour expression, his attempt to correct himself hadn't made things any better. "Besides, this is the Zenobians' home world," he added. "I'd think as long as they're happy with the company's performance, a bunch of Alliance bureaucrats don't have much to say about it."

"Don't be so sure of that, sir," said Beeker. "Have you looked into the precise terms on which Zenobia joined the Alliance? I would be very surprised if the natives of a new world were allowed to come in without major concessions to the powers that be—of which the regulatory bureaucracy is a not insignificant constituent. Having gotten a toehold on this world, the AEIOU is bound to do all it can to increase its power and influence here. No sensible person could expect otherwise."

"Hmmm …" Phule frowned. "I think I'm going to send Chief Potentary Korg a note about these people, emphasizing that they came without our being informed. From the way he acted when I told him about the hunting party, he's pretty touchy about what off-worlders try to do on Zenobia …"

Phule was interrupted by the buzz of his communicator. "Captain, we've made contact with the incoming ship," said Mother. "Just as you thought—it's those fat cats Ambassador Gottesman sent here. You want to talk to them, or shall I send them away?"

"Oh, thanks, Mother," said Phule. "Of course I'll talk to them—put them through." Then a new thought crossed his mind. "Umm ... actually, give me a moment to think about where to have them land. I'd rather not have the AEIOU people notice them."

"It'll be rather a challenge to keep someone from noticing a nearby shuttle landing, sir," said Beeker. "At least, I can think of nothing short of having them alight on the opposite side of the planet, which hardly seems compatible with the ambassador's orders to treat them as honored guests."

"You're right," muttered Phule. "Wait a moment! Why don't we invite the AEIOU people to tour our base, show them all the latest environment-friendly features built into it ..."

"It's still a barbarous locution," said Beeker.

"And while they're indoors, the bigwigs' shuttle can land without the AEIOU team noticing it," Phule continued. He was grinning, now. "We just have to keep the two groups from noticing one another! Mother, you call the AEIOU team and extend the invitation—nicely, mind you! I'll talk to the hunters and stall them while we get the environmentalists out of the way. If we play our cards right, we can keep them from ever knowing of each other's presence. And maybe we can even persuade the AEIOU that we're really nice guys, after all."

"It's a really stupid idea, but it just might work," said Mother. "I'll do my best, sweetie. But if they bring Barky, all bets are off."

"I doubt we can get them to leave Barky behind," said Phule. "Well, just warn everybody—particularly the non-humans in the company—that he's coming, and that they might want to watch their step."

"In case Barky decides to drop a little pollution on his own?" asked Mother. Before Phule could answer, she said, "I'll pass the word, sweetie-poo. Hold on, now—I'm patching the hunters through." There was a light crackling sound from Phule's wrist communicator, and a red LED glowed.

"Hello!" said Phule. "This is Captain Jester of Omega Company. Welcome to Zenobia! I've got my people preparing a landing area for you, so I'm going to ask you to take one more orbit of the planet."

Beeker rolled his eyes. He knew, as surely as he knew Zenobia's sun would rise the next morning, that there was going to be more trouble. And he knew perfectly well whose job it was going to be to get Phule out of it. He sighed. He'd taken the job with open eyes, and there was no point getting annoyed about it now. Still, the boy ought to have learned *something* by now ...

CHAPTER EIGHT

Journal #688

My employer, for all his dedication to the military life, was at bottom a businessman. In that, he resembled his father. He also resembled that gentleman in a firm conviction that his own view of the world was fundamentally accurate, and that others who did not share it were in need of correction. Unlike his father, he was at least willing to give those others sufficient data to arrive at such a correction. It did not occur to him that others might interpret the same data differently ...

It must have been some such motivation that induced him to invite the AEIOU inspection team to tour the Legion base camp. The fact that, to all appearances, they had come to the planet with the express purpose of shutting down that very camp seemed to carry no weight with him.

Surely he can't have been so foolish as to believe that an afternoon's VIP tour would be enough to overcome the chief inspector's evident belief that a military unit was by its very definition incapable of adhering to environmentally correct policies.

o o o

"Welcome to Zenobia Base," said Lieutenant Rembrandt, smiling as she met Chief Inspector Snieff and her AEIOU team in the courtyard. Phule had chosen her and Sushi, who had the closest approximation of all his legionnaires to something resembling diplomatic temperament, to make up the greeting party.

The three AEIOU inspectors, accompanied by Barky, the Environmental Dog, had walked from their camp to the Legion base. Phule had, of course, offered to send a hoverjeep for them, but Snieff had turned him down peremptorily. "Nonessential energy use is a crime against posterity," she snarled. "The Legion should have a greater sense of its role in preserving precious resources."

Now Chief Inspector Snieff looked suspiciously at Omega Company's modular base camp unit. "I see a great many artificial materials being used here," she said. "That must have had a high energy cost." She and her two assistants were wearing uniforms of some coarsely woven natural fiber.

"We don't have very much choice in a semiarid setting," said Rembrandt. "The Zenobians insisted that we site our base camp here, so as not to use up territory they considered more valuable. As you may know …"

"The Zenobians should consider all their territory untouchable," said Inspector Slurry. "If the locals can't recognize its value, it's our mission to show them. We have already had ample occasion to marvel at the wildlife in this area …"

"That's funny," said Sushi, with a broad smile. "I've had quite a few encounters with the wildlife out there. As best as I can recall, I was usually too busy trying to keep the little beasties from biting or stinging me to have much time left to marvel at them. Do you have some kind of secret vermin repellent, or do the local critters just respect your proper green attitude?"

"Sushi!" said Rembrandt. Phule had instructed them to avoid antagonizing the visitors.

"That's all right, Lieutenant," said Inspector Gardner, with a grin—apparently the only one the AEIOU team had brought with it. He turned to Sushi, and said, "We get our share of bites, too. The main trick to avoiding them is to learn when the various animals are actively feeding and stay out of their territory then. If we absolutely have to work in a certain area when the local bug equivalents are active, we wear protective clothing."

Snieff nodded. "After all, our blood could be poisonous to them—which means their bites would do them a lot more harm than us. This is their world, after all—we would be remiss if we exposed them to danger."

"I don't know," said Sushi. "I bet the other animals on the planet don't think twice about squishing a bug that's trying to bite them. Why, when we were traveling through the desert with Flight Leftenant Qual ..."

"Why don't we take our visitors to meet the captain?" said Rembrandt, cutting Sushi off in midsentence. She'd already heard how Qual had used his stunner to clear annoying vermin from the legionnaires' path during their desert mission a few months before, and she didn't expect the AEIOU team would find the story enlightening. She was also under strict orders to get the inspectors inside the base before the hunting party's shuttle began its landing approach. "I think you'll be surprised at some of the environmentally friendly features built into the module," she said, pointing toward the closest entrance. "If you'll follow me inside ..."

"Woof!" said Barky. The Environmental Dog had been sitting politely nearby, generally ignoring the activity in the camp around him. Quickly, Rembrandt turned, hoping there wasn't going to be trouble. Phule had warned everyone in Omega Company that the dog was coming to visit. That gave the nonhuman legionnaires, or anyone else to whom Barky seemed to have taken a particular dislike, the chance to make themselves scarce. That didn't mean that Barky might not take a particular dislike to yet another member of the Omega Mob ...

There stood Mahatma, smiling his beatific smile at the Environmental Dog. "Hello," said the little legionnaire. "It is not often that a famous animal star visits Omega Company."

Rembrandt took a deep breath. So far, at least, Barky didn't seem to be taking exception to Mahatma's presence. But she knew Mahatma too well, especially his uncanny ability to find the single most unsettling question to ask in any given situation. That might not make Barky angry, but she couldn't be sure that Chief Inspector Snieff wouldn't sic the dog on him if she thought he was getting impertinent. And Mahatma could get very impertinent ...

"Mahatma," said Lieutenant Rembrandt, "weren't you supposed to be on perimeter guard duty just now?" Maybe he'd get the hint ...

But Mahatma wasn't taking any hints. "I wonder why the inspectors risk bringing a genetically engineered animal to this world?"

Rembrandt stepped forward, putting an arm around Mahatma's shoulders. "Uh, I'm sure the inspectors know exactly what they're doing ..."

"Oh, we can speak for ourselves, Lieutenant," said Chief Inspector Snieff, with a predatory smile. "Of course Barky is genetically engineered," she continued. "But since there are no other creatures of his species here, there is no chance of his passing on his genes, and therefore no threat to the Zenobian environment."

"On worlds with other dogs, we take additional precautions, naturally," added Inspector Slurry.

"Naturally," said Mahatma, still smiling broadly.

"Well, shall we go see the captain?" said Rembrandt, attempting to herd the environmental inspectors toward the entrance to the base module. It was only a matter of moments before Mahatma sprung his inevitable follow-up question, which was likely to be even more unsettling than the first one.

She wasn't fast enough. "Of course, there are other ways for those genes to get into the environment," said Mahatma.

Slurry looked at him quizzically. "I'm not sure what you mean ..."

Mahatma's smile got even wider. "There are many hungry beasts on this planet," he said. "What if one of them ate the poor Environmental Dog?"

"Ate Barky?" said Snieff, her jaw falling.

"Be very, very careful," urged Mahatma. "I am sure the AEIOU would not want to be responsible for destroying an unspoiled ecology because it let its famous mascot roam about unguarded." He smiled and bowed, and turned away, leaving the three inspectors dumbfounded.

Rembrandt said once more, "Shall we go see the inside of the base?"

"Yes, by all means," said Snieff, looking around apprehensively. "Come, Barky—stay close to me!"

"Woof!" said Barky, the Environmental Dog, lifting a hind leg to give his ear a vigorous scratch.

O O O

"A slots system?" Ernie sat up, an eager expression on his face. "Y'know, if he's really got one, that's like money in the bank. People have been looking for a way to cut the house odds in slots for centuries ..."

"Ernie, we're talking about Victor Phule, the arms dealer," said Lola. "This is a man who already has more money in the bank than most small planetary governments. He's the last person in the galaxy to need a system for beating slots."

"Hey, maybe he's like, diversifying," said Ernie. He took a sip of his cold beer, and added, "You know, in case the old arms business goes through some hard times. I hear wars are a bit scarce nowadays ..."

"Right, and the food business might hit a patch of real hard times, too," said Lola, scornfully. "Whatever reason Victor Phule has for playing those slots, it's not because he needs the money— or the exercise, either. If we can figure out his game, there's a good chance we can get in on it."

"What if he's just having fun?" asked Ernie. "You know, even a rich guy must like to let his hair down and stop pinching every last penny. Some guys tool around in space yachts, some play the rocket races—maybe the old boy gets his splats out by throwing five scra- goonchies into a slot and pulling the handle. Hey, he can afford it."

"It's such a dumb idea, it might even be right," admitted Lola. She paced back and forth in her stocking feet, thinking out loud. "But we can't ignore the chance that he's up to something bigger, Ernie. Besides, he's the closest person on the station to the guy we're supposed to be snatching. He could be the whole key to our getting off of Lorelei Station with our hides intact, not to mention coming out ahead of the game. It's worth our time and effort to scope out whatever it is he's doing, and look for a way to turn it to our own advantage."

"I'll buy into that, I guess," said Ernie. He spread his hands apart, palms up, and said, "Thing is, how are you gonna find out what he's doing? You already asked him flat out, and you don't wanna believe the answer he gave you. So what've ya got that's better?"

"I don't know—yet." Lola peered out the window of their modestly priced room. The view was nothing special; another block of workers' living quarters like theirs. Then again, nobody came to Lorelei expecting to see natural beauty, unless the showgirls in the casinos fit that description (some did). Lola drummed her fingers on the plastiglas, then turned to Ernie, and said, "Victor Phule is the real thing. Even a small fraction of his money could put us on Easy Street. But we can't afford any mistakes. The one thing I don't want to do is alert him—or more likely his bodyguards—that somebody's keeping an eye on him. So I need you to do some of the spy work. You think you're up to it?"

"Sure, sure," said Ernie, stretching. "You know me ..."

"That's why I'm worried," said Lola. She walked over and put her hand on Ernie's head. "This bodyguard isn't some third-rate musclehead," said Lola. "I don't know where he came from, but he's very smooth, and very professional. He's likely to remember my face a good long time. So I've got to be really careful where and when I pop up."

"I get the picture, babes," said Ernie. "What you want me to do is peek over the old boy's shoulder, try to figure out his system, but keep the guard from noticing. Nothin' to it ..."

"Wrong!" said Lola, and she smacked her hand on top of his head. "You couldn't fool this guard if he spotted you six dry martinis and a fake beard. I'm sorry, Ernie, he's just way out of your class. And nearly out of mine, I think. But I've got a plan ..."

"Yeah, sure," said Ernie, rubbing his head where she'd hit him. "Your last brilliant plan blew up in our face, with nothing to show for it until we got sent back here to finish the job right—at our own expense. What kind of dope do you think I am?"

"A smarter one because of what's already happened," said Lola.

"And so am I. Listen to this."

Ernie listened, skeptically at first, pointing out objections to Lola's plan. But gradually he began to nod, then enthusiastically to offer suggestions of his own. Finally, after nearly an hour, he said. "All right, you win. It's worth a try, especially considering we got nothin' else to try."

"Good," said Lola. "Now, here's what I want you to do first ..."

O   O   O

The shuttle was already on the ground, and the dust of its landing mostly settled, when Gears guided the Legion hoverjeep over a low hill and came into sight of it. There were a couple of men at work unloading large cases of equipment from an open hatchway, and another stood studying a map under the shade of the shuttle. The afternoon sun was beating down fiercely, without a trace of cloud in the sky.

Lieutenant Armstrong stood up in the passenger seat and waved. "Hello the shuttle!" he called. Phule had chosen him to greet the hunting expedition while he and Lieutenant Rembrandt escorted the AEIOU inspectors on a tour of the Legion base.

The landing party turned and stared as Gears brought the hoverjeep down a short distance away from where they stood. As it touched down, Armstrong leapt out and strode over to the newcomers. "I'm Lieutenant Armstrong, Omega Company," he said, extending a hand. "Welcome to Zenobia!"

One of the hunters, a stocky man with short gray hair in a vaguely military style, stepped forward and took Armstrong's hand in a crusher grip. "A pleasure to meet you, Lieutenant," he said. His voice was an incongruous combination of rasp and drawl. "I'm L.P. Asho. We hear tell there's some mighty good hunting hereabouts. Looking forward to seeing what kind of wild and wooly critters you all have for us to shoot."

"Wild is no problem, Mr. Asho," said Armstrong. "But I don't think you'll find very much in the way of wooly on Zenobia. The animals here tend to have mostly scales ..."

"Har har! Fellow's got a good sense of humor," said Asho. "Here, let me introduce you to the other fellers—this is Austen Tay-Shun—he's a big-ass lawyer, but he ain't all that bad, y'git to know him. And over there's good ol' Euston O'Better. You prob'ly heard of him, on account he's the richest son of a gun on Tejaz."

"Uh, pleased to meet you all," said Armstrong, shaking the men's hands as they were offered to him.

Asho's description notwithstanding, Tay-Shun was a small, wiry man with penetrating eyes. He gave Armstrong a steady look, and said, "Interestin' country here. You don't suppose there's any chance we could hire one of the natives for a guide, do you?"

"I suppose it's possible," said Armstrong. "To tell the truth, we haven't really had contact with any of them other than the military. I think they've put us out here in part to isolate us from their civilian population." He tried to remember if he'd even set eyes on a Zenobian other than those in Flight Leftenant Qual's unit. To the best of his knowledge, he hadn't. Was that also intentional on the Zenobians' part? He wasn't sure.

"Not very friendly of 'em, I'd say," drawled Asho. "Well, if we can't get a native, we'll just do the best we can without. How soon can we light out for the killin' grounds?"

"Fairly soon, I'd think," said Armstrong. "Captain Jester wants to schedule a briefing as soon as convenient with you, and then we can get you to the designated hunting areas."

"Briefing?" Austen Tay-Shun interrupted. "What, does your captain think private citizens are subject to military discipline?"

Armstrong cleared his throat. "Mr. Tay-Shun, Zenobia is an inhabited planet, with its own laws and government. The Zenobian government retains the right to decide which off-world visitors may visit their world and under what conditions. By inviting the Space Legion to operate here, they have effectively given us the right to bring in what personnel we consider necessary to the mission. Now, at the request of your friends in the State Department, Captain Jester has persuaded the Zenobians to permit you to hunt the local animals in designated areas, provided you follow certain rules. I think you'll agree that knowing what the rules are will make it a lot easier to follow them. So this briefing is simply an opportunity for the captain to tell you what's expected of you and to answer any questions you may have about Zenobia."

"Long-winded cuss, ain't he?" said Euston O'Better, a tall, shambling fellow with a grin that suggested unplumbed depths of ignorance. He emphasized his point with an elbow in Tay-Shun's ribs. "But what the hell, let's go meet this captain so we can get it over with. The sooner I can start shootin' a few critters, the better, sez I. I ain't even *seen* no dinos yet."

"*Dinos* might not be the right term," said Armstrong, glad of a chance to change the subject. "The local sophonts do resemble certain species of dinosaurs, but the other fauna we've seen are pretty varied. Why—" He broke off suddenly, as a strange being came into his view. "What in Ghu's name is that?"

The creature that had emerged from the hunters' shuttle was furry, long-eared, round-faced, and about two-thirds Armstrong's height. It was evidently some kind of sophont, because it was wearing a large backpack and a loose black garment that had a remarkable resemblance to ... a Space Legion uniform? Armstrong watched openmouthed as it approached him. It stopped a short distance away, came to attention, and saluted—rather smartly, Lieutenant Armstrong thought. As he stared openmouthed, the new sophont said, "Legionnaire Recruit Thumper reporting for duty to Omega Company, sir!"

"Legionnaire? Thumper?" said Armstrong.

"Oh, yeah, we forgot to tell ya," said L.P. Asho. "The gov'ment asked us to give the bunny a ride here, since there wasn't no other ships coming this way. He wasn't really much trouble, and I guess he's yours, now."

"I'll be doggoned," said Gears, who'd stood back and watched the conversation between Armstrong and the hunters without comment. "Every time you think you know what to expect in Omega Company, it just gets weirder. Throw your pack in the jeep, buddy—I guess you'll be riding back to camp with us."

"Yes, sir," said Thumper, who still had the recruit's automatic (and generally accurate) assumption that everybody and everything wearing a Legion uniform outranked him.

"Save the *sir* stuff for officers," said Gears. "I'm Gears, and since the lieutenant still seems to be gaping for air, I guess I'm the one who's got to welcome you to Zenobia—and to the Omega Mob. And I don't know what kind of outfit you come here from— but I can guarantee you it's a whole lot different here."

O O O

The monitor of Sushi's computer displayed a rapidly changing series of not-quite-random characters, and the speaker emitted a tantalizing series of hisses and grunts, which the autotranslator stubbornly declined to render into anything that the three men in the room could make sense of. Sushi and Lieutenant Rembrandt had delivered the AEIOU inspectors to the captain, at which point Sushi had remembered that Rev was coming by today for a progress report. Fortunately, the officers were willing to dispense with his services for the rest of the afternoon. Unfortunately, what Sushi had to report to Rev was not exactly progress …

"Looks like nothin' but garbage to me," said Do-Wop, "Hey, Soosh—you sure that ain't just somebody's unshielded belt sander, or maybe a can opener?"

"Well, it's the wrong frequency for that," said Sushi. "I know this is some written document off the Zenobians' Web, or whatever they call it. But until we can get the translator to recognize the input as some kind of articulate language, it might as well be garbage."

"Well, we know the translator works on spoken Zenobian," said Rev. "We can all understand Flight Leftenant Qual, or at least most of the time. So the written language shouldn't be all that much harder." He paused and looked at Sushi. "Should it?"

"I'd need to know a lot more about written Zenobian to tell you, Rev," said Sushi. "I suppose one of us ought to ask Qual just how their writing system works. If it's straight phonetic, the translator ought to be able to make sense of it sooner or later. If it's not … well, if it's not, then we could be way over our heads, guys."

"I'm over my head just listenin' to this stuff," said Do-Wop. "Do you know what he means, Rev?"

"Mostly," said Rev. "What kinds of things are you worried about, son?"

"We don't know how many languages the Zenobians speak, or who speaks what," said Sushi, counting on his fingers. "Maybe the ruling classes speak a different language from the ordinary people. Maybe their older books are in the same language as their modern ones, maybe not. I mean, there were some religions on Old Earth that used a whole different language for their sacred texts than the people spoke in everyday life. Maybe ..."

"That's way too many maybes," said Do-Wop, a concerned look on his face. "Y'know, you keep runnin' your mind so hard, you're gonna get a really rotten headache. What I do, is whenever my brain starts running around in circles, I go get myself a couple-three cold brews and stop thinkin' for a while. You oughta do that, Soosh. You don't watch it, you'll be just like an officer."

"Yeah, yeah," said Sushi. "And if I don't do this job, I'll have to go back to work on something a lot less interesting. The problem we have right now is to find out how the Zenobians' written language works, which means doing some fieldwork with the only Zenobians we have handy. Who's gonna go talk to Qual?"

"He's bound to get suspicious if I ask him anything about their writing," said Rev. "And when that happens, he starts messin' with my head—at least, I think that's what he's doin'. Anyways, his answers don't hardly make sense. One of you boys is gonna have to go ask him for me."

"Well, I'm out," said Do-Wop. "I can't understand half of what *you* guys are talkin' about, let alone Qual. I think his translator's buggy, the way it screws up words."

"Buggy translator ..." mused Sushi. "You know, that gives me an idea. I think I know just the trick to get Qual started talking about spoken and written Zenobian, without him suspecting what Rev's up to."

"And what's that, son?" asked Rev.

Sushi grinned. "I'll tell you after I've found out whether it works. Which I'm going to go find out right now. See you later!" And out the door he went, leaving Rev and Do-Wop staring at each other.

After a moment, Do-Wop shrugged. "Guess this is as good a time as we're gonna get for some cold ones. Gotta stop them headaches before they start. Catch you later, Rev." And he went out the door as well, leaving Rev alone.

Rev turned and looked at the shifting characters on Sushi's computer monitor, squinting as if it might help him discern a pattern in the rapid flow. After a while, he shook his head and blinked. Everything was tantalizingly close to making sense ... And yet none of it did. He put his hands in the pockets of his not-quite Legion-issue jumpsuit, turned to the door, and sauntered out. For now, he would have to leave it up to Sushi. If Sushi couldn't solve the problem, he'd decide what to do then. Until that point, Do-Wop's advice actually sounded good. He stopped and looked in a mirror, taking a moment to touch up his hairdo. The King had always made it a point to keep up his appearance. Finally satisfied, he turned and headed down the corridor toward the officers' club, whistling softly to himself.

O O O

Thumper's departure for the Legion base was delayed while Lieutenant Armstrong persuaded the hunters to stay and set up their camp instead of coming immediately to see the captain.

"We'll take you there this evening," Armstrong told the hunters, smiling. "Captain Jester just sent me to make sure you had everything you needed, and it looks as if you do. Since that's straightened out, I'll head back to the camp, and you'll be seeing the captain as soon as he's free."

"I can't imagine what your captain's got to do on this here planet that's so important he can't talk to some of his constituents," said Austen Tay-Shun, who seemed to be the leader of the hunting party. "We've contributed ..."

"Excuse me, sir," said the lieutenant, whose smile had abruptly vanished. "The captain isn't an elected official, so of course he doesn't have any constituents. And I don't recall hearing that the Legion ran on political contributions."

"Well, sonny, we've contributed a whole *shitload* to the folks that give the Legion its orders," said Tay-Shun. "I reckon they'd be right concerned to find out that the Legion don't pay no never mind to their constituents' needs. Why, I'm surprised the captain didn't come out himself instead of sending his messenger-boy."

"Mr. Tay-Shun, I will attribute your remarks to ignorance, and overlook them on that account," said Armstrong, frostily. "I have given you my word *as an officer* that Captain Jester will receive you as soon as he has completed certain urgent business, and I should think that would suffice. Now, Mr. Tay-Shun, if there is nothing else …?"

The hunters took the hint at last, and the hoverjeep headed back to the Legion base, with Thumper riding on the back seat.

O   O   O

Thumper wasn't sure just what to expect from Omega Company. Probably because he'd spent much of his time in basic training under the illusion that the Legion actually worked the way the recruiting brochures had told him, his fund of Legion rumor and gossip was possibly even smaller than that of the average recruit. Belatedly, he'd realized he needed to catch up. But by then, he was leaving Legion boot camp, a passenger in a civilian ship that just happened to be headed his way. Somebody had called in a favor, and Thumper was the beneficiary—or so he hoped.

The civilians on board were all humans, like most of those he'd met since leaving his home world. None of them seemed to know very much about Omega Company, or its commanding officer— and in any case, they had very little to say to Thumper. They were much more interested in telling improbable stories about their hunting exploits. This struck Thumper as an incredible waste of time, since none of them seemed to believe any of the others' stories—or even to listen to them, very much. And since he showed almost no interest in the subject that dominated their conversation, they quickly stopped trying to impress him.

That was all right with Thumper. He needed time to reassess the lessons of basic training, which evidently went well beyond such superficial matters as marching, saluting, and running the obstacle course. All that he'd managed as well as anyone in his squad—in fact, according to Sergeant Pitbull, he'd completed the obstacle course in record time. But by showing how fast he could run the course, he'd made enemies, which made no sense to him—even after his buddies sat him down and tried to explain it to him.

One thing he did understand: making enemies had gotten him in trouble with General Blitzkrieg, which in turn had gotten him sent to Omega Company. That at least made sense, once he learned of the general's long-standing grudge against Captain Jester and Omega Company. That story was apparently known throughout the Legion, although Thumper hadn't heard as much as a peep about it until his assignment to Omega came through. Only then had the other recruits taken him aside and told him what they'd heard. And Thumper's ears had stood on end, and his eyes grew wider and wider.

The only problem was, the stories contradicted each other on almost every point. Some said that Omega was a dumping ground for the dregs of the Legion, and its CO a certified madman who turned every Legion rule on its head. Others said it was the softest duty a legionnaire could get, with routine assignments to fancy resort worlds and officers who let all discipline go by the boards. And others said it was the one unit in the Legion where a legionnaire wasn't strapped in with archaic rules and mindlessly enforced regulations; where a sophont with some imagination and ambition might find a niche for himself.

Thumper had taken advantage of his copious spare time on the voyage to research Omega Company and Captain Jester on the Web, and what he found there was every bit as contradictory as the rumors he'd heard. A long string of news reports from Jennie Higgins made Captain Jester look like the kind of hero Thumper had always thought of as the essence of the Legion—the active, resourceful leader of an intrepid band. But other reports portrayed the captain as a laughingstock, and his company—to quote the governor of one planet where they'd been stationed—as "the idiot bastard offspring of a travesty and a calamity." Thumper had to look up a couple of those words in the human dictionary. He still wasn't sure what to make of it when he found out what they meant—or whether he liked what it meant for him.

But like it or not, here he was, riding the last couple of kilometers to his destination on the back seat of a Legion hoverjeep. Gears chattered the whole way back to the camp, pointing out various features of the desert and asking Thumper how he'd come to be assigned to the company. "You know, you're the first sophont of your kind I've seen," he said, turning around to look Thumper in the eye. "We got some Gambolts in the company, a couple Synthians, a Volton—and all kinds and shapes of humans, of course. But you're the first—what did you say your species was?"

"I'm a Lepoid, from Teloon," said Thumper. "I guess we look like some kind of Old Earth animal called a rabbit. In basic, the sergeant called me things like *Bunnyears* and *Cottontail*. Do the sergeants here make fun of people and call them names?"

"Captain don't like that," said Gears. "People do it anyway, but if they get too nasty, they can get in trouble. Mostly it's just funnin' between friends."

Lieutenant Armstrong was more aloof than Gears—perhaps his confrontation with the hunting party had something to do with that. Still, the lieutenant's first reaction to Thumper had been a kind of shocked silence, and he had never really done much in the way of welcoming him to the company. Thumper wondered whether Armstrong was uncomfortable with nonhumans, though Gears's mentioning that legionnaires of several other races belonged to the company seemed to rule that out. Well, unless Armstrong was his immediate superior, that seemed unlikely to be a problem.

Thumper's train of thought came to an end as the hoverjeep crossed into the Legion camp and came to a stop. "Well, here we are," said Gears. He pointed toward a large woman sitting at a portable desk, shaded by an awning. "You'll need to report to First Sergeant Brandy, I guess—that's her over there. She'll tell you where to go and what to do."

"Thanks!" said Thumper, grabbing his duffel and jumping out of the hoverjeep.

"No problem, buddy," said the driver. "And good luck!" He started the jeep back up and headed off. Thumper shouldered his duffel and began walking toward Brandy. He still had no idea what Omega Company held in store for him, but he was about to find out. And this time, he was determined not to throw away his opportunities.

CHAPTER NINE

Journal #695

My employer's single stroke of genius was his perception that running his Legion company was in principle no different from running any other kind of business. Well, perhaps "genius" overstates the case, but certainly the discovery was something no one else in the military seems to have stumbled upon. This meant, among other things, identifying key personnel and making certain that their loyalty was secured by the most direct means.

I am quite certain that my employer would have been unable to parse the admonition "Thou shalt not muzzle the ox when he treadeth out the corn," let alone identify its source; but he showed a keen understanding of it in practice. This understanding was particularly evident in his handling of the Supply sergeant, one Chocolate Harry.

O O O

Chocolate Harry yawned and looked around his office. Somewhere or another he'd put a catalog of custom hovercycle parts, little things that might add the perfect finishing touch to his beloved Hawg. Where had he put it? He riffled through the top couple of inches of a stack of magazines and catalogues on his desk, then stood and went to one of the file cabinets. But the thought of dealing with the chaos he knew he'd find inside was almost enough to chill his enthusiasm. He kept meaning to set up his database engines to connect him to the major hovercycle supply houses, but it was too much like work …

His hand went halfway to the handle of the most likely drawer, then he drew it back. Before he ordered up any new parts, he really needed to give the Hawg a bit of a ride to see just how it was running. It'd been a few days—as good as Omega Company had been to him, he'd fallen in the habit of actually giving his job priority over his hobbies. The old Chocolate Harry would never have approved. But Captain Jester had made a very persuasive case for the advantages of taking care of Legion business—very tangible benefits, as it happened. And the captain had no qualms about letting the noncoms have all their traditional prerogatives … including the little rakeoffs Harry had become accustomed to.

Still, it *had* been a few days since he'd revved up the bike. It wasn't good for it to sit idle. Harry turned his gaze out the window, to the semiarid landscape beyond the Legion camp. It was a clear day, but not too hot, and there were miles of open territory out there, just begging for somebody to cruise through them at full throttle. Harry shrugged. "What the hell," he said, and touched a button on his wrist communicator. "Yo, Double-X! I'm taking a couple hours off," he said. "Gotta check out the Hawg, give it a real shakedown. Anything comes up, you can handle it—or make it wait until I'm back. Got it?"

"Sure 'nuff, C. H.," came the raspy voice of Harry's Supply assistant. "Got it covered. Have a good ride—see you in a couple."

Harry nodded. He knew he could trust Double-X not to mess up too seriously if something complicated came up in his absence. He pushed the starter button on the hover unit and listened critically as the antigrav units warmed up. Satisfied at the low purr, he mounted the bike and put on his helmet, then keyed the remote to open the Supply dump's delivery bay door. It slid noiselessly open. Harry edged the throttle up a notch, put the propulsion module into slow forward setting, and edged the Hawg out the doorway into the late-morning sunlight.

A few legionnaires waved to the Supply sergeant as he came into sight on the hovercycle. Chocolate Harry grinned and waved back, then rolled his left wrist slightly, revving the engine just enough to remind the onlookers of the Hawg's power. A quick motion of the right hand, and he was in gear, soaring off into the desert in search of whatever adventures awaited him. Well, to tell the truth, there weren't usually any adventures, but out in the open air, it felt as if the chances were a lot better than at his desk in the Supply depot.

At first Harry took a familiar path—a broad, level swath where he could push the hovercycle close to its top speed without worrying about obstacles. He leaned forward, lowering his profile as the Hawg cut into the dry wind, enjoying the speed for its own sake. Out of the corner of his eye he could spot small desert animals belatedly scurrying out of the way of this noisy intruder. He'd never seen any living thing much bigger than the palm of his hand—there *was* nothing larger than that in this part of the planet, according to the Zenobians.

He came to a halt on a low rise, where he wheeled the bike around to get a look back toward the camp. The landscape around the Legion base was flat enough that even a slight hillock gave a long view in all directions. Harry normally didn't spend a great deal of time admiring the view, however. In his opinion, the desert landscape was just so much worthless real estate. Not even the locals had much use for it—as evidenced by the fact that they'd given it to the Legion for a base.

This time, though, there was something new in the picture. In the middle distance, just south of the Legion base, there was a green canopy—a tent of some sort, Harry realized. It only took a moment for him to remember the scuttlebutt he'd heard from the command office. Captain Jester had finally found out that all the support he'd gotten from his buddies in the State Department came with a hefty price tag: namely, giving a party of big-time politicos the run of the planet for hunting. Harry could have told him it was going to cost— in fact, he'd be surprised if this was the only payback in the deal.

Of course, that was only part of the story. Visitors from off-planet wouldn't have all the stuff they needed to handle local conditions. Chocolate Harry was just sure they'd have to have all sorts of supplemental provisions and supplies. The right color camouflage to match the local landscape, for example. Harry had plenty of it. They'd probably want extra liquor, and ammo, and bait ... Harry was sure he could get hold of all that, too. Harry smiled. This could be the best opportunity to come his way since he'd cornered the market on purple antirobot cammy ...

He revved his engine and started off toward the distant tent.

O   O   O

Sushi found Flight Leftenant Qual with a crew of his fellow Zenobians, working with the large device that had been the focus of their attention for the last several days. Exactly what its purpose was, Sushi had never learned; he assumed the captain had some general notion what the thing did and why the Zenobians were setting it up in the middle of a Legion camp.

"How's everything going, Qual?" said Sushi, walking up to the group. "Good to see you today."

"Ah, Rawfish," said Qual, flashing the disconcerting smile that reminded everyone of his race's carnivorous proclivities, "The Sklern is obstinate today, but a tightening of the Zorn Modulator should resolve that issue. Or so one hopes. Mechanical onerosities can be recalcitrant, even with a good crew."

"I know what you mean," said Sushi, surprised even as he said it that he *did* follow the Zenobian's general drift. "In fact, that's sort of what I came to see you about."

"Ah, does your species have its own Sklerns?" The tip of Qual's tail began twitching. "We were not aware of it."

"Nope, we're Sklernless, far as I know," said Sushi. "It's one of our own machines I want to check out. Your auto-translator has been giving us some flaky output lately, and I wanted to see if we could recalibrate it."

"Flaking outpost?" Qual's eyes opened wider, and he stared at the miniature device hanging from a strap around his shoulder. "I have not seen any signs of it."

"Well, there you go," said Sushi, grinning. "That's just the kind of thing I was talking about. The translator usually adjusts itself automatically, but it's not necessarily perfect. In your case, you were the first of your species to get one, and there must have been some glitches because we didn't have any previous samples of your language. Anyway, it's been doing subtle mistranslations, probably in both directions, for quite a while now. That could be dangerous in an emergency. Best to catch it before anybody's life depends on it."

"Oh ho, I comprehend," said Qual. "To state the facts, I thought some of you humans were saying very strange things, but I attributed it to your extremely bizarre cultural attitudes. But if it is merely a mechanical delusion, correction would be a boon to both species. How do you intend to adjust the device?"

"Well, to do it right, I need some information on your language," said Sushi.

"Ah, I am but a simple air warrior," said Flight Leftenant Qual. "The subtleties of semantics are beyond me. Perhaps you need a certified scholar of language."

"Don't sell yourself short," said Sushi, breezily. "You've been speaking your native language since you were a kid ..."

"Not so," said Flight Leftenant Qual. "Our people do not acquire language until they are nearly grown, and each finds his own way. And some ways are very strange indeed. But the better a Zenobian speaks, the greater rights and duties that one can achieve. Chief Potentary Korg is the great power that he is because he is the most admired speaker on all the planet."

Sushi stared at Qual for a long moment, then shook his head. "If I didn't know you better, I'd think you were giving me the business. In fact, I'm still not sure you're not trying to pull the insulated fabric over my eyes."

"It is a verity," said Qual, and the other Zenobians working with him, who had followed the conversation with apparent interest, flipped their tails from side to side—a gesture that the legionnaires had learned meant the same to the Zenobians as a nod to humans. "Perhaps your translator problems arise from this feature of our language."

"It sounds like a good recipe for problems," said Sushi. "Do you mean that everyone speaks completely differently?"

"Oh, not completely so," said Qual. "Careful guardians will expose the adolescents in their charge to the most admired speakers, hoping to influence their mode of speech. It works, to some degree. I myself was made to listen to the speeches of Korg's predecessor, Grand Potentary Zarf. I believe that was a large factor in my rising to officer rank so quickly."

"Amazing," said Sushi, shaking his head. "So how do messages that have to reach a lot of people get sent? Do you have some kind of common language that everybody understands?"

"Oh, yes," said Qual. "But it is curious that you ask, Rawfish. That is a language that everyone knows, but no one speaks."

"What the ...?" Sushi frowned. "If nobody speaks it, how can you communicate in it?"

"Very easy," said Qual, and the other Zenobians again flipped their tails. "It is a language for the eyes only, which we use to record knowledge that everyone must know. However a Zenobian speaks, he will have learned the written language first."

"Wow," said Sushi. "That's exactly the reverse of how humans do it—and, as far as I know, all the other species in the Alliance, too. Let me get this straight—you're telling me that the written language has no spoken equivalent?"

"Oh, no, that is the beauty of it," said Qual. "It has as many equivalents as there are different ways of speaking. Every Zenobian knows the meaning of a written message, but the way of rendering it into sound is left to the speaker's own choice. A matter of taste, I think you humans call it."

"Uh-huh," said Sushi. "Excuse me, Qual, but this has just boggled my mind. I'm going to go think about it over a drink or two, and see whether I can make any sense of it. Do you mind if I come back later and ask you some more questions?"

"Oh, no," said Qual. "It is invariably an amusement to talk to you, Rawfish."

"Thanks, I think," said Sushi, and he wandered off in search of his coworkers on the Zenobian language project. He already had a good idea where to find them ...

O   O   O

"All right, how does it look now?" said Ernie. He stepped out into the center of the little hotel room so Lola could inspect him. She stood with her hands on her hips, inspecting the dress suit he wore. "You still look more like an out-of-shape bouncer than a high-stakes player," she muttered. "To tell the truth, I don't think it's the suit that's the problem—it's you."

"Hey, I *am* an out-of-shape bouncer," Ernie said brightly. "It's been a few years since I worked the door anywhere, but don't go taking me for granted—I'm in better shape than it looks like, baby. You oughta know that ..."

"It's not what I know that matters, it's what Victor Phule and his bodyguards think," said Lola, frowning. "If they knew what I know, they wouldn't even let you in the casino—forget about striking up a casual conversation with a gazillionaire. We're stuck with trying to make you look like somebody respectable. Are you sure you can't shave any closer?"

"Not unless you want my face to look like the insides of a watermelon," said Ernie. "Hey, why don't you just put a dress on me and try to pass me off for a cocktail waitress? Maybe he'll go for that one ..."

"Yeah, you're right. I'm stuck with the raw material I've got," said Lola. "Besides, this *is* Lorelei. He can't expect all the people he meets—even the rich ones—to be from his own social class. I wonder if he'd believe you as a construction magnate, self-made from the ground up?"

"Forget it," said Ernie, impatiently. "You wanted an actor, you should've hired somebody off a tri-vee stage. Now, do you have any other improvements on the scam, or are we goin' to get any real work done today?"

Lola threw up her hands. "Oh, the hell with it," she said. "You're right—we're not going to get anywhere if I spend all my time trying to get your act perfect. You'll go over to the casino, talk up Victor Phule, and see if you can figure out what he's up to—if anything at all. Keep an eye out for his son—he's the one they're paying us to snatch—and make sure the Legion guards don't get too suspicious. I may need you to go back there again, and I can't do that if they throw you out of the place as an unsavory character."

"Yeah, yeah, and I won't scratch my ass in front of the marks, neither," said Ernie, sullenly.

"I'd settle for your using civilized grammar," said Lola. She shook her head, then relaxed, and said, "All right, then. Try not to lose all your money, you big dumbbell. And call if you're going to be later than midnight getting back."

"Ah, the old guy prob'ly ain't even up that late," said Ernie. Then he grinned, and said, "I'll call, though. Wish me luck!"

"You'll need all you can get, you goofball," said Lola, and gave him a punch on the biceps. Ernie just grinned more broadly, and ambled out the door toward the bus line that would take him to the Fat Chance Casino. Lola watched the door close, then shrugged and went over to her computer. She couldn't do much about Ernie's part of the job besides sit and worry, but she could get to work on other parts of the plan. She sat down and began working. Before long, she'd even forgotten that she ought to be worried about Ernie.

O O O

Chocolate Harry's hovercycle coasted down the slight incline into the camp and came to a halt outside the largest tent. There was nobody in sight.

"Hey, hey!" called the Supply sergeant. "Anybody home? The man you need to see is here to be seen. You want it, I got it—c'mon out and let's talk turkey."

A bleary-eyed face appeared between the flaps of the tent. "Who the hell are you?" it said, staring at Harry's considerable bulk and his black Legion uniform.

"Chocolate Harry—*Sergeant* Chocolate Harry, of Omega Company. The man in charge of supplies—which on this planet, means the main man you need to know. You the dude that's buyin' for this outfit?"

The face came out in front of the tent, accompanied by a beer-bellied body. The man looked around as if to make sure the two were alone, then said in a quiet voice, "Not for the whole outfit, but maybe for myself. I'd be interested in some military-grade guns and ammo—something that can knock over some of the big critters I hear tell they have on this planet."

"Knock 'em over?" said Chocolate Harry, rubbing his hands together. "No sweat, buddy—I can sell you the same weapon the locals use. *Guaranteed* to coldcock anything that walks, runs, swims, or flies. How many you gonna want?"

"Just enough for me," said the fellow, lowering his voice even further. "One, with the ammo—enough for a couple weeks' hunting. Can you do it?"

"Like I said, no sweat," said the Supply sergeant. He wondered briefly why a hunting party would come to a distant world without the weapons it needed to do the job. Did they come from one of the worlds where private ownership of arms was banned? "Say, it ain't any of my business," he said, "but it's kinda funny you'd come all this way without any guns."

"Oh, hell, we got lots of guns," said the hunter. "I'd jes' like to get somethin' a little bit better than store-bought—for myself, anyway. If the other boys want to get their own, that's their lookout."

Chocolate Harry wasn't quite convinced; what if they'd come to a world without a conveniently corrupt Legion Supply sergeant? Would this fellow have settled for the "store-bought"? Or was he trying to obtain the military weapons for some purpose other than hunting? Then he shrugged it off—it really wasn't his business. If there was money to be had, that was all he cared about. He smiled, and said, "It'll run you fifteen hundred bucks, though. And you gotta keep quiet about it—this is Legion issue, top secret stuff. Word gets out I sold it to you, both our asses are gonna be in the cooler for a *lo-o-ong* time."

"Price isn't a problem," said the fellow. "By the way, Sarge, the name's L.P. Asho. And you don't have to worry about me passin' along any secrets. I do lots of big government contracts, so I know how to zip the lip. I'd hope you'll do the same for me—I get the idea your boss don't like us playin' with guns."

"He's the *last* dude I'm gonna tell, believe you me, Asho," said Chocolate Harry. "Now, guns ain't the only thing I can put in your hands. You folks need any fancy food or drinks? I got real Galactic Bohemian from New Baltimore, in the bottle or in the keg. Or I got genuine scotch whisky from Aldebaran IV—they even got sheep to pee in the water, give it the Old Earth flavor. Or maybe you boys need some pills ..."

"Naah, we brought all that kind of stuff with us," said L.P. Asho. "Maybe if we run low—good to know there's a local source for the better things in life. But say—you wouldn't know where I can find a good poker game, would you? The other boys can't play worth a damn, and I wouldn't mind that so much if they didn't *know* they can't play, which means they *don't* play—unless it's for the kind of money I throw the guy who opens a door for me in a fancy restaurant. And that ain't hardly poker at all, in my DB. A fella likes a little real action, where's he s'posed to go on this planet?"

Chocolate Harry rubbed his chin. "Gee, I dunno. Most of the guys in Omega Company don't have those kind of bucks, either," he said. "We do have a little game every now and then, if you're looking for some action. Not a lot of money, y'understand—the Legion doesn't pay all *that* much, not even to fellows like me who've been pulling our weight for a good long while. But if you and your buddies are interested in something a little livelier, maybe we could get a few of the guys to show up for a five-buck ante ..."

"That's the kind of stuff I like," said Asho. "What do y'all play?"

"Dealer's choice," said Harry. "Mostly pretty tame stuff like Anaconda or Hold 'Em. Every now and then something a bit funkier, like Aldebaran, or Texas Chainsaw ..."

"So if a fella came in with a different game he didn't mind explainin' the rules, you wouldn't have a problem with that?"

"Oh, no, not at all," said Chocolate Harry, grinning. "Why don't I see how many of the boys I can scare up. Would tomorrow night be cool?"

"Very cool," said L.P. Asho, with a predatory grin. Chocolate Harry grinned right back at him, then revved the hovercycle and roared back toward the Legion base.

After a few moments, Euston O'Better came out of one of the tents. "What the hell was that noise?" he asked.

"Legion sergeant invitin' us to play poker," said Asho.

"Poker?" O'Better frowned. "Hey, I came here for the hunting, not cards."

"Sonny, this is the best kind of hunting there is," said Asho. "Sucker hunting—and I think I just found me a big one." He rubbed his hands together and smiled—a very nasty smile.

O O O

First Sergeant Brandy hadn't seen the AEIOU team arrive, nor had she watched the hunters' shuttle landing, out in the desert. She'd been too busy with her squad of new legionnaires—none of them raw recruits anymore, but most of them still unseasoned, by her lights. This morning's training exercise had gone all haywire, and now she had to figure out how to make it work tomorrow morning. It had started out simply enough: she'd broken the squad into two groups, then sent one of them into the desert to prepare an ambush and, after a decent interval, sent the other to try to find them without falling into the ambush. The spirit of competition should have spurred them to do their best, and in the process, both groups should have learned a good bit about the terrain around the camp and how to operate in it.

Except the first group had gotten lost right away, in spite of its maps and instruments. That wouldn't have been all that bad, if they'd just chosen a more or less suitable site, set up some kind of position, and waited to ambush the second team when it came to find them. No such chance. Instead, Roadkill had gotten into a discussion with Brick about which way they were originally supposed to go, and most of the rest of the squad had taken sides with one or the other. Meanwhile, the other squad, which admittedly had the somewhat tougher job of finding the first, got itself lost even more thoroughly than the first. When Brandy had finally gotten annoyed and sent out a search party, she'd found the second team trudging through the desert—in an almost perfect circle around the first party.

In fact, the only thing both squads had done according to orders was to maintain comm silence so as not to alert the "opponents" of their position. And, since nobody had kept an eye on the emergency comm frequency, both groups were utterly unaware that Brandy had been trying to recall them for several hours before she'd given up and sent out the search party. Which, to her utter annoyance, had promptly gotten *itself* lost. It had taken most of the afternoon to finally get everybody found and back on base—luckily with no injuries worse than sunburn. And all this while the captain was entertaining the AEIOU team, which was snooping around the base looking for reasons to find Omega Company guilty of environmental offenses (with Barky ready to attack suspected polluters), *and* while trying to keep the AEIOU team from noticing the party of bigwig big-game hunters that had landed just south of camp and apparently insisted on instant VIP treatment. All this was enough to turn Brandy's mind, yet again, toward the prospect of an early retirement … and maybe, this time, Captain Jester wouldn't manage to sweet-talk her out of it.

So Brandy wasn't really paying attention when an unfamiliar sophont in a Legion uniform came up to her, dropped a duffel bag, came to attention, and saluted. "Legionnaire Thumper reporting for duty, Sergeant!" it said.

Brandy looked up from the Training Progress Report she'd been in the process of deciding how to fill out. The new arrival was about a meter and a half tall, dressed in regulation Legion black (although a good bit less stylish than the standard Omega Mob version of the uniform), and had long ears, big eyes, and a ridiculously cute wiggly pink nose. She stared for a moment, then blurted out, "Where the hell did you come from?"

The legionnaire looked puzzled. "Uh, do you mean originally, Sergeant, or just now?" Its voice was high and squeaky, though not unpleasant. And it didn't use a translator.

Brandy shook her head. "Radicate that," she said. She thought back a second and retrieved the new legionnaire's name from memory. "Thumper, what I mean is, what are you doing here? Nobody told us there were any new troops coming."

"Sergeant, as far as I know I'm the only new member sent to this company," said Thumper. "I came with the hunting party that just landed. I understand they owed someone important a favor …"

"Huh," said Brandy. "And that meant giving you a ride. What makes you important enough to get a trip on a civilian space yacht?"

"Uh, I think it's because I got in trouble with a general," said Thumper. He went on to tell a complex, but predictable story of showing up his buddies in basic training and being made the scapegoat for a practical joke on General Blitzkrieg. At the end, he said, "But I think maybe somebody thinks I'm all right, after all—my drill instructor said Omega Company is really one of the best in the Legion."

"*The* best, Legionnaire," said Brandy, proudly. She set her paperwork aside and stood up. "You are now a member of *the* best company in the Space Legion, and you better not forget it. But why don't you pick up that bag and follow me? I know where there's a vacant bunk. Then we can start showing you how things work in Omega. We do things a little differently around here ..." She stalked off toward an entrance to the modular base, with the new recruit close behind her. Hope sprang eternal. Maybe this one would be able to go out in the desert without getting lost ...

O   O   O

Sushi toyed with his drink, then said, "Have you ever seen written Chinese?"

"Can't say that I have, son," said Rev. "Thought that was some kind of food, to tell you the truth."

Sushi managed not to roll his eyes. "The Chinese were an Old Earth people who spoke like seven or eight different languages," he said. "Mandarin, Cantonese, a bunch of others you don't need to know the names of ..."

"Why not?" said Do-Wop, with an evil grin. "I bet you don't even know 'em all."

Sushi shot Do-Wop a withering glance. "Will you give a guy a break when he's trying to explain something? I think you've been hanging out with Mahatma."

"Hey, you know me, Soosh," said Do-Wop. "Ever eager for knowledge ..."

"Yeah, because you've got none of it to spare," answered Sushi.

"All right, fellas, you're strayin' from the point," said Rev, raising his palm to stop them. "What were you sayin', Sushi?"

"Anyhow, they spoke all these languages, and speaking one didn't give you more than a guess at understanding the others. But they were all *written* the same way. The written symbols represented the meaning of the words, not their sound, so a Mandarin speaker could pretty much read a document written by a Cantonese speaker, even if he couldn't understand the spoken language. It's sort of the opposite of the old-time European languages, where a reader could get a rough idea how a message in another language would sound, even if he didn't know what it means."

"Weird," said Do-Wop. "Why'd they do a stupid thing like that, Soosh?"

"Actually, it's not that stupid if you have a big empire with several different spoken languages," said Sushi, shrugging. "That gives you two choices—either make everybody learn one common spoken language, the way the Romans did, or have one common written language, the Chinese way."

"You left one out," said Do-Wop. "Autotranslators. You don't even need to have the same kind of ears for them to work ..."

"Sure, except the ancient Romans and Chinese didn't have autotranslators," said Sushi.

"You're jivin' me, Soosh," said Do-Wop. "The Romans had *everything,* man. They were like Italians, only with a better army and space force ..."

Sushi rolled his eyes. "I hate to tell you this, but the Romans didn't have a space force, either ..."

"*What?*" Do-Wop's mouth fell open. "*Fangul',* Soosh, you can't tell me that shit with a straight face ..."

Rev raised his hands. "Gen'lemen, gen'lemen," he said, in a calming tone of voice. "We're strayin' off the point again. Sushi, you were tellin' us about how the Zenobians write, weren't you? I'd surely like to hear more about that."

"All right, here's the deal," said Sushi. "From what Qual said, it seems as if the Zenobians learn to read before they learn to speak. They're descended from predators—well, in a sense, they still are predators. So the young ones depend on their vision more than most other sophonts. Well, maybe the Gambolts would be similar … I don't know much about their language, either, except the translator works for *them*?"

"All right," said Rev. "So the Zenobians learn to read first. I reckon that would mean the written language ought to be pretty easy to understand, then."

"You'd think so," said Sushi, nodding. He took another pull on his beer. "But that brings me back to Chinese. I've heard people say that Chinese is actually very easy to read—that all you have to do is look at the writing as pictures, and when you see what the pictures are, you know what the writing says."

"Why, that's perfect," said Rev. "So we ought to be able to read Zenobian even without a translator."

"Yeah, sounds great, doesn't it?" said Sushi. "Except it doesn't work quite that way. The pictures are too sketchy—four lines sort of in a box might be a house, or a dog …"

"Sounds like they couldn't draw very good," said Do-Wop. "Hell, even I can draw a house and a dog so they look different, and I ain't no Michael Angelo."

"Michael Angelo? Who's that?" said Rev.

"Italian artist, best there was," said Do-Wop. "He laid on his back for twenty-five years, painting fiascos on the ceiling of some big church …"

Whatever else Do-Wop might have had to say about Michelangelo, he was prevented by Sushi spraying a fine mist of beer out of his mouth as he fell out of his seat, laughing uncontrollably.

CHAPTER TEN

Journal #703

T aking the visiting *AEIOU* inspectors on a tour of the Legion base was an operation that required a great deal of delicacy. My employer took every effort to ensure that the visitors were shown everything that might show the company in the greenest possible light, and as little as possible that might reflect discredit upon its environmental practices. After letting Lieutenant Rembrandt steer the inspectors through the less sensitive areas of the compound, the captain himself joined them to show off the more highly technological departments. This was where, in his opinion, his influx of his own funds had had the greatest effect in improving the company's performance. He didn't necessarily reckon on the inspectors' believing otherwise.

O O O

"And this is our comm center" said Phule, showing the AEIOU inspection team through the doorway. "All official communications, and most unofficial ones, come through here."

"How much energy does it use?" asked Inspector Slurry, eyeing the large panel of readouts above Mother's console.

"Less than you'd think," said Phule. "In a military field base, we have to be prepared to operate in emergency conditions. One of the first things an attacker is going to try to hit is the power supply. So in a pinch, we have to be able to run our entire system on the power we can produce ourselves. That puts the premium on efficiency."

"Efficiency is a relative term," said Inspector Gardner. "It tends to vary depending on what the person using the word is trying to sell you. Just how much power do these systems use in a normal day's activities?"

Phule paused just a second before answering. "Our exact power requirements are classified, but I think it's safe enough to tell you that we can run the entire base indefinitely on solar energy, which of course there's plenty of out here in the desert. And there are backup systems in case we get a run of bad weather, natural or otherwise. Again, you'll have to pardon me for not giving details."

"Well, solar is acceptably green, for the most part," said Chief Inspector Snieff. "I do want to find out about these backup systems, though. I'll have you know that I have made a study of most of the ways one can generate and store power, and the majority of them are very suspect, environmentally. I would hate to think …"

Whatever Snieff would have hated to think, her revelation was interrupted by a loud exclamation from Barky, the Environmental Dog, who had wandered through the comm center, sniffing the equipment and eyeing the personnel, and had finally found his way to the door of the officers' lounge. There he had halted, staring inside the door and growling, which no one had quite noticed until he let loose with a series of loud barks.

"What in space …?" said Phule. He strode over to the door and looked inside to see what had caused the dog's reaction. There, to his surprise, stood Tusk-anini, on top of a chair, his head scraping the ceiling. The Volton was scowling down his long snout at the Environmental Dog. "Uh-oh," said Phule.

"Tell famous doggy would be most healthy for him to stay distant," said Tusk-anini calmly, but emphatically. "I no want to be hurting little Earth animal. But I tell you now—doggy tries to bite, Tusk-anini doing what he needing to do."

"Barky!" said Inspector Gardner. "Come on, fella—leave the nice sophont alone. He can't help it if he smells …"

"Tusk-anini no smell," said the Volton. "*Doggy* smell. Tusk-anini *stink.*"

"Now, let's not take things too literally," said Phule, stepping gingerly between Tusk-anini and Barky, now apparently pacified. Inspector Gardner was down on one knee beside the dog, scratching him between the shoulder blades and holding lightly on to his collar. "Would it be fair to say that Barky's nose is perhaps a little too sensitive, Inspector Snieff?"

The AEIOU inspector sniffed. "Barky is a genetically enhanced ultracanine, highly trained to discern the smells of pollution and other assaults on the environment. If some of the sophonts in your company carry odors like those of common pollutants, it may be no surprise that he reacts to them with hostility. Would it be fair to say that perhaps some of your legionnaires need to bathe more frequently, Captain Jester?"

"Begging your pardon, Chief Inspector, I seriously doubt that is the problem," said Beeker. "If I may be permitted to say so, I can testify, based on personal observation, that the bathing facilities on this post would be the pride of many private athletic clubs."

"Maybe," said Inspector Slurry. "Probably waste water, too."

"I think I can respond to that," said Phule, grinning. "This base module is about as water-efficient as you can contrive, Inspector. A military unit in an arid environment can't afford to take water for granted. We recover, reuse, recycle, and recondition every possible drop of water. In fact, about the only way we could do better would be to capture the perspiration of our legionnaires working outside the base. And if we really needed to do that, I suspect we could find a way to do it ..."

"Undoubtedly by throwing even more money at it," said Snieff. "Have you ever sat down and calculated how many resources your company requires to maintain this exorbitant lifestyle?"

"Oh, yes," said Phule. "I think you'd find the figures very interesting. If you compare us to units of similar size, on similar missions, you'll find that Omega Company actually has a significantly less negative impact on the environment than a typical military operation. Granted, I've solved a lot of our problems by spending money—but it's *my* money I'm spending, not the government's, and I make very sure I get what I'm paying for."

"Never minding money," said Tusk-anini. "Why don't you taking Barky dog away so Tusk-anini can finish reading book? Am halfway through Old Earth classic and want to know how it comes out." He pointed to the thick volume on the floor. The spine of the book displayed the curious word, *Dhalgren*.

"Woof!" said Barky, the Environmental Dog, sniffing the book, but then Inspector Gardner clapped his hands, and a few moments later, the Environmental Dog and all the other visitors left the Officers' Lounge to Tusk-anini. With a snort of relief, the Volton stepped off the table and picked up his book. He wasn't quite sure where the story was leading, but on the whole it wasn't any stranger than most of the other human literature he'd read.

Which, he thought as he settled down, wasn't saying very much ...

O   O   O

The Fat Chance Casino was crowded as Ernie made his way through the gaming rooms. No surprise there; according to the local newstaper, several large space liners had just made their regular stopovers at Lorelei, and the travel-weary passengers were eagerly getting what they'd come for: first-class dining, lavish entertainment, and high-stakes gambling. The sight of all the expensively dressed suckers with fat credit accounts made Ernie's mouth water. It was every grifter's dream, and there were plenty of grifters willing to take advantage of it. Except in the Fat Chance Casino, where Captain Jester had ordered his security forces to clamp down on anything that might cut into the players' enjoyment—or the house's percentage.

He stopped at the bar and ordered a drink—a tall glass of quinine water with a twist of lime. No alcohol tonight; that had been another of his promises to Lola. Instead, he'd brought along an Aromacap: a tiny capsule filled with an aromatic oil that, rubbed on the skin, conveyed the exact odor of an expensive brand of imported gin. If the marks—or casino security—thought he'd been drinking heavily, they were likely to underestimate him. Better yet, as long as he stuck to Aldebaran Amber Gin, Ernie had a fair chance of convincing Lola that he'd been using the Aromacap instead of knocking back a few G'n'T's while he was supposed to be working. But this time, Ernie had promised Lola to stay straight. More importantly, he'd promised not to do anything that might draw the attention of security—either the casino's or Victor Phule's very professional bodyguard. That meant resisting the temptation to pocket any loose change that might be lying around, such as waiters' uncollected tips or customers' unattended handbags. And it meant not carrying any of a number of devices meant to increase the odds in his favor, devices generally frowned upon both by the casinos and by those players who were naive enough to expect that everyone else in the game was playing by the rules. Especially in the Fat Chance, the ownership took exception to such devices—and its guards seemed to have a better-than-average record at spotting them in use.

In most places, he'd have taken his chances and figured on tipping the security guards to turn a blind eye. But the Fat Chance Casino's policy was to expel any cheaters it caught not just from the casino, but from Lorelei itself—and its guards were apparently tip-proof. If Ernie and Lola were identified as cheats, their chances of completing the mission that brought them here shrank very close to zero—as did their chances of convincing a certain Mr. V to let them keep breathing. That was good enough to convince Ernie to keep his hands to himself and leave his educated dice at home.

His specific mission tonight was to find either of the Phules, Willard (A.K.A. Captain Jester) or his father Victor. In principle, that was a no-brainer. He knew what both men looked like and had a fair idea where, in the public parts of the casino, they might be found this time of day. In practice, as his previous experience with the younger Phule had taught him, the job was far from easy.

On their previous visit to Lorelei, Ernie and Lola had laid a subtle trap to kidnap the captain of Omega Company, and on the space liner away from Lorelei Station, found themselves in custody of an Andromatic robot whose features were a dead ringer for Captain Jester's. The situation had fallen entirely apart when the robot had commandeered an escape pod and left the space liner entirely. Luckily, nobody on board ship had managed to connect them to the incident, or else (in addition to their other troubles) they might now be trying to figure out how to come up with the replacement value of a deep-space escape pod.

Ernie had no idea whether the robot had been recovered or replaced; certainly the Phules could afford to do either. But barring information to the contrary, he and Lola agreed that any Phule they encountered had to be considered a possible robot. Since their contract had said nothing about robots—since, in fact, Mr. V had been emphatically uninterested in hearing about their misadventures—the two kidnappers needed to be sure they were getting the real thing. And with a high-priced bodyguard standing nearby, an experimental poke or pinch to determine the subject's reaction would *not* be a good idea.

Ernie drifted nonchalantly through the casino, stopping to look at the play at a table here or there, occasionally placing a small bet on a whim. If anyone were watching, they were likely to check him off as a bored dilettante, with no fixed purpose. But he gradually made his way toward the higher-priced rooms, where his quarry was likely to be playing, or watching the action. What would happen when he found one of the Phules remained to be seen. But he'd think of something, he was sure. He could always think of something.

O O O

"Well, I believe you've seen our whole camp," Phule said to the AEIOU inspectors. "I can see it's getting close to dinnertime; could I persuade you to stay for a taste of Omega Company's cooking? I think Sergeant Escrima is as fine a chef as you'll find in this arm of the Galaxy …"

"Is the food organic?" asked Slurry, a dubious expression on his face. "We absolutely insist on that."

"I believe you can take it for granted that Sergeant Escrima's offerings fulfill that requirement," said Beeker, his chin inching upward. "In fact, it is all but impossible to obtain nutrition from inorganic substances."

"The Nanoids seem to do just fine with sand," said Phule, grinning. "But I think you're missing the point, Beeks." He turned back to the AEIOU team. "In fact, Escrima insists on only the freshest and purest ingredients—I ought to know, since I'm the one paying for them. And he prides himself on being able to supply a satisfying meal to anyone who walks into the mess hall. At the moment, he's responsible for feeding members of at least five different species and I don't know how many ethnicities. So I'm sure you'll find a wide selection of dishes that meet your requirements—unless you insist on your food being bland or overcooked, in which case he'll probably come after you with a red-hot skewer. Would you like to join us?"

Inspector Gardner chuckled. "I've been eating camp food for long enough that I'm tempted to take you up on it. Unless your chef's an even worse terror than you say ..."

"You may be certain he's a terror, sir," said Beeker. "But I'd advise you to take up the captain's invitation nonetheless. The food is the best on the planet."

"Given the alternatives, I'd be very surprised if it weren't," said Gardner. "Even so, I'd love to join you. But I can only speak for myself. Chief, do you think we can eat here, or do we need to go back to our own camp?"

"Eating here would help conserve our own food supplies," added Slurry. "And it would give us a chance to evaluate the Legion's energy efficiency and waste management procedures."

"You shouldn't judge the Legion as a whole by us," said Lieutenant Rembrandt, earnestly. "To be as clean and green as we are, you have to have a CO who cares about something besides kowtowing to the top brass. Most Legion companies spend so much time trying to avoid getting on the wrong side of headquarters that they can barely achieve their basic mission, let alone worry about the environment."

"Thank you, Lieutenant," said Chief Inspector Snieff. "But I believe I'm going to make my own decision on this company's environmental practices rather than accept the testimony of an undoubtedly biased party. Granted, I haven't found any blatant destruction of vital habitats, or flagrant pollution of the environment—*so far*. The lack of evidence doesn't mean this company isn't guilty."

"What a convenient system," said Beeker. "Guilty until proven innocent—it must save you ever so much trouble."

"We nearly destroyed Old Earth by giving the anti-environment forces too many loopholes," retorted Snieff. "The AEIOU has sworn never to let that happen again."

"Perhaps you should consult the local inhabitants before you make your decision," said Rembrandt. "The captain has worked very closely with the Zenobians to minimize the impact of this base on their planet. If they're satisfied, why is it your concern?"

"Locals can be very shortsighted," said Slurry. "It's our business to think of the long term."

"Well, at the moment, I'm not thinking any farther ahead than dinner," said Phule, stepping forward to cut off any reply from his officers. "If you all want to join me, now's your chance—and I cannot only promise you the best food on the planet, but one of the best meals you'll ever eat."

Gardner and Slurry both looked at Snieff, but apprehension was clear on their faces as their chief wrinkled her brow, trying to decide. Some of the legionnaires who'd overheard the discussion shook their heads, or grinned ruefully. Escrima's cooking had spoiled them for the kind of rations the AEIOU contingent had undoubtedly brought with them to Zenobia. The inspectors would be sorry if they missed it—but they'd be even sorrier if they accepted the invitation, and then had to go back to their own cooking.

At last, Chief Inspector Snieff shrugged, and said, "Very well, Captain, we'll dine with you tonight. It's late enough that by the time we returned to camp we'd be behind schedule for our meal. I suppose we will simply have to trust this Legion cook to make us something moderately healthy and not too extravagant."

"I think you can trust Escrima for that," said Phule, with a knowing smile. "Come with me!" And he turned and led the AEIOU inspectors toward the mess hall.

O O O

Mess Sergeant Escrima, undisputed ruler of Omega Company's kitchens and dining hall, hadn't been told to expect company for dinner, but that didn't matter. Every meal that came out of his kitchen was a special occasion, as far as he was concerned. And when he learned that the visitors were humans, he shrugged. For someone who regularly cooked for Synthians, Gambolts, and a Volton, that was no challenge at all.

Sure enough, the captain's guests had found plenty to put on their plates as they went through the line. One of the AEIOU inspectors, a severe-looking woman, restricted herself to plainly cooked vegetables and rice; Escrima, watching from behind the counters, thought she could use a little fattening up, but kept his opinion to himself. If she didn't appreciate his sauces and meat dishes, she wasn't worth talking to, anyway, he thought. As long as she didn't say anything, he'd leave her alone.

The others took a wider sampling of the cuisine, and seemed excited to find so many tasty choices in what they must have expected to be a typical military mess. That made Escrima feel better; he always enjoyed surprising visitors who thought that institutional food was required by some cosmic law to consist of subpar ingredients, unimaginative recipes, and bad cookery.

Even Barky, the Environmental Dog, was relatively easy to please. An interplanetary tri-vee star could have gotten away with being much more temperamental—even ace reporter Jennie Higgins had been known to get picky about her dinner selection— but the legionnaires of Omega Company (at least the ones who dared get close to his teeth) oohed and ahhed to see such a famous animal in their midst. And so, with a good dose of fan appreciation as appetizer, the ever-environmentally aware Barky settled right down with a medium-rare prime vege-rib and seemed as happy as a clam in unpolluted water. Escrima grinned. Most cooks—even the specialists in vegetarian cuisine—had a tough time making vege-beef taste like anything but recycled cardboard (which it mostly was), and then only by disguising it with enough marinade and sauces to swamp a space liner. Only a genius like Escrima could serve it up plain and make it not just edible but delicious.

He'd been more worried by another variation from the normal routine tonight—the unannounced arrival of a new legionnaire of a species not previously represented in Omega Company. Escrima pulled down his trusty copy of *The Practical Chef's Encyclopedia of Culinary Preferences and Nutritional Requirements of Sophonts Around the Alliance* and looked up the entry on the new arrival. It'd be just his luck to be short of some nonsynthesizable nutrient the Lepoids required, with no way to get it but express delivery at exorbitant prices. And since the entire expense would be to feed just one legionnaire, some bean-counter in headquarters was likely to gripe at the expense. That was tough luck, as far as Escrima was concerned. They should have thought about that before they'd sent a Lepoid legionnaire to Zenobia. His job was to feed 'em, and screw anybody who didn't like the expense.

But after flipping through several cross-references and charts of substitutions, scowling as he matched the names of the exotic ingredients with their common equivalents, Sergeant Escrima sat back and smiled. Feeding the new guy was going to be a piece of cake, after all. Carrot cake, to be exact.

O   O   O

Thumper's introduction to Omega Company was progressing at whirlwind speed. In the short time he'd been at the company's Zenobia Base, he'd already met the first sergeant, who'd shown him to a comfortable barracks room and explained how Omega Company did things. He was going to be paired with one of the other legionnaires on base, not just as a roommate, but as a partner. This was one of Captain Jester's innovations, though Thumper didn't quite understand the reason for it. But eventually he'd get it, he knew. He was a smart Lepoid, and had the grades in school to prove it. Things hadn't gone quite so well in basic training, but that had been his first exposure to mass human psychology. Now he had a better idea what was going on. Or so he thought ...

The mess hall was open for the evening meal beginning at 1700 hours, the same as in basic. Here, though, the legionnaires apparently had the option of going to eat at any time between then and 2030, instead of being assigned a set (and usually too short) time slot during which they had to report for their meal. Having had his last meal just before the human hunters' shuttle landed on

Zenobia, Thumper was starved. He finished stowing his gear, washed his paws and combed his whiskers, and stepped out into the corridor, hoping the mess hall was close by—and easy to find.

It was. At the end of the short corridor leading to his barracks room, Thumper turned left and almost immediately saw the double doors of the mess hall in front of him. There was a small group of legionnaires standing around chatting just outside the doors, while a stream of their comrades walked through. Not really knowing anyone yet, Thumper stepped past them and took a tray. He was unavoidably conscious that the conversation in the group behind him had stopped just after he had passed, then resumed in a lower tone.

It didn't take a genius to figure out what had caused it. *New guy,* they were undoubtedly saying. *New guy.* Well, he *was* a new guy, here at least. Before long, he'd get a chance to show them just what kind of guy he was. And if he'd learned anything from his last talk with Sergeant Pitbull, he thought they'd be glad to have him on board. Meanwhile, his stomach reminded him, he hadn't eaten in hours.

There was a food service line ahead of him, with absolutely wonderful aromas wafting out to the nostrils of the waiting legionnaires. Thumper stepped into line and took one of the trays—which, he was surprised to see, was not the ugly standard-issue plastic that everyone in Legion basic had used. Instead, these trays came in a variety of pastel shades with geometrical designs that might actually enhance the user's enjoyment of eating. Even more surprising, they all managed to be attractively clean, rather than unappealingly sterile. Thumper hadn't been in the Legion very long, but he already knew enough to recognize that this wasn't typical of mess halls.

He stepped into line behind a tall legionnaire—almost all of them were a lot taller than he was, but he was used to that, too—and peered over the edge of the counter at the food. There was a selection of raw vegetables, the kind the humans called "salad." He took a large helping of that, and an equal amount of cooked greens—which, for the first time since he'd joined the Legion, weren't boiled beyond recognition. He wondered how Omega Company got enough fresh vegetables to supply the mess hall; he hadn't noticed a garden patch on his way into the base. But that didn't mean there wasn't one away from the route he'd traveled. It was just a real treat to see fresh veggies once again. It almost felt like home.

Best of all, there was no sergeant standing there to tell him what to take, or how much, either. Omega Company apparently let its legionnaires eat whatever they wanted. That was a really triff idea, thought Thumper. He couldn't remember a time when there wasn't somebody telling him what to eat, beginning with his mother. He was ready for a change.

He looked around the room for a place to sit—he'd only met a couple of members of the company so far, so he had nobody in particular to look for. Plenty of tables had empty seats, so he had his choice of dinner companions. Then he caught a whiff of something he hadn't in his fondest dreams expected to find this far away from home. *Carrot cake*—his favorite dessert!

Thumper followed the delicious aroma to its source, a serving station piled high with desserts of all kinds. He recognized some of them as distant relations of the offerings in the mess hall back in basic training—obviously far more palatable, even to his nonhuman taste buds. But it was the carrot cake that he craved, that promised his taste buds all the delights of home.

He was so intrigued by the aroma that he didn't even notice when the trouble started.

O O O

"Well, boys, it looks like we're not makin' a whole heap o' progress with this," said Rev, setting down his glass. "I reckon we ought to call a halt and go get some food in our bellies."

Do-Wop knocked back his half-full glass of beer and set it down with a wistful look. "If you say so, man," he said. "Hey, I was just gettin' started. But a little chow don't sound so bad, when you come right down to it."

Sushi, who'd had only one drink, stood up and said, "I'd even settle for a big chow, but I don't think Escrima cooks that recipe. I suspect some of the guys would vote to put Barky in the stewpot, though."

"Now, now, son," said Rev. "The King wouldn't like to hear you talk that way about a fellow star, 'specially not a dog. You talk nice about Barky, y'hear? That lil' ol' pup's a surefire hit anytime he's on a vidscreen."

"Star or no star, he better stay away from me," said Do-Wop. "C'mon, if we're gonna stand around and jabber, I'm gettin' me another brew."

"Hey, I've been ready," said Sushi, punching Do-Wop in the shoulder. "Come on, let's go find out what Escrima's cooking."

The three of them entered the dining hall together, took trays, and made their selections. Rev and Sushi went for chicken (there was a choice of Southern fried or curried) with rice, while Do-Wop loaded up his plate with butterfly pasta in a rich alfredo sauce and crisp broccoli tips.

The trio were on their way to the drink station when the trouble started.

Sushi was the first to notice anything out of the ordinary. "Who's the new guy over there?" he asked, pointing to the dessert line. The others turned their heads to see what he was talking about. There was a small figure in a regulation Legion jumpsuit, considerably less dashing than the special uniform Captain Jester had ordered for Omega Company to wear. Sushi just barely had time to notice that the new company member (he assumed that was what the newcomer had to be) had long floppy ears when a familiar sound came from behind them.

"Woof! Woof!" said Barky, the Environmental Dog, baring his fangs and charging full speed in the direction of the little legionnaire.

Chief Inspector Snieff leapt up and called out, "Barky! Sit! Bad dog! Sit!" But nobody, least of all the Environmental Dog, was paying much attention to her at this point.

The three Legionnaires made an altogether praiseworthy effort to get out of the dog's way, but (inhibited by full trays of food) they were nowhere near nimble enough. As Barky's well-fed bulk crashed into his shins, Do-Wop's tray tilted, then tipped directly over, dumping a plateful of steaming hot pasta with alfredo sauce on his legs, the floor, and onto Barky's bare back. That set off a chorus of woeful howls—from Do-Wop and Barky both.

Barky spun around to find whoever was attacking him. But the wet floor offered no traction, and so the famous Environmental Dog slid full speed into Sushi's legs. That, inevitably, sent Sushi tumbling into Rev, and both men went down in a heap. At the same time, their trays hit the floor, scattering chicken and rice in all directions. There were gasps and shouts from those within range of the flying food, and all over the mess hall heads turned to see what the disturbance was about. They hadn't missed anything to speak of; the chain reaction was just beginning to pick up momentum.

Chocolate Harry, going back to the main serving line for seconds, turned his head to look at what was happening behind him and inevitably put his foot in exactly the wrong place—on a stray chicken leg—and went down with a *basso profundo* shout of "Goddamn son of a bitch!" in an avalanche of table scraps, dishes, and cutlery. One of his forks bounced twice, flipped over one and a half times, and arrived prongs first in the close vicinity of Barky's tail, sending the galaxywide star Environmental Dog off yelping in the direction of the dessert stand, where Thumper still stood, surveying the catastrophe unfolding around him with eyes growing steadily wider.

One look at Barky was enough to convince Thumper that he had come to the wrong place at the wrong time. With the finely honed reflexes of a recent graduate of Legion basic training, Thumper dropped his own tray and took off for the nearest cover as if his life depended on it. Unfortunately, Barky's canine instincts were aroused by the sight of something running, and he redoubled his speed in an attempt to catch the fleeing Lepoid. Meanwhile, an infuriated Chocolate Harry had begun gathering up various articles from the floor around him and throwing them (with an obligato of curses truly worthy of a veteran Legion sergeant) in the general direction of the Environmental Dog.

Unfortunately, Harry's aim was about what one would expect of a Supply sergeant who had moved the trash basket next to his desk so as to avoid bending over to pick up the paper wads that missed their target. One of his hastily flung chicken bones caught Do-Wop square in the chest. Harry couldn't have picked a worse target on purpose. Never one to back down from a perceived challenge, Do-Wop scooped up a handful of pasta with alfredo sauce and fired it back at Chocolate Harry.

Do-Wop had no better aim than Harry. His improvised missile went far and wide, hitting Double-X (who had just turned to see what was happening) full in the face. The legionnaire dropped his tray and fell backwards into the main food station, knocking it over and scattering the contents across the floor and hitting (among others) Super-Gnat, who had been right behind Double-X.

That was the final spark to set off an explosion. Super-Gnat snatched up a boiled potato and fired it off. The spud hit Do-Wop directly in the snoot. Temporarily blinded, Do-Wop stepped on another gob of alfredo sauce and fell back on top of Rev, who had almost managed to get up on all fours. The pair went down with an impressive splash in the spilled pasta—but not before Do-Wop managed to fire off an unaimed breast of chicken that landed on a nearby table, knocking a pitcher of orange juice onto the laps of Roadkill, Street, and two of the Gambolts. Almost immediately, food was flying in every direction. Half of Omega Mob enthusiastically joined in, and the other half broke for the exits.

Meanwhile, Thumper and Barky were racing around the mess hall as if their lives depended on it, with the AEIOU inspectors following in a dogged attempt to prevent their intergalactic media star from injuring himself. Some of the legionnaires, whether angered at the inspectors' perceived interference in their operation or simply aroused by the challenge of moving targets, concentrated their fire on the AEIOU team, adding to the already considerable chaos.

Mess Sergeant Escrima, an irascible sort in the best of times, emerged from the galley red-faced, with an enormous cleaver in one hand. He took in the scene in a glance, and let out a thunderous roar in some language that, perhaps fortunately, none of the other members of the company understood. Before he took another step, Barky, the Environmental Dog, bowled headlong into Escrima, knocking him off his feet. Escrima went down into a pile of stewed tomatoes, sputtering curses, and threats of bodily harm. A split second later, he retrieved his cleaver and jumped up to join the chase.

This, of course, was the very moment at which an unsuspecting Captain Jester, A.K.A. Willard Phule, and his loyal butler Beeker chose to enter the mess hall …

CHAPTER ELEVEN

Journal #711

A sufficiently obstinate conviction is immune to all demonstrations of its falsity—in fact, they are the best means to harden the conviction, no matter how wrongheaded, into an unshakeable credo. And when two or more persons who hold such convictions come into contact, there is no hope of any such thing as communication or mutual enlightenment. The best one can hope for, in my experience, is to keep collateral damage to an acceptable minimum.

O   O   O

Predictably enough, Victor Phule was in the High Rollers' Lounge, where the games were scaled to the ultrarich, and the security discreetly steered away anyone whose pockets weren't deep enough—although not until they'd had a glimpse of the upper crust. Every nickel-dime punter who walked in the doors of the Fat Chance had a dream of breaking the bank and going home in a private space yacht. Giving them a brief look at the big-time players in action reinforced the glamour that was an essential part of any casino's appeal. *Let 'em dream, as long as they don't touch,* was Tullie Bascomb's credo. And almost everything in the Fat Chance reflected the veteran casino manager's words.

Ernie found it very curious that the richest man in the place—there was no question at all that Victor Phule fit that description—was playing the least glamorous game of all, the quantum slots. Ernie wondered about that, and about the fact that the casino had set up a row of slot machines here in a room where the players were more likely to prefer roulette and baccarat. You didn't need to know very much about the business to see that something funny was going on.

Ernie's latest theory was that, by ostentatiously playing high-priced slots, Victor Phule hoped to entice other high rollers to drop an occasional token into the machines—which notoriously offered the worst payoffs (or, from the house's point of view, the highest profits) in any casino. The casino stood to make a substantial gain if it could find a way to make the slots fashionable for the big spenders. A few thousand here, a few thousand there—that could add up to a nice sum of money quickly enough. If that was all that was going on, there wasn't likely to be any chance for Ernie to get an edge. But if Victor Phule was doing more than just playing the shill … Well, that was what Ernie had come here to find out.

The major flaw in the picture of Phule as a shill was that he totally lacked charisma. If the managers of the Fat Chance wanted to convince patrons that the slots were an exciting way to gamble, they could hardly have picked a worse role model. Pumping his tokens into the machines, shirt-sleeved Victor Phule had all the glamour of a middle-aged file clerk trying to avoid reinjuring a bad paper cut. Unless you knew who he was, there wasn't a hint of his money and power. So why was Phule out here working the slots, when he could undoubtedly sit in an easy chair sipping cold drinks and earn more money in half an hour from his businesses and investments than he was likely to win in the biggest payout these machines offered?

Wait a minute, Ernie thought, with the stunning awareness of someone who's overlooked an iceberg in a swimming pool. Just how big *was* the payout on these machines? What if the casino was offering enough to give even Victor Phule a rush of adrenaline every time he yanked the handle?

Casinos always make it a point to list the payout on the front of the slot machines, to remind the customer just how much he stands to win in the unlikely event of the symbols actually lining up right. Trying to appear as casual as possible, Ernie strolled up to one of the machines at the other end of the bank that Phule was playing, reaching in his pocket as if he might be interested in trying his luck.

"Sorry, my friend, these machines are in use," said a calm voice at his side. Ernie turned to see a compact, competent-looking man with eyes that looked as if they could've cut a clean hole straight through a planet. *The bodyguard,* he thought.

"Hey, no problem," said Ernie, genially. "Just taking a look at the payout, to see if it's worth my while to play. I can always come back after you're done."

"The payout's fine," said the bodyguard. "But the price is a bit steep. You might do better over at the roulette table—it's only a hundred dollars a spin, there." His manner was as casual as Ernie's, although it was perfectly clear he was doing his best to discourage anyone else from playing this bank of machines. That was enough to eliminate any idea that Phule was shilling for the house. No shill would stand in the way of a customer anxious to drop a few tokens in the slot. *Thousand-dollar tokens,* Ernie realized, looking at the machine he was standing next to.

Then he saw what the payout was, and in spite of himself, he let out a low whistle. "Whoa, are these guys kidding?" he asked. "A partner's share in the casino—that can't be for real."

"Oh, it's completely legitimate," said Victor Phule, stepping up to the machine next to Ernie. "I made certain of that, you can be sure. I'm not going to throw my money away for nothing."

"I guess *not,*" said Ernie, stepping back to give Phule room to pull the lever. He was fully aware of the bodyguard's steady glare as he said, suddenly putting on his best imitation of an educated accent, "Sorry, I don't mean to cramp your style."

"That's all right," said Phule. "I've about done my six-hour stint for today. If you've a mind to play these machines after I'm gone, feel free. I don't think anyone besides me has been trying them, though. Shame. A few more players would shorten the odds against someone's winning."

"Well, I guess I got nothing against being part owner of the casino," said Ernie, feigning an interest much milder than he really felt. "I'd have to turn it over to somebody else to run, though. I've got too many other balls in the air back home to stay around here to watch one more small business."

"Here, then, have a pull on me," said Victor Phule. "If you hit the jackpot and don't want it, you can always sell it back to me." He reached in his pocket and tossed Ernie a silver-colored metal token. Ernie stared at it in disbelief. It was heavier than it looked from a distance. In the center of each side was a hologram, showing a roulette wheel that spun as the token was tilted to different angles. Around the rim in raised letters it read: "Fat Chance Casino— $1000." Smaller print added the phrase, "Redeemable in Alliance funds at any window."

The bodyguard was scowling even more fiercely, but Ernie gave the token a flip, and said, "Oh, all right. Just one spin. If I win anything, I'll give you half."

He dropped the token in a slot and pulled the lever. The symbols began to spin in front of him …

o   o   o

"All right," said Phule, shading his eyes with his left hand. "Explain to me just what happened at dinner."

Rembrandt stood at the foot of his desk, looking just as unhappy as her superior officer. "Well, Captain," she began, "we warned all the nonhuman members of the company to avoid the dining hall until Barky and the AEIOU group were gone. It looks as if Barky has some particular grudge against nonhuman sophonts—you'd think they'd have trained that out of him, but there it is. What nobody had picked up on is that we've got a new member in the company, Thumper by name. He's a Lepoid from Teloon …"

"And nobody remembered to warn him about Barky," Phule finished the sentence for her. "Or me about him, either. I had such a perfect plan, too. We'd give the AEIOU inspectors a nice guided tour of the base, pointing out all the neat environmental things we're doing. Then we'd feed them a better meal than they get in their own camp, let the troops make friends with Barky, and send the inspectors home with everybody feeling good about each other."

"Yes, sir," said Rembrandt, not lifting her gaze to meet his.

Phule shook his head, then continued in a quiet voice. "The worst thing is, it almost worked. Even after Barky had his run-in with Tusk-anini, I thought we'd managed to smooth it all over. Then this Thumper walks into the mess hall, and Barky takes off after him like ... *like a dog after a rabbit*. And now we've got another incident on our hands, just as I thought we were about to make some real headway."

"Escrima didn't make it any better," said Rembrandt, quietly.

"No, I guess not," said Phule. He raised his hand to grip the bridge of his nose, as if his sinuses were paining him. After a bit he looked up, and asked, "The new recruit—Thumper—is he all right?"

"Yes," said Rembrandt. "He's pretty fast—maybe faster than Qual, from what I saw last night. Barky never had a chance to catch him."

"The canine made an astounding effort, though," Beeker observed quietly. "I've rarely seen such a ... *dogged* pursuit."

Rembrandt groaned. "Well, it was in character," she conceded. Then her eyes opened wider, and she said, "But that reminds me, Captain—Legionnaire Thumper wants to speak to you personally."

Phule nodded. "Oh, of course. Is he here? Bring him in, then."

Rembrandt went to the door and beckoned to the waiting Legionnaire, and a moment later Thumper came into the room. Phule took a moment to size up the new member of his company, whom he'd seen before only in the chaotic action that had taken place in the mess hall earlier that evening.

Thumper stood just under 1.5 meters tall, if you counted his long ears—which in any case were hard to ignore. His eyes were the second most prominent feature of his face: big and brown, nervously checking out the room as he entered. His incisors were prominent, and below his twitchy pink nose were long, catlike whiskers. His feet were long, too—or perhaps it was the obvious adaptation of his entire lower legs for speed that made them appear so. The instant reaction any human child would have had upon seeing him—or any other of his Lepoid race—was "big bunny." Phule had to consciously restrain himself from allowing a goofy grin to spread across his face. And he couldn't help wondering whether there was a fluffy white tail under that black Legion jumpsuit.

Phule somehow managed to keep a straight face as the Lepoid came to attention at the foot of his desk and saluted—rather smartly, he thought. "At ease, Thumper," he said. "What can I do for you?"

The Lepoid appeared to relax fractionally. "I'm not sure, sir," Thumper said. "I've always wanted to be a legionnaire. But now that I'm in the Legion, I keep having problems with superior officers. I got sent here because General Blitzkrieg thought I'd ruined his uniform …"

"The general had you sent here?" Rembrandt asked. "That explains it, then. He's been trying to make trouble for us ever since he sent the captain here …"

"I hope you don't mean that the way it sounds, Lieutenant," said Phule, with a grin. Before Rembrandt could protest her innocence, he turned to Thumper, and continued, "What just happened in the mess hall wasn't your doing, Legionnaire. We thought we'd warned all our non-human legionnaires to take their meals after Barky had left, so as to avoid something like what happened. But you were new here, and nobody thought to include you in the warnings. I'm sorry about that, and it shouldn't have happened. But it's no more your fault than your being a member of a species that the dog wanted to chase. So relax—nobody here holds it against you."

"Thank you, sir," said Thumper. "But there's another thing …" He paused.

"Go ahead, Thumper," said Phule. He'd already noticed that the Lepoid spoke excellent Standard, without using a translator.

Thumper took a deep breath. "As I said, sir, I've wanted to be a legionnaire ever since I was growing up. But what I've seen so far in the Legion hasn't been at all like what I expected."

"I know what you mean," said Phule, with a quiet smile. "Day-to-day life in the military actually tends to be pretty boring …" He looked at the expression on Rembrandt's face, and added, "Well, maybe this company is an exception."

"I consider that rather an understatement, sir," said Beeker, his eyebrows raised.

Rembrandt cleared her throat. "Perhaps we ought to let Thumper finish what he's saying, sir," she said.

"Ahh, of course you're right, Lieutenant," said Phule. "Please, Thumper, tell us what you were about to say. Sorry for the interruption."

Thumper's ears twitched, and he looked open-eyed first at Rembrandt, then at Phule. "I was going to ask how I could get out of the Legion and go back home," he said. "Everything that's happened to me since basic training had convinced me I'd made a really bad mistake. But I think I just changed my mind. I mean, I never heard an officer admit he was wrong about something, or apologize to an enlisted legionnaire. I've gotta think about this. So if you don't mind, I think I'll withdraw my request to speak to you, sir."

"All right, Legionnaire Thumper," said Phule, carefully. He hadn't seen much of the little Lepoid in action—just that one incredible burst of speed in the dining hall—but he'd read the report from Sergeant Pitbull, who'd been Thumper's drill instructor in basic. Pitbull's report was obviously phrased so as not to set off too many alarms if a certain Someone in Legion Headquarters happened to see it, but reading between the lines, it was full of praise for the diminutive recruit. Maybe Headquarters had done Omega Company a favor without intending to do so. It wouldn't be the first time that had happened.

He chuckled, then added, "Go look around the company and see if you like what you see. If you still want to get out of here after you've had a good look at us, I'll make sure nobody stops you. But give us a chance. I have the idea you might fit into this company better than you think."

"I'll give you a fair chance if you'll give me the same, sir," said Thumper, coming to attention and saluting with a crispness that reminded Phule that the recruit was fresh out of basic.

Phule returned the salute, and added a smile. "You've got a deal, Thumper."

O   O   O

"Somebody remind me where we were before the roof fell in," said Sushi. It was early in the evening after the food fight in the mess hall, and there was a prominent shiner under Sushi's right eye, where a too-enthusiastically thrown apple had nailed him. He'd gone to the autodoc, which had dispensed a couple of pain pills and a tube of cream that would take down the swelling, but the discoloration would still last a couple of days.

"Tryin' to learn how these here Zenobians can write before they can talk," said Rev, who'd fallen to the floor early and managed to avoid being hit by anything solid during the food fight. "And, to get right back to square number one, tryin to find out somethin' about this here character name of 'L'Viz in their mythology, which is what got me started on this whole fuss and botheration."

"Yo, Rev, you really think there's some kinda connection?" asked Do-Wop. He'd somehow managed to avoid any damage other than a thoroughly besmirched uniform, despite being one of the prime instigators and most active participants in the mess hall fracas. "I mean, the dinos and humans never even met until just a couple-three years ago. Don't make sense that they'd know squat about your guy, the King. What d'you think, Soosh?"

"It seems farfetched to me, too," Sushi admitted. "But tell me, Rev—why haven't you just asked Flight Leftenant Qual what it's about? He's got to know."

"Sure he does," said Rev. "In fact, I tried 'xactly that, and the little leftenant clammed up quicker than a politician on the witness stand. The long and short of it is, I gotta find out on my own."

"All right, I guess that makes sense," said Sushi. "It just doesn't sound like Qual to me. But what if it does turn out that the Zenobians had their own analog of the King? It'd be the most sensational discovery since it turned out the Synthians have a game exactly like human chess, only with a nine-by-nine board and an extra piece on each side, and the pawns reverse direction when they reach the back row, instead of promoting. Who could resist the chance to be in on a discovery like that?"

"Me for one, if they were givin' away free beer across the street," said Do-Wop. "I mean, don't get me wrong, Rev—doin' this job is way better than KP, or nighttime guard duty. But I don't think it makes a whole bunch of difference how it turns out, y'know?"

Rev looked at Do-Wop with one eyebrow arched. "Well, Do-Wop, if this here project don't move you, I could always cut you loose. 'Course, if you were hangin' out in the parade ground doin' nothin' in particular, ol' Beeker might remember just who it was who was flingin' the cheese sauce that got all over the captain's uniform. I won't claim I've had to pull any strings to keep you off'n some kind of punishment duty, but it could happen, y'know. It could happen."

"Aw, c'mon, Rev," whined Do-Wop. "You know the captain wouldn't do that to me. He's a laid-back dude ..."

"Sure," said Rev, shrugging. Then he added, with a hint of significance, "But Beeker jes' might be the kind to hold a grudge."

"You think so?" asked Do-Wop, now visibly worried. "Jeez—I wonder if there's any way I could make him forget about what was goin' on there ..."

"Why don't you jes' let me take care of it, son?" Rev put his hand on Do-Wop's shoulder and spoke in his most sympathetic voice. "The captain knows I don't have no kind of ax to grind, except maybe to see that the King's good people get treated fair and square. You do a good job for me, and I'll make sure nobody ever says *boo* to you."

Sushi chuckled. "And if my buddy joins the Church of the King, you'll make double sure nobody bothers him, right?" he said, with a knowing grin.

"Why, Sushi! I'm surprised you would suggest such a thing," said Rev. "Everybody in Omega Company is my concern, you know that."

"Right, but the ones with pompadours, sideburns, and pouty mouths are a little bit more your concern," said Sushi. "Don't worry about Do-Wop, Rev. I think I've known him long enough to have a pretty good idea what he does best."

Do-Wop looked up with a surprised expression. "Hey, thanks, Soosh. I didn't know you thought that much of me."

"...which is goofing off," Sushi finished.

"Yo! That ain't fair!" said Do-Wop, punching his buddy on the shoulder. "I thought you was gonna defend me!"

"You've known *me* long enough that you should've known better," said Sushi. "But seriously, Rev, you don't have to worry about Do-Wop. He knows a good deal when he sees one, and this is about as good as he's going to get in the Legion. Trust us—we'll get you results, if anybody can. Now, here's an idea I just came up with ..."

Rev and Do-Wop bent close to listen, and soon their heads were nodding.

O   O   O

"Pssst—Harry sent me," said a shadowy figure just beyond the perimeter of Zenobia Base.

"Yeah? What's the word?" said Double-X, who'd volunteered for sentry duty on this part of the perimeter. Rembrandt had been mildly surprised that the Supply sergeant's assistant was volunteering for anything at all, but she'd shrugged and put Double-X on the duty roster. Anytime somebody actually wanted to take on nighttime guard duty, it was one fewer warm body she'd have to cajole into doing it. And while she'd probably wonder about the reason for the unusual request, the captain's policy was to give the troops a good deal of slack, and she wasn't about to overrule him.

"Bird is the word," said the voice from beyond the perimeter.

"What's the bird?" said Double-X.

"Thunderbird," said the voice, somewhat exasperated. "Hey, can we come in now? This password stuff is silly."

"Aww, you know we gotta do all this stuff in the Legion, man," said Double-X. "You got it right, anyhow. Come on in—but hurry, we don't want the wrong folks to see you."

"We're comin'," said L.P. Asho, stepping out of the shadows. He was followed by Euston O'Better and Austen Tay-Shun. All three were wearing dark coveralls—not quite Legion black, but good enough to reduce visibility on a dark night. The three men stopped just inside the perimeter, then Asho asked, "Which way's Harry's place?"

"Straight ahead," said Double-X. "The Supply shed's right behind that big Zenobian machine—watch out you don't trip over it. I don't know whether you can break anything 'sides your toe, but you wouldn't want to find out the hard way."

"Weird-lookin' thing," said O'Better. "What's it do?"

"Damfino," said Double-X. "They call it a *sklern*, and if you know what that means you're one up on me. Hurry up, now, 'fore somebody spots you."

"We're going, don't worry." The three hunters moved off toward the supply shed, leaving Double-X alone on the perimeter. He watched them go, then settled back down to wait. He'd be off duty in another three hours. With any luck, the off-planet suckers would still have some money left by then. If what Harry said was right, they had plenty to lose. If they'd already been cleaned out, well, those were the breaks. He'd have to take his chances with the usual crew.

O   O   O

"Four thousand dollars?" Lola's jaw dropped. "Victor Phule gave you *four thousand dollars?*"

Ernie grinned, and he tossed the four Fat Chance Casino chips lightly from hand to hand. "To tell the truth, it was only a thousand." He stopped and laughed. "*Only!*—and that was really just a loan to play the slots. For a goof, I guess. I won nine thou, and gave him back his one plus half the winnings. So he came out ahead of the game, too."

"All right, but he had no way of knowing you were going to win," said Lola. "Why'd he give you money to throw away in one of those stupid slots?"

"He was gonna play it if I didn't," said Ernie. "I think he was just using me to change his luck or something. Or maybe he did know it was going to come up a winner—if he's shilling for the casino, maybe he'd have some way to rig that, figuring that if I do hit a winner, I'll put the money, plus some of my own, back in the machine trying to win again."

"And just as likely, you'll walk away and cash it in," said Lola, frowning. "Which is exactly what you did—except you didn't cash in. Why not?"

"I wanted him to think I don't need the dough that bad," said Ernie. "I'm pretending to be a guy with a few bucks of my own. If I cash the chips in right away, it looks like I'm hungry for the money. If I just throw a few thou in my pocket like small change, and walk out like it's too much of a pain in the ass to wait in line to change 'em, it makes the scam look better. Next time I walk in there, Phule will think I'm one of the big boys, just like him. And the chips are good anytime—you could go cash 'em in, one chip at a time, and nobody'd know any better."

"Don't be so sure about that," said Lola. "They may have them marked some way. In fact, they may even have them sending out a signal so they can tell where you've gone with them."

"Ahh, you're being paranoid," said Ernie. "They wouldn't go to the trouble to rig something that fancy for somebody like me."

"Don't be so sure," said Lola. "Remember, we're dealing with two guys who can very easily get their hands on all the latest military and spy hardware. Or are you forgetting just what it is that the Phules do for a living, besides running a casino?"

"Shit, that's right," said Ernie. He stared at the chips for a second, then suddenly stepped over to the bed and stuck them under a pillow. "You think they're bugged?" he whispered.

"If they really are, we're dead ducks already," said Lola quietly.

"Shit!" said Ernie, more vehemently. He stared at the pillow, then turned back to Lola. "I should've known better than to let that old skinflint slip me those phony chips. What the hell are we gonna do now, Lola?"

Lola sat on the windowsill, back to the window. She stretched her arms up and folded her hands behind her head, then said, "We don't have a lot of choices. Either they've got us pinned or they don't. If they're bugging us, they already know enough to kill any chance we have of our plans working. If that's true, we might as well cut and run—and take our chances about Mr. V catching up with us again. I don't like that idea, although four thousand dollars would give us a fair head start."

"Assuming the Phules don't have their security boys waiting to bust whoever tries to cash in the chips," said Ernie, his voice still low. He shot a glance at the pillow covering the chips, as if he expected it to do something unusual. It didn't cooperate.

"Right," said Lola. "The other choice is just to go on with the plan, on the theory that nobody knows nothin' about us and everything's exactly what it looks like. I don't especially like that idea, either, but at least it leaves us with something to play for."

"Yeah, I guess I can see that," said Ernie. He thought a moment, then said, "What if we're wrong about that?"

Lola shrugged. "If we're wrong, we find out just how good Phule's security guards are and just how serious they get with somebody who tries to do what we're planning on doing. At least there's a chance they'll put us someplace Mr. V can't get to us very easily. Maybe he'll even accept it as an occupational hazard if we're locked up somewhere and not come down too heavy on us."

"Yeah, right," said Ernie, gloomily. "So which way do you want to play it, then?"

"Dead straight," said Lola. "Go on back to the casino, joke with Victor Phule about forgetting you'd won, and drop those chips right back in the slot."

Ernie was flabbergasted. "Throw four thousand pazootlers back down the hole? Do I look like a dimwit to you?"

"Yeah," said Lola. "But for a moment, there, I thought maybe you were getting the idea. I'll explain it again. You've got to look as if you don't *care* about a few lousy chips. Then Phule won't think you're just out to get his money. Then maybe he'll start telling you what's really going on with his son, who's the one we want anyway. Get it?"

"I got it," said Ernie, sourly. "It just seems like we could hold back one or two chips, in case of emergency."

"Ah, come on, be a sport," said Lola, with a grin. "Besides, if you pull that lever just right, you might win. *Then* you'll thank me."

"Su-ure, and maybe Victor Phule will disown Junior and put me in his will," said Ernie. "What did you figure the odds against that jackpot were? Twenty billion to one?"

"Yeah, but somebody's got to win it," said Lola brightly. "Why not you?"

"Better me than anybody else, that's for sure," said Ernie. "Except I know better than to hold my breath."

"Go play it anyway," said Lola. "We don't have any other choices, so we might as well have fun with the one we do have."

"Aw right, but don't blame me if I come back broke," said Ernie, and he headed out the door and back to the casino.

O   O   O

"Great Goombah, who dealt this drutz?" growled Euston O'Better, scanning his cards. The game was Red Comet Stud, High-Low, with a buy after the last down card.

"Your good buddy over there," said Chocolate Harry, who was sitting behind an impressive pile of chips. "You don't like 'em, throw 'em in. Otherways, there's a bet on the table you gotta call—or raise."

"I ought to fold," said O'Better. "But I guess I'll look at one more card." He shoved a red chip into the center of the table.

Chocolate Harry shrugged. "Ain't no law I ever heard of says you gotta play if you're afraid of losin'. And that's the only gamblin' tip you're gonna get from me." He shoved in a blue chip. "Raise you five."

"Call," said Sushi, whose own pile of chips was slightly smaller than Chocolate Harry's, but still a good bit larger than when he'd bought into the game.

L.P. Asho, in the dealer's seat, looked at his cards. "What the hell, it's only money," he said. "Your ten"—he slid a blue chip into the pot—"and mine." He added a second blue, grinning.

"That's what I like to see," said Harry, beaming. "Man knows how to play the game. You still in, Street?"

"Not with these cards I ain't," said the legionnaire, turning his cards face down. "Can't get high or low either one. Why don't somebody invent a game where middle hand wins?"

"You can call it when it's your deal," said Harry. "Meanwhile, we got cards and money on the table, and time's a-wastin'. You in, Mr. Tay-Shun?"

Austen Tay-Shun took a sip of his drink—bourbon and cactus juice—and contemplated first his own cards, then those visible in the other hands. "I like what I see," he said. "Call."

"You can't like it that much or you'd raise," said Harry. "Your turn, O'Better. Fifteen bucks to play, jet out for free. What'd'ya say?"

"I *said* I'd see another card," said O'Better, putting in two chips. He looked like a man whose word of honor has just been impugned.

Which of course was exactly what Chocolate Harry was banking on. "Here's the raise," he said, "and last raise for another blue one." *Plink* went his chips into the pot. Sushi rolled his eyes and folded, but the three hunters all called, with varying degrees of enthusiasm. The game had been going like this all night long.

"More cards, Mr. Dealer," called out Harry. "Make 'em good— I don't want to hear no complaints about how folks came to Chocolate Harry's to play poker and couldn't get a hand to play!"

"Yeah, yeah," said Asho, turning over another card for each of the players. "Read 'em and weep."

"That's what the farmer said," said Tay-Shun. "Or was it 'Weed 'em and reap'? Har har." He shoved a red chip into the pot. "Five."

Euston O'Better snorted. "I don't know what's worse, your jokes or my cards. And that's a mighty sad comment on this hand." He tossed his hand in and pushed back his chair. "Gotta get me another brew."

"Help yourself—we got plenty of it," said Chocolate Harry, gesturing toward the cooler in the back of the Supply shed. He turned back to his cards and shoved two chips into the pot. "Your nickel and my dime."

"Sarge is nickel-dimin' us to death," said Street, looking enviously at the growing pot.

Chocolate Harry snorted. "A man wants to take the boodle home, he got to feed the pot," he said. "You don't have to play the game if it's too rich for your blood—we got a lot of folks on base would like to take some of this money if you ain't up to it. Hey, Soosh, you think Do-Wop's up for a game?"

Before Sushi could answer, Street said, "I didn't say I was givin' up my seat. Just kibitzing, is all."

"Whatever you say," said Harry. "Didn't want to see a man jump in over his head."

"Sure you did," said Sushi, leaning back in his chair to study the visible cards. "You run a poker game every few days, and I never yet saw you tell somebody he couldn't play because he wasn't good enough. Or rich enough, for that matter. You might be the most democratic sergeant in the Space Legion, when it comes to taking other people's money."

"Well, I'll take that as a compliment," said Chocolate Harry. "Even though I have to say you're wrong. You give me my choice, I'd much sooner take a rich man's money than a poor man's. And the reason why is easy …"

"Because there's more of it to take," said Sushi and Street in unison.

Chocolate Harry frowned. "What's wrong with you boys, steppin' on all a man's best lines?"

"Just tryin' to save you the effort," said Street, grinning—broadly. "You workin' so hard as it is …"

"Hellfire, there's a game goin' on," said Austen Tay-Shun. "You boys playin' or not? It's your bet, ain't it, L.P.?"

"I'm callin'," said the dealer. "You in or out, buddy? If you ain't holdin' anything better than you're showing, you best get out while you still got some skin left."

"There's one more card before the buy," said Tay-Shun, unfluttered. "Plenty of time to get better. Call."

The call went around the table and Asho dealt the remaining players one card each, face down. "All right, pay dirt!" said Tay-Shun, peeking at the card he'd gotten.

"You might have the dirt, but I'm the one who's takin' home the pay," said Chocolate Harry, with a broad grin. He was showing three queens in his face-up cards.

"We'll just have to wait and see on that there question," said Asho. "You can brag all you want about your popgun, but don't expect it to carry no weight with somebody that's got a cannon."

"That's the truth," said Austen Tay-Shun. "There's gas and there's neutronium, and a man that don't know which one's which better keep tight hold of his wallet. I bet twenty-five."

Chocolate Harry looked at Tay-Shun's cards. "Must be goin' low. Bump it twenty-five."

"And another twenty-five," said Asho, shoving three blue chips into the pot and grinning broadly.

Tay-Shun raised another twenty-five. "Looks like we got you whipsawed, Sarge," he said.

Chocolate Harry chuckled deep in his throat. "You talk bad, but it's the cards that get the last word."

Sushi had been kibitzing the game, waiting for the next deal. Perhaps that was why he noticed that O'Better, after folding his hand, was taking a long time to fetch himself a beer. He looked around the shed and spotted the absent player standing by a rack of weapons. He had a beer can in his hand, all right, but his attention was raptly focused on the military hardware.

Casually, Sushi made his own way back to the cooler, got himself a cold one, and sauntered over to stand next to O'Better. "You look like a man who knows his way around a gun," said Sushi.

"Huh?" said the hunter, startled. "Oh yeah, yeah—gotta have some serious weapons if you're gonna hunt big game, heh heh. I surely do admire some of the stuff you Legion boys have got, though."

"Yeah, I guess it's pretty exotic to civilians," said Sushi. "We use it all the time, so it's nothing special to us. Then again, we have specialized requirements—most of this stuff would be no use for you. You don't get much of a trophy if you blow the whole animal to constituent quarks, do you?"

"Naw, I reckon not," said O'Better, with a guffaw. "But there's trophies and trophies, y'know? And with some of the critters I hear tell this planet's got, maybe just stunnin' the critter so's you could cut off the head would be fine ..." He waved his hand in the direction of a Zenobian stun ray—a weapon that, as far as Sushi knew, was still available only to Omega Company, thanks to the captain's father's munitions plant.

"Stun it? Yeah, that'd be triff, if there was some weapon that would do it," said Sushi, watching O'Better's reaction carefully. But before the Tejan could say anything, a voice came from the card table. "Hey, Euston, you playin'? We're dealin' Chainsaw ..."

O'Better gulped, and said, "'Scuse me." He headed back to the card table, obvious relief on his face. But Sushi couldn't help but note that both Tay-Shun and Asho were staring daggers at their fellow hunter.

O   O   O

Ernie sauntered into the Fat Chance Casino as if he owned the joint. Well, why not? Looking and acting confident—putting up a good front—was one of the main weapons in a con man's arsenal. If nobody thought to question him, he was home free. And, after all, right there in his pocket were chips worth $4000 that he was planning to play with. That gave him just as much right to be there as anybody else—more than most of the other customers, if the amount of money he had meant anything.

His first stop was at the cashier's window, to change one of the thousand-dollar chips into fifties. The smaller denominations would allow him to gamble with the money over a longer stretch of time, although he'd still be betting amounts significant enough to distinguish him as a big-time player—an "elephant," in the casino workers' slang. He would reserve the remaining big chips to play Victor Phule's thousand-dollar slots, allowing him—or so he hoped—to strike up a further conversation with the weapons magnate.

Ernie was looking forward to renewing that acquaintanceship. He still had hopes of finding out exactly what Phule's real plans were. They couldn't possibly be as stupid as trying to win a jackpot big enough to break the bank, as Phule had insisted he was doing. And just maybe, he could find out where Willard Phule was, so he and Lola could decide whether or not to change their original plan of kidnapping the young Space Legion captain who was majority stockholder in the casino. Whether they could convince the people who'd hired them to go along with a change in plans was another problem. Ernie preferred not to think about that one, just now.

He sat down at a blackjack table and played a few hands. The cards weren't running his way, and he ended up dropping three hundred dollars in fifteen minutes. It was hard to keep his hands from shaking; here he was, frittering away more than his entire daily budget before Victor Phule had tossed him a chip and told him to play the slots. A person with any brains at all would probably pocket the money and get the hell off Lorelei. But, of course, Ernie wasn't going to do that. Lola was the brains, and she'd told him to come back here and play with it. She didn't have to tell him twice.

He stood up and wandered over to a roulette table; he'd get worse odds, but the game was more in line with the high roller image he was trying to project. A perky redhead with a really spectacular figure was watching the action—waiting for two or three blacks in a row, then sliding a large bet onto the red, figuring it was more likely to come up now. Ernie had heard somewhere that it didn't make any difference how many times one color came up, the odds were still the same old fifty-fifty on the next turn of the wheel. That didn't make sense to Ernie. If you couldn't trust the law of averages, there wasn't any point to gambling at all.

Ernie bellied up to the table alongside the redhead. He slipped a fifty-pazootie chip out of his pocket and placed it on the red, right next to hers. Startled, she looked up at him. He grinned at her, not worrying for the moment about what Lola would have to say if she found out about it. *Hey, I gotta play the role,* he told himself.

The croupier announced the end of betting with the traditional incomprehensible phrase in some forgotten Old Earth language. Impulsively, Ernie pulled a second fifty-buck chip out of his pocket and put it atop the first just as the wheel began to spin. The redhead's eyes widened, and she turned a very curious sidelong stare at him before returning her gaze to the wheel.

Ernie caught himself involuntarily holding his breath as the wheel spun. He made himself relax. If he was supposed to be a big spender, a hundred bucks shouldn't be a big deal to him. Hell, a thousand shouldn't be that big a deal. In a little while, he was going to go throw that much into a slot machine in a couple of pulls, and unless he got really lucky, he wasn't ever going to see it again.

The wheel slowed, and the redhead leaned forward, showing off a nice stretch of décolletage. Ernie wondered if it was for his benefit, and decided it probably was. He chuckled, and managed to keep from turning right around to stare at her. As interesting as she might be, he had to remember his real purpose here. More importantly, he had to remember what was likely to happen to him if Lola found out he'd been fooling around with some bimbo in the casino. Yes, those were the words she'd use. Then she'd use considerably harsher words directed at him. And unless he got very lucky, the harsh words might be followed by a stream of very hard objects flung in his direction.

It probably wasn't worth it, Ernie thought, even as the roulette wheel came to a stop and showed the ball resting in a red slot. He—and the redhead—had won. She let out a whoop, and gave a little jump, brushing up against him—on purpose, he was sure. He was going to have to be very disciplined. He was going to hate it, but that was the price a fella had to pay.

Even so he managed to smile as the redhead brushed up against him again and turned her big eyes his way as he scooped up his winnings.

CHAPTER TWELVE

Journal #714

The most common question asked of a legionnaire—at least, by civilians—is "Why did you join the Legion?" The most common answer, in my experience, is "To get a fresh start." While that answer may not be strictly true in every case, it does possess a great deal of psychological validity. A genuine fresh start in life is a rare thing indeed; even the illusion of a fresh start can lead to a significant alteration in a person's outlook. And in fact, more than almost any other institution in society, the Legion does offer a fresh start to those who come to it in search of one.

The fact that so few of its members take any significant advantage of the opportunity is hardly to be held against the Legion.

O   O   O

Thumper bounded out of bed; it took him only a moment to reach the jangling wake-up alarm and turn the buzzer off. That was all it took to remind him that he was in a new place. It also reminded him, inevitably, of everything that had happened the night before. He shook his head; there was no changing what was past. He quickly washed up, threw on his black Legion jumpsuit, and went out to find some breakfast. Then he would report to Sergeant

Brandy's training squad, as she had instructed him the previous afternoon. It was good being allowed to eat before having to stand in formation—Thumper decided that this was another one of the ways Omega Company was a significant improvement over Legion basic camp.

He loaded up his tray and turned to look for a seat at one of the tables. To his surprise, there were a couple of legionnaires beckoning to him from the nearest table. "Hey, new guy, come sit with us!" said one of them—a small human with a hairless head and a wide smile.

Encouraged, Thumper took one of the empty seats at the long table. "Thanks for the invitation," he said. "My Legion name's Thumper. What about you guys?"

"I am Mahatma," said the one who'd invited him. "And until you came, I was one of the new guys in Omega Company. So you have caused me and my friends to become veterans, for which we owe you many thanks."

The others introduced themselves: a small human named Super-Gnat, and her partner, a Volton named Tusk-anini; two Gambolts named Dukes and Rube; and two other humans named Roadkill and Street. As it turned out, several of them, including Mahatma, were also members of Sergeant Brandy's training squad, to which Thumper had been ordered to report after breakfast. "Is this going to be anything like Legion basic?" Thumper asked.

Mahatma smiled. "I went through basic training with Brandy, so I have nothing else to compare it to," he said. "Sergeant Brandy can sometimes be obstinate, but she is usually capable of adapting to circumstances."

Tusk-anini snorted, and said, "Mahatma has not seen many other sergeants. I have. All of them were tough, and Brandy is tough, too. But better than most sergeants, she understands that not all sophonts are just humans with funny faces. That is a good thing to know, for a sergeant."

"But she will make you work hard," said Rube. "I hear you are a fast runner and a good jumper."

"Well, I guess so," said Thumper. "They told me I set a camp record for the obstacle course in Basic."

"Ah, yes—the obstacle course," said Dukes, brushing crumbs out of his whiskers with one paw. "Captain Jester has us run the obstacle course, too. I believe that we do it differently from other Legion companies. It will be interesting to hear what you say after you run it with us."

"Uh-huh," said Thumper, suddenly cautious. "I guess we'll see what it's like when it comes up." He sensed some deeper meaning behind the Gambolt's comment, some unspoken subject he'd best not commit himself on until he saw its complexities firsthand. He took a forkful of salad to chew on, hoping that someone else would pick up the thread of the conversation.

But the only one who spoke was Mahatma, who simply smiled, and said, "Oh, yes, we will certainly see."

And with that, Thumper had to remain contented until one of the squad looked up at the wall clock, and said, "Uh-oh—time to get moving. Don't want to make the new guy late on his first day here."

"Ahh, why not?" said Roadkill, grinning. "Make the rest of us look bad if he bein' always on time. Oughta start out on the wrong foot like the rest of us."

"Not correct," said Tusk-anini, shaking his huge head. "If new guy starts out on wrong foot, he doing it on his own. That what Omega Mob be all about—from each according to his inability, to each according to his misdeeds."

Super-Gnat looked up at her partner in awe. "Tusk, I don't know what you've been reading, but I somehow don't think it's a manual of military procedure. You're right about one thing, though—the new guy's gotta make his own mistakes. Go ahead, Thumper—the others can be as late or early as they want, but you need to be on time today. And good luck!"

The others at the table laughed, but they all stood up along with Thumper. "OK, new guy, follow us," said Street. "Brandy be waitin'." And together they filed out of the mess hall toward the parade ground for Thumper's first full day with Omega Mob.

O O O

The observer in the Fat Chance casino's control center turned away from the monitor screen and called out to her superior. "Looks like Toni's got a live one," she said.

"Let's see," said the manager. She stepped up behind the observer's chair and leaned forward, looking at the monitor. "That guy again," she said. "Yeah, we've been watching this bozo for a good while now. Has all the marks of a grifter, but nobody's seen him doing anything we can nail him for—yet."

The observer leaned back. "Maybe he's running some kind of game outside the casino, then coming in to gamble with the take. I can't believe he came by that kind of money honestly—to throw a hundred bucks on the table like it didn't matter."

"*As if,*" the manager—who was a stickler for grammar—corrected her. "Well, we don't know where his original stake came from, but we can blame the old man for giving him enough to play at the big tables."

"The old man?" the observer looked up in surprise. "What do you mean?"

The manager grunted, then said, "This guy walked up to Victor Phule when he was pumping chips into the thousand-dollar slots. For whatever reason, Phule seems to have taken a shine to him. So he tossed him a chip and asked him to play it for him—to change his luck, I guess. The guy wouldn't take it at first, but Phule told him they'd split anything he won. Damned if the guy doesn't score an eight-for-one, and come out four thousand ahead. This morning he changed a thousand into smaller chips—those thousand-buck chips are all marked—and that's what he's playing with now."

"Uh-huh," said the observer. "Well, it looks as if he's winning a little bit of his own. Red just came up twice more, and he was down on it both times."

"Shit," said the manager. "I hate it when these guys win. Let's just hope Toni can persuade him to let it ride a little longer—we don't want this guy getting too far ahead of the game. He's too slimy for my taste—and I'd just as soon not give him enough money to try something really big."

"Like what?" asked the observer. "I mean, he looks like a slimeball, but so far the worst I've seen him do is stare at Toni's boobs—which she's trying her best to get him to do, anyhow."

"Well, we've got a little bit of history on him," said the observer. "He and a woman were here a few months back, and we had a couple of flaky security incidents involving them—nothing we could make any kind of case on, but suspicious. And they left the station very suddenly, didn't check out or anything. Everything was paid up, so we didn't follow it up—but I'm wondering if we shouldn't have.

"He won *again,*" said the observer. "That's sixteen hundred he's ahead, now."

"Let him just keep playing," said the other woman, leaning forward to stare at the monitor. "Better yet, let him bump the bets even more. C'mon, Toni, that's what you're here for. Get him to put his whole wad on the red." She spoke as if the redheaded woman—whose job description fell somewhere between "shill" and "undercover security guard"—could actually hear her. *Maybe she can hear,* thought the observer. It wasn't unknown for the floor agents to wear equipment both to send and to receive messages.

Whether Toni had heard the supervisor or simply grasped what the situation demanded, the observer never found out. But she leaned over to the object of their scrutiny and said something in his ear. He grinned, stupidly. Whoever this guy was, suave wasn't in his repertory at all. Then he reached in his pocket and pulled out a handful of chips. He looked at them, shrugged, and put them all out on the red section of the betting layout. Even from the observation cameras lodged in the ceiling lighting fixtures, it was obvious that there were three thousand-dollar chips in the stack.

"Yes!" hissed the supervisor. "He's betting everything he has. C'mon, black!"

"Black, yeah, c'mon black," echoed the observer. Rooting for or against one of the players wasn't really professional, but there were times even the most hardened casino hands got involved in the play. And nobody could really object if they were rooting for the bettor to lose.

The wheel spun, and the spectators at the table leaned forward, holding their collective breath. So did the two unseen spectators high above the action. The wheel gradually slowed, and the ball's motion brought it down into the slotted section until it came to rest in one division ...

O   O   O

"All right, red again!" shouted Ernie. Suddenly there was a stunned silence around the table as the other bettors realized what had happened. The croupier turned a sour look toward the wheel as he watched Ernie scoop in his winnings—now totaling over ten thousand dollars. But it wasn't the wheel's fault, or the croupier's, either. Ernie was on a hot streak. He knew the feeling, and it was hard to keep from grinning.

It went against all his instincts to pick up his chips when his luck was running. But out of the corner of his eye he'd seen Victor Phule walk by, and that reminded him what he'd come here to do. As tempting as it was to take another shot at doubling his money, he had work to do, and messing up this job was likely to get him in the kind of trouble he couldn't sweet-talk his way out of. He'd almost be better off coming home with the redhead—her name was Toni—who'd been egging him on to bet the house on the roulette table. At least, if he did that, Lola would vaporize him on the spot, without stopping to ask questions.

Toni looked up at him now, a rather attractive pout on her lips. "Hey, what are you—chicken? Come on, let it ride one more time. I've got a really strong feeling, red's coming up again!" She put her hand on his arm, tempting him to stay.

"Sorry, babe, gotta go," said Ernie, reluctantly shrugging off her hand. "Important business."

"Aww, and I thought you were a real man," said Toni, fixing him with her most seductive stare. Behind her, the croupier was getting ready to spin the wheel. Toni pointed to the betting layout. "Show me what you're made of, big boy."

"Well ..." Ernie was torn between putting his chips back on the table and following Victor Phule toward the bank of thousand-dollar slots where he'd won his bankroll to begin with. He glanced at the wheel; the croupier stood there with the ball in his hand, smirking at Ernie, just asking to be taught a lesson. Ernie's hand moved in the direction of his pocket, and he turned back toward the table, almost involuntarily.

But just as Ernie began to turn, a big man shoved his way into the space Ernie had vacated, plopping a small pile of ten-dollar chips on the table. Ernie looked around and quickly spotted another clear space, a few feet away. He stepped quickly forward, but just as he did, someone tapped him on the shoulder. He turned around to see a cocktail waitress with a tray full of glasses. "Bring you something to drink, sir?" she chirped. "It's on the house."

"Sorry, honey, nothing now," said Ernie, forcing himself to smile. He quickly turned, only to find that the space he'd seen before was now occupied. But there was Toni at the far end of the table, beckoning him. He started forward—why were there so many people around the table all of a sudden?—and reached the open space beside Toni just in time to hear the croupier Call, *"Les jeux sont faits!"* Toni shot him a disgusted look, but the wheel was already spinning. Resignedly, Ernie turned to watch the wheel. If it came up red again ...

It spun, slowed, and after what seemed like hours came up on thirty-two—*black*. Ernie had just missed losing all his winnings—and the rest of his bankroll, as well. A cold sweat broke out on his forehead as he realized how close he'd come.

After a moment of stunned silence, Ernie reached into his pocket and pulled out a chip. Without even looking at it, he handed it to the cocktail waitress who'd distracted him just at the crucial moment, then walked away in the direction Victor Phule had gone in.

The waitress stood openmouthed, staring at the hundred-dollar chip in her hand. Before she could tuck it in her tip pocket, a hand touched her elbow. She looked up to see Toni, who'd been trying so hard to get Ernie to let his bets ride on red. "Don't spend it all in one place, sister," said the shill, with a tight-lipped smile. Seeing the worry on the waitress's face, she added, "No, don't worry—nobody's going to take it away from you. But a word to the wise—you just got really lucky. Most of the time, you'll make better tips if you *don't* stop the customers from playing. Now, you'd better get back to work. I know *I* have to."

Toni turned back to the roulette table, making it a point to squeeze up against the new big spender who'd taken Ernie's place. Maybe she'd have better luck getting *this* one to let his chips ride until the odds caught up with him ...

O   O   O

The Zenobian sun was just a hand's breadth above the horizon as Phule stepped out into the parade ground of the Legion base for his morning run. The early-morning desert air was crisp and cool, belying the furnacelike temperatures Phule knew by now to expect by midday. The company's prefabricated base module was climate-controlled, of course, and it had a thoroughly modem gym and spa built into it. Phule would have accepted nothing less for his money. But he still felt a certain exhilaration when he did his running outside under the blue sky, with real planetary soil under the feet. If nothing else, it made him feel more in touch with the world he and Omega Company had come to help.

As was his habit, Phule turned and scanned the horizon in every direction. As usual, there was little to see that differed from what he'd seen the day before, or any of the other times he'd looked out on the landscape surrounding Zenobia Base. The small cluster of cirrus clouds to the west looked very much like the clouds that had been there yesterday morning, although he knew better than to believe they were actually the same. As much undue excitement as Phule had been through the last day or so, he was actually rather pleased to find at least one thing that was exactly as he expected. With Omega Company, that was the exception rather than the rule. Especially after last night's debacle in the mess hall ...

Phule had just begun to stretch out his leg muscles when Lieutenant Armstrong emerged from the base module. He and Phule had been keeping each other company during the morning run for several months now. They were close enough in age and physical condition so that neither held the other back, and of course it was good policy to have a companion along in case the unexpected happened—a sprain or some more serious injury was always possible, even in the controlled environment of the gym.

Outdoors, in a desert environment, it would be foolhardy to risk it without help close at hand.

"Good morning, Captain," said Armstrong, nodding. Before Phule could reply, a series of loud sounds came from the desert east of the base. *Pop pop pop! Pop pop!* Armstrong turned his head that way and said, "What the devil ...?"

"That's gunfire, Lieutenant," said Phule, suddenly alert. "And unless I'm completely turned around, it's coming from the direction of the hunting party. What do they think they're doing?"

"Well, sir, I suspect they think they're hunting," said Armstrong. "The sport does involve shooting guns, you know ..."

Phule peered at his lieutenant. "You haven't been taking sarcasm lessons from Beeker, have you?" he asked. Then he shook his head. "No, that would require a sense of humor. The point is, as far as they're concerned, neither we nor the Zenobians have given them permission to fire any weapons yet. And I wasn't about to give them that permission until we got them someplace where our AEIOU friends can't hear them banging away. Come on, Lieutenant, let's go read them the riot act. It's just far enough to make a good run."

"Yes, sir," said Armstrong, catching up with his captain, who had already taken off at a steady pace. "Uh—shouldn't we have some backup, sir? I mean, those people are *shooting*."

"Yes, Armstrong, and we're going to tell them to stop," said Phule, looking back and grinning. "We're the Legion, remember? We can handle it. In fact, it's our job to handle it. And if we get there quickly, there's still some chance that Inspector Snieff and her friends haven't noticed the noise."

"What if they have, sir?" Armstrong still looked worried.

"We'll just have to convince them that we were the ones doing the shooting," said Phule, skipping over a small dry streambed in the way. "That shouldn't be too hard. After all, we are a military unit. It's our *business* to fire our weapons every so often."

"Snieff will start quoting some regulation we're breaking," said Armstrong, doing his best to stay abreast with Phule. They were now out of the cleared area immediately around the base, and the ground had become rougher.

"Sure," said Phule, dodging around a low, bush-like native plant. "One thing you find out in the business world, Lieutenant. You can't do *anything* without breaking one regulation or another. That's how the game is played. What makes the difference between success and failure is figuring out how to get your job done with as little interference as possible from the people who want to enforce the regulations. And that's what we're going to do here."

"Yes, sir," said Armstrong. He jumped over a low rock and kept moving in pace with his captain.

Up ahead, another loud report broke through the calm morning air. Phule gritted his teeth. Whoever was doing the shooting, he hoped they had enough sense to make sure what was in the line of sight before they pulled the trigger.

He hoped he wasn't going to find out he was wrong the hard way ...

O O O

Hurrying a bit more than was comfortable, Ernie caught up with Victor Phule just at the entrance to the High Rollers' Lounge, where the thousand-dollar slots had been installed. He slowed down the last few steps to give himself a chance to appear unruffled and relaxed. "Hey, how's it going, buddy?" he said, as if greeting someone he'd known since childhood. "Any luck today?"

Eddie Grossman took a quick step forward, glaring at Ernie through narrowed eyes, but Victor Phule raised his hand, and said, "Relax, Eddie—you don't need to worry about this fellow."

"Mr. Phule, you're *paying* me to worry about this fellow, and everybody like him," growled the bodyguard, but when his boss shot him an exasperated look, Grossman shrugged and stood back. Still, he kept his eyes focused on Ernie, ready to move in case of trouble. Victor Phule had the right to give him orders, but he was prepared to ignore those orders if it looked as if he was about to lose his client—not to mention his job.

Ernie, who had an excellent idea what was likely to happen if he made the wrong move, grinned broadly. He intended to be very careful not to do anything that the bodyguard might decide to interpret as unfriendly. "It looks like I'm on a hot streak today," he said. "Been cleaning up over at the roulette table all morning."

"Good for you," said Victor Phule. "The owners don't know it, but they're giving money away hand over fist. My idiot son thinks the way to run a casino is to give the best odds on the station. I'm trying to show him the error of his ways. A few lucky customers taking home big jackpots ought to put the icing on the cake."

"Well, I'm all for that," said Ernie. "Can't let these young whippersnappers think they know everything," he added, as if he were somehow old enough to be entitled to the sentiment.

"His biggest mistake was running off and joining the Legion instead of settling down to business," growled Phule, only half-listening. "Now he thinks he can run a business from halfway across the Galaxy. Well, I won't say it can't be done, but you need some real experience under your belt, real business experience. None of this rah-rah save-the-universe crap."

Ernie, whose business experience consisted almost entirely of scams and petty theft, nodded sagely. "No substitute for knuckling down and getting your hands dirty," he said. "Not a job for weak sisters."

"Just so," said Victor Phule. "Say, how'd you like to take another crack at the slots? If you're on a lucky streak, you're just the man I need. If you win a big jackpot, it'll show the boy the consequences of setting the odds too much in favor of the customers."

"Sure, why not?" said Ernie. He was enough ahead of the game that he could afford to throw a few tokens into the slots and still have a little nest egg so that he (and Lola) could afford another couple of weeks on Lorelei. By then, he hoped, they'd have made some kind of breakthrough. If not ... well, as usual, he'd deal with the problem when his other choices ran out.

He followed Phule into the elephants' lounge. As usual, nobody was playing the thousand-dollar slots. Even the most well-heeled bettors generally considered it foolish to drop that much on such a low-return bet. Other than Phule and Ernie, there hadn't been more than the occasional dabbler, who typically put in one or two tokens, then went on to play something that delivered better odds. Which was almost everything else in the Fat Chance Casino.

"All right," said Ernie, fishing in his pocket for the thousand-dollar chips. He had ten of them, now. He picked a likely-looking machine—not that there was any noticeable difference among them—and put a chip into the slot. He grabbed the handle, then turned to Phule. "Say, by the way—what's a partner's share of the casino stock actually worth? Must be pretty valuable, considering they're charging a thousand bucks for a chance to win it."

"I guess it's valuable enough, if you want that kind of property," said Victor Phule. "Probably fifty or sixty million, if I were going to guesstimate."

"I see," said Ernie. All of a sudden his palms began to sweat. He looked at the machine he'd just pumped a thousand dollars into. *Fifty or sixty million,* Victor Phule had said. Of course he'd dreamed of having that kind of money, but actually having it had never been remotely probable. *Fifty or sixty million* ... He pulled the handle and the machine display became a whirl of rapidly changing symbols.

He eased up on the handle, and one of the electronic "wheels" stopped on a golden bar that framed the words "FAT CHANCE" in bright blue letters. The other symbols continued to change rapidly. He waited, trying to feel the right moment, then gave the handle a little jiggle and watched a second "FAT CHANCE" golden bar appear. *All right!* he thought. Now, any symbol but a lemon would give him a decent return for his play. The machine was of course carefully calibrated not to turn up another gold bar. The first two were supposed to make him think he'd just missed, and pump another token—or a dozen or more—into the machine. But a bell or a cherry or a rocket ship were always possible ... He gave the handle a little pull toward him, then released it. The final wheel came to a stop.

It was a third golden bar, with the words "FAT CHANCE" in bright blue letters. A bell started ringing somewhere very close, and, after a pause, tokens began pouring out of the machine.

Victor Phule stood openmouthed, speechless. But he was nowhere near as surprised as Ernie, as a loud siren added its noise to the bell, and happy music began playing. In front of his face, a sign was flashing off and on: "SUPER JACKPOT!!!"

That was echoed in the back of his mind by a little voice saying, *Fifty or sixty million,* over and over and over …

CHAPTER THIRTEEN

Journal #723

T he fascination of some men—it is invariably men—with implements of destruction never ceases to amaze me. While all collectors are by definition fanatics, the connoisseur of weapons takes this quality to an extreme. Even if one grants in principle the historical, and (I will even grant) the artistic appeal of certain weapons, surely no civilized person can entirely forget their gruesome purpose.

I find it particularly paradoxical that these aesthetes of destruction insist on having the finest weapons possible at their command. As if the victims would somehow be insulted to learn that their demise had been brought about by bargain-basement artillery, with secondhand ammunition!

O O O

Phule and Armstrong came in sight of the hunters' camp just as another loud explosion shook the air. Armstrong involuntarily ducked. "Great Ghu, I hope they're paying attention where they point that thing," he said. "It sounds like a cannon."

"For all we know, it is," said Phule. "According to Ambassador Gottesman, they've come to Zenobia planning to shoot some dinosaurs. I don't even want to speculate on what kind of weapons they thought they'd need for that."

"Civilians," grumbled Armstrong—just before another, even louder explosion caused him to duck again. "What the hell?"

"It came from over there," said Phule, pointing to the left of the row of three luxury-grade Ultra-tents facing them. "Let's find out what's going on."

They found the hunters in a group, huddled around a selection of weapons ranging from antique firearms to what looked alarmingly like a milspec rocket launcher, supposedly unavailable to the civilian trade. "Let's try this one," said one of the group. "The salesman told me it'd knock anything up to five thousand kilos right off its feet."

"Five thou?" said another. "Hell, if they got real dinos on this planet, not that I've seen hide nor hair of one ..."

"You won't, either," said Phule, stepping forward. "The local fauna are pretty diverse, but I've yet to see anything with hair—at least nothing indigenous."

Startled, the hunters whirled around to face them. "Captain Jester!" said the man who'd spoken first. "We didn't hear you coming."

"I'm not surprised, with all the noise you've been making," said Phule, with a smile. "You really ought to wear ear protection if you're going to be using those big cannons. By the way, would you mind pointing that one the other way?" He gestured toward the large-bore double-barreled rifle the hunter was cradling under one arm.

"Oh yeah, sorry," said the hunter—Euston O'Better, Armstrong recalled. He shifted the weapon to one side, and said, "It ain't loaded, anyways." To prove his point he pulled the trigger. The weapon roared, and O'Better nearly fell backwards from the recoil. At the same time, a gaping hole appeared in one of the Ultra-tents.

"Hey, why don't you watch where you're shooting?" came a woman's voice from inside the tent, shortly followed by the emergence of a compactly built brunette in shorts. Her hair was up in curlers, and her expression could have curdled milk at a hundred yards. "Oh, hello," she said, "I didn't know we had company."

"Captain, this is my wife Dallas," said one of the other hunters, Austen Tay-Shun. "And don't you worry, honey—we'll make sure Euston doesn't shoot you again."

"With that thing, once would be enough," said the woman. Then she turned to Phule, and a pleasant smile replaced her frown. "Hello, you must be Captain Jester. I'm Dallas Treat. And who's this handsome young man with you?"

Phule introduced the blushing Lieutenant Armstrong, then turned back to the hunters. "Gentlemen, what just happened is a good example of why I came out here. It looks to me as if you need to pay a lot more attention to weapons safety generally. For example, not knowing whether a weapon is loaded before you pull the trigger ..."

"Ahh, it's not such a big deal," said the third hunter, L.P. Asho. "It could've happened to anybody."

"It darn near happened to *me*," said Dallas Treat. "What do you need all those big guns for, anyway?"

"I tol' you, honey, we came to this planet to hunt the biggest game in the whole galaxy," said Tay-Shun. "If you're fixin' to go toe to toe with the big 'uns, you better have your boots on."

"What's that have to do with guns?" said Dallas, pouting. "Sometimes I think you say things that don't make any sense just to make me feel stupid."

"Honey, you don't hardly need help with that," said Tay-Shun. "Now, if you'll pardon me, I need to talk with these here Legion officers that come to visit ..."

"We're not really here for a social visit," said Phule, cutting him off. "I just have one point to make. You are not allowed to fire weapons indiscriminately as long as you're this close to our base. I'm going to insist that you stop shooting until you're someplace where you can't hurt one of my people by accident."

"I see," said L.P. Asho. "Tryin' to get rid of us, are you?"

"Mr. Asho, I want to get rid of anything that puts my people in danger," said Phule. "If you won't use weapons responsibly, that definitely includes you. I can't make you go home, but I *can* take your weapons away as long as you're in territory under my command. Or I can be a good deal of help."

"How's that?" asked O'Better.

Phule waved in the general direction of the Legion camp. "If you think you need weapons practice before you start hunting, I can give you guest privileges at our base firing range, with Legion instructors. Or if you'd prefer, I can help you move your camp out to a remote area with plenty of game, where you can fire away as you please. Your choice. But you just can't go popping off this close to my base; you don't even know where my people are, at any given time."

"All right, I take your point," said Tay-Shun, quieting Asho, who seemed ready to protest again. "I reckon we aren't quite ready to move out into the country just yet; we'd like to hire a native guide or two for when we do move. You think you can help us with that?"

"Our Zenobian liaison officer could probably help," said Phule. "But will you promise to put the guns away, or at least not to use them except at our range, until you're away from our base?"

"Fair enough, Captain," said Tay-Shun, and turned to look at the others. After a moment, they nodded reluctantly.

"Good, then," said Phule. "I'll talk to my local contact and see if he can connect you up with a guide or two. And if you want to practice, just let me know, and I'll arrange for you to use our facilities. Thank you for your understanding, gentlemen. And now, I'm afraid Lieutenant Armstrong and I need to get back to base."

"All right, then," said Tay-Shun. "Just get us that native guide, and we'll be out of your hair right quick."

"Can't be any too soon for me," muttered Armstrong, as the two officers turned. Phule shot him a warning glance, but he'd spoken too quietly for the hunters to hear. Together, they began jogging back to camp.

O O O

Willard Phule was back at his desk, eating a late breakfast and reading the daily performance summary of his investment portfolio, when his wrist communicator buzzed. That in itself was enough to alert him that something unusual was going on. The routine at Zenobia Base was sufficiently settled, by now, that Mother was unlikely to put a call through to him at mealtime for anything short of a genuine crisis.

On the other hand, the last few days had been characterized by a series of minicrises, involving Barky, the AEIOU team, the training exercise that had gone haywire, the "guests" that State had sent for him to entertain … Warily, Phule lifted his wrist close to his mouth, and said, "What is it, Mother?"

"I've got Tullie Bascomb on the line, sweetie," came the saucy voice. "I told the old *goniff to* call back when you're awake, but he just says it can't wait. Shall I tell him to go away?"

"Oh, Tullie's all right," said Phule, idly wondering where Mother had picked up Yiddish insults. "If he says it's important, I'm not going to make him wait."

"All right, but if he spoils your digestion, you know who to blame," said Mother. Phule nodded, silently, waiting. Something told him that Tullie's call arose from the fact that his father was on Lorelei Station, sticking his nose into the casino business. He hoped Victor Phule wasn't being too tough on the staff …

Abruptly, Bascomb's voice came through the speaker of the wrist communicator. "Captain, everything's hit the fan," he growled.

"Hit the fan?" Phule was nonplussed. "What's going on there, Tullie?"

"I'll tell you what's going on," said Bascomb. "Between your know-it-all father and some third-rate con artist we never should have let into the joint …"

Phule could hear shouting in the background, and Bascomb said, "Excuse me a second, Captain," and the line went quiet; evidently Tullie had pressed the mute button. Then, after a pause, Bascomb returned and began speaking again. "All right, Captain, this whole screwup was my idea, and I've got to take the heat for it. You've got my resignation as of right now, if you want it …"

"Wait a minute," said Phule. "Con artist? Screwup? Resignation? Tullie, I don't have the faintest idea what you're talking about. Will you go back to the start and tell me the whole story?"

"All right," said Bascomb. "It all started with your father …"

"I'm not surprised," said Phule. "Go ahead, Tullie."

"You remember we set up the thousand-dollar slots to get him to play, and you authorized a really big prize to lead him on? We all figured the odds were so long there wouldn't be a bug's chance on a hot griddle of our actually having to give the prize ..."

"Yes, I remember," said Phule. He suddenly sat bolt upright. "Don't tell me ..."

"I *am* telling you, Captain," said Bascomb. "But that's not the worst of it. Your damn-fool father wasn't satisfied with playing the slots himself, he had to go and give his chips to other people to play for him. Now I've got some smirking greaseball sitting in my office ..."

"Hey, buddy, show a li'l respect," Phule could hear a muffled voice say in the background.

"All right, all right," said Bascomb, resignedly. "Captain, the long and short of it is this: this guy sitting in my office is named Ernie Erkeep, and I'm sorry to tell you that, thanks to your old man, the bum now owns a controlling share—what used to be *your* share, in fact—in the Fat Chance Casino. Here, I'm tired of looking at the sleazy bastard. Why don't you talk to him while I go get myself a couple of stiff drinks?"

And the speaker again went silent while Phule sat looking stupidly at his wrist, waiting for someone on the other end to say something.

O   O   O

Thumper and the group of legionnaires he'd eaten breakfast with arrived in the center of the parade ground just before Sergeant Brandy emerged from the modular structure that was the main building on Zenobia Base. The Top Sergeant of Omega Company was one of the largest humans Thumper had ever seen, although she was a good bit shorter than the Volton legionnaire named Tusk-anini.

"All right, people, this is the Legion. Let's see something I could mistake for a formation," said Brandy, resignedly. She flipped through papers on a clipboard as the squad lined up, with only a minimum of grumbling. Thumper took a place in the middle of three rows, toward one end, waiting to see what would happen.

He'd been in formations before, and had learned not to be either too eager to catch the leader's attention or too obviously trying to escape it.

When everyone was more or less in place, Brandy looked up, and said, "We don't usually do roll call—I know all of you by now. But we've got a new guy today, and I think it'd be a good idea to call roll until he gets an idea who everybody else is, and you get to know who he is. So sound off when I call your names—you've all done this before, so don't make things any harder than they've gotta be."

"Sergeant, I have a question," said Mahatma, raising his hand in the front row.

Brandy rolled her eyes. "Gimme a break, Mahatma! Can't it wait until after roll call? I'd like to get through at least that much before the philosophical seminar for the day."

"But I just want to know how hard things have got to be," said Mahatma. "Do Legion regulations specify the degree of difficulty of roll call?"

"As a matter of fact, they do," growled Brandy. "They say you're supposed to answer when I call your name, unless you aren't here, in which case I mark you absent. Is that hard enough for you?"

"Maybe not for him, but it's a real challenge for some of these grunts," came a voice from the back of the formation.

Brandy glared. "Shut up, Roadkill," she barked. Then, after a pause, she added, "Haven't you feebs figured out I know your voices by now? OK, come on, let's hear a nice clear answer when I call your names. Brick?"

"Here, Sergeant," said a thin human female just in front of Thumper.

Brandy put a mark on her pad and continued. "Cheapshot?"

"Yo!" said another voice from the ranks.

Brandy dropped the hand with the clipboard to her side and glowered. "Look here, Cheapshot, we're trying to show Thumper how we do things in Omega Company. How many times have I told you not to answer 'Yo' when I call the roll?"

"Bunch of times, Sarge," said Cheapshot. "Never convinced me, though. You wanna show the new guy how we do things in Omega, you gotta include the bad with the good, right?"

"Cheapshot makin' sense," said another voice, and Thumper could hear still others murmuring their agreement.

Then Brandy said, "Shut up!" and the murmurs stopped. "OK," she said, "maybe you've got a point, Cheapshot. I'll agree that there's a lot of good things about the Omega way, but this is one of those times when I just want the good old Legion way. Believe me, there'll come a time when you'll thank me for this."

"If we thank you now, will you stop?" said another voice from the ranks.

"SHUT UP!" said Brandy, before the murmurs could get started. "If you just want to screw things up, I can make you stand here all day and never get to the fun stuff. I was gonna take you out to the obstacle course today, so Thumper can get a look at how Omega runs it."

Suddenly the entire formation fell silent, and Thumper could see the spines of his fellow legionnaires straighten as they came to attention in a way they'd only hinted at before. Even Cheapshot stood up straighter, and said, "I meant, *Here, Sergeant!*"

"That's a lot better," said Brandy, bringing up the clipboard and checking off the legionnaire's name. "Dukes?"

The rest of the roll call went so smoothly that even Thumper was impressed. What was it about the obstacle course that had such influence over Omega Company?

Whatever it was, he was about to find out …

O   O   O

Qual and his squad of Zenobians were out in the central compound of Zenobia Base again, busy at work as Sushi walked up to them. "Hey, what's new, Qual?" he said, waving to the Zenobian Flight Leftenant.

Qual looked up from the piece of equipment he and his crew were working on. It was apparently called the *Sklern*. At least, that was what Qual had told Sushi it was. But after hearing Qual explain how no two Zenobians spoke their language in exactly the same way, Sushi wasn't sure he could assume that the words Qual told him for local objects had any universal validity for other Zenobians.

The explanation still didn't quite make sense to him. But today, he had other things to think about, in particular Rev's quest for the mysterious 'L'Viz.

"Oh ho, welcome, Rawfish!" said Qual. "All goes rippingly with us today, our alignments are exemplary!"

"Uh ... triff," said Sushi. Then, recognizing an apparent opening, he went on, "Really interesting machine you guys have here. What does it do?"

Qual's face assumed what Sushi took to be a serious expression. "Much of what it does is organized," the Zenobian officer said.

It took Sushi a moment to make the mental connection between the translator's wording and Qual's probable meaning. "Oh, I didn't mean to pry into military secrets," he said. "Just curious about the apparatus, y'know."

"Oh, no offense received," said Qual, calmly. "In fact, I will tell you as much as I am permitted. The *sklern*—the meaning of the name is of course obvious—is in essence merely a triaxial projector of nonrandomized heebijeebis. As you can undoubtedly see, it is of considerably higher power than such units produced for the consumer market."

"Right," said Sushi, little wiser than before. He thought he grasped at least one point, though. "So this is basically the latest milspec version of one of your standard bits of hardware."

"Outstanding, Rawfish!" said Qual, slapping Sushi on the lower back. "Your intellectual capacity is, as usual, of the highest grade."

"Er, thanks, Qual," said Sushi. He didn't think he knew much more than before he'd asked, but maybe if he mulled over Qual's answer he'd come up with something. Meanwhile ... I've got a favor to ask you guys," he said. "We're still trying to figure out how to adjust these translators to give the best results so you guys can understand us and vice versa."

"That is hardly mandatory," said Qual. "Misunderstanding is a fact of life. If you were a Zenobian, you would accept it as it is."

"Maybe," said Sushi. "But as it happens, I'm a human, and an inquisitive one at that. So I can't help tinkering with stuff that doesn't work quite the way it ought to. Here's what I'd like to do."

He pulled a small rectangular black object out of his pocket. "This is a minirecorder I'd like you guys to turn on while you're talking about things. It'll give us a good sample of your normal conversation, with three or four of you talking at once, and then we can analyze it for common patterns. Is that OK?"

Qual looked at the minirecorder with lidded eyes, then turned to his crew and spoke a few sentences. They replied, and a brief conversation ensued. "We will do it," said Qual. "But only if you show me how to turn it off. I hope you understand me, Rawfish, my friend—sometimes we need to talk about things we do not want others to hear."

Sushi nodded. "Sure, I know what you mean. Even friends need privacy once in a while. See this red switch? Slide it to the left—toward this red LED—and it's off, back to the right, and it's on."

Qual took the device and slid the switch back and forth, then asked, "There should also be some way we can resolve what it has recorded, and remove it if by mischance we have forgotten it was working while we talked."

"Yeah," said Sushi. "This is the playback switch, and this is the erase button. Let me show you ..."

A few minutes later, with Qual and his crew satisfied they knew the workings of the recorder, Sushi said his goodbyes to the Zenobians and walked back to report to Rev. Rev and Do-Wop looked up at him as he entered the room. "They took it," he said.

"Good," said Rev. "Were them boys suspicious?"

"Maybe a little, but I showed them how it worked," said Sushi. "That seemed to satisfy them."

"Good," said Rev again. "I hope you didn't show them how *everything* worked."

"No way," said Sushi. "Unless they're experts in Terran milspec hardware, they'll never figure out that it's a transmitter as well as a recorder—and that you can't turn the transmitter off. You should be getting their signals now."

Sushi and Rev smiled at each other. They turned to the receiver Sushi had rigged up on a bench in Rev's office. Sure enough, a little light was blinking, showing that the unit was receiving. Attached to it was another small box, automatically recording every word the

Zenobians said within range of the recorder Sushi had given to Qual. Now all they had to do was wait …

O O O

"You won *what?*" For once, Lola's openmouthed surprise at Ernie was not for his having done something stupid. Just the fact that he *hadn't* done anything stupid—at least, not anything she knew about yet—was sufficient cause for surprise, as far as she was concerned.

"I won the casino," Ernie repeated, smirking. "Er—at least, a big share of the stock. The old man told me my share is worth maybe fifty million smeltonians."

"I still don't believe it," said Lola. "They wouldn't offer that big a prize. Even if the odds are close to impossible, the risk of losing is too big …"

"Hey, *you* come down to the office with me and talk to the casino guys," said Ernie. "That's what I came to get you for, anyway. They want me to sign papers, do all sorts of other stuff. I may be dumb, but I ain't dumb enough to sign somethin' I don't understand. That's what you're for."

"To sign something you don't understand?" Lola raised an eyebrow. "That applies to just about anything more complicated than a bar chit, and I'm sure not signing any of those for you. Well, if Phule's lawyers are as good as the rest of his staff, I doubt *anybody* could understand the papers they're going to want us to sign. We'll probably have to find a lawyer of our own to tell us what we're getting into—and I don't know who the legal heavies are on Lorelei. But give me a couple of minutes to fix my face, and we'll go see what they're trying to put over on us."

It took Lola more like half an hour. She changed into a dark designer suit that stamped her as a no-nonsense professional who insisted on getting the absolutely best quality without worrying about her purchases going out of fashion within three weeks. Lola had picked it up last year from an acquaintance who fenced for a haute couture shoplifting ring, and considered it worth every penny it had cost—a serious outlay of money even after the five-finger discount. Her makeup took longer—she wiped it off and started over twice before she nodded and turned away from the mirror. In the end, she looked about five years older than her usual style—and ten times more formidable. Nobody was likely to underestimate her, not now.

It took her another fifteen minutes of browbeating to get Ernie to change into something that might induce the Fat Chance Casino's legal staff to take *him* seriously. Then they boarded the local hoverbus and headed back to the casino. The Lorelei buses catered mainly to casino workers, and the vehicle was nearly empty, this being the middle of a shift. "What's our plan?" asked Ernie, keeping his voice low just in case the driver was spying for the Fat Chance.

"I don't really have one yet," said Lola, shrugging. "Find out what they're offering, and figure out how much more we can get by being a pain in their butts. That's what negotiating's all about."

"Well, they gotta make good on their promise, right?" said Ernie. "They say I own a hunk of the casino ..."

"And if you believe that, I've got a couple of nice planets for sale, cheap," said Lola. "The best thing we can do is go in there expecting the worst, and let them surprise us by doing better. And if we can keep them from figuring out just where we're coming from, maybe we can even fool them into offering us something they didn't plan on."

Ernie nodded. "I got it," he said. "We play the dumbs, and wait for them to screw up."

"Uh ... not quite," said Lola. "Your job is to sit there looking as if you're in charge, but let me do all the real talking. Just pretend I'm your lawyer, and you don't make any move involving money or your rights without my say-so. And I don't commit you to anything until I think we've got the best deal they're going to give us. Got it?"

"Sure," said Ernie. "Just what I said before—we play the dumbs and wait for them to screw up."

Lola sighed. "OK, have it your way," she said. "Just let me do all the talking."

The hoverbus changed lanes and came to a stop. Across the street was the Fat Chance. Smiling bravely, Lola took Ernie's arm and steered him out to the sidewalk. *This isn't going to be easy,* she thought to herself. Then again, the alternatives all looked a lot worse ...

O   O   O

"If you don't mind my saying so, sir, I find it difficult to understand your father's involvement in this scheme," said Beeker, over a hot cuppa tea. "It is hardly in character."

"Oh, I'd have to disagree, Beeks," said Phule, looking up from his Port-a-Brain computer. "Dad's always had a stubborn streak—when he's got a point to make, he insists on ramming it down the throat of anyone who doesn't instantly agree. I didn't even mind giving him a chance to win my share of the casino, even though it was a long shot. Dad could run the place as well as I ever did, and the troops will still get the dividends from their shares."

"And now you've delivered a controlling share to some unknown gambler, like a handout to some beggar on the street," sniffed Beeker. "What if he tries to run the casino himself? He's likely to run it into bankruptcy in no time at all."

Phule scoffed. "Oh, he can't do anything significant without winning a stockholder's vote. The fellows in Omega Company would never back him—they know Tullie and Lex and the others too well to turn them loose just because the new fellow wants to make a change."

"Do they?" asked Beeker, sharply. "What if this new fellow claims a new management team could increase profits? Or what if he offers a price for their shares that's too good to resist? It wouldn't be the first time stockholders have gotten greedy when somebody dangled cash in front of their noses."

"Oh, it's not impossible," said Phule, leaning back in his chair and looking at his butler. "We still don't know very much about this fellow—but I doubt he's got the capital to pull off that kind of trick. If he did, I think we'd have heard about him before he showed up at the Fat Chance."

"A very dubious assumption, sir," said Beeker. "The fellow could come from almost anywhere. If I were in charge of the casino,

I'd be checking the databases to see if he has a criminal record anywhere in the Alliance."

"I think we can trust Tullie Bascomb to find that out for us," said Phule. "In fact, I think that's one of the things we'd know by now, if there were anything to concern us. My suspicion is that the big winner's just a regular fellow—maybe a salesman, or a small businessman—who wanted to play with the high rollers and ended up getting luckier than he had any right to. When he realizes he's in deep water with all the big fish, he'll listen to reason and let the professionals handle things."

"It would be pleasant to think there was such an elegant solution," said Beeker. "Unfortunately, sir, in my experience the ability to recognize that one is out of one's depth is a rare commodity—especially among those most in need of such insight. Far more common is an indomitable thickness of skull bordering on complete absence of gray matter."

Before Phule could answer, Mother's voice came over the intercom. "Captain, we've got trouble," she said. At that very instant, Chief Inspector Snieff of the AEIOU burst through his office door. She was one step ahead of Lieutenant Rembrandt, this morning's OD. "Captain, I demand an explanation of this outrage," Snieff barked.

"Do you, Chief Inspector?" Phule's eyebrows rose ever so slightly. "And what outrage do you want me to explain? I haven't noticed any outrages in particular, unless maybe you're talking about your dog."

"Aha!" said Chief Inspector Snieff, pointing a finger at the captain. "And exactly why do you mention our beloved mascot, Barky, the Environmental Dog?"

"That ought to be pretty obvious," said Phule, staring at her. "He's been attacking my people ever since he set foot on this planet."

Snieff pulled herself up into a fair semblance of wrongly accused innocence. "Barky never attacks unprovoked," she said. "He only responds to pollution, or to direct harassment. He would not attack your people unless they were causing some kind of ecological problem. And he is trained not to injure the suspects he apprehends, merely to hold anyone who has detectable levels of a carefully delimited list of pollutants on their person, or in their belongings, until one of the human members of our team arrives to take charge."

"I'm sorry, Inspector, but you'll have to find somebody else to swallow that line," said Phule. "Your dog was chasing one of my legionnaires all around the dining hall just last night. *You* saw him, too—you were there."

"I am surprised at you, Captain," said Snieff. "The incident was clearly provoked by your legionnaire."

Beeker, who had been sitting quietly until now, snorted and said, "Provoked? Good Lord, madam, provoked in what way? By walking to the salad bar to get his dinner?"

"I *saw* him taunting poor Barky," said Snieff, lifting her chin and looking down her nose at the butler.

Beeker looked up at her, and said quietly, "Madam, you might discover more insight into the unfortunate animal's lack of manners by looking to the character of his human guardians than by postulating any provocative acts by his unlucky victims. If your dog is so poorly trained that he responds to this supposed taunting, then an objective observer would have no choice but to interpret that as proof of malfeasance on the part of his handlers."

Acting quickly, before Snieff could respond to Beeker's indictment, Phule smiled, and said, "Have a seat, Inspector. Tell me what the trouble is, and we'll try to sort it out."

Snieff glared at Beeker, then settled into a chair next to Phule's desk. "I'll get directly to the point, Captain. The last two days, I have heard your people firing weapons out in the desert—no doubt shooting at the local wildlife, possibly even harming it."

"I beg your pardon, ma'am," said Rembrandt. "If our people are shooting at something, you can be dead certain they're harming it. That's what weapons do, you know."

"Easy, Lieutenant," said Phule, raising a hand to quiet Rembrandt. He turned to Snieff. "Yes, Inspector, our people do shoot weapons out in the desert. Weapons training is an important part of the Legion's job, you know. But we aren't shooting at any local fauna—or the local flora, either, in case you're worried about that. We have a regulation practice range set up out beyond the perimeter. If you'd care to inspect it, I think we can even let you and your people fire a few test rounds ..."

"I think *not*," said Snieff. She stood, abruptly. "However, I do intend to make certain your people aren't taking potshots at the local animals. Be very careful, Captain. You military types may not think much of the AEIOU, but we have considerable power of our own when we decide to put to use. Good day." She turned and stalked out of the office, nearly knocking down Rembrandt as she went past.

"Well, well," said Phule, after the door had closed behind her. "I think we're going to have to do something about those hunters sooner than I planned."

"I wouldn't delay, sir," said Rembrandt, shaking her head. "She may be annoying as all get-out, but she's right about the AEIOU's power. And we're already way over on the wrong side of her. If she ever gets wind of a real violation, we could be in worse trouble than anything Headquarters has ever thought up for us."

"You're right, Remmie," said Phule. "We've got to get those hunters out of the vicinity. The only problem is where we're going to move them *to* ..." He rubbed his chin, then raised his wrist comm to speaking range and said, "Mother, find Flight Leftenant Qual for me. I think it's time we made use of his local knowledge again."

"Your wish is my command, sweetie pants," came Mother's mockingly sultry voice. Phule sighed. At least one thing was still more or less normal around Omega Company.

O O O

Brandy and the training squad—plus a handful of other legionnaires who seemed to have nothing better to do—hiked a couple of kilometers out into the desert. Thumper gazed curiously at the exotic landscape around him—this was only the third planet he had been to in person. And, of course, the incident with General Blitzkrieg had resulted in his entire basic training squad being confined to camp—so he'd seen very little of Mussina's World beyond the Legion boot camp and the spaceport.

One thing for sure—Zenobia was certainly different from the urban areas where he'd grown up, on his home world Teloon. He knew there were deserts and mountains and arctic tundra there, of course—he'd studied the geography of Teloon in school. But being there was a whole new experience. He'd joined the Legion to see the galaxy—and here it was, right under his long furry feet. If only his mama could see him now!

Finally, Brandy turned around and called out, "All right, squad, take five. We want everybody in shape for the obstacle course."

The little group gratefully complied. The walk had been short enough, over mostly level terrain, but hauling along full combat gear—as per Brandy's orders—made it a bit of a chore nonetheless. Looking around, Thumper wondered what they had stopped for. The landscape here looked pretty much the same as every other chunk of desert they'd marched past: interesting in a wild and foreign way. But there was no sign of the kind of obstacle course Thumper had run in Legion basic.

More surprising, when Thumper turned around, was the sight of a large fraction of Omega Company standing behind the training squad. Had they all heard of his record-setting obstacle course run back on Mussina's World? Were they here to see if he was as good as he claimed, or had they come hoping see him put in his place? Even the captain had come along. All the hints his fellow trainees had dropped about the obstacle course at Omega Company being *different* suddenly came back into his head. Just what was he going to have to do to prove himself to his new company?

Thumper looked out into the desert again, wondering whether Omega Company might have created an obstacle course using only the natural terrain. Thinking about it, he realized it might be a logical response to the different environments the Legion must find on the different worlds it was sent to. If Omega Company was going to operate on Zenobia, it made plenty of sense to train in Zenobian conditions …

His thoughts were interrupted by Brandy calling the squad to attention. "All right, people, form up and listen up!" She paused a moment while the Thumper and his fellow trainees gathered in front of her, then went on, "We have a new member of the company, one that's never run the obstacle course with us before. Now all of you know that we in Omega Company have our own way of running the course—and it's the best damn way in the Legion!"

Thumper wasn't quite sure what she was talking about, but he joined in automatically with the rest of the squad in a general cheer. Legion Basic had taught him that was a good thing to do, even when he didn't understand what everybody else was so enthusiastic about. He seemed to attract enough unwelcome attention from the sergeants and officers without asking for more.

Brandy nodded. "Now, some of you may have heard that Thumper set a record on the obstacle course in Legion basic. That's good—Omega Company wants the best legionnaires we can get."

"How'd Do-Wop get in?" yelled someone from in back of the group, but Brandy ignored the voice, and went on.

"But now we're out in the field, and what matters is getting the job done," she said. *"Everybody* has to get through the course, not just the two or three fastest guys."

"Right on, Sarge," said another voice from the back of the group—or maybe it was the same one. This time, others rumbled their agreement. Thumper began to wonder whether he'd been quite so wise to own up to his record-setting performance in basic. Not that these legionnaires seemed to hold it against him. But there was obviously a different standard in effect with Omega Company. He began to wonder just what was going to be demanded of him here.

"OK, then, here's the drill," said Brandy. "Thumper, you and the three Gambolts are the fastest here. So your job is to get out ahead of the rest, identify all obstacles, and decide how to get them out of the way for the rest of the guys. If you can't do it by yourselves, come back to the group and get help."

"Yes, Sergeant," said one of the Gambolts—his Legion name was Rube, Thumper remembered. "How about the machine guns? You want us to take them out, or do you have another team for that?"

"Mahatma and Brick will do that," said Brandy. "All right, the course runs directly west two hundred meters, then takes a turn to the northwest for another two hundred. You'll start at my signal—ready: go!"

The Gambolts looked at Thumper, then all four of them slapped paws together. "All right, let's roll!" growled Dukes, and together they dashed off into the desert. Behind them there was a roar as the remainder of the squad—and most of the spectators—fell in behind them.

At last Thumper began to understand—*this* was what Omega Company was about! He grinned and began moving forward, proud to be part of the team.

CHAPTER FOURTEEN

Journal #727

n a truly orderly universe, a once-in-a-trillion-chances event ought to have the common courtesy to wait for someone to make a few million attempts to bring it about before manifesting itself. It says something very unpleasant about the universe we live in that such an event can just as easily occur the very first time someone tries to bring it about.

O O O

Two men were waiting for Ernie and Lola in the Fat Chance Casino offices. One of them introduced himself to Lola as Tullie Bascomb, chief of gambling operations. The other she already knew: Victor Phule, who wore an uncharacteristically pained expression. He looked Lola in the eye, and said, "I remember you! What are you doing mixed up with this fellow—or have you been all along?"

"That's really not germane to our business today, Mr. Phule," said Lola. "In fact, I might ask you what you're doing here today—I didn't know you had a direct interest in your son's holdings here on Lorelei."

Bascomb answered before Victor Phule could speak. "Mr. Phule is here as a witness to the events that were responsible for the situation we're in today. But you should know that I'm fully empowered to act for the Fat Chance Casino Corporation—in fact, this is pretty much a formality. I'm pleased to say that we're ready to give you two million dollars free and clear—cash, check, gold, or Fat Chance Casino chips. We'll hand it over just as soon as you sign a few papers." He gestured toward a sheaf of documents lying on his desk.

"Two million?" said Lola, raising an eyebrow, while frantically signaling to Ernie to keep his mouth shut. "That isn't quite what we came here expecting, Mr. Bascomb. The terms of your prize offer were very explicit. A partner's share ..."

"Do you really think so?" said Bascomb, with a predatory grin. "As it happens, two million is a very generous payout. To tell you the truth, I'm not even quite sure what you think you've won. The terms of the jackpot on the thousand-dollar slots were never precisely spelled out ..."

"That doesn't matter," said Lola, crisply. "I hate to correct you, Mr. Bascomb, but I have done some research into the Interplanetary Commercial Code as it applies to Lorelei Station. Your local government has managed to get in a number of provisions I'd have to describe as highly unfriendly to consumers, but I can assure you there are still some very explicit penalties for deceptive advertising, especially as applying to prizes offered in the casinos."

"That may well be, young lady," said Bascomb, shaking a finger. "I won't argue the ins and outs of the law with you here. The bottom line is, we've got some damn fine lawyers—damn expensive ones, too—to argue our position. How are you fixed in that department? We can afford to tie you up in court for an awful long time."

Lola stared him down. "And what do you want to bet the other casinos won't be licking their lips when they find out that Fat Chance is trying to renege on your super jackpot? Especially after you've been stealing half their business by offering the best payouts on the station. The publicity value ought to be worth jillions to them. Come to think of it, they might even be willing to contribute to our legal fees ..."

Tullie Bascomb frowned. "Are you threatening us?"

Lola laughed, lightly. "Oh, no, Mr. Bascomb. Just reminding you that your casino isn't the only game in town. I think Captain Jester knows that, even if you don't. It's too bad *he* isn't here to talk to me. I bet he'd be a lot more reasonable ..."

Victor Phule gritted his teeth. "If the boy were reasonable, we wouldn't be in this mess at all," he growled. "I swear, the brat hasn't done a sensible thing in years, starting with joining the Space Legion and abandoning the name his parents gave him. You'd think he'd have more respect for his own family ..."

"Now, Mr. Phule," said Bascomb softly. "Let's try to keep our focus on the issue at hand ..."

"Hey, I don't think he's that far out of line," said Ernie, speaking for the first time since the meeting had begun. "I know what it's like when you don't get any respect from people. Believe me, I know."

Victor Phule looked at Ernie and nodded. "Yes, I expect you do," he said. "It's ironic—a fellow builds up something by his own efforts, and all of a sudden everybody around him thinks they know more about it than he does. I've seen it all too often ..."

"Hell, that's what happens when you let somebody else try to run your life," said Ernie, sympathetically. "I bet if you and I just sat down together, without any middlemen, we could get this whole problem straightened out in jig time. Come to think of it, why don't we go have a drink and do just that? We'll probably be back with a done deal before these two are finished calling each other names."

"You've got the right idea, old boy," said Victor Phule, standing up. He put a hand on Ernie's shoulder. "Come on—I'm buying. We'll have things sorted out in no time at all."

Tullie Bascomb looked up in alarm as Ernie stood up, grinning. "Hold on, Mr. Phule. The captain hasn't authorized you to strike any agreements with these people ..."

Lola was already on her feet, hands on her hips. "Ernie, I can't let you make any deals without my advice."

"Oh, encapsulate it," said Victor Phule, waving a hand. "You two buzzards want to dictate every pixel of this agreement, but that's the stupidest possible way to go about things. I'll tell you what's going to happen. This gentleman and I will sit down together and find a solution we can both agree on. Then we'll bring it back to you two to fiddle with the details. I'm sure there'll be plenty of detail work left for you. But for now, you're going to leave it up to the principals. And Bascomb, if you don't like it, you can call up my son. I suspect he'll tell you to step aside and let two gentlemen arrive at something we can all live with. Come on, Ernie. Let's go get a drink."

He walked out the door arm in arm with Ernie, leaving Bascomb and Lola staring after them, openmouthed.

O   O   O

Sushi was wearing a set of headphones and carefully adjusting dials on his device when Do-Wop walked in. "Hey, man, what's up?" said Do-Wop. "We figured out what Qual and his homeboys are talking about yet?"

"Shh," said Sushi, pointing to the device. "I've finally got them pretty well tuned in. And I've learned one thing already. Qual was right—they all speak slightly different versions of their language."

"Huh. Who'd've thunk it?" said Do-Wop, pulling up a chair. "What are they jabberin' about?"

"Mostly technical stuff so far," said Sushi. "Adjusting that machine—the *sklern*, Qual called it. And in between, joking about something—here, you give a listen." He took off the headphones and reached up to turn on a speaker.

"Ve ought to rotate it two *grimbugs* upward," said one Zenobian voice.

"Two and a fifth," came another—this one recognizably Flight Leftenant Qual. "That'll just clear the faffleweed cluster."

"Vorking on two and a fift," answered the first voice. Then, in a different tone, "Hey, Flort, didja view the Tail-vippers last sundown?"

"Sssst, dey raise a stench in my nostrils," said a third voice—apparently Flort. "Dey haven't had an efficient leaper since Blurg retreated to his domicile."

"Watch it, Zoot," said Qual. "Don't overcrank …"

"Tightly vocussed at two and a fift," said the first voice again. Then Zoot added, "Don't underrate Kloog. Ven he's in the league a little longer been, an exemplary leaper he'll be."

"Kloog is widout grace," growled Flort. "He could take lessons from a *gryff*."

"This shit don't make no sense," said Do-Wop, drumming his fingers on the table next to the equipment.

"I think they're talking about some kind of sports team from their home city," said Sushi. "Hard to tell exactly, because the words don't all translate into anything we have an exact equivalent for."

"That's for damn sure," said Do-Wop. "I think Rev's lookin' for a weefle in a viddleworf. If it wasn't such a sweet deal workin' for him instead of pulling regular Legion duty, I'd tell him so myself."

Sushi looked at him with raised eyebrows, then said, "Well, I don't see any percentage in ruining a good scam, either. But you know, even if Rev's ideas never pan out, this whole Zenobian language thing is fascinating. If I could figure out a way to rig translators to deal with it, I bet there's a lot of money to be made. So I'm not just in this to get out of other work. And if you're not just looking for a new way to goof off, it could work out to benefit you, too."

Do-Wop looked doubtful. "I dunno, man. You listen to a bunch of crazy stuff long enough, you could maybe end up crazy yourself."

Over the speaker, Flight Leftant Qual's voice said, "Now doxen up the regulator for a test projection."

"Gott it, Leftenant," said Zoot. Then, after a pause, "Regulator energetically doxened; ready to project, sir."

Do-Wop waved a hand. "See what I mean? Nothin' but crazy stuff. Maybe it's worth a million, I dunno."

"Kloog seems graceful enough for me," said Zoot over the speaker. "The purpose is not the senses to bedazzle, but to advance the pellet."

"Kloog cannot retain da pellet in his claws long enough to advance it," said Flort. "He raises a continual stench in my nostrils."

"Maintain the doxenization or we will be forced to recommence," said Qual, sternly. "Your sporting chatter can be retained for a more propitious occasion."

"Double vision, Flight Leftenant," said the other two Zenobians, almost in unison.

"Double vision?" said Do-Wop. "I told ya, this is crazy stuff. You keep listenin' to these lizards, you're gonna end up with scales on your ass."

"So should I tell Rev you're tired of working on this project?" said Sushi, with a mischievous expression. "I hear tell Remmie's asking for volunteers for a heavy construction squad …"

"Uh, hey, Soosh, just kiddin'," said Do-Wop. "Lizard talk is the real deal for me. What did you say you wanted me to do?"

"Well, for starters, you could run down to supply and get about a dozen blank recording cartridges," said Sushi. "We don't want any of this immortal Zenobian conversation to get lost just because we ran out of cartridges, do we now?"

"Cartridges comin' up," said Do-Wop, and headed out the door.

Sushi watched him leave, chuckling, then put the headphones on again. Maybe there was a way to broaden the standard semantic filtering circuits …

O   O   O

"What do you think they're up to?" asked Lola. She and Tullie Bascomb were nursing twin glasses of syntha-scotch on the rocks in his office, waiting for Victor Phule and Ernie to return.

"Hell, I'd just like to know where they *are,*" said Tullie. "No sign of 'em in the casino lounge, and the security system says that nobody's entered Mr. Phule's room in the last three hours. They must be outside the Fat Chance, and I don't like that one damn bit."

"Neither do I," said Lola. "I hope they at least took Mr. Phule's bodyguard along with them."

"Well, there's no sign of him, either, so that's the way to bet," said Tullie. He took a long sip of his drink, then glanced at the computer monitor on his desk. "Just how far do you trust your guy, by the way? Is he going to listen to sense once they come back to us?"

"I trust him just about as far as you trust your guy," said Lola, staring at him over the rim of her own glass. "Which, from the way you've been talking, is about as far as you can throw a small asteroid two-handed."

"That's what I was afraid of," said Tullie, glumly. "I've got one advantage over you, though."

"What's that?"

"My guy is my boss's father," said the casino manager. "He can get me in a bunch of trouble, and he's as stubborn as any man I've ever seen. But I don't think Captain Jester is gonna fire me just on the old man's say-so. Not unless he's got some reason to believe I've really screwed up. Your guy, on the other hand …"

Lola grimaced. "Yeah, does the phrase 'loose cannon' mean anything to you? And since he's the one who pulled the handle on that machine of yours, Lorelei law says he's the one who gets the last word. Well, I've talked him out of stupid things before, and I can do it again."

"Lorelei law is an extremely flexible instrument," said Tullie Bascomb, grinning. "Considering who made it, that shouldn't surprise anyone. I think we can work with that."

"As long as you don't work with it to cheat my client out of what he's got coming to him," said Lola, firmly. She stared at her empty glass, then looked up, and said, "What exactly are the terms you were offering on that jackpot?"

"If you want to know the real truth, we didn't expect anybody but Victor Phule to win it," said Bascomb. "We set up that whole bank of slots with odds that ought to have dissuaded anybody with brains from playing it, and a price that should've clinched the deal."

"What were you doing that for?" asked Lola, setting down the glass.

"The old skinflint got the idea that our payouts were too generous," said Tullie. He'd emptied his glass quite some time before. "Victor Phule thought he could prove it by playing a system, and we decided to let him—teach him a lesson the hard way. Captain Jester approved it, too. But who the hell expected a billion-to-one shot to pay off in less than a week?"

"Well, I'm just as glad it was my guy who hit the winner," said Lola. "Remember, though—I'm here to make sure the casino honors its promise. You offered a share of the casino, and that's what you're going to deliver. Or I'm going to yell so loud they hear it on Altair IV."

"Yeah, yeah, I hear you," said Tullie. "We'll play it as honest as we can afford to, don't you worry. What worries me is whether those two *gentlemen* are going to cook up something neither one of us can live with."

"A gentlemen's agreement between those two is the last thing we need," agreed Lola. "But if Victor Phule doesn't have the authority to cut a deal for the casino, why are you worried about him running off to talk with Ernie? If he can't bind you to anything, you've got nothing to lose ... Right?"

Bascomb leaned back in his chair and stretched his arms above his head. "One thing you learn in this business," he said. "You've always got *something* to lose. And there's always somebody standing there ready to pick it up and run away, the minute you drop it. So you cover all your exits, is the only way to play the game. Which is why I'm worried about the old man—and about your guy, too."

"They're wild cards," said Lola, nodding.

"Worse than that," said Bascomb. "I can figure the odds on a wild card, and make allowances for it. Your guy—I thought I had some idea what he was, but now I'm not so sure."

"I've known him longer than most people, and sometimes he scares even me," said Lola. "What about Victor Phule?"

"I don't even want to *think* about Victor Phule," said Tullie. He reached for the syntha-scotch. "Which is why I'm havin' another drink. How about you, sister?"

Lola nodded again. "First good idea I've heard today," she said.

o o o

"Hey, Soosh, quittin' time," said Super-Gnat, sticking her head through the door. Behind her was Tusk-anini, with a baleful stare that might have worried Sushi if he hadn't recognized it as the Volton's habitual expression.

"Sure," said Sushi, stretching his arms above his head. "It doesn't look as if anything's going to happen here, anyhow. Give me a minute to put it on auto for the night, and I'll be right with you."

"All right," said Super-Gnat. "Just don't make Tusk start counting, OK?"

Tusk-anini's scowl became even more menacing. "Why no counting? I count good as anybody," he said.

"Yeah," said Super-Gnat, grinning. "Now all we have to do is teach you when not to do it." She gave him a friendly elbow in the short ribs.

While the two legionnaires bantered, Sushi quickly ran through his routine to set up the listening apparatus for automatic recording of the Zenobians' conversation. He didn't expect to find any great amount of material when he came back. The natives tended to end their workday around the same time as the legionnaires. In fact, Flight Leftenant Qual was often seen in the lounge, having a drink with the captain and the other Legion officers before dinner.

Almost without thinking, he glanced at the translated text scrolling across his computer screen before turning off the display for the night. That was when the word "L'Viz" jumped out at him. "Hold on a minute, guys," he said. "Something weird's happening here ..."

"Sure, like that's anything new," said Super-Gnat. "This whole outfit is about the weirdest experience I've ever had anything to do with."

"Uh-huh," said Sushi, peering intently at the screen. He spoke a soft command, and the text scrolled backwards. He leaned closer, muttering softly.

"Uh-oh," said Super-Gnat. "This looks like one of those minutes that turns out to be all night long. Hey, Soosh, are you comin', or not?"

"He standing still, looks like to me," said Tusk-anini.

"Yeah," said Sushi, turning around to meet their gazes. "Look, guys, something really interesting just came up. It'll take me a little while to figure out. Why don't you go ahead and I'll catch up with you."

"Sure," said Super-Gnat, shrugging. "We'll save you a seat. Just don't expect us to save you any beer."

"Yeah, OK," said Sushi, obviously only half-listening. Then he said, more to himself than to any listener, "Why didn't I think of this before?"

But Super-Gnat and Tusk-anini were already gone.

O O O

"Where in Ghu's name *are* they?" Tullie Bascomb stared through bloodshot eyes out the window of his office at the neon-lit landscape of Lorelei. He and Lola had been waiting for Victor Phule and Ernie to come back for over six hours. Several discreet (but increasingly urgent) searches of the hotel and surrounding area had produced no sign of the two delinquents.

"Your guess is as good as mine," said Lola. "I'd have bet on the nearest bar, but we've tried that—the nearest dozen bars, I think. And you say they're not in Mr. Phule's room."

"Security says so, and I trust my security people," said Bascomb. "More than I trust Victor Phule—let alone your guy."

Lola set down her drink—she really didn't need any more, not if she wanted to have some semblance of her wits about her when Ernie and Phule Sr. returned with whatever crazy deal they'd agreed on—assuming they *did* agree on something. She looked Bascomb directly in the eyes, and said, "Look, my guy just wants you to deliver what you said you were gonna pay to the jackpot winner—a partner's share of the casino stock." She paused. "I don't see how it's *our* problem if you didn't intend for him to win. Not if you're running an honest business, the way you claim you are."

Bascomb drew himself up straight, and said, with as much dignity as he could muster after four stiff drinks, "I wish I had any reason to believe *you* two are as honest as the Fat Chance Casino. We're as honest as anybody in this business—a lot more honest than most—and if you've done your homework, you ought to know that."

"All right, I'll give you that much," said Lola. "The point is, my client Mr. Erkeep is entitled to the jackpot for the machine he played. The casino has no rules posted concerning any eligibility for prizes or jackpots other than having to be of legal gambling age—which on Lorelei means tall enough to reach the handles of the slots. My client qualifies."

"What if he obtained the winning chip fraudulently?" said Bascomb. "We've got precedents covering that ..."

Lola shook her head emphatically. "Fraudulent? How do you get fraudulent? Vic Phule gave Mr. Erkeep a chip to gamble with, he played and won, and gave Mr. Phule back half his winnings—as agreed up front. The remaining chips were his to do with as he wanted. He could've thrown them into a trash disintegrator if he'd wanted—in fact I bet you'd like that."

"Nah, not really," said Bascomb. "There's always a small percentage of chips that never get cashed in. The customers take 'em home for souvenirs, or lose 'em down a drain or someplace else where they never get found. Sure, it's money we don't have to pay out, but the legal beagles and the bean counters get headaches about it. They always worry that somebody's gonna show up one day with a huge spacechest full of chips and clean out the bank. Outstanding liabilities, they call it. And when they worry, that gives *me* headaches."

Lola stared hard at him for a long moment, then nodded. "OK, I guess I *do* believe you," she said. "But if you're so worried about what the bean counters and the shysters think, why'd you even offer a deal like the one Ernie won? Didn't they scream bloody murder?"

"We never asked 'em," said Bascomb. "I thought it up, and Captain Jester approved it himself, and that was good enough. We didn't expect anybody but the captain's father to play at such lousy odds. And if by some quirk of the odds, the damn machines did pay off, the captain didn't see anything wrong with passing a share of the casino to his old man. As long as it stayed in the family, he figured he wouldn't have to worry about how it was being run."

"What, he thinks his whole family has the golden touch?"

"No, he just thinks they're smart enough to leave something to the professionals when they can't do it themselves," said Bascomb. He shook his head, and continued, "Now that I've put him in the hole this way, I wouldn't blame him if he decided to get in some new professionals to run the joint." He sighed and took another sip of his drink.

"Well, you're not fired yet," said Lola. "Look, as long as my guy gets a fair shake out of this, he's not going to let them cut you loose."

"Easy for you to say," said Bascomb. "You think you're going to have any influence on what Captain Jester decides to do? Your guy may think he's won a partner's share, but control of the casino still rests with the majority of the stockholders. And I wouldn't bet on them listening to anybody but the captain."

"Hey, I don't want to see you in the ejection pod," said Lola, reaching over and putting her hand on his forearm. "We just have to find something the two of us can agree on, and when Phule and Ernie come back, we convince them it's what they really wanted all along. If you can get Mr. Phule on board, I'm sure his son will listen to what he says."

"If he does, it'll be the first time in years," said Bascomb. "But I agree, we've got to be ready with something sensible before our principals come back with their proposition. What do you think of this idea ..."

The discussion went on into late hours.

CHAPTER FIFTEEN

Journal #732

T|he rationalist is convinced that every sophont is at bottom predictable, acting according to consistent (if not necessarily already well-known) rules. The mystic, for his part, believes that every creature conceals within its breast some element of the wild and unpredictable. Of the legionnaires who play parts in this ongoing chronicle, perhaps young Sushi best characterizes the former point of view, with Rev perhaps the most obvious advocate of the latter.

The realist (a label I believe I may fairly apply to myself) is aware that both of these philosophies have merit. Most of us are predominantly creatures of habit and pattern; but even the quietest of us has depths, from which the most unexpected actions can sometimes emerge ...

O O O

Tonight, Thumper was standing perimeter guard duty for the first time. Brandy led him out to the position he'd be occupying, to show him the ropes and give a word or two of advice.

"The biggest thing to remember is that you've got instant comm contact with Mother, if anything weird happens," said Omega Company's Top Sergeant. "Don't worry about bothering her—first of all, she loves to talk, and second, whatever's going on, she's probably talked to a lot of legionnaires in exactly the same spot you're in—so she may have a pretty good idea what's happening. And third, if you really do need help, she can get it to you faster than anybody else. Got the picture?"

"Yes, Sergeant," said Thumper, peering out into the darkness surrounding the base. He felt small and alone, even with the Zenobian stun ray he cradled in his arms.

Brandy nodded. "And the second thing to remember is, even though we're on a strange planet light-years away from your home or mine, there's not really much that *can* go wrong. The only other humans on the planet are the AEIOU team, over there, and the hunters who brought you here. And none of them are going to invade the camp—though if those hunters get boozed up, they might do something stupid. The Zenobians are our allies—in fact, they're the ones who invited us here. And the Nanoids—the microscopic colony intelligence that the captain and Beeker found out in the desert—nobody's seen them since the captain sent his robot double to deal with them. Not much chance they'll decide to come back on your watch. As for the local animals, they pretty much keep their distance. If in doubt, buzz Mother, then shoot to stun if you think you're being threatened."

"Right, Sergeant," said Thumper. He was doing his best to sound confident and competent.

"OK, then, you're on your own," said Brandy. She gave the new legionnaire a friendly soft punch in the shoulder. "Garbo will be here to relieve you in four hours. Do your best to stay awake until then."

"*Yes, Sergeant!*" said Thumper, grinning a little bit now as Brandy headed back in toward the modular base building. His Lepoid eyes were already adapting well to the darkness, and he could see the vague outlines of some of the larger specimens of the local vegetation out against the starry horizon. After a couple of minutes, he heard the faint sound of the door to the base building opening and closing. Now he really was alone.

Thumper looked around in all directions, taking his time to make sure he didn't overlook anything. Finally, satisfied that he wasn't under observation, he took a deep breath, and, as quietly as possible, slipped out across the perimeter of Omega Base into the cool desert night.

O O O

"Hey, kid, wake up," said a loud voice in Lola's ear. "We're back!"

"Ernie!" Lola sat bolt upright, her eyes suddenly focused. "You idiot! Where've you been all this time?"

"Hey, take it easy," said Ernie, backing away a pace. "Mr. Phule and I just went someplace quiet to talk things over without any audience or interference, OK?"

"No, it's not OK!" said Lola. She suddenly became aware of Victor Phule standing slightly behind Ernie, and Tullie Bascomb in his chair behind his big desk. Bascomb was rubbing his eyes; so at least she hadn't been the *only* one to fall asleep. "What time is it?" she asked, lamely trying for a graceful change of subject.

"Three in the morning," said Victor Phule. "Reminds me of old times, staying up to the wee hours to hammer out details of a deal. Exhausting, but there's nothing more rewarding. Why, I remember the foundry strikes of '58—we negotiated around the clock and finally convinced the union scum they'd lose thirty-five hundred jobs if they didn't settle! The rascals tried to put the best face on it for their followers, but it was all on our terms in the end, of course."

"Wonderful," said Lola, with a frozen smile. "And did you two uh, hammer out a deal this time?"

"Sure did," said Ernie. "Here's what's going down ..."

"Wait a moment," said Tullie Bascomb, sitting up straighten "We can't just wing it on something this important. Have you got anything written down, or shall I call in a stenobot?"

"Ahh, we don't need no stenobot," said Ernie. "Mr. Phule and me have got a gen'lman's agreement ..."

"Send for the stenobot," said Lola, cutting him off. "I don't want anything these two *gentlemen* have agreed on slipping between the cracks while everybody's getting a good night's sleep and sobering up."

"And just maybe we will have a few little suggestions on how to make the language more precise," said Tullie Bascomb, with a smile that would do a piranha proud. He pushed a button on the desk and winked at Lola, who gave him a slight nod in return. She wasn't anywhere near as confident as Bascomb seemed to be. They'd come up with a more or less workable understanding, but there was still the chance that Victor Phule and Ernie would dig in their heels, either together or separately. Especially after Phule's bragging about the good old days of union-busting …

A side door slid open and a small officebot glided through, with an almost inaudible whirring sound. It rolled over and stopped next to the desk, waiting. Bascomb said, "Record," and a light began winking off and on. "All right, Mr. Phule, Mr. Erkeep, tell us what you've arrived at. Once it's in memory, we can look at it and see what needs to be twiddled."

"Very well," said Victor Phule, sitting up and clearing his throat. He looked at Ernie. "I'll explain this, and Mr. Erkeep can confirm it." He waited for Ernie to nod, then continued. "What we've agreed on, in principle, is a buyout. Mr. Erkeep agrees to assign his share of the casino stock to me, and renounces the right to any input into the day-to-day operation of the business."

"I don't wanna go to an office every day and sit through all those business meetings," said Ernie, spreading his hands apart. "Suits make me look fat, anyway."

"Your lip's going to look fat if you didn't get something worthwhile in return," said Lola, staring hard. She turned to Victor Phule. "Just how large is the share of stock you want him to assign you?"

"I was getting to that," said Victor Phule, smoothly. "The jackpot my friend here won was sixteen thousand shares of stock, from the portion that was held by my son, Willard—as Mr. Bascomb told us earlier today."

"And what's the current market value?" asked Lola, a suspicious expression on her face.

Phule tucked his thumbs into the lapels of his jacket. "Well, since this is a closely held stock that isn't normally traded on the open market, that's a bit of a tricky question," he began.

"Oh, *su-ure*," said Lola. "I think I'm going to insist on an independent confirmation of whatever value you claim."

"Hey, hey," said Ernie, making shushing motions. "Don't queer the deal, Lola. You haven't even heard what we're getting ..."

"All right, I'll listen," she said. "But it better be mighty good."

Victor Phule raised his brows and said, "Our best estimate of current market value is 250 dollars a share. That would yield a gross value of four million dollars for the shares in question."

"Yess!" said Ernie, pumping a fist into the air.

Lola thought for a moment, then said, "Your previous valuation was a lot higher." She stared pointedly at Phule. "Something like fifty million dollars, if my client quoted you correctly."

"Well, you can't really hold me to that," said Victor Phule. "That was an off-the-cuff estimate. These figures are much more scientific ..."

Lola cut him off. "For a thousand-dollar bet, that makes that only a four-thousand-to-one jackpot. Not very impressive odds, if you ask me."

Victor Phule held up a hand. "You haven't heard the whole agreement," he said. "We are also prepared to pay an annual royalty of one percent of par value per share for twenty-five years, for a total of another one million dollars in deferred payments if the stock remains at its current value. Naturally, the payment could fluctuate, but under good management, I'd expect the value to go steadily up."

"I tried to get him up to fifty years, but he wouldn't bite," said Ernie, sheepishly.

Tullie Bascomb shook his head. "I'm going to have to run this past the captain, but I think he'll okay it. I don't see where he has a lot of choice. Is that everything? I can have the stenobot print it up and send it to the captain. Are you satisfied with the terms, Miss?"

Lola exchanged a quick glance with Bascomb. She was amazed. These two clowns had somehow managed to come up with a workable scheme—one she could actually live with. There was, of course, no point in Ernie's having a serious interest in any kind of legitimate business, let alone a casino. He'd run it into the ground in record time if he ever tried to manage it. And he'd be robbed blind if he tried to hire somebody to run it for him. Lola knew that. And Tullie Bascomb, who was as shrewd an operator as she'd ever laid eyes on, probably knew it, too. So a flat buyout was the most sensible deal they could have asked for. The only question was whether they could realistically jack up the buyout price any higher.

After a moment's reflection, Lola decided not to press her luck, and shrugged. "I think we can live with that," she said. "Are there any other conditions you haven't told us? Any reason we can't pick up our money and go as soon as the captain's OK comes through?"

"No, that's the whole deal," said Ernie, and Victor Phule nodded.

A high-pitched mechanical voice spoke—the stenobot. "The agreement is subject to two legal restrictions that have not been made explicit. Shall I include them in the memo to Captain Jester?"

"Uh—legal restrictions?" Lola was frowning, now. "Just what are those?"

"First is the security and exchange commission registration fee for transfer of stocks. Since the stocks are being transferred twice, the fee is doubled. It comes to twelve hundred dollars."

"Twelve farkin' hundred? No way!" said Ernie.

"You cannot own the stocks without registering them, and you cannot sell the stocks unless you own them," said the stenobot, in an irritatingly pedantic tone.

"I don't care," said Ernie. "I'm not payin' no fees."

"We'll pay the fees," said Tullie Bascomb, raising a hand. "What else?"

"Lorelei casino regulation statutes require winners of all jackpots in excess of ten thousand dollars to have their holo image taken and put on file for use in casino publicity. A copy will also be kept on file in the station police headquarters."

"That's a completely unacceptable condition," said Lola. "Mr. Erkeep will not allow his image to be used."

"Aww, why not, Lola?" said Ernie. "I always wanted to see my picture on the cover of a mag—even if it's the back cover, in an ad."

Lola grabbed him and pulled his head down close to her mouth. "You want Mr. V to see that image?" she hissed in his ear. "Or have you forgotten just why we came back here?"

"Oops, that's right, no pictures!" said Ernie. "Completely unacceptable condition!"

"Uh, I'm afraid we're gonna have a problem with that," said Bascomb. "The casino security system automatically takes a picture of all big winners. It's been on file with the police ever since the jackpot bell went off. And unless our publicity department is asleep on the job, I'd bet they've been sending it to every media outlet in the galaxy, too."

"Oh, shit," said Lola, with utter sincerity. Abruptly she stood up. "Come on, Ernie, we're out of here," she said, and before anyone else could say a word, the two of them stalked out of the office, leaving Bascomb and Phule standing openmouthed.

O O O

"Captain, there's something you need to know," said Sushi.

Phule looked up from the screen of his Port-a-Brain. Sushi was leaning against the frame of his office door, looking dead tired. "Come on in and sit down, Sushi," he said, deactivating the computer screen. When the legionnaire was seated opposite him, he said, "From the way you look, it's fairly important. I hope it's not bad news ..."

"It is if we don't do anything about it," said Sushi. "But I think I know what we can do—if we're quick enough, and if I'm right about what I think the Zenobians are doing."

"This is getting complicated," said Phule. "Why don't you go back to the beginning and tell it straight through? Maybe that'll make it easier to figure out."

"All right, there are a couple of parts to it," said Sushi. "First of all, I've figured out what those so-called hunters are really here for."

Phule sat up and pushed his Port-a-Brain aside. "Now that's something we've been wondering about ever since they showed up. I didn't think they acted all that interested in getting out into the wilds and finding game. What are they up to?"

"Yes, I've been wondering that myself," said Beeker. "They certainly aren't here for the cultural experience."

"Nor for the waters," said Sushi. "In fact, as best I can tell, they're here to spy on us."

"Spy?" said Beeker. "To steal military secrets? If young Mr. Phule will pardon my saying so, I find it difficult to believe that the commanders of the Legion would entrust this company with any highly sensitive information. For that matter, even if there were such secrets to be found, to whom would they be sold? The Alliance has no enemies that I know of."

"Well, Beeks, that may be," said Phule. "On the other hand, I'm inclined to give a certain amount of weight to Sushi's suspicions— at least until I find some reason to doubt them. What makes you think they're spying, Sushi?"

Sushi cleared his throat. "Captain, I happened to be present at a highly unofficial gathering where the hunters and some of our personnel were present ..."

"Chocolate Harry's poker game?" said Phule, raising an eyebrow. "I knew they showed up there, and I heard that Harry took a good bit of their money, which is fine with me. If they don't know any better than to gamble with a veteran Legion sergeant, that's their bad judgment. But what secrets could they be looking for there?"

"Weapons, Captain," said Sushi. "You may forget—Omega Company has become the de facto testing unit for your father's munitions line. Every experimental weapon in the Legion comes to us first, and Harry's got samples of everything sitting right there in his Supply depot. It seems to me that every time one of the hunters dropped out of a hand, he'd go over and ogle the hardware. My best guess is that these guys are from a rival weapons manufacturer, trying to grab samples of Phule-Proof's latest products to knock off. Or maybe they're trying to supply a revolution somewhere, maybe on their home world."

Phule leaned back in his chair and crossed his arms over his chest. "Well, that's certainly possible. I've pretty much given Harry blanket permission to turn a buck any way he sees fit, as long as the company doesn't run out of anything it needs. So if he's sold them a few spare weapons, I don't see how it hurts us. He's probably hit them with an outrageous markup—I wouldn't be at all surprised if they paid more than if they'd gone directly to the factory. At Harry's prices, it's going to be one very expensive revolution, if that's what they have in mind."

Sushi considered a moment before responding. "I didn't hear them trying to talk Harry into selling them anything, although it could have happened after I left. I think maybe they just plan to come back and help themselves some time when nobody's looking. It's not as if Harry guards the place all that carefully."

"Hmm … that's a different story, Sushi," said Phule. "I'll certainly have to look into it. Stealing from the depot? I don't see how they expect to get away with something that blatant. If there's enough reason to think they're going to try that, I'll just order them off the planet."

"I would advise caution, sir," said Beeker. "Remember who sent them here: your friend in high places, Ambassador Gottesman. I don't know whether the ambassador is their accomplice or their dupe, but I do recall that he appeared quite anxious to ensure that you would extend the company's hospitality to them. One ought to be very certain of their criminal intentions before expelling them summarily. You do not have so many influential friends that you can afford to alienate one of them without excellent reasons."

"I see," said Phule. He mused for a while, then asked, "What if I get the Zenobians to demand that we kick them out? Chief Potentary Korg didn't particularly want them here to begin with. I suspect he'd welcome a good pretext to send them packing. If Sushi's right, I wouldn't mind it myself."

"That is quite understandable, sir," said Beeker. "However, you are in a somewhat difficult position. Ambassador Gottesman may take it amiss if you appear to take the natives' side against your own species. Even if we can find solid evidence of intended malfeasance, these rascals may be sufficiently well connected to defy us. Better if we could resolve the matter without their becoming aware of our part in foiling their intentions."

"Which brings me to the second half of my plan," said Sushi. "Have you noticed the machine that Flight Leftenant Qual and his team are working on—the Sklern?"

241

"One could hardly help noticing it," said Beeker. "It seems quite an eccentric device, although I've yet to fathom its purpose. Ah … but perhaps you were going to inform us on that point, young man?"

Sushi smiled. "Why, yes, Beeker. Not only that, but unless I've completely misunderstood everything so far, I think it's the whole answer to your problem."

"Now you've got me really interested," said Phule. "I tried to get Qual to explain it, but I couldn't understand the first thing he was saying. Either he was giving me double-talk, or that stupid translator was acting up again."

"Funny you should mention that," said Sushi. "As it happens, that's exactly the problem that led to my finding out what the *Sklern* really does. It started when Rev got an idea about trying to get the Zenobians to listen to his spiel about the King …"

O O O

"What we really need is to find out what those people want," said Tullie Bascomb. "They were all ready to accept a buyout at something like eight cents on the dollar, and they walked on it when we told them their pictures had gone out as part of the casino's standard publicity package. That doesn't make sense."

"Well, it looks very much as if they don't want publicity," said Rex, who was in charge of the Fat Chance Casino's lavish entertainment program. "That doesn't make a lot of sense to me; but then again, I've never been one to pass up a chance to get my face in front of a holo camera. You never know when somebody'll come along with a job offer you can't refuse."

"Funny you should use that phrase," said Bascomb, drumming his fingers on the desk. "I wonder …"

"Wonder what?" barked Victor Phule, who'd been sitting with growing discontent during the casino managers' meeting. "I negotiated the deal, good old Ernie accepted, and it was your harebrained publicity department that queered it by forwarding his picture to the media without asking anybody whether it had been cleared. Send me to talk to him and that woman, and I can have them both eating out of our hand in no time flat."

Bascomb grunted. "Hell, if you hadn't stuck your nose in, and left deal-making to somebody who knew the rules everybody else was playing by, we'd have had the whole thing settled two days ago," he said. "Now, if you'd let me finish what I was about to say ..."

"Gentlemen, this is getting no place," said Doc, the former character actor now playing the role of commanding officer of the Fat Chance Casino's security force—a picked squad of actors in black uniforms, backed up by a few Legion veterans to supply real muscle on the off chance they had to deal with anything worse than an unruly drunk. "Why don't you both back off instead of butting heads every thirty seconds? We might even figure out something to do, if the rest of us could get a word out of our mouths."

Victor Phule and Tullie Bascomb glared at one another for a moment, but by their silence they appeared to accept Doc's reprimand. Doc nodded. "Now, Tullie, what was the point you were about to make?"

Bascomb laid his hands on the table, palms up. "I've got an idea why Erkeep doesn't want his name in the media, and maybe an idea what we can do about it," he said. "I think he's on a hit list somewhere, and he's afraid the publicity's going to give away his location."

"There ought to be ways to deal with that," said Rex. "Our makeup people can fix the winner so his own mother wouldn't recognize him. And I suspect, with Mr. Phule's help, we can find ways to get him and the young lady to almost any destination in the Alliance without attracting undue attention.'

"That's fine, if the people looking for them aren't too mad at them," said Tullie. "But from the way they reacted, I suspect it won't be enough."

"I don't get it," said Victor Phule. "I mean, Ernie is a fine fellow—salt of the earth, if you know what I mean—but I don't see us as having an infinite obligation to him. Pay the fellow off, whatever it costs, and give him and his lady first-class tickets to wherever they want to go, and that's all. Story over."

"It'd be nice if that *was* the whole story," said Doc. "But I'm afraid the ending wouldn't be anything we'd want to take credit for. Maybe I'm getting softheaded in my old age, but I'd like to think we'd take better care of somebody we promised we'd make a part owner of the casino. And I think Captain Jester would agree with me."

"Perhaps he would," said Victor Phule. "That doesn't mean it's a sound business decision."

"Well, when you get right down to it, the captain put his own shares up for grabs at our urging, and lost them despite some pretty long odds," said Rex. "And good business decision or not, maybe just out of basic consideration, he ought to get some say in how we treat the fellow that won them. Even if it wasn't the fellow we originally meant to win." He glanced significantly in Victor Phule's direction. Phule snorted, but said nothing.

"That makes sense to me," said Tullie. "Why don't we give the captain a call and see what he suggests? It's midevening, his time—so unless that planet's got a lot more nightlife than it looks like on tri-vee, he ought to be within hailing range of his desk."

"You're bound and determined to involve him, so I see no point in wasting my breath," said Victor Phule. "Go ahead—but don't expect the boy to have anything sensible to say. I'd lay odds we'll be no better off when you've talked to him than we are now."

"I'd take that bet," said Tullie Bascomb, reaching for the phone.

O   O   O

"That's the sticking point," said Tullie Bascomb to Phule. "I thought your father had talked them into accepting a buyout for a fraction of actual value—I have to give the old rascal credit, for once. I figured they'd hold out for at least ten million, more likely twenty, but he had them ready to bite on five! I was having a hard time keeping a straight face. But once they learned the casino had taken Erkeep's picture, they hollered bloody murder and walked out."

Phule sighed. The problem with the casino shares was not solving itself as smoothly as he'd expected. He didn't particularly mind having lost them; he'd never have put them up as a prize if he'd cared that much. Besides, it was probably a good idea to hand his father some of the responsibility for keeping the business profitable for the members of Omega Company, who were the real majority stockholders. The old fellow's business experience was nothing to sneeze at, even if it was in a different industry. Meanwhile, Phule could keep his attention focused on managing Omega Company—and his own portfolio.

But who'd have thought the jackpot winner would turn down a quick and easy payment of several million dollars just because the casino had taken his photo?

"There has to be an explanation," said Phule. "Have they made any kind of counteroffer?"

"No, that's what has me puzzled," said Bascomb. "They just walked out and left us trying to figure out where we'd gone wrong. At first we thought they'd figured out how low our offer really was. It was only when the stenobot played back their conversation that we even got a clue what the problem was."

"Have they stayed in touch?" asked Phule. "I can't imagine they'd give up that easily, when everything else seemed to be in place."

"My guess is they'll be back within a couple of days at the outside," said Bascomb. "I called to run a few scenarios past you, to see how you want to handle them."

"Tullie, you don't need to ask me about every detail of the business," said Phule. "You're where you are because I trust your experience and your common sense. Use them, and don't worry about me second-guessing you."

"It's not you I'm worried about, Captain," said Bascomb.

There was a long pause.

Phule finally said, "Is it Dad you're worried about? I don't think you need to. He's run a business for most of his life, and made it one of the most profitable in the galaxy ..."

Bascomb cut him off. "And because of that, he thinks he knows everything there is to know about the business I've been running most of *my* life, and making a damned good profit at. It's because of him that we're in this mess, Captain. That's why I want you signing off on our plans to handle the most likely reactions from Mr. Erkeep."

Phule sighed. "All right, I understand," he said. "If I know Dad, it's not going to make much difference. I'm the one he thinks is incompetent, Tullie, not you. In fact, I wouldn't be surprised if he'd gained a degree of respect for you by now. But I'll give you what you need to cover yourself, if you think it'll help. Tell me what you're looking at."

They spent the next half hour going over different scenarios Bascomb had sketched out, with Phule making occasional comments, but for the most part simply approving Bascomb's plans without modification. On one occasion, Beeker broke in with a suggestion that both Phule and Bascomb immediately recognized as better than anything they'd thought of. Finally, Bascomb said, "All right, I think that covers everything I can foresee. Any other suggestions, Captain?"

"No," said Phule. "If they manage to pull any more surprises out of their hats, you'll just have to deal with them according to your best judgment. Don't feel you have to call me—I trust you, Tullie. And if Dad has any problems with that, tell *him* to call me. All right?"

"I'll tell him, Captain," said Bascomb. He chuckled, then said, "And I wish I could listen in on that conversation," before he broke the connection.

Phule turned to Beeker with a wry grin. "Well, I hope that's the worst problem we have to deal with today," he said.

The butler raised one brow. "I still find it anomalous that you would so easily part with your stock in what must be one of the more profitable of your investments, sir. Are you really so certain your father can handle it as well as you can?"

"He can if he keeps his hands off, which is all I've really done," said Phule. "Besides, Beeks, I intend to write off the shares as a promotional expense, which in my tax bracket will be almost more valuable than the shares themselves. And there's no shortage of profitable investments. Speaking of which—what do you think of Sushi's description of this Zenobian *Sklern*? I'd bet we could get the off-planet marketing rights to it for a song ..."

O O O

The nighttime desert air was still bone-dry, but on the cool side, as Thumper made his way along a well-trodden path out of Zenobia Base toward his destination. Brandy had shown him where the electronic sensors of the perimeter defenses were, and with that knowledge in his head, it wasn't too hard to dodge around them. He'd know soon enough if he didn't dodge around one; the perimeter alarm would alert Mother, who'd signal him to go investigate the disturbance—and send backup just in case it wasn't something he couldn't handle by himself. That would pretty much put an end to this little unauthorized excursion.

If he didn't run into anything unexpected, he'd be back in camp well before his relief guard showed up. And he was confident he could convince Mother he was still at his post, if she decided to call him on the wrist comm to chat, or (just as likely) to check up on how well he was managing to stay awake. His new friend Mahatma had told him Mother was often like that, going out of her way to make sure the newer legionnaires didn't get into trouble when they weren't actively looking for it. That was good to know—but just now, he didn't need anybody to hold his forepaw.

A dim light in the middle distance pointed out the way to his goal. He struck off in that direction, and shortly found a smoother path going his way—the clean-swept ground mark of a recent hoverjeep passage. He considered for a moment whether he needed to worry about leaving footprints, then shrugged and stepped onto the path. If he succeeded, nobody would pay any attention to a stray set of Legion-issue boot marks. And if his plan fell through, they'd have a lot more to worry about than figuring out who'd been along this trail—and when.

He was almost to his destination. He slowed down, making sure he could see everything in his pathway. (The night-vision goggles Brandy had given him for sentry duty brought out the landscape almost as clearly as in bright daylight—although there were funny color substitutions, especially where a large rock or other object glowed warmer than its surroundings.) There, a short distance ahead, was what he'd been expecting: a low-lying shape to one side of the trail, glowing brightly with the warmth of a living body. He came to a halt, not wanting to intrude on the other's territory.

"Hello," Thumper said softly. "You can probably see me as well as I can you. Can we go somewhere to talk where we won't wake everybody else up?"

"Why should I trust you?" the other said, in a strangely familiar guttural voice. "Why are you here, anyway?"

"To talk to you," said Thumper. "I'm by myself, in case you hadn't noticed."

"You have weapons."

"Sure do," said Thumper. "It's part of my job to carry them. If I wanted to use them, I would have sneaked up on you from downwind and got you before you knew where I was. You know I could do it."

There was a pause, as if the other were thinking things over, then the voice said, "Follow me." The bright shape ahead got to its feet and began to walk quietly away from the camp it had been guarding. Thumper followed, at a distance.

Perhaps a hundred meters from the camp, the figure turned and faced Thumper. "All right, this should be safe," it said. "What does a legionnaire want with me?"

"I told you, I want to talk," said Thumper. "What do you have against the Legion?"

"Stinking humans," growled Barky, the Environmental Dog. "Make other sophonts do all the work, take all the credit."

"Not everybody in the Legion's human," said Thumper. "There's me, for one. And the Gambolts, and the Volton, and the Synthians."

"All the leaders are human," said Barky.

"That's true," said Thumper. "Especially the commanding general. I got in trouble with *him* back in basic training. But that's a long story, and it's not what I came here to talk about."

Barky said nothing, waiting.

"All right," said Thumper, shrugging. "All I really need to say is that you and your humans are doing your jobs, and we're doing ours, and there's no reason we need to be enemies. Have you caught us polluting or destroying the environment?"

"Not yet," said Barky, reluctantly. "But if you do your job, sooner or later it will hurt the environment. War is not healthy …"

"For living things," Thumper said. "I learned that in school. They had us watch your show a lot."

"Then you know what I mean," said the Environmental Dog.

"Sure," said Thumper. "But we aren't here fighting a war. In fact, I don't think there's a war anywhere in Alliance space we could be going to fight. So we've got to do other jobs. If the other guys are telling me the truth, what we're doing here is keeping a war from getting started."

"I'm sure that is very wonderful," said Barky. "You will no doubt be able to tell me how bringing more soldiers and weapons to a place where there is no war is going to keep one from starting."

"Some of the other guys can answer that better than I can," said Thumper. "I came out here to talk about something else, though. Answer me this: Your job is to fight pollution, but is it better to fight it, or to prevent it from happening at all?"

"You know the answer to that," growled Barky. "What are you telling me?"

"I'm telling you something you'll be very interested in hearing," said Thumper. "Listen to this ..."

Thumper spoke quickly, skipping over all but the most crucial details. But Barky only interrupted him with questions twice. By the end, the Environmental Dog was growling and gnashing his teeth. "All right, you've convinced me," he said at last. "You can count on me."

"Good," said Thumper. "We'll let you know when we need you to help." He turned and headed back along the trail to his guard post. It was with considerable relief that he discovered that his little excursion hadn't been noticed at all.

Or so he thought. He settled into his assigned guard post, ready to spend the rest of his shift doing the duty to which he'd been assigned. He had a feeling of accomplishment—he had done his part to counteract what he saw as the greatest threat to the missions of both the Legion and the AEIOU here on Zenobia.

A more experienced legionnaire might have noticed the shadowy figure that had trailed him all the way to the AEIOU camp and eavesdropped on his entire conversation with Barky. Perhaps a more experienced legionnaire would have circled back to observe the AEIOU camp after he had announced his departure. Then he might have seen that his conversation with Barky was just the beginning of the evening's events …

CHAPTER SIXTEEN

Journal #744

T hose of us who spend much time with the class of humans who travel to distant worlds to pursue golf, bird-watching, mountain climbing, or underwater fandootery, cannot fail to note how little interest these people have in the sophonts native to the worlds they visit. At best, they poke gentle fun at their customs and language; at worst, they consider them lesser races to be pushed out of the way when they happen to inhabit a particularly valuable sand trap or fandooter's reef. Curious, then, how their attitude changes when one of the locals presents himself in the role of a native guide—and how uncritically they accept the native's qualifications for a task that none of them would dare undertake without considerable special training.

O   O   O

Euston O'Better sat at a camp table in the center of the hunters' campground, scanning a rough topographical map of the eastern part of the main Zenobian continent. It was rough because it had been downloaded from the landing craft's navigational computer, which had scanned the surface during their approach to the current landing site. O'Better was almost certain that the Legion company had better maps, but those were currently unavailable to him. The

Legion captain had smiled and hinted at military secrets. "We'll try to get a civilian-legal map printed out for you," he drawled, but nothing had so far come of it.

The natives undoubtedly had maps, too, but the hunting party had yet to meet an actual Zenobian. They'd all seen them on the tri-vee, of course. They looked like little dinosaurs, O'Better remembered, although they reportedly had a primitive spacegoing technology. And Willard Phule—Captain Jester—had talked them into a sweetheart deal with his father's company.

There was a roundish feature on the map, about fifty kilos west of the camp, that had looked a lot like a salt dome when they'd flown in over it. That might indicate subsurface mineral deposits, in which O'Better had a professional interest. But they had to get out into the desert, where the Legion wasn't looking over their every move, before he could find out whether there was anything more to it. He'd have to do some seismic testing, and that required making few loud noises—more than they could get away with this close to a military installation. Especially one whose leader had reportedly negotiated an exclusive on trade rights with the natives. Out in the desert, nobody'd notice—and if they did, the "hunters" could always explain it away as gunfire. After all, if you were trying to kill a dino, you needed a real big gun—didn't you? And, thanks to the crooked Supply sergeant, they were going to be trying out some *really* big ones this time out.

He smiled and rolled up his map. Hunting dinos was fine, especially if it gave him the chance to test a few otherwise unobtainable weapons. His friends at BigBoum Armaments would be very interested in his report on the capabilities of the new weapons Omega Company was supplied with—thanks to the company commander's father, who just happened to be the CEO of Phule-Proof, BigBoum's main competitor. And if at the same time he managed to get a lead on some unexploited mineral rights that he could possibly convince the ignorant natives to let him exploit—why, there was a lot to be said for combining business with pleasure.

He had just decided it wasn't worth trying to get the computer to enhance the printout—if only because he wasn't sure he really knew *how* to get the stubborn machine to do what he wanted—when a high-pitched voice said, right behind his left ear, "Hello, you are leader of the hunting humans?"

O'Better turned to see a reptilian face with a mouthful of sharp-looking teeth, and nearly jumped out of his skin. "Wh-who the hell are you?" he asked.

"I am Qual, your hunting guide," said the creature, grinning ferociously. At second glance, O'Better saw that it was wearing a battered straw hat and ragged camouflage. "A friend with big ears told me of your need, and so here I am standing."

"OK, you're the guide," said O'Better. He turned toward the tents, and shouted, "Hey, guys, our guide's here!"

The other hunters emerged, looking curiously at the little Zenobian. O'Better turned back to Qual, and said, "It's about time you got here—we've been settin' on our duffs just waitin' for you. Couldn't get squat done without a native guide."

"Oho, this is why you sit," said Qual. The Zenobian peered about the camp, then said, "These are your hunting companions? We should converse so I can determine what part of our planet offers the creatures you desire to kill and eat."

"Oh, I don't know if we'll want to eat any dinos," said L.P. Asho, looking curiously at Qual. "Though I suppose if they were tasty, we might think about it ..."

"Not eating?" Qual's mouth opened wide, showing his teeth again. "If not eating, why shooting?"

"Well, we figured we'd mount 'em ..."

"Human not talking sense," said Qual, making a noise that sounded suspiciously like laughter. "Mounting much better when alive. Then they still can move ..."

Austen Tay-Shun scratched his head and changed the subject. "What do they taste like, anyway? What kinds do you folks eat?"

"The small ones, of course," said Qual. "They taste much like the Old Earth bird known as chicken. And they are not known for deciding to try to eat you instead."

"Well, it's the big ones we want, anyway, Qual," said O'Better. "Where would you go if you wanted to find some of them?"

"There are some astonishing specimens at Lhort's Stretch," said Qual. "It is where I would certainly go first."

"Great, that's the place for us then," said L.P. Asho. "How do we get there?"

Qual rubbed his chin, pondering. "From my home, I would take the red trackway," he said. "It costs a smacker and a half, but one needn't pay to store the scooting-thing."

"Trackway? I don't get it ..." said Asho.

"It is a public conveyance," said Qual, grinning. "One waits at a designated corner, the trackway vehicle comes, and one boards ..."

"Ah, it's some kind of damned *bus,*" said O'Better. Then he stared at Qual, hands on hips. "Wait a minute, Qual. Do you go hunting at this place?"

"Oh, no, all the creatures are protected," said Qual. "It is a place for the young ones and the savants to observe them."

"A zoo," said Asho, disgusted. "Listen, Qual. We want to go someplace where we can shoot the stupid dinos, not just look at 'em. That's what we're here for, and that's what we want."

"Oho, that is distinct," said Qual. "You humans are very strange, but now this makes a certain sense even to me. In fact, you are very near one of the very best places to find some very large creatures."

"Aw right," said Tay-Shun. Then he narrowed his eyes, and asked, "Can we shoot 'em?"

"Why, yes, if you have the weapons," said Qual. "But let me see all your trappings, so I can determine whether all is in readiness. If you have a lack, I know a person who can supply it. With any fortune, we shall be stalking large creatures before a matta can hop twice."

"What's a matta?" asked L.P. Asho.

"I dunno, what's a matta wit' you?" said Qual, grinning.

The three hunters stood there scratching their heads until Qual said, "But make haste! The game's afoot." He ducked quickly into the nearest tent, where a loud screech greeted his entrance.

"Oh, hellfire," said Euston O'Better, as Qual bolted from the tent, dodging a high-heeled shoe thrown at his head. Another just followed, but by then he was out of range. "Guess we should've told Dallas the native was here. You know how spooky she gets sometimes."

Qual looked accusingly at the hunters, but simply said, "Perhaps you should bring out your trappings for me to look at here. Is more dangerous inside than I suspected."

"Little feller, you don't know the half of it," said Euston O'Better. His companions nodded, gravely.

O O O

"Damn it all," said Lola. She'd been pacing furiously back and forth in the little hotel room on one of Lorelei's back streets, away from the casino district. Ernie, sitting on the bed, swiveled his head back and forth, watching her. She reminded him of a shuttlecraft in a crowded spaceport. Which, unless somebody got a really bright idea, might be the next scene the two of them would be seeing.

She stopped and stared out the window at the distant gleam of neon. "For a short while there, we had the whole game won," she said. "I knew it was too good to be true."

"Too good to be true?" Ernie repeated, stupidly. "Mr. Phule and the other casino bosses were all ready to give us five million spifflers, just to go away and leave 'em alone, and you call that too good to be true? We could've lived like kings, anywhere in the Alliance."

"Yeah, and had the mob on us the minute we let down our guard," snarled Lola. "If only the stupid casino publicity department hadn't sent our picture out to the galactic media. If Mr. V and his boys were ready to murder us before, what do you think they'll be now?"

Ernie shook his head, trying to conjure up an answer that could do justice to the probable wrath of the mob enforcers who'd come to their apartment back on Bu-Tse to remind them of the job he and Lola had left undone on Lorelei—capturing Captain Jester (A.K.A. Willard Phule), and delivering him into the hands of the syndicate. So he and Lola had come back to Lorelei, but the job was still undone. And now ...

Whatever answer he'd been about to offer was aborted by the hotel room's door suddenly swinging open.

"Hello, Ernie," said the heavyset man who walked in. There were two other men behind him, who stood barring the door, which until just a moment ago had been soundly locked. While they were simply standing there, there was very little doubt what they were there for— or what they would do if either Ernie or Lola made a wrong move. The man removed his hat and turned to the window. "And Miss Lola. A pleasure to see you both here. But enough small talk—I've come to see what progress you've made on your assignment." He paused frowning. "You have made progress, correct?"

"Well, yes, of course," said Lola, making an effort to put on a cheerful smile. "As it happens, we were just about to lay down plans for the final phase of our operation here, and since you're here, I'm sure your input would be …"

"DON'T GIVE ME THAT BULLSHIT!" roared Mr. V—for that was who had come to visit them, unannounced and certainly unwanted. He waited for a moment, then continued in a quieter (but no less menacing) tone, "You two have been paid good money, and as far as I can tell you haven't done a damn thing to earn it. Now, that's just not right, is it, boys?"

There was no response from the two men blocking the door behind him, and Mr. V turned to look, a puzzled expression on his face. It wasn't normal for his underlings to forget their lines, especially when he'd prompted them so clearly. They were exactly where he'd stationed them, but their faces had assumed blank expressions, and even as he watched they slumped slowly to the floor. "What the hell … ?" said Mr. V.

His answer came from a little man in a black jumpsuit who poked his head around the doorframe. "Mind if I come in?" he said, stepping over the two fallen thugs. Cradled in his right arm was some sort of exotic device—from the look of it, a weapon.

"Who are you?" Mr. V's voice was harsh, but his expression looked anything but confident. His eyes stayed fixed on the weapon in the little man's arms.

"Mostly people call me Doc," said the man, with a bright smile. "I'm security chief at the Fat Chance Casino. Which may give you some idea of what I'm doing here, not to mention why I just stunned your muscle boys." He patted the weapon he was carrying. "One of the good things about working for the Legion is you get some really nice hardware."

Mr. V and Ernie were both taken aback by this information, but Lola nodded, and said, "You've been keeping us under surveillance, right?"

"Well, since you won the jackpot, we have," said Doc, with a wink. "Didn't want one of our partners to walk around Lorelei unprotected. There are some mighty rough characters on the station, y'know."

"Yeah, we noticed," said Ernie. "So what happens now?"

"Well, Tullie Bascomb would like you two to come down to his office—he's got a proposition we think will be to everyone's advantage. As for you"—he turned to Mr. V—"there's a squad of legionnaires out in the hallway. They'll take you and your boys down to the spaceport and put you on the next ship out. Tell them where you're staying, and they'll get your luggage on board. And, oh yeah—don't plan on coming back."

Mr. V was livid. "You won't get away with this!" he shouted.

"Sure I will," said Doc. Two solidly built men in black jumpsuits came through the door. Doc nodded to them, and said, "He's all yours, men. Don't hesitate to zap him if he gives you any trouble."

"Right-o, Doc," said one of the two, stepping forward to put a hand on Mr. V's shoulder.

"Good, I knew you'd see it my way," said Doc, as a sullen Mr. V stepped to one side and, at the casino guards' signal, raised his hands above his head. Doc turned to Ernie and Lola. "Now, shall we go see what's up at the casino?"

They followed him out the door, stepped over the slumbering mob heavies, and went down the stairs with him. Neither Ernie nor Lola said anything the whole way back to the Fat Chance Casino.

O O O

"Here is the hunting ground," said Qual, softly. "It is now requisite to be very careful and quiet. The game's afoot! And you know what that signifies!"

"Hell, no," said L.P. Asho, testily, but Qual had crept ahead out of earshot, so he turned to Austen Tay-Shun, and muttered. "The damn critter's been sayin' that all day long, like it meant somethin'. You got any idea what it means?"

"I think it's a quote out of some Old Earth writer," said Tay-Shun. "Prob'ly Sheik Spear—that old buzzard seems to have wrote almost everything."

"How's a Zenobia lizard know Sheik Spear's stuff?"

Tay-Shun shrugged. "Maybe he just said something similar, and the translator turned it into poetry. Be quiet, now—for all I know, you're like to scare the critters so they come chargin' at us, and I don't want no part of that."

"You see any critters?" whispered Euston O'Better. "Damn if I can see anything like a dino …"

"In this light, I'm damned if I can see my hand in front of my face," said Asho. "There could be all sorts of critters out there and we'd never…"

"SHHH!" said Qual, and the three hunters jumped. The Zenobian guide had crept back practically on top of them, so quietly that none of them had noticed. "If humans aren't being very careful and quiet, all is for nought. I am guiding like a good native, but humans must do their part. Follow!" And before any of them could ask a question, Qual turned and vanished into the semidarkness again.

The hunters, chastened, moved in the general direction he'd gone, hoping the trail wasn't too difficult to follow. Some of the places he'd led them through today *had* been almost too much for the humans, with thick briarlike tangles of underbrush, small biting flying creatures that seemed to have an appetite for human flesh even though they hadn't evolved to eat it, and another small creature whose nest they seemed to have threatened, and which noisily kept trying to repel them until they were far out of its territory. It had been quite a challenge for the three humans to keep up with Qual.

"I don't know how the hell we're supposed to find the damned dinos if we can't see 'em," Asho muttered again. "Why, they might be sneakin' right up on us …"

"Come on, you know somethin' that big would make a lot of noise," whispered O'Better.

"Hey, some of the most dangerous Old Earth dinos were little fellers, not much bigger than you or me," said Asho. "Take that lizard boy Qual, for example. If he was huntin' for us, you think you'd hear him? He could take a big bite out o' your butt before you knew he was in the same county ..."

"He could take a bigger one out o' yours," said Tay-Shun. "Now, why don't y'all do like he says and hush up. At least then, if some dangerous kind of critter tries to sneak up on us, at least we'll have some chance to hear it."

"SHHH!" said Qual, who'd sneaked up on them unnoticed again. When the hunters were done jumping, the Zenobian said, "Game is very close. We wanting to surprise it. Follow me, and be very, very quiet."

Dutifully, the hunters fell into single file behind Qual and crept forward through the tall alien vegetation. Now Qual carried a dim handlight of some sort—more for the hunters' convenience than for his own, it seemed. The little Zenobian's vision was evidently as good in the starlit night of his home world as theirs was in full daylight. Perhaps the sunglasses he habitually wore in bright sunlight were another consequence of his night-adapted vision.

The party came into a moderately large clearing, perhaps twenty meters across. The sandy soil was soft and loosely packed here. "Look!" said Qual, shining his light on a depression in the ground. It was an enormous footprint.

"Ghu almighty, what kind of critter made that?" said Asho. "It must be enormous ..."

"That is game we hunt," said Qual. "The mark is fresh, so we are very up close to it. It went thataway." He pointed to the left.

"How did somethin' that big walk past us and we didn't even hear it?" said Tay-Shun, falling in behind Qual, who had wordlessly begun to stalk in the direction the footprints pointed—they could now see that there were more of them.

"Here's another footprint," O'Better whispered, turning back over his shoulder. He pointed down. "This mother's *big*—you boys got your guns ready?"

"Sure do," said L.P. Asho, brandishing the Legion surplus weapon he'd gotten from Chocolate Harry's arsenal. "Who gets first shot?"

"I dunno—I reckon we all oughta be ready, in case it charges. When we see it, we better spread out so's we all have a clear shot in case it charges or somethin'. If we get time to think about it, we can decide who's got the hammer then."

"Good plan," whispered O'Better. "Can anybody see anything? It's darker than the inside of a horse ..."

"SHHHH!" said Qual, turning around. "I sense the game just ahead," he whispered. "It is in a small clearing. I will turn out the light, and we will all step forward—utterly quietly, or it may respond unpredictably. Everyone is to expand sideways, so we are having direct view before I turn on light."

The hunters stepped forward into the clearing, suddenly aware despite the darkness of some huge living creature there in front of them. Asho held his stun ray at the ready, and to either side he could hear his friends moving into place. "Now!" whispered Qual, and turned his light on to a brighter beam.

Asho stared upward, where the beast ought to be, startled at the sudden brightness in the clearing. *Where was it? Had it heard them and escaped already?*

"What the hell ..." said O'Better, expressing the puzzlement all of them felt. They swung their heads in all directions, looking for the huge creature that must be directly in front of them. "Where's the critter?"

"Down there!" said Qual, pointing. Sure enough, there on the floor of the clearing, directly in front of them, sat the creature they had been trailing. It was a stubby creature, more or less the size of a lounge chair. At first glance it looked like nothing so much as the enormous paw of some huge beast of prey, cut off just above the ankle. At the top, a pair of bulbous eyes on thin stalks swung toward the sudden light, staring at the hunters for just a moment. Then, before any of them could react, the huge appendage flexed its toes and bounded out of the clearing, too swiftly for any of them to get a shot off.

"What the hell?" said Asho, making up in vehemence what he lacked in originality. "I never seen anything like that before. What was that thing?"

Qual turned to them, and said, grinning toothily, "Didn't I tell you? It is just as I said: *The game's afoot.*"

"Look here, Qual, this won't do at all," said Euston O'Better. "We'd be pure and simple laughin'stocks if we showed up back home with that kind of thing as a trophy." The hunters had returned to the camp, and the three of them were sitting with the Zenobian around a small camp stove, warming up coffee for the humans.

Qual grinned, showing his intimidating array of daggerlike teeth. "You did not explain this to me," he said. "What kind of game is it you search, then, if the *snool* is not it?"

"Hell, dinos!" said L.P. Asho. "The big mothers—you know, like tranasaurs or brontosaurs. You got 'em here, don't you?"

"Big mothers?" Qual looked puzzled. "My own mother is rather large, perhaps twenty centimeters taller than the average female, and proportionately weighty. But I do not think she would like being hunted …"

"L.P.'s just usin' a figure of speech, is all," said O'Better, hastily. "He don't *really* want to shoot nobody's mother, do you now, L.P.?"

"Well, I gotta think about that, Euston," said Asho, rubbing his chin. "Eddy Joe Hollub's mom was always real mean to me back when I was a kid …"

"Har, har!" said O'Better. "L.P.'s full of jokes, ain't he? But seriously, Qual, a big hairy jumpin' foot's pretty unusual, but I don't think it's quite the kind of thing you can be proud of havin' shot, y'know? It don't make a very smart trophy."

"I think not," said Qual. "The *snool* is a very stupid animal. It rarely knows whether it is coming or going …"

Austen Tay-Shun cut him off. "Nah, we don't want the *animal* to be smart—we want it to look impressive as a mounted trophy. You know, big and fierce, like that."

Qual's eyes opened wider. "Big and fierce? Aha, why did you not say so? I can find you many such beasts."

"All right," said Asho, setting his coffee cup loudly down on a flat stone. "Now we're cookin' with raw antimatter. What kind of critters are we talkin' about, and how soon can we get a shot at 'em?"

"Oh, these are very large beasts," said Qual, his eyes rolling as if to suggest their magnitude. "They are bad-tempered and always hungry. I do not know whether a wise sophont would go looking for them on purpose. The best way to deal with them is to be somewhere else."

"Whoo-ee, that sure sounds nasty," said Asho. "Do they have big teeth, or claws, or somethin' else like that?"

"Teeth, and claws, and horns, and a sharp, sharp barb on the tippy-tip of the tail," said Qual, putting his hands over his eyes. "I think you are very smart humans. Listen to me; you go hunt for these animals, maybe they get the smart idea to come hunting for humans instead. And if that happens, the beasts having all the fun."

"Whoo-ee," said O'Better. "I reckon we oughta stop and think about that one, boys."

"I knew you would be smart humans," said Qual. "Now, I can find you nice safe things to hunt, like *gryff* ..."

"Damnit, we don't want safe!" bellowed Asho. "What are you boys, men or miffles? We come here for just two things, to get us some samples of Phule-Proof's new models and to hunt some big ol' critters."

"Shh!" said O'Better. "The boy here might tell somebody!"

"Shee-it, Euston, the boy ain't gonna tell nobody," said Asho. "He don't know anybody at Phule-Proof to go yappin' to. But he sure does sound like he can take us to some serious big game—I mean, fierce-lookin' critters with teeth and claws. I don't want to come home with nothin', but I don't want the folks back on Tejas to think I shot some poor old woman's milk cow, neither."

Qual seemed to slump, and he said in a voice that, even through the translator, sounded subdued. "If you are so anxious to seek danger, then I will take you. But do not tell me I did not give you all fair warnings."

"Fair or not, I'm ready to roll," said Asho. "When do we go, and what do we need to take."

"Tomorrow we go," said Qual, in what sounded like a doleful tone. "Bring your most powerful weapons. Get a good sleep—we leave at dawn. And if you have any business to settle, do it now. We seek the most dangerous beasts on Zenobia, and there is no promising that we will prevail."

"Yee-hah!" hollered Asho, tossing his hat in the air. The other two hunters managed a smile, too, although they were a good bit less exuberant. As for Qual, he flashed his teeth—an expression that might mean almost anything—and vanished into the dark.

CHAPTER SEVENTEEN

Journal #748

Having spent as much time as I have in the employment of those who have acquired their fortunes in one form or another of commerce, I have learned at least this much about how these somewhat enigmatic persons think: The average person looks at a deal, and asks, "What's in it for me?" The successful businessman asks, "What's in it for everybody?"

It is the ability consistently to find a satisfactory answer to the latter question upon which the greatest fortunes are built. And that particular ability is one that Mr. Willard Phule, known to the Legion as Captain Jester, possessed in full measure.

O O O

Doc ushered Lola and Ernie through the Fat Chance Casino's lobby, up the elevators to the executive office level, and into a conference room where Tullie Bascomb and Victor Phule sat waiting. "Good, good, glad you're here," said Tullie, indicating two chairs drawn up opposite his desk. "Thanks, Doc."

"You're not the only one who's glad," said Lola, sinking into one of the chairs. "Your security chief got there just in time to save us from a fairly nasty experience. Which, by the way, is very much related to our problems with your buyout offer …"

"Well, I suggest you wait until you hear what we're offering," said Bascomb. "Drinks?" He waved toward a nearby cart bearing several ornate bottles, an ice bucket, and assorted glassware.

Ernie's mouth opened, then snapped shut as he saw the look on Lola's face. The elbow she dug into his rib made her meaning plain, just in case he'd missed it. "Uh, no thanks," he said.

"All right, then, we'll get straight to business," said Bascomb, with a twinkle in his eye. He'd noticed the elbow. "I think the captain's come up with a plan that addresses your problems fairly directly," he continued.

"He has?" Lola's brow furrowed. "What does he know about our problems, anyway?"

"Well, you'll probably want to ask him that," said Bascomb. "All he told me is that he figured out what was going on when he debriefed a robot that used to work here."

"A robot." Lola opened her mouth, then shut it again. After a moment's thought, she continued, "Well, that's certainly interesting. But maybe we should save that subject for later and find out what the captain's offering."

"Good idea," said Bascomb. "As a matter of fact, he's decided to improve the original offer a good deal. We'll buy out your 'share' in the casino for $7.5 million. But instead of the annual royalty, he's offering the two of you full-time paid executive positions with the Fat Chance. The salary is pretty generous, but not outrageous—and the job description ought to be right up your alley. Basically, the captain wants you two to supervise our cheat-detecting operation. He figures you know the scams as well as anybody—and we'd rather have you on our side than working against us."

"I suppose we ought to take that as a compliment," said Lola. "If I were looking for a regular job, I guess it'd be as good as anything …"

Bascomb smiled. "There's more, in case you hadn't guessed. Figure in complimentary lodgings and meals in the casino hotel, and—I think this might be of particular interest to you—complete access to all of our facilities and services, including security."

"Security," mused Lola. "Now, that just *might* be something we can talk about. I was certainly impressed by the way Doc and his people took care of a little problem we ran into back at the hotel."

"Nothing to it, Miss," said Doc, smiling broadly. "Just doing our job." He poured himself a glass of cold water from a pitcher on the bar cart and settled down to drink it in a soft chair facing Bascomb's desk.

"The offer would also include access to some of the best plastic surgeons and uh, image consultants, in the business—just in case you want to be a little bit harder to spot. And you might also like to know, we've managed to recall the photos that PR had sent out, before the stories were distributed—at least most of them. And we managed to tweak the few stories that did run to imply you were off to parts unknown to enjoy your winnings. The long and the short of it is, the captain thinks you're good at what you do, and he wants you on the Fat Chance team," said Tullie. "And as it happens, Mr. Phule agrees with his son."

"That's right," said Victor Phule. "I must admit I'm not quite certain what it is old Ernie does, but he's clearly very good at it. And Miss Lola is very sharp."

"Thank you," said Lola, looking at Tullie Bascomb. "But you must realize, gentlemen, this is all very sudden. Could my client and I have some time to discuss it in private?"

"Why, of course," said Bascomb. "If you'd like, we can arrange for a private dining room so you can discuss it over a meal. On the house, of course."

"Thank you very much, but I think we'll be able to come to an answer with just a little walk around the block," said Lola. "We can celebrate with a meal if we decide to accept."

"Sure," said Bascomb, nodding. "If you'd like, we can have a couple of security people keep an eye on you—at a distance, of course."

"Again, thanks but no thanks," said Lola. "We won't stray that far outside the casino. And unless I'm mistaken, the only people who had anything against us are already out of the game—at least, for the time being."

"All right, then," said Bascomb. "I'll be here when you're ready to talk."

Lola and Ernie said nothing until they were all the way down to the bottom floor in the elevator and out the doors. There, Lola set off at a brisk pace, with Ernie struggling to catch up despite his longer legs. Finally, after they'd turned a corner and put the casino's front entrance out of sight, he said, "All right, what's the problem? Are we gonna take the bait or not?"

"I don't know what other choice we have," said Lola. "Unless you want to head off for no place in particular and hope to stay one jump ahead of Mr. V and his boys. They're really going to be mad at us, now."

"Yeah," said Ernie. "I don't want to be anywhere they can find me. Unless I've got more guns on my side than they do on theirs."

"Which is exactly what's attractive about Phule's offer," said Lola. "We'd be stuck on a space station, where the company isn't necessarily my kind of people, and where we'd pretty much have to give up hustling and play by the books. And that could get dull after a few months. But with the Legion in charge of security, the Fat Chance has got more muscle than some small planets I've been on. The syndicate originally hired us to try to snatch Phule because they knew a direct attack wasn't going to work. Now, it looks as if an indirect attack's not going anywhere, either. So odds are we'd be safer here than anywhere else we can afford to get to, even if Mr. V and his boys know exactly where we are."

Ernie walked silently for a few paces, then stopped, and said, "That all makes sense to me. So what are we waiting for?"

"For one thing, to make sure it's what we really want," said Lola. "Are you ready to take a job, even a really good one with better pay than you'd ever make hustling? Are you ready to stay in one place for the rest of your life, even if it is a first-class resort hotel and casino?"

Ernie grunted. "You make it sound pretty good," he said. "But is that the whole deal?"

"What do you mean?" asked Lola.

Ernie's expression was, for once in his life, dead serious. "I mean, are you gonna take the deal? Are you gonna stay here? Because if you're not, it don't appeal to me."

Lola's eyes grew wide. "Good Ghu," she said. "If I didn't know better, I'd think that meant …"

"Don't think," said Ernie. "Just let me know. Are you gonna take Phule's offer?"

Lola reached out and took Ernie's hand. "You know, in spite of all the downsides to it, I think I just might." She smiled, and Ernie smiled back at her. Together they turned and walked to the Fat Chance Casino.

○ ○ ○

Qual had guided the three hunters' all-terrain hovervan across a long stretch of semiarid country to the spot where the Zenobian claimed the most dangerous creatures of his planet could be found. In addition to the four passengers, the van was loaded down with weapons and ammunition, as well as various other supplies, purchased at Chocolate Harry's backdoor commissary.

Finally, near midday, Qual pulled the van to a halt in the shade of a stand of Zenobian "trees" that, except for their orange coloration, bore a disturbingly close resemblance to giant stalks of asparagus—at least to the hunters, who had previous experience with asparagus. A native of the planet, like Qual, undoubtedly considered them just ordinary trees.

"Here is our destination," said Qual. "There is a water hole just beyond that hill. The beasts we are hunting arouse themselves from slumber in the later afternoon and visit the water hole, then go hunting. Our notion is to set up an asylum near the water. From there the brave hunters can likely snipe at the unwitting beasts for quite some time before the inevitable raging counterattack."

"Inevitable?" Euston O'Better scoffed. "These weapons we're toting may have something to say about that."

"They may," said Qual, opening the van door and getting out. He turned, and added, "Then again, the beasts may not be inclined to listen."

A blast of superhot, desert-dry air greeted the hunters as they tumbled out behind their guide. "Whoo-eee!" said Austen Tay-Shun. "Whoever told us this was a desert world sure knew what he was talkin' about. How do these big critters live in this kind of heat all day?"

"As I told you, they lie in a shady spot and slumber through the worst of the heat," said Qual. "Your visual organs will not detect one of them, this time of day. Indeed, if you detect one of them at all, this time of day, it will be through the unlucky accident of stumbling over it where it sleeps. You may have a brief period in which to regret your misfortune before you are devoured."

"You're tryin' to scare us off, aren't you?" said L.P. Asho. He slapped the heavy weapon he had just unloaded from the hovervan's tailgate, and added, "Well, I guess it'd work with some folks. But here's somethin' you better remember—those folks ain't from Tejas!"

"You're not in Tejas anymore," said Qual. "But we expend time to no end. Let us transport our supplies to the vicinity of the water hole."

Each of them shouldered a heavy pack—they'd spent the morning loading them, under Qual's supervision—and headed toward a well-defined path through the asparagus trees. These gave enough shade to reduce the effect of the afternoon sun for a few moments, but soon the party was out in the open again, headed slightly downhill. Below them, the scrubby alien vegetation grew slightly thicker, betraying the presence of a source of water, although the water itself remained invisible from this distance.

The hunters had worked up a considerable sweat when Qual finally called a halt. "From here we can survey the approaches with elegance," he said. He pointed to the left. "In that patch of tall grasses we will erect our asylum."

The patch of vegetation—which, viewed close-up, had only a faint resemblance to grass—sat atop a low ridge, giving a clear view of everything below. There Qual put the hunters to work, cutting the vegetation from the center of the patch and setting it up in a thicker wall around the perimeter. In the little clearing thus created, the hunters set up poles to hold a canopy to keep off the sun, and spread blankets over the stubble to allow them to sit comfortably. Toward the downhill side of the blind, Qual set up a miniature vid-eye and portable screen to give them a view of what went on by the water hole. Then they settled down to wait for the game animals he had promised.

The three hunters watched in fascination until they began to realize that almost nothing worth watching was going on down by the water. The only creatures braving the midday sun were too small to be exciting—at least, to humans who have come across several light-years in search of Really Big Game. A xenobiologist might have found the interaction of various Zenobian species—many of which might never have been observed by anyone from off-planet—sufficiently interesting. But it was just under an hour before L.P. Asho set his weapon aside on the blanket next to him, cracked open a beer, and pulled a deck of cards out of the pocket of his shooting jacket. The three humans ordered Qual to alert them if anything worth their time showed up at the water hole, and got down to some serious poker.

O   O   O

"Come on in and take a look at this," said Sushi. "It'll answer a lot of questions."

Phule, Beeker, Rev, and the two lieutenants stepped into the crowded workshop. Most of the space was filled with equipment that, even if its purpose wasn't immediately obvious, was at least made up of recognizable components. But in the middle of a bench toward along the back wall sat a piece of equipment that instantly drew attention to itself.

In fact, Armstrong immediately blurted out, "What in the world is that thing?"

It was a good question. To begin with, nobody could have mistaken it for anything of human manufacture. Its most familiar feature was what appeared to be a display screen similar to that of an Alliance computer, but its shape and proportions—a long oval in "portrait" orientation—were clearly different from those of human devices. The material of the case enclosing it was of a rough, mottled texture—more like natural rock than the smooth exteriors human designers favored. And what appeared to be its controls were neither knobs, buttons, nor sliders, but stubby bars that projected at different lengths from the top of the unit.

"Well, Lieutenant, this is something we should have gotten a long time ago," said Sushi. "I'm surprised nobody in Intelligence has been after us to get them some of these."

"Maybe so, sonny, but I'm still downright stumped," said Rev. "How about lettin' us in on the secret?"

"I do believe it's some Zenobian equivalent of a tri-vee set," said Beeker, peering at the device. "To tell the truth, I'm rather disappointed—I thought better of the little saurians. But I suppose it was too much to hope that a technically competent race would have the good taste to forgo creating its own version of the mass media, once it had the capability."

"Beeker's got it," said Sushi. "And if it'll make you feel any better, it looks like Flight Leftenant Qual has about as low an opinion of the Zenobian's mass entertainment as you do of ours. He gave me this machine—their name for it translates as *viewbox*—last night, when I asked him about one of their popular shows. This set was supposed to be for the officers' quarters of their little base here. But he's the only officer, and the enlisted Zenobians have their own viewbox. Qual said he has more amusing ways to destroy brain cells than watching the stuff they show. So he didn't see any problem in letting me borrow it for a while. Of course, it took most of today to adapt it to our power sources and add a translator to the output, but it's mostly working, now."

"I follow you so far," said Lieutenant Armstrong. "But what do you want it for? Are you going to watch whatever silly thing the Zenobians do instead of gravball?"

"That's not such a bad idea," said Sushi. "I'll add it to the list. But first I wanted to find something I heard the Zenobians talking about earlier today. I think Rev will be interested in this ... Excuse me a moment while I try to get this crazy machine working again." He turned around and began fiddling with the controls of the viewbox.

The speaker emitted several whistles, pops, honks, and crackles, and the screen on the front of the unit began to display apparently random splotches of color. Sushi peered at it, fiddling with one of the controls, and eventually the image resolved into the recognizable close-up image of a grinning Zenobian, swaying back and forth. "Take my eggs—please!" came the mechanical voice through the speaker, followed by the sound of an audience laughing and applauding.

"What's that all about?" asked Rembrandt.

"No idea," said Sushi. "Remember, I've only been watching this for a couple of hours. It's all new to me, too." He pushed another control, and the picture changed.

This time the view was of an outdoor scene, with two Zenobians riding at a breakneck pace on the backs of a pair of large reptilian creatures. They came to a third native, who stood by the side of the path they were following, at a point where it divided. The dismounted native pointed down one fork, and said, excitedly, "The miscreants followed yonder trail!" At this, the two mounted Zenobians directed the beasts they were riding down the indicated path.

"That seems familiar," said Armstrong, peering at the screen.

"Depressingly so, in fact," said Beeker, looking down his nose at the images.

Sushi changed the controls again, and the image shifted to what looked like a large indoor arena, where an excited crowd of Zenobians stood on ramps surrounding a smaller group of the natives, wearing contrasting costumes of bright primary colors and running at top speed from one end of the central area to the other, knocking each other down and biting the opponent's tails in what looked like nothing short of an all-out riot. An off-camera commentator shouted, "Garp has the nodule; he hurls it to Wafs; that worthy cradles it cleverly, avoiding the snap of Brotch! The Guardians are at a turning point!" It was easy to guess that some sort of team sport was in progress, but none of the watching humans could make out what was supposedly being passed around, let alone the object of the "game." Perhaps the translator was at fault, or perhaps the game had hidden subtleties.

After a few more moments of incomprehensible mayhem and even less coherent commentary, Sushi again changed the controls and brought in another "channel"—that apparently being the closest equivalent in human communications to the different settings of the viewbox. "Ah, here's what I was looking for," he said, and stepped back to let the others see.

This image was radically different from any the watchers had seen so far. In fact, to everyone's consternation, it showed not a Zenobian, but what appeared to be a human—although greatly distorted, as if scanned through a defective input device. The colors were washed out into shades of black, white, and shimmering gray. The jerky movement was accompanied by a shrill, relentlessly thumping sound track. But even the grainy, unrealistic image was clear enough that, after a moment's glance, every eye in the room turned to look at one person. And that person stared in openmouthed disbelief at what was on the viewbox screen in front of him.

"Wait jes' one cotton-pickin' minute, Sushi," said Rev, at last. "Are you tellin' me that these-here Zenobians are showin' the *King* on their viewboxes?"

"I'm not telling you—I'm showing you," said Sushi. "But if I had to guess, I'd say we're probably seeing an Old Earth broadcast that made its way across the intervening space to here, back when the Zenobians were just beginning to explore the electromagnetic spectrum—however long ago that was. We'll have to check the light-distance between there and here to find out when they could have first seen it. But I think we've got the answer to the question you asked me to research, Rev. Now, at least, we know who 'L'Viz is."

Sushi put on his most sympathetic expression and turned to Rev. "You see, there's no mystery at all. It's all perfectly rational and scientific—just old signals that the Zenobians somehow received and interpreted in their own way. Sorry, Rev. I guess this is a disappointment." He felt sorry for the poor company chaplain, who'd pinned so many hopes on the Zenobians' apparent veneration of 'L'Viz.

But Rev seemed not to notice. He was still staring at the viewbox. Finally, he turned. "No mystery, Sushi?" he asked, a smile now playing on his lips. "No mystery? Why, I guess I gotta disagree with you on that, son. These here broadcasts left Old Earth countless years ago—back in the age of the King himself, as any fool can see. And somehow they traveled night and day, runnin' all the way, just like a mystery train, tryin' to get right here to Zenobia—just as the little folks who call this world their home was ready to receive 'em. You want to call that perfectly rational and scientific? Well maybe you believe that. But I say, the King done jes' what he set out to do."

Rev turned and bowed to the officers, who all stood there openmouthed. "Now, gentlemen, if you'll excuse me—I gotta spread word to the faithful!" And he turned on his heel and left the room.

Beeker and Phule made coughing sounds to cover up what might have been laughter. But Sushi spread his hands, and said, "Well, there's one more proof—it all depends on how you look at the data."

O   O   O

There were a good dozen beer containers tossed into a corner of the shelter, and a large pile of dollars in front of Euston O'Better, when Qual caught their attention with a penetrating hiss. "Creatures approach," he whispered.

"Whoa," said L.P. Asho, turning to look at the view screen. Sure enough, there was activity visible in the hollow below their hunting blind. A herd of small hopping animals with kangaroo-like forefeet was swarming around the water—it was hard to tell their exact size without some standard for comparison, but they seemed no more than a meter or so in height. Intermixed with them were a few larger creatures—horned quadrupeds, perhaps twice as tall at the shoulder, and three times longer than their height, if you counted a substantial-looking tail.

"What are those damn things?" asked O'Better, crowding forward to examine the screen.

"Shhh!" warned Qual. He continued in a dry whisper. "You are seeing *sprvingers* and *gryffs*. They are a distance away, but they hear excellently. And the large creatures we hope to ambush hear even better. Quiet is obligatory if we are to accomplish anything."

In fact, several of the animals had paused in their activity, and were peering around as if alerted. One or two of the larger ones—

the *gryffs?*—were staring straight at the hunting blind, although the hunters had taken considerable pains to make it indistinguishable from the rest of the nearby vegetation.

"So these ain't the ones we're looking for," said Asho, in a much lower voice. "When do they show up?"

"When they desire to," said Qual. "Sooner than we really want, I expect."

"Hell, bring 'em on—I'm ready for 'em," said Asho.

"If you continue to make so much noise, they will be here sooner than you think," said Qual, very softly. "But I don't think you will get very much chance to shoot at them."

"All right, L.P., let's listen to the native guide," said Austen Tay-Shun. "Let's bide our time so we can get a really good trophy. I'm a few bucks down, anyways—if the critters take their time, maybe I can win some of it back."

"That is the best plan," said Qual. "Softly, softly, catch a *sproinger.*"

The hunters returned to their cards—and their beer—as the sun sank gradually lower in the west, and the heat of midday began to wane. For his part, Qual remained by the view screen, watching carefully, every now and then softly warning the card players to keep their voices down.

Finally, as the rim of the sun stood just a hand's breadth above the horizon, Qual let out another hiss. "Here is something different," he added in an almost inaudible whisper, pointing to the view screen.

"What is it now?" said L.P. Asho, but when he turned around and saw the screen, his mouth fell open, and he said nothing more. There on the screen was possibly the largest animal any of the three hunters had ever seen, on this world or any other. It had the general conformation of one of the Zenobian natives, but scaled up to nearly thirty meters in height. Its teeth were long and pointed, and its claws were almost the length of an adult human being. The hoverjeep-sized *gryff* lumbered away from it in panic, scattering like slow-motion mice before a cat. "What the hell is *that?*" gasped Asho.

"It is a *grggh,*" whispered Qual. "It has not sensed us yet."

"Is that what we're hunting?" asked O'Better, in a quavering voice.

"Until it begins hunting us, yes," said Qual. "Perhaps our weapons are adequate to repel it; this is one of the small ones."

"Repel it?" L.P. Asho's jaw dropped. "I don't want to repel it, I want somethin' for my trophy room."

"Shh!" said Qual. "We do not want to attract it any sooner than we must. It may have pack mates in the vicinity."

"Pack mates? You mean there might be more than one of these things?"

"They hunt in packs," said Qual. He peered at the screen. "I do not see another, yet; perhaps it is not hunting. That would be a rare piece of luck."

"Rare? What do you mean?"

"*Grggh* are constantly hunting," said Qual. "Do you think a beast can achieve those dimensions by restricting its caloric intake?"

"I guess *not*," said Asho. "Damn, I'd love to have that sucker's head in my trophy room. Couldn't get much more than that in without rebuildin' ..."

"Hell, we'd have trouble gettin' it back to the ship, let alone liftin' off with it," said Austen Tay-Shun. "And that's not even thinkin' about trophies for the rest of us. *I* ain't goin' home with nothin' to show for it."

"Silence!" hissed Qual. "Something approaches!"

"Wha ...?" said L.P. Asho, but before he could complete the thought, the roof of the hunting shelter disappeared skyward, and a large, tooth-filled visage leaned down inquisitively toward the little group. The mouth opened, and a wave of heat—accompanied by the worst stench imaginable—filled the little shelter. With a choral scream of terror, the hunters bolted.

CHAPTER EIGHTEEN

Journal #751

While I have never been attracted to a military career, my employer's tenure in the Space Legion has given me ample opportunity to assess the qualities requisite for success in that branch of life. I do not think I flatter myself excessively if I state that I might have done better than most, had I been placed in such circumstances. Many of the necessary qualities of a gentleman's gentleman would serve, with little need for adaptation.

In fact, I doubt one officer in ten could match the average butler in the ability to tell when one's position has so grievously deteriorated that nothing remains but to make one's escape without undue regard for one's dignity. Indeed, in my experience, the higher one rises in the military rank, the more conspicuous is the lack of this invaluable quality.

On the other hand, the hunters from Tejas, whom I had never before observed to be in the possession of any outstanding virtue, proved to be quite sensible when it came to mounting a timely retreat. Indeed, they did it every bit as well as any general could have, and with a good bit less fuss.

O   O   O

Phule's hoverjeep pulled up to the hunters' camp just as Euston O'Better dashed out of his tent carrying a huge duffel bag. Ignoring the captain—and Beeker, who sat observing the scene with raised eyebrows—O'Better rushed breathlessly over to the shuttle and tossed the bundle through the cargo hatch. Then he turned and headed back to the tent.

"Good morning," said Phule, in a conversational tone.

O'Better jumped as if someone had set off a small explosive in his near vicinity. He landed facing the hoverjeep, at which point his mind apparently managed to process it as something not likely to eat him, and he snapped, "Durn it, you oughtn't sneak up on a fellow that way." Then, realizing there was no immediate threat, he relaxed, and said, "Sorry, Captain, but we've had a bit of a scare. Your planet's got some mighty ferocious critters on it, y'know?"

"Well, it's not really my planet," said Phule. "And I can't say I've really had time to do a proper survey of the local wildlife. Of course, the Zenobians do tell stories …"

"They don't do the critters justice," said O'Better, closing his eyes and shuddering. "Not even close … but I'm sorry, Captain. I guess you didn't come here just to chitchat, and to tell you the truth, I don't have a lot of time myself. What brings you out this way, Captain?"

No sooner had he finished speaking than Austen Tay-Shun and L.P. Asho dashed out of their tents, each carrying a large bundle that they proceeded to stow in the cargo hold of the shuttle. They turned, then, noticing the hoverjeep, lined up behind O'Better, staring at Phule and Beeker, with unmistakably unfriendly expressions.

The silence built for a long moment before Phule broke it. "I'm sorry, Mr. O'Better," he said, scratching his head. "It looks as if I'm interrupting something. Were you gentlemen getting ready to move out?" He stepped out of the jeep, peering casually around the campsite. Sure enough, much of the fancy equipment that had been visible on his previous visit was out of sight—presumably packed up and stowed away in the shuttle.

O'Better grimaced, then said, "What the hell—there's no point telling anything but the truth. What happened is, me and the boys went out in the sticks with your local guide, plannin' to get those big trophies we'd come here lookin' for. So, naturally enough, we asked the native boy to take us where the really big critters were. And when he did, we found out we were in way over our heads—that's all, Captain. *Way* over our heads. I don't know how the natives manage to keep from being eaten right up by some of the critters we seen. We brought some pretty serious weaponry with us, but I'll tell you this—I don't reckon there's anything short of siege artillery that'll bring one of those monsters down."

"Monsters?" said Phule. "I grant I haven't spent much time researching local fauna, but I'd think Flight Leftenant Qual would've warned us of anything really dangerous. I hope they aren't going to become a nuisance to the camp."

"Well, if they do, your boys are goin' to find out just what your weapons can and can't do," said L.P. Asho, sullenly. "Ain't nobody payin' me to stand and get chewed up like a light snack, but maybe the Legion is willin' to give it a try. You're welcome to it. As for us—we're gettin' the hell out while we still can."

"Well, I'm sorry to hear that," Phule began.

Asho cut him off. "You damn well ought to be. We come here not just for a little huntin' and recreation, but to look into this planet's mineral development potential, which I reckon it has a lot of. But there ain't nobody goin' to sink his money into a place where his people are goin' to get et up by Godziller if they make a wrong step."

"Godziller?" said Phule.

"You heard the man," said O' Better. "If the Legion takes matters in its own hands and exterminates the monsters, there may be some room for investors to move in and develop the place good and proper. But short of that, I'm keeping my money in my pocket. Now, Captain, if you'll pardon us, we'd like to get loaded and lift off before the creatures come looking for us." He and the others turned and went back into the tent.

"Creatures?" said Phule. He looked at Beeker. "Exterminate?"

"I'm sure I don't know what they're talking about, either, sir," said Beeker. "I have a strong suspicion who will know, though. If I may be so bold, shall we return to camp and speak to Mr. Qual?"

281

"Qual!" said Phule. "I think you're right, Beeker. Let's go see if we can get to the bottom of this. For starters, I think we're going to talk to Sushi." He hopped back into the hoverjeep, just as Asho and Tay-Shun began to strike the tents. By the time the hoverjeep was over the hill, they'd already gotten the first one folded and ready to pack into the shuttle.

"So all those funny lights in the desert are Qual's doing," said Phule, bemused.

"Yes, sir," said Sushi. He leaned forward, both his hands placed casually on Phule's desk. "That big machine of theirs, the *sklern*, is a hologram projector, programmable in real time, that they invented for psychological warfare. They were using our camp to test it, figuring this might be a useful base for it if the Nanoids ever became a hostile force."

"I ought to be annoyed that he didn't bother to tell me what he was doing, especially considering the trouble it got some of our people into," said Phule.

"I'd guess he was under orders not to," said Armstrong, the officer on duty. His rigid posture was the exact opposite of Sushi's. "Even allies have secrets from each other, you know. I wouldn't be at all surprised to learn that Legion HQ has a detailed plan for invading Zenobia if our friendship suddenly falls apart at the seams." He looked at Phule, who sat staring back at him without saying anything. After a moment, Armstrong looked away. "But I suppose that's none of my business until the situation arises," he added, lamely.

"Which none of us expects to happen," said Phule, quietly. He turned back to Sushi. "You've put me in something of an embarrassing spot, as well, you know," he said, wagging a pointed finger. "Spying on Qual could sour relations between us and the Zenobians. Even if Qual doesn't take it as hostile, his superiors might. Now we have to figure out what to do if Qual finds out about it,"

"More importantly, we have to figure out how to prevent him from finding out about it," said Armstrong. "If they don't know that we know about their secret project, they can't hold it against us that we found it out by spying on them, if you follow my logic."

"I don't think so, Captain," said Sushi. "Qual wouldn't have set the thing up right in our faces if he was trying to keep it secret—let alone using it to help us get rid of those so-called hunters. That'd require a good bit of conscious duplicity, and I don't think the Zenobians think that way."

"If you've figured out how the Zenobians think, you're a couple of steps ahead of the rest of us," said Armstrong. "Half the time, I can't even figure out the plain sense of what they're saying, let along what might be behind it."

"Well, that's something we found out from the project Rev's been running," said Sushi. "Or rather, the project he recruited me to run for him, more or less, trying to find out about the Zenobians' legend of 'L'Viz. Well, you saw yesterday what that came to—I thought Rev was going to be disappointed when he realized it was just a delayed copy of something he already knew about. He managed to turn it his own way, though. But that's not the whole story. Along the way, I've found out some very interesting things on my own. Things about the Zenobians' language, which is a lot weirder than I expected."

"I'm not surprised," said Phule. "I've probably spoken to as many of the natives as any human alive, and even with translators I wouldn't rate the communication as very fluent. A lot of the time what they say has nothing to do with what I've been saying. It's as if we're carrying on two separate conversations."

Sushi grinned. "Believe it or not, a lot of conversations between one Zenobian and another seem to be like that, as well. I know—I've been listening to quite a few of them talking. Their society doesn't seem to have a common language in the same sense that ours does."

"In light of certain locutions I've heard from the members of this company, I would consider it a debatable proposition that *we* have a common language," said Beeker. "Why, just this morning I heard one of the legionnaires say ..."

Phule's intercom buzzed. "Hold on a second, Beeks," he said, and lifted his wrist to his mouth. "What is it, Mother?" he asked.

"Flight Leftenant Qual wants to see you, cutie," said the saucy voice of Comm Central. "Ordinarily I'd have just sent him down, but seeing as how you have people in your office ..."

"Ah, perfect! Send him in, Mother," said Phule. "No problem. In fact, I think he can clear up a few questions for us."

"Just make sure he's answering the same questions you're asking, lovey," said Mother. "I'm sending him down."

"Great," said Phule, and he broke the connection, smiling.

"I sure hope so, Captain," said Lieutenant Armstrong. He was definitely *not* smiling.

o o o

A few moments later, Flight Leftenant Qual entered. For the first time any of the legionnaires could remember, he was in mufti—a ragged outfit, half camouflage and half what looked like homemade garments. A straw hat that might have been stolen from an out-of-work farmhand completed the ensemble. "Greetings, Captain Clown!" he said. "Acting on the advice of your legionnaire Thumper and the famous Environmental Dog, we have completed a worthy mission this day."

"So I hear," said Phule. "Uh, why don't you tell us about it, Qual, so we can get your viewpoint on the whole thing?"

"Of a certainty," said Qual. "The entire business began when Rawfish approached me as my team was calibrating the *sklern*. At first, I could not understand his purpose, although I believed it had to do with learning our secrets."

Sushi blushed. "Oh, no, that was totally the farthest thing from my mind," he said.

"Don't put yourself in a binder, Rawfish," said Qual. "The *sklern* is not a secret project, or we doubtlessly never would have come to your base to set it up."

"Not a secret?" Phule looked puzzled. "Your crew acted really evasive every time I or one of my people tried to ask what it was and why you were testing it here."

"Oh, I see what the problem was," said Sushi. "It's what I've been telling you about the Zenobian language, Captain. No two Zenobians speak exactly the same way, so our translators don't work the way they're designed to. With most other sophonts, the differences between one speaker and another are pretty minimal, but if I've understood what Qual says, Zenobians vary all over the chart."

"And if the Zenobian gentleman is so hard to understand, how do you know that you do understand him?" asked Beeker. Everyone ignored him.

Armstrong wrinkled his brow. "You know—this could have security implications, Captain," he said.

"You're right, Armstrong," said Phule. He was grinning, now. "And I think I've got just the way to make use of that phenomenon."

"Make use of it?" Armstrong's eyes opened wide. "How in the world can we make use of an inability to communicate?"

"You're not thinking big enough," said Phule. "Modern industry and business need secure communication. Every businessman in the galaxy would give his eyeteeth for a really secure code. But as Sushi has shown us more than once, modern computers—in the right hands, and with a little bit of time—can break any code that's been devised."

"Well, maybe not *everything*," said Sushi, shrugging. "But I'd be willing to promise a pretty good success rate against most of the commercial stuff I've run across."

"From what I've seen, I'd rate you a lot better than *pretty good*," said Phule.

"Yes, Rawfish is a most intelligent human," agreed Qual, wagging his tail.

Phule grinned. "I'm sure he appreciates the endorsement. But here's my point, Sushi—how well would you do with an encrypted signal when the clear text was two Zenobians speaking in their own language?"

Sushi looked at Phule a long moment, then said, "It'd slow me down a *lot*. I mean, in most communication you assume the two sides are speaking the same language, and with two Zenobians that's only mostly true. If you run it through an encryption circuit, on top of all that—I can't say my equipment would never figure it out, but it could sure make things tougher."

"Exactly what I thought," said Phule. He turned to Beeker. "I think we're sitting on a dilithium mine here, Beeks. Remind me to look into it—I've been looking for another high-yield investment, and this just might be it. I'm sure we can figure out ways to structure it to benefit the company, as well."

"Yes, sir," said the butler. "I've already thought of a few useful directions to explore."

"And do I correctly speculate that there will be benefits for the local sophonts, as well?" asked Qual, showing his teeth in a fearsome reptilian grin.

"Absolutely," said Phule. "We can't neglect the people that make the whole thing possible. Besides, I owe you a real debt of thanks—getting those hunters off-planet is going to save me all kinds of headaches."

"It is but a smallness, Captain Clown," said Qual. "When Famous Barky and I learned from Thumper the true purpose behind their excursion, it was much to my pleasure to frighten them away. They scare very easy. I use image of my own egg-mother, exploded fifty diameters and made uglier. She glad to help, but thinks it makes her look fat. Best of all, it provided muchly useful training with the *sklern* for my subordinates."

Phule chuckled. "I'll bet it did," he said. "And thank your mom for me. Now if we could just figure out some excuse to send a few scary critters over to the AEIOU inspectors' camp ..."

He was interrupted by the buzz of his communicator. "Excuse me, gentlemen," he said, lifting his wrist to speak. "Yes, Mother, what's the story?"

"Another visitor, sweetie," said Mother. "One of those AEIOU snoops. Shall I have him sit here for a couple of hours?"

"No, as it happens, we were just talking about the inspectors," said Phule. "Why don't you send him in?"

"OK, silly boy," said the saucy voice from his wrist speaker. "But it's your funeral," she concluded, and cut the connection.

O O O

"Hello, Captain," said the AEIOU inspector. Phule looked up in surprise. Chief Inspector Snieff had been the spokesperson for the AEIOU team in all their meetings. But now Inspector Gardner had come to visit. "I hope I'm not interrupting anything," he said.

"Your whole team's been interrupting things ever since you arrived," muttered Armstrong.

Phule ignored him, "Not really," he said. "What can we do for you, Inspector?"

"Actually, I just came to tell you that we've finished our investigation," said Gardner. "We'll be packing up and leaving as soon as we can get a launch window."

"Finished?" said Beeker. "Excuse me, sir, but you've hardly had enough time to build any kind of case against us."

"Yes," said Phule. "In fact, I was under the distinct feeling that Chief Inspector Snieff was under orders to uncover as many violations as she could."

"Well, given the info we had coming in here, she was ready to shut down the whole camp and sic Barky on anybody who didn't like it," said Gardner. "But when we got a close look at things, it was pretty clear that we weren't going to find anything beyond token violations. You've basically got a clean report, Captain—I'd call that pretty impressive, considering the business you're in. Military bases and good environmental practices aren't often found under the same roof, but I have to admit you've done it."

"Hmff," said Beeker. "Exactly how did you arrive at that conclusion, if I may ask? I must say, it appeared as the chief inspector was determined to see everything in the worst possible light."

"I guess she was," said Gardner. "But she got overruled, and that's that."

"Overruled?" Phule frowned. "I thought she was the leader of the mission."

"Well, Snieff has the title, sure enough," said Gardner, looking a bit embarrassed. "And she can get pretty literal-minded about the rules, sometimes. That's not always bad—if we need to shut down a real environmental threat, we need every tool in the box. When we first arrived here, we were all expecting a major environmental impact case, and the chief had us all fired up about stopping polluters. Like I said, she gets literal-minded. So Barky came here ready to beat up on the bad guys, and that probably had a lot to do

Robert Asprin and Peter J. Heck

with his hostile attitude when he first met everybody. And when one of your guys showed him there wasn't really any problem, it took him a while to adjust ... But when push came to shove, it was Barky that called the shots. He can't be wasting his time someplace where there's nothing to be found. He's got his career to think about, after all."

"Career? That pooch?" Armstrong looked at Gardner as if he'd been speaking a particularly obscure dialect of Zenobian. "What career does he have besides biting legionnaires and chasing anybody who doesn't look sufficiently human?"

Inspector Gardner shook his head, wearily. "Doesn't look sufficiently human? Listen to yourself, Lieutenant. Yes, Barky's genetically a dog; but don't forget—he's a tri-vee star, too. And it's not just training—his intelligence measures just above human-average,"

Armstrong snorted. "Above average? On what scale?"

"The same one the Legion uses to assign recruits to various specialties," said Gardner. "With the right training, Barky could probably do *your* job. In fact, he told me he'd like to give the Legion a try some time ..."

"*Told* you?" Armstrong's jaw fell. "You mean that pooch can talk?"

"Sure," said Gardner, grinning. "That's one of the modifications. Except it's in a much higher register than our ears normally hear in—we have special implants so we can understand him. But some races can hear him just fine—your Lepoid legionnaire, for one. The little guy came out and tipped Barky off as to what those hunters were planning. Of course, he'd already learned that Barky could talk during that food fight in your cafeteria. They had quite a time of it, then."

A large grin came to Sushi's face. "That's a major understatement," he said. "I wish I had video of Barky chasing Thumper around the mess hall ... it'd be worth millions!"

"Oh, sure, I wouldn't mind seeing that again myself," said Gardner, chuckling. Then his face turned serious, and he added, "Of course, if you had something like that, you'd have to go negotiate rights with Barky's agent. And that could be pretty

288

tough—a big star like that doesn't work for free, you know."

"Of course not," said Phule. "Neither do my legionnaires, if you want to get down to that. So if any such video should ever emerge, we'd expect our performers to be properly compensated. But we're talking hypotheticals, I assume." He smiled broadly.

"As far as I know, yeah," said Inspector Gardner. "But hey, I almost forgot. Barky wanted to show you guys there's no hard feelings, and to apologize for being a bit rough on everybody. He wants you to know he was just doing what he thought was his job."

"Just doing his job?" said Beeker. "That's all very well, sir, but one would think that if the little fellow wants to make his apologies, he could come do it himself instead of sending a substitute."

Gardner slapped his hand against his forehead. "Oh, I should have told you—he *did* come, but we thought he ought to wait until we'd found out what his reception would be before bringing him into your captain's office. He's waiting outside with the woman at the desk."

"With Mother?" said Phule. He raised his comm to his wrist, to hail her.

But before he could say anything into the wrist comm, his office door burst open, and a small furry missile came through, leapt to the top of his desk, and began vigorously licking his face.

Inspector Gardner chuckled. "See, Captain? I told you he wanted to show everybody there's no hard feelings." He pulled out a pocket camera and quickly snapped a picture of the pair. "That ought to look great on tri-vee," said Gardner.

"Woof!" said Barky, the Environmental Dog, turning to show his best side to the camera.

EPILOGUE

Damnit all!" shouted General Blitzkrieg, throwing the sheet of color printout toward the trash basket. It missed, and landed face up, showing a glossy image of Barky, the Environmental Dog, and the heroic Captain Jester of the Space Legion. That one image had ruined the general's entire day. He turned to Major Sparrowhawk, who had just brought in the day's news printouts for him. "Those AEIOU morons were supposed to bury Omega Company in red tape, not give them more favorable publicity. Why are Jester and that ugly mutt on the front page of my paper?"

"Cute sells papers," said Sparrowhawk, resignedly. It was one of a large body of significant truths that were about as much use to General Blitzkrieg as a trombone to a porcupine. Just for starters, it required the ability to recognize Captain Jester as cute, a perception for which the general was seriously unsuited.

The general snorted. "To hell with cute," he growled. "I don't have any use for those green-nosed ecofreaks to begin with—all they know how to do is come in where they aren't wanted and tie a man's hands with so many regulations he can't do his job. So why the hell do they suddenly make like best buddies with Jester and his pack of blithering incompetents? You can't tell me *they're* not violating every regulation ever written. That's why they ended up in Omega Company, damnit."

"Well, General, now that you mention it, I did some research and found out something you may not know about the AEIOU team that went to Zenobia. Their leader is Chief Inspector Snieff ..."

"Sure, Senator Snieff's sister," said the general, nodding. "Bit of a sourpuss, unless she's changed since I met her. And a full-bore nutcase on the environment. I'll give her one thing, though—she takes her job seriously. My God, she takes it seriously. I wouldn't think the likes of Jester could sweet-talk her out of throwing the book at him."

"Exactly right, sir," said Sparrowhawk. "The senator got her the job, of course, and nobody's got the guts to stand in her way, even though she's a bit extreme even for the agency."

"'A bit extreme' is one hell of an understatement," said General Blitzkrieg. "I met her at a dinner party in the senator's home, and the poor fellow who had to sit next to her looked like he wanted to go home and snort some insecticide. I think he must have done something to piss off the senator ..."

"Yes, sir," said Sparrowhawk, wondering (not for the first time) who she'd managed to piss off to get the assignment as Blitzkrieg's adjutant. "As it happens, sir, there's a bit more to the story. Inspector Snieff happens to affect the higher-ups in her own agency the same way as she does everyone else."

"And serves 'em right," growled the general. Then his brow raised a fraction of an inch. "You mean she's too screwy even for the damned tree huggers? I'm surprised they can tell the difference!"

Sparrowhawk patiently explained. "General, the higher-ups in the AEIOU may be officially required to act as if they care about other planets' environments, but they quite naturally care a good bit more about their own careers. Most of them *are* political appointees. And generating terabytes of bad will because of literal-minded enforcement of unpopular policies isn't good for anybody's career. Letting Chief Inspector Snieff run around the galaxy unchecked would be a recipe for disaster."

"Anybody can see that," snorted Blitzkrieg. Then his eyes opened wide, and he said, "Wait a minute. This is starting to sound familiar. She's too crazy to give any real responsibility, and too well connected to kick out ..."

"Yes, sir, just like Captain Jester," said Sparrowhawk. "So they put her in charge of a special team, with a couple of levelheaded veterans to make sure she can't do anything irreversible, and with Barky, the Environmental Dog, their biggest media star, to give the team a positive PR profile. In a sense, it's their version of Omega Company. And while she's nominally the commander, it's just a sham. And the system seems to work. That Barky is apparently every bit as smart as he is cute."

"God save me from cute," said the general, with a groan. He pounded a fist on the corner of his desk. "Between Omega Company and the Snieff woman, the Zenobia operation should have been declared an environmental disaster. And now it's a photo op, with Jester and that fleabag hamming it up. If I see any more cute for a week, I swear I'm going to be sick."

"Yes, sir," said Sparrowhawk. "Shall I send in your morning appointments?"

"You might as well, though I'll be damned if I'm in much of a mood for it," said Blitzkrieg. "Who's on the list?"

Sparrowhawk looked at her clipboard. "Mrs. Biffwycke-Snerty, for the Retired Officers', Refugees', and Orphans' Relief Organization. She wants you to give a speech at their fund-raising affair."

"Fine, send her in," said Blitzkrieg. "Always glad to help out the good old veterans."

And never reluctant to spout off in front of a captive audience, thought Sparrowhawk. She nodded and left the office.

A moment later the door opened to admit a portly matron, a familiar figure at charity balls. "Oh, General, I *do* hope you'll be able to address the RORORO fund-raiser next month," she warbled, in a voice at least an octave above her natural range. "We have such a *wonderful* program planned, and you would be just the *perfect* one to speak for the Legion."

"Why, I'd be delighted," said the general, rising to extend a hand. "There's nothing closer to my heart than the welfare of the

Robert Asprin and Peter J. Heck

retired officers. I'll tell my adjutant to make it a firm date."

"Oh, I'm *so* pleased," said Mrs. Biffwycke-Snerty. "Now we have something for all our clients. You for the officers, and Mr. Vodoh-Deo, who's done just so *much* for the Jivan refugees—and you'll *never* guess whom we've persuaded to come for the orphans!"

"I haven't a clue," said Blitzkrieg, already mildly annoyed that he wasn't to be the sole attraction.

"It was such a *coup*," said the socialite. "Priscilla Ann Hoglinton *just* happens to know the executive producer of the IGT network, and I told her we just *had* to have someone for the poor children, and she went in and talked to him, and you know how tough these producers can be, but sure enough, Priscilla Ann just *prevailed* upon him, I swear I don't know how, and he said he'd do everything he could for RORORO. And now we've got just *the perfect* celebrity to make this the best fundraiser *ever!*"

"And who would that be?" said Blitzkrieg, throwing caution to the winds.

"Why, *Barky*, the Environmental *Dog*, of course! He's just so *cute* ..." Mrs. Biffwycke-Snerty chirped.

General Blitzkrieg's wounded bellow was audible three buildings away.

ABOUT THE AUTHOR

Robert Lynn Asprin was an American science fiction and fantasy author, best known for his MythAdventures and Phule's Company series. As an active fan of the genres, he was a member of the Society for Creative Anachronism, a co-founder of the Great Dark Horde, and founder of the Dorsai Irregulars. He was nominated for the Hugo Award for Best Dramatic Presentation for *The Capture* in 1976.

Asprin died in 2008 at the age of 61 having published over fifty novels and several short stories.

Peter Jewell Heck is an American science fiction and mystery author, best known for his "Mark Twain Mysteries" and Phule's Company series. He was an editor for Ace Books and is a regular reviewer for Asimov's Science Fiction and Kirkus Reviews.

IF YOU LIKED ...

If you liked No Phule Like an Old Phule
you might also enjoy:

Phule's Errand
Robert Asprin

Fifth Foreign Legion #2: Honor and Fidelity
Andrew & William H. Keith

The Worker Prince
Bryan Thomas Schmidt

OTHER WORDFIRE PRESS TITLES BY ROBERT ASPRIN

Phule's Company
Phule's Paradise
Phule Me Twice
A Phule and His Money
Phule's Errand

Our list of other WordFire Press authors and titles is always growing.
To find out more and to see our selection of titles, visit us at:

wordfirepress.com

CPSIA information can be obtained
at www.ICGtesting.com
Printed in the USA
LVHW092255150319
610881LV00001B/54/P

9 781614 754602